Vasily Mahanenko

THE BEGINNING

*Books are the lives
we don't have
time to live,*

Vasily Mahanenko

DARK PALADIN
BOOK#1

Magic Dome Books

The Beginning
Dark Paladin, Book # 1
Copyright © V. Mahanenko 2017
Cover Art © V. Manyukhin 2017
English Translation Copyright ©
Alexandra Tussing 2017
Published by Magic Dome Books, 2017
All Rights Reserved
ISBN: 978-80-88231-22-6

TABLE OF CONTENTS :

CHAPTER ONE

BIRTH OF THE PALADIN

THE ARMY OF ORCS led by Yargul headed to the tall forests of Idilrance. The wood elves were planning to bring a great mage of the past back to life – the one who had destroyed half of the world, so the orcs decided to interfere and show the whole world once again who were the true rulers of Zalta. Along enormous chords the army of orcs was moving towards the woods without even noticing...

"QUIT PICKING YOUR NOSE, you grunt! Three laps around the drill field once we get back to the base!" The sergeant's booming voice jerked me out of my dreamland. The orcs evaporated from my imagination like a ball of ice cream on a server under peak load – fast and frying the motherboard in the process. Clinging to the side of the APC I stared at the mountains gloomily: four hours in a dusty metal box never made anyone happy. Particularly on a narrow road. When I started imagining horrendous monsters under every shrub it became clear: my brain needed a reboot. The orcs came to my rescue, saving me from the monotony of the ride, but the sergeant destroyed them ruthlessly, totally blowing all the fun. I wouldn't be able to run three laps after a ride like this. Not even if I walked. I wasn't sure about crawling, but I wouldn't want to have to find out.

Scheduled patrol of the area around the base on three APCs was our commander's weekly fun. Sometimes he made arrangements with a platoon of contract troopers from the neighboring base to ambush us "to keep the grunts on their toes." On those days a dozen or so powerful fighters would attack us and knock us out – purely for instructional purposes. So that we would not lose our edge! Those of us who managed to roll off from the vehicle onto the ground and start shooting blanks at the appearing "enemy" the troopers did not bother: these soldiers were considered to have lived up to expectations. We were shooting blanks; only the commander had live ammo. Of course, the middle APC also had the battle large caliber NSV machine gun, but no one was allowed to even come close to it. There was just that one time, in the mountains, when the commander let us take a couple of shots from that wonder of military technology. It would be impossible to convey the feeling of great power completely controlled by you! At that awesome moment I felt like I could level the mountains, only provided the machine gun had enough ammo! Sadly, this only happened once in the whole year of service and by now it felt like a dream. Sweet and pleasant, but still a dream. The rest of the time we either waited for the troopers to attack or trundled along narrow roads. How very romantic!

"You crowbag, is your bag hanging down?" The hoarse rough voice of lance-corporal Fagov came from the other side of the APC, and the privates on his side guffawed in unison. Some stand-up comics, my ass! Fagov was the worst wacko old-timer in the platoon and taking it out on the newbies for his sordid childhood. He managed to take the top spot even among his peers. When a huge thug, almost two meters tall, whose face brightens with intelligence only when he is straining to take a crap, is hanging over you it's hard not to acknowledge him as a leader. There was an unspoken rule among the privates: never argue with Fagov. He would yell some, wave his arms in the air, hit you a couple of times, but it would only take a minute for his attention to switch to something else. His attention span was something remarkable – like a baby's.

Lieutenant Sintsov, our platoon commander, included all three of his squad sections in today's patrol. Twenty-seven knuckleheads and three sergeants. You didn't need a crystal ball to understand: today was when he planned the massacre of the innocents. Sintsov must have arranged it with the contract guys again! Formally we were listed as paratroopers, but it was beyond me to

see a hidden paratrooper among the brush and stones
– a real professional and not a cheap imitation like us.
I didn't even try. Instead I quietly sat at the side of the
APC, didn't bother anyone, clutched my useless
assault rifle dreaming of elf girls, hot shower, soft bed
and treating my surroundings as if they were just a
figment of my sick imagination.

"Did you go deaf, you?" Amazingly, Fagov had
not forgotten about me. "Think you're immortal?"

"Check that!" shouted Sintsov from the second
APC. "Smarty-pants, if you keep picking on the young
ones, I'll send you to the right place right away.
They'll make the first part of your name very true very
quickly! Shut up and look sharp! Homemade
Rambo..."

In reality all of the above was conveyed in
highly specialized military curse language that most
of the army speaks. Most of what I understood were
prepositions, and I guessed the overall meaning based
on the emotional content. Before I joined the army I
practically never had to curse so actively, so any
communication with the lieutenant turned into an
educational session. He managed to shoot out such
strings of obscenities that my eyebrows crawled up
and a smile appeared on my face: Sintsov combined
incompatible things, but it all worked out so smoothly
that I was just left in wonder at the capabilities of the
Russian language. I was sure that no other language
could possibly deliver, with such flourish and
effectiveness, a single thought into the soldiers'
minds.

"Return to base!"

The command that sounded about five minutes later triggered a unanimous sigh of relief: no massacre today. The troopers never attacked on the way back – considering that extremely rude. The troops were returning to base, so it wouldn't be right to interfere with them. Looking forward to resting soon, the soldiers relaxed and were smiling feeling like they were nearly home...

But suddenly ...

I never understood why the leading APS was thrown into the air. There was no explosion, no noise or dust – but suddenly the huge metal vehicle bucked like a nervous horse and rolled over. I clung harder to the side of my vehicle, stunned, staring at the blood that appeared from under the machine. Several soldiers were crushed! To death! What kind of blasted training could that be when people were being killed?! Some force pulled on my boot making me fall on the ground. The sergeant. Cursing like mad he was grabbing the grunts, pulling them down from the vehicle, kicking them to force them to lie low to the ground. Hanging on to the useless assault rifle I was nervously seeking the enemy who must have lost it. After the drill someone will get it real bad!

"Issue live ammo!" came a shout from Sintsov, making me hug the ground harder. What did he mean, live ammo? There was a set of live ammo in each APC; it could be accessed only by the senior sergeant, but to issue live ammo on patrol? Had Sintsov taken a hard hit on the head?

"Catch!" as soon as the magazine with red tape wound around it fell in front of me I heard the lieutenant's wild scream:

"Get down!"

I didn't stare at the magazine, I pulled it under my body, raised my head and saw one of the soldiers running to the nearest line of trees. He almost made it. When the trees were just within reach, the private suddenly stopped, standing straight still and then, like an activated cracker, burst into hundreds of small bloody pieces.

"It blew Vas up!" Fagov screamed in a panicked voice, "— A-a-a! Take it, bastards! You're all dead!"

To say that I was shocked would be a gross understatement. The sight of the exploding body just turned my brain off. I turned into a motionless mannequin, dumbly staring at the bloody boots: all that was left of the soldier. Chaos broke around me: shots, screams, orders to cease fire, but none of that existed for me. Just the boots stained with blood. Then, suddenly, silence fell. It was so terrifying, so physical, that I let go of the assault rifle and pushed my face into the ground, as if trying to dig deep into it. It seemed that the silence would cause my eardrums to rupture at any moment! The silence!

The overturned APC with several crushed bodies under it suddenly exploded into shards turning into a huge shrapnel bomb. If I had not pushed my head into the ground fighting the overpowering silence, a huge chunk of the armor would have become my personal guillotine. The silence dissipated, replaced by pleas for help, screams of pain and the monotonous hum of a working transformer. I lay on the ground completely unsure what to do – we were never taught anything like that in boot camp. I didn't see the enemy; all the fire came from our side. From fear my muscles were so cramped that every move was painful. All I was able to do was to clutch my useless assault rifle. As if it were a life ring. Live ammo was near me but it did not even occur to me to switch magazines. I dully noticed that my shoulder was ripped practically to the bone; there was a lot of blood but I felt no pain at all. As if someone had switched it off.

"Retreat!" I heard from somewhere ahead. "Cover us!"

Who was I supposed to cover, and from what? What was I supposed to do generally?! One of the sergeants jumped up on the second APC, turned the machine gun in the direction in which the column had been moving and took a few shots, looking like he knew what he was doing. After this all hell broke loose.

Here is a sergeant, standing and shooting at something. Bang, and there is no sergeant. Only the rain of bloody scraps tells you that a moment ago there was a person here.

Here are three surviving privates from the first APC jumping to their feet and running towards us. Bang, and they are gone. Just the bloody rain again, without a single shot. What are they shooting at us?!

"Private! Follow me! On the double!" I heard the squad sergeant's order next to my ear.

I lifted my head dully and looked at our sergeant without seeing him.

"Get up, damn you! Swap the magazine and

follow me! Quick!

I was not sure what affected me: the clear command, the sergeant's awful appearance, the sight of exploding soldiers, or Fagov frozen between the APCs, staring with terrified huge eyes at the soldiers exploding next to him and not even attempting to drop to the ground. Maybe he thought he was a hero. Who knows? I sprang to my feet, switched the magazine to live ammo and, without thinking that I too could turn into bloody rain, started for the APCs. The only way to provide cover was the machine gun; the assault rifle would not help much. The most important thing was to make it there.

Several steps away from the vehicle I tripped, ploughing the stony road with my face. My arms immediately came into motion, lifted the assault rifle and aimed it at a man slowly walking down the road. His arms were covered with unnatural fire. Actually, they weren't his arms – the man's fists were covered in blue and gold flames as if two magical fireballs had flown into our world by mistake and stuck to the stranger's hands. The dark cloak streaming behind him and the hood covering his face made him look like a character from some computer game. A Warrior Mage.

The man took another step, raised his hand and just a few steps away from me another bloody cloud formed; the sergeant's remains showered the ground.

"A-A-A!" I screamed, pushing the trigger. For the first time in my life I was shooting at a living person, but at that moment the thought did not bother me in the least. If this prick was to blame for everyone around him exploding and dying, he must be stopped.

I sent bullet after bullet at the man coming towards me, but something weird was happening. At the shooting range, on average I hit 40 points out of 50 but now all my shots went nowhere. It's not like I missed him – they just dissipated! Small fiery flashes appearing right in front of the walking man indicated that my aim was good, but the shots produced no result at all. I'll be damned! This freak had some kind of mean protection device! A normal assault rifle wouldn't do it, I would need a more powerful weapon!

The NSV!

Two dark cords of fog swiftly snaked from the enemy's hands. They bent around the APC that I was using for cover and rushed onward. A scream of horror joined the cries of pain. I turned my head and saw the APC of my squad floating about two meters off the ground. It started growing smaller. Like a balloon that had lost all its air. "Back to the taxpayers!" A thought flashed through my mind, and then blood started pouring from the shapeless heap of metal. Someone had stayed in the vehicle to the last.

"All the way!" Sintsov rushed with a wild roar from somewhere behind the bushes. Shooting at the oncoming enemy using one hand, as the bullets produced the fiery flashes which I recognized, the lieutenant was carrying several grenades in his other hand as he ran towards the enemy. He's right! If it's impossible to destroy the defense from outside you could try to blow it up from the inside!

Having seen Sintsov I threw away the spent assault rifle and jumped onto the APC. Fear left me when the lieutenant appeared: now I knew with certainty who I was supposed to "cover" and from what. I am a soldier who must fulfill his duty until the end! The whole side of the vehicle was covered in blood but it didn't bother me anymore; there would be time to throw up later. If there was a "later". I had never thought that in a critical situation like this I would be able to act calmly and rationally. Having reached the machine gun I aimed it at the enemy and nearly lost all my determination: the lieutenant was being torn in half! With just two hands! Along his body, completely ignoring the armor vest! Sintsov's torn-off arms were lying on the ground a few meters away: he never made it with the grenades.

"All the way!" I whispered, tightening my fingers on the trigger. The enemy turned and I was overpowered by hellish pain. I felt as if I was skinned alive, doused with salt and thrown on hot embers while acid poured over me. Pain dimmed my mind, something warm trickled down my legs, I could not move a single muscle. I was unable even to draw in some air for a scream. At the edge of my consciousness I felt the NSV start shooting. If I were to die, I would die fighting.

I was rammed in the chest and thrown a few meters back; both my arms were torn off. The last thing I saw before fainting was a bloody fountain gushing from where the enemy's head had been. The torn-off arms still pushing on the trigger did it: the enemy was destroyed. The rest was not my concern...

All the way!

New user initialization in progress
Choose a name

Darkness retreated instantly, as if someone had thrown a switch. A moment, and I became aware that I was lying on my back staring at a snow-white ceiling. I felt no headache, no sleepiness, no nausea – the standard symptoms of vodka overindulgence. The only thing breaking the pattern of my usual world were strange messages obscuring the ceiling. Perhaps they were the reason for me finding myself in the hospital: someone had figured out that I had a bout of DTs. I could also feel that something was not right with me: the battle I had dreamt about was so bright and vivid that it seemed real. Ha! Why would warrior mages show up in our reality? They would only appear to someone who was seriously intoxicated.

Choose a name

The apparition refused to disappear, thus confirming its unnatural origin. It was amazingly similar to a standard game message used by all computer games, and it kept floating in front of my eyes. Even when I closed them to rest from the whiteness of the hospital room. I would have to report this to a doc, that I'm having residual hallucinations. Perhaps they'd give me some pills? I opened my eyes and finally looked around. White walls, white ceiling and the white floor on which I was lounging so comfortably. Everything was white. Even my clothes were white. I noticed with significant relief that my arms were still attached to the right places. The nightmare I had just gone through was so realistic that I was in doubt for a few seconds. But no, my arms were in order and working properly, so there had not been any mage. Besides, how would something like that appear in real life? This is no game after all.

Choose a name

Blasted thing! Oh well, that would not do! Something needs to be done with my head or else they will stick me in a loony bin for sure. Could this be a test? The guys had been saying that close to our base there was some kind of a top secret facility; could it be that I'd been shipped off to there? The brainiacs there figured out that I have a gaming problem and so they fitted me with undetectable lenses similar to G*-Glass and were now sending their messages to me? Perhaps they were now watching me and placing bets on how soon I would start bashing my head against the wall.

"Sergey Lemeshev!" I stated my name clearly, wanting to proceed to the second part of the test.

You cannot choose the name used by you during life

Choose a name

During life?!

"This is not funny!" — I screamed, trying to

fend off the panic "what kind of a stupid joke is that?"

Name chosen "This is not funny"
Save changes?

When two huge buttons backlit in white —
"OK" and "Cancel" — were added to the messages, I
could not take it any longer and tried to pull the
lenses out of my eyes. May they all rot in hell! I never
agreed to that, and did not want to keep taking part
in this absurdist theatre. Pretend I am dead, my ass.
For jokes like that people end up in court in a flash!

Waiting time expired, changes will be reset
Choose a name

The buttons disappeared. But they took my
self-control with them: there were no lenses. I clawed
at my eyes mercilessly, but the messages would not
even budge, as if they appeared directly in my head.
As if they were outside of this world. Just like me!
"NOOOOOO!" I screamed bitterly, refusing to
believe the obvious: the battle had been real. I
happened to die at the hands of a warrior mage, and
the place where I came to was purgatory.
On this note my consciousness could not take
it anymore and faded, sending me into a faint. The
mind refused to accept my own death.

Choose a name

I did not know for how long I stayed

unconscious. But at some point in time I came to, and realized that it was not a dream. Not a figment of my sick and feverish imagination. Not someone's mean joke. I really did die, and now for some reason it was proposed that I take a new name. I wanted to howl and scream, close my eyes and leave this nightmare forever, but the persistent message would not leave. Quite the opposite – it became brighter and shone more intensely as if it worried that I might have missed it. Besides, it grew larger, by now filling most of my field of view. I looked at the silver letters with open hatred, and growled the first name that popped into my head:

"Yari! Yaropolk!"

Over the last seven years this name had become so much a part of me that many called me that even in real life. Few remembered that the skinny guy was named Sergey, but many knew me as Yari or Yaropolk. The Paladin of Light, damn it! I registered with that name in all the computer games, which were the reason, by the way, why I ended up in the army after college rather than getting a fine job. To be more precise – because of which I decided to serve a term in an army that would definitely not offer any online games, so I could get rid of my game addiction. I used to spend ten hours a day playing those games, forgetting about the real world, so the idea to do a term in the army where no online games would be available for sure seemed ideal to me. Since the games were the reason why I ended up dead, let them atone for this at least by that name.

Name chosen: "Yaropolk", short name "Yari"
Accept changes?

Two buttons appeared and I realized that unless I pressed "OK" immediately, the changes would reset again and I would have to stare at that loathsome message some more. Unable to figure out a better way, I stared at the button, mentally commanding it to push itself. I recalled a situation from my life: there was a time when I had sat in front of my cat for the longest time and tried to hypnotize him in a similar way. I wanted the stupid animal to succumb to my superior mind and start talking, but all I got was a cat who lost interest and turned away from me, and a broken cup that I shattered in my rage. As an ESP I was not much.

Once I replayed in my head the situation with the cat and compared it to my current situation, I started laughing so hard I bent over. I had never laughed like that before. All the comedians in the world stood in no comparison to my yawning cat and my rage. Laughter swelled within me, trying to bubble over and show its overwhelming emotional power to the entire world.

Name accepted
Character race determined
Character is being generated

At some point the wild uncontrollable laughter was replaced by tears; I completely shut off the "manly" side, which was supposed to be strong as granite and not feel any excessive emotions, but which was drowning in tears. I died. I will never see my relatives and friends. Some bastard in the magic coat destroyed me like a fly, tearing my limbs off before killing me. And now I am in a purgatory for gamers, where they are made into computer game characters; this process does not resemble anything else. Such a simple hell for hardcore gamers – to stay an NPC for the rest of eternity.

Character generation complete

I wanted to tell everyone to get lost, but suddenly someone turned off the light, and my consciousness along with it. Something blinked and I heard some voices nearby:

"...the patient is steadily declining. We are struggling, but there is no improvement so far."

"Is there any hope?"

"No. He was treated too late. We can keep him going for a couple more days but then he will slip away."

"That's a pity. This soldier saved fifteen people and destroyed the enemy. Another hero to be rewarded posthumously. I've seen so many of them already..."

Something blinked again and the voices changed:

"...final journey. He will live forever in our memory!"

"My son, my darling..."— the familiar voice of my mother, full of tears, sounded right next to my ear, followed by a burning touch of lips to my forehead. Hey, mom, I'm alive!

Something clunked dully, then I was jolted and found myself again in the room with white walls.

Choose character class

Bastards!

A colorful window popped up in front of me, showing a lengthy list: mage, hunter, priest, druid, warrior, fighter... hundreds if not thousands of lines appeared before me; once I focused my gaze on one of them an image instantly appeared. A mage casting lightning bolts; a shaman calling on the spirits; a warrior crushing all around him; a druid working with plants. I stared at the dance of the images, but basically couldn't see anything. After I heard my mother's voice I felt so low that I mumbled without even listening to my own words:

"Paladin."

Leaving for the army I did not give much thought to what my mother's life would become if she stayed alone with my twelve-year-old sister. But now it felt like a band tightened around my chest: mom was slaving at two jobs to make sure there was food on the table and clothes for us; she did everything she could to make sure her babies knew no hardship. She forgave me constant gaming and mediocre grades. She rejoiced when I entered college and shook her head in bewilderment as I decided to join the army, but never said a word against it. According to her, I would need to choose my own path... So look where all that choosing landed me...

Current class: Paladin
Initial settings complete
Character level: 1

A status bar, standard for games, appeared at the bottom of my field of view once again, informing me that I had gone into the game. Emotions faded as tears dried up, so I decided to take another couple of minutes to assess the abilities of my character. If I was destined to continue as a computer unit, I should know what it could do.

Drawing on the experience I already had pushing buttons, I stared at the icons in the status bar and issued a mental order: "Open". Immediately a semi-transparent window appeared, covering practically my entire field of view.

Yari, Paladin, human. Level 1 player. Points needed to progress to next level: 1000. There was also something called "Specialty", but it wasn't clear what it covered or what advantages it conferred. There was Energy. What was that for? Another unknown. I could not help noticing the absence of the familiar indicators: Strength, Intelligence, Agility, Endurance and Life reserve. All games had these five core indicators in some way or another. Sometimes it was even considered that games without these words were perceived to be deficient, but the game in which I happened to end up could not care less about that. Energy was a be-all and end-all here...

By the way: where was I?

Judging strictly by how I felt, I was still alive. I could hear – I made a noise to verify that, just in case. I could see: the white walls served as confirmation. I could feel and breathe – I could do anything! I could even think! The conclusion was obvious: I had no idea what was going on.

If I were a gamer, then where was my character? If I were a character then where was my gamer, and why did I have a certain degree of freedom? If I was both gamer and character at the same time, how could that be possible? And finally – even though it was a rhetorical question anyway, but still – what would happen if I were killed?

The questions went unanswered. No window appeared with a detailed description of the game, nor did I see a specially trained character who would bring all the newbies up to speed. There was nothing besides the semitransparent window and the white room. I bit my lip in annoyance; the pain I felt was quite real. I kept studying the tabs.

Spell Book. A book appeared in front of me, floating in the air and iridescent. Now it was blank, but a strange feeling of recognition overwhelmed me. Right! This was the Spell Book from the game "Heroes of Might and Magic III!" Exactly like it! The same massive book with the pages yellowed from age, sporting several currently inactive bookmarks and funny icons. Someone's into plagiarism! Either the HoMM3 developers or the game itself!

Generally I was very glad to see that magic could be used in the game. I would bring forth the truth by my sword as well as by my word. I liked

Paladins because they were universal: in each game I've played this class was capable of performing all sorts of functions: tank, healer, fighter. Role selection depended exclusively on how many of your fingers were thumbs. If you had just the right number of them, you could become a healer or a tank. If you had a few too many, shaky and crooked and liable to keep your character in some puddle of fire — only the fighters for you, only hardcore. Mostly, the hardcore task would be for the healers trying to cure the twit with the last drops of mana and screaming into the mike to get that moron to come out of the fire. Besides, afterwards the healers would be the ones having to put up with "The healers suck! They can't do nothing! Ham-handed noobs! I'm leaving!"

Location map. While it had several available scales, in all the modes my map was covered in fog. There was not a single hint as to where I was or where I needed to go. Very informative indeed.

Personal inventory. A small shimmering shelf invited me to put something on it. It was so tiny that it would house three or four books, not more. Five centimeters long and ten wide; my personal inventory storage space reminded me more than anything of the line I read at the initial screen: "Newbie".

Initial character familiarization is complete. Are you ready to start the game?

I looked at the buttons angrily and smiled without humor. To hell with you! If my fate is to become a game character, there is no sense in delaying it. Sooner or later it will happen anyway.

Accept!

An electric shock jolted me, making me faint. Once I felt my body once again, I realized that I was lying on my back. In complete darkness. And I could not move a single body part. I was not even breathing!

If I could have drawn some air, I would have screamed with all my might. Not because I was afraid of darkness – because I was afraid to stay like that for the entire rest of eternity. What if my role was that of a paladin locked in a tomb, never to be found? Hundreds, thousands, millions years of solitude! While you could go mad here in a week!

"Shit, that's new," – suddenly my solitude was broken by a hoarse voice – "looks f...ing fresh."

"Squint, what if there's no shit there? Why should we bust our ass for nothing?"

"Shut the f... up! I saw the old hag at the funeral – she was crazy as f...! Could have easily thrown something in with that bastard. Look, what if there's a medal there? That's no shit! Petrovich'll give us a couple of bottles of vodka for it, and maybe some money too!"

Body control will be available after return to world. Wait.

I was found! Guys, friends, pull me out – quick! I am here! I am alive!

The wild fear that had washed over me a few moments back was replaced by complete happiness. I didn't even bother with the thought that I was in a coffin; the joy from knowing that the darkness would soon recede filled my whole being. Somewhere at the periphery a thought flashed that since I was lying in a coffin the diggers must be grave robbers, who would not want to have extra witnesses. They could hit me over the head with a shovel or hoe sending me back to the grave. This time for good. But all of that flashed somewhere at the back of my mind and vanished right away: the anticipation of returning to the world pushed everything else aside.

"Squint, I'm f..ing tired of digging! Why in hell did they have to dump him so deep in?"

"F..ed if I know! Come on, there's just a dick's width left! Suck it up and dig harder! Here it is!"

There was a sound of metal hitting metal.

"I got the box! Whack it here, it'll bump the lid."

Full body control reached. Game world: Earth. Local time: year 2015

Have a great game!

Absolute darkness dissipated replaced by the twilight of a summer night and the dim light of a lamp. In addition, there were two dirty bearded mugs staring at me with interest from above.

"That was an ugly one for sure," one of the diggers drawled, and I was immediately overwhelmed by a wave of sensation. I felt the cold, something sharp pricking my back, clumps of earth sliding down, but the most important thing I felt was that I really needed air.

"Aaaargh!" I sighed noisily, stretching my back.

Like a young inexperienced diver coming to the surface after holding on underwater without breathing for two minutes. Colored sparks jumped in my vision, my head was swimming, so I sat up purely on reflex, pushing with my hands on the edge of the coffin. With my hands! I had hands! And arms! Two normal working moving arms! This fact cleared my head, the sparks faded and I was finally able to see my saviors, frozen at the far edge of the grave.

"Hi," — that's all I was able to say before bending over in a fit of coughing. My chest felt tight, breathing was almost impossible and it felt as I was coughing out what was left of my lungs. Each breath came in with a wheeze, the sparks happily regained their places in front of me, and instead of dizziness there was a huge message that obscured my entire field of view:

Negative effect sustained: "Tomb dust". Consequences: uncontrollable coughing fit. Duration: unlimited; resets for 30 seconds every 5 minutes. To neutralize the effect drink any liquid.

"Water,"— I croaked, having read the message on something like the fifth attempt. Judging from how I felt, I had already coughed out my lungs and now it was my stomach's turn. — "Gimme water!"

The coughing would not stop. All thoughts vanished from my head, space contracted to a point and sucked in the entire world around me like a black hole. All I had left was the word "water" that I mumbled like a mantra.

I recovered instantly, as if someone had thrown a switch; there were no consequences from the fit. A number appeared in front of me: "30"; in a second it was replaced by "29". The countdown! It was resetting! I had only 28 seconds to find liquid and relieve that damned cough! I jumped to my feet, noticing the grave was empty. My rescuers had vanished somewhere, leaving me alone. Ignoring the dirt I started climbing out of the grave, surprised by how deep it was. It was a couple of meters at least! In any case, even when I stood on the edge of the coffin only my head showed above the grave edge. I did not know how tall my new body was, but the old one was a meter seventy three. They really did put me six feet under!

No matter how much I tried I was unable to climb out. Judging from the marks on the soil the grave robbers had used a ladder which they did not forget to take with them. The good thing was they did not whap me over the head with a shovel. Realizing that I would not make it I started digging holes in the wall: I would use them to step up the next time.

"Water!"

The second fit was worse than the first. Once I saw the countdown once again I was surprised to feel wetness on my hands. I stood up, leaning against the wall, as I was tired, and looked at my hands. Hmm... in the moonlight I could see black glistening trails. I smelt it. Nothing. No smell at all. The timer had gone down to twenty when I licked my hand carefully. So what was it?

Liquid consumed (blood) is not sufficient to neutralize the negative effect. Constraint: own blood is not suitable to neutralize the negative effect.

WHAT?! A fit of nausea twisted me in knots right there in the grave. The thought that I would be drinking someone's blood was beyond my ability for self-control.

Water! Oh, well, to hell with water – I'll take blood!

The third coughing fit settled my priorities. I climbed out of the grave with one clear thought: the nearest source of liquid would be mine! It did not matter what – or who – it would be. I might not survive the fourth fit.

"I'm not going there!" I heard someone's voice just as I climbed out of the grave.

"Yes you will!" – a menacing growl stated in response. "Have you gone f...ing mad with your movies? What f...ing zombie?! You should quit drinking, idiot!"

"Petrovich, f..k me if I'm lying, it's true! Look, Squint still can't get over it!"

I was so weak I was swaying from side to side: apparently, each coughing fit produced a cumulative effect. I was stumbling on my own feet, my head was ringing, so I could not understand who was talking: the digger or someone else. I could not even figure out all of the words. I looked around; seeing no puddles nearby I steeled myself and started running towards the voices. I needed some kind of liquid and I only had twenty one seconds to get it.

"Water!" I rasped, tumbling into the door of a simple trailer. Most likely it was the office of the local custodian. I did not care what they would think of me – the most important thing was to drink something within the ten remaining seconds. Something, anything! I stopped still at the entrance, looking around the room. I needed something, bottle, kettle... a glass or even a toilet. I would stoop to drinking from the toilet bowl if it meant I could make it within the ten remaining seconds.

Two pairs of eyes were staring at me. Another person was sitting in the corner howling and rocking from side to side. Having found no liquid – there was nothing even on the table – I looked at the people. I'll be damned!

"It's him!" — the skinny guy with the beard screamed — "It's the zombie!"

"Hey chap, who are you?" the voice I heard was quite calm, although wary, and the description appeared right above the man's head:

Sergey Petrovich Selivanov. Level 3 Reading skill needed to learn the other parameters.

5...
"Fellow, do you understand me at all?"
4...
"Gimme water!"
"What? Talk more clearly!"
3...
"Water!!!"
"Petrovich, what is he mumbling about?"

2...

Bastards! I hate you! I don't want this!

1...

"A-a-a-a!" — the bearded one screamed again; then his screams became more distant. I didn't care: I was frantically swallowing hot salty blood from Petrovich's neck that I bit. I could not remember how I ended up next to him. I paid no attention that the huge guy was not trying to push me aside – I was reaching for the only source of liquid I could see. I would not have survived the fourth coughing fit.

Negative effect "Tomb dust" is neutralized.

NPC Sergey Petrovich Selivanov has been destroyed. You receive +1 Experience

You drank blood of a live creature. Negative effect sustained: "Poisoning" Duration: 10 minutes.

You have not completed initiation; therefore, you can change race. Races available: Vampire. Accept changes?

Only the two buttons – "Accept" and "Reject" – helped me retain my sanity. They reminded me that everything happening around was no more than a game, no matter how real it seemed. I had not killed a person; I killed a common game NPC. The graphics of this one were a little more advanced than the games I was used to playing, but it was still a blasted game!

There was no new coughing fit and the counter disappeared; however, that didn't make me feel better: pushing Petrovich's still warm body aside I pushed two fingers down my throat and pressed on the bottom of my tongue to induce vomiting. My body bent in a cramp, trying to remove the source of irritation. Bloody slime mixed with something white poured onto the floor. Once I realized that these were pieces of Petrovich's skin I had swallowed while biting him, I bent over in another heave. The second fit was followed by a third one, and then a fourth. I threw up until my throat started burning with stomach acid and the salty sweet taste of blood in my mouth became acrid. Suppressing the fifth heave I crawled to the wall on all fours. Too weak to stand up I collapsed where there was no blood, vomit or dirt. My head throbbed, my stomach felt like I would throw up again, my muscles felt like lead, as if I had been exercising for too long. There had only been one time when I had felt so horrible – from food poisoning. The sausage I ate had been spoiled. Curling into a fetal position since I didn't have the strength to do anything else, I finally paid attention to the buttons. Since they were the only thing that kept me from just curling up and dying.

The buttons never went anywhere; moreover, they stayed in the center of my field of vision regardless of the direction in which I looked. Even when I closed my eyes trying to escape this nightmare for just a moment, the buttons were fixed in front of my internal vision, laughing at common sense and logic. They lured, they shimmered, they longed to know my choice, vibrating with impatience! I felt with my entire being that the longer I delay my choice the worse I would feel. The game system wanted to know how I was going to advance in that blasted game.

I suppressed the initial desire to press "Cancel". Given that I had actively played a number of games before ending up here, it would be very stupid to reject something before finding out what its attributes were. What are the advantages of the race "human"? What would be the advantages of the race "vampire"? What constraints do both of these races have? The questions appeared in my head despite my awful state, but there were no answers to them. Just the buttons kept shimmering in front of me. Losing it completely I shouted:

"Information! I need comparative information on the races. That's the only way I can make a choice."

The last sentence came out garbled as my innards started burning as if they were on fire. I had no idea what was happening to my body now, but I felt clearly that in the next few minutes I would be dead. I did not know if this game offered respawn or if I would just disappear completely, but I did not want to find out. If I was given a second chance at life it would be silly to let it end in just thirty minutes.

Request is granted. Access to Temple of Knowledge is provided.

For the duration of study of comparative attributes time for player Yari is suspended.

The pain vanished completely. Along with it vanished the blood, the vomit, the trailer, and the world around, Everything that had surrounded me just a few second ago just vanished! What appeared instead was the white room where I had been previously. Except that now, unlike during my previous visit, a gray haired man of uncertain age was present. He could be fifty to infinity. Actually, it's the latter that I was inclined to believe the most. All the Christian pictures showing god right after the creation of the world contained that very image: white flowing clothes, gray hair, kind and understanding gaze. Could that really be him?

"Welcome to the Temple of Knowledge, young recruit," — the old man said, spreading his arms in a welcoming gesture. — "You have requested information on the comparative characteristics of two races: human and vampire. Your request was reviewed and ruled justified. The information you need is in this scroll. Study it."

A glass coffee table appeared in front of me with a small sheet of paper on top of it.

"Where am I?" — I blurted out, subconsciously expecting to hear a squeaky rasp. But no, my voice was quite normal. Amazing – a second ago I was writhing with horrible pain and now there was not even a phantom trace of it. As if my consciousness had been detached and relocated to a different place, leaving just the empty shell to suffer.

"Three questions on subjects unrelated to the initial query lead to a ban on access to the Temple of Knowledge for a year. You shall receive an initial warning. For the next unrelated question you will receive a penalty. Pay attention, young recruit."

Damn! Shut up and be quiet! I had just received a very clear illustration of the expression "A man's ruin lies in his tongue." The old man standing in front of me instantly lost the veil of divinity: HE could not possibly be so indifferent to His creations. I surveyed the surrounding space thoroughly. There were no indicators suggesting a time limit for staying in the Temple of Knowledge; I settled down in front of the coffee table. I decided against reaching for the paper sheet: there were no guarantees that as soon as I got it in my hand I would not be thrown back into my body suffering from pain. If someone or something suspended the time for me, I would do well to thoroughly think over everything that happened to me..

Judging from the appearance of my surroundings, I was indeed placed within a computer game, through some incident combining the functions of character and player. Or supposing that I was a player. It was quite likely that in some other world there was a zitty nerd in glasses sitting in front of a monitor and controlling me, making me go in one direction or another. On the other hand, if I were under someone else's control there would not have been the option to choose a race. Immediately after I had killed Petrovich I should have been turned into a vampire and received a whole heap of info on my new race. However, that was not the case, and I was allowed to visit the Temple of Knowledge. A gamer is not likely to take it well to have a character that decides on his own what path to choose for development. Or it could be a type of game where the character makes decisions independently and the gamer only determines the main direction for development? Damn! You could really wreck your brain on this!

I hadn't spent much time in the game itself, if it could be called that. Even though I was conscious only for a few minutes, now that I was recalling my sensations and the overall environment I could state with certainty: the game did not differ from the world in which I had lived for twenty-three years. Remembering the strange opponent that I had managed to destroy would lead me to conclude that I had been living in the game even before I died. Because it was just an ordinary mage that came out to fight our platoon. Protective magical sphere, flaming hands, the APC soaring into the air... the whole scene of my death looked too much like a fight between a mage and some peasants with pitchforks. Besides, one peasant had managed to stick his pitchfork straight into the mage's head.

The first question that came up – did I kill him or send him for respawn? Does it exist in this game at all? If so, what is the cost to the player – does he lose a level? Is he rolled back to the starting point in development? Does he transfer to a respawn point? Will he try to avenge his death? Why was I made a player? Is it because I killed another player? Or because I sent him for respawn? Swarms of questions popped up in my head, but they all went unanswered. No one hastened to me with an open embrace to explain the core rules of the world in which I had ended up. The old man became still as a statue. During the entire time that I was sitting on the floor he never moved, waiting while I read the crumb of knowledge allocated to me and returned for more suffering. I was allowed to become one sheet of paper wiser. How could there be anything more valuable than that?

I leaned closer to the paper and read a couple of short paragraphs.

Human. Unpopular game race (0.0092% of all players). Commonly occurs in the following game worlds: "Altair" (82.3376% of players, dominant role in governing the world), "Gliax" (57.0093% of players, dominant role in governing the world), "Earth" (7.4471% of players, advisory role in governing the world). In other game worlds humans constitute less than 1% of the total number of players; have no influence on governing the world. Positive features of the race: adaptability to the environment is 180% of normal. Negative features: initial level of physical and energy state is 20% of normal; rate of increase of attributes is 20% of normal.

Hm... that is a rather interesting description that brings up more questions than it provides answers. Earth is just a game world among others. So, we are not alone in the universe after all and there are other locations where other people live? Not little green men that every second earthling secretly wants to see but just normal people that look exactly like us? Scientists and ufologists of the Earth of my past would have given several decades of their lives for this information. Stop! Now is not the time for figuring out where and how people live. That's not what I am here for. Even without reading the description of the bloodsucker I could tell that humans were weaker on all accounts. Disadvantages were too great and it was unclear whether they were offset by adaptability. What was it needed for, anyway? I wondered if I were to ask the old guy a question on terminology, would be consider it a question on an *"unrelated subject"?*

Vampire: popular game race (3.4419% of all players.) Common in 42 game worlds <list of worlds>, playing the dominant role there. In another 172 worlds <list of worlds> represents over 5% of players and takes an advisory position. Absent in 5 game worlds. Positive features of the race: initial physical condition is 150% of normal, elevated resistance to mind energy, accelerated recovery of attributes during nighttime. Negative features: initial energy level is 1% of normal, in daylight rate of attributes recovery is 1% of normal; requires blood consumption at least 1 time per week.

This was the end of information. No classes, directions of development, locations for study and training – there was nothing more. Those in charge of the game considered that in order to make a decision it would be enough for me to have a brief overview of the areas where the races are common and a few words on their features. Very informative indeed!

"You have read the comparative characteristics of the two races," stated the old guy. I was right: they were going to take me back as soon as the information was in my brain. Who am I to stay in such a "sacred" place? A level one player unable to decide what would be better: a human or a vampire? On the other hand, why unable? I have already sorted it out for myself.

"You must make a choice. In order for it to be a justified one you will be taken back. Remember: the doors of the Temple of Knowledge are always open to seekers."

Something flashed in front of my eyes and the whiteness of the Temple of Knowledge was replaced by the dirty floor of the trailer covered in blood and vomit.

You have not completed initiation; therefore, you can change race. Races available: Vampire. Accept changes?

The pain returned together with the message. My body curled into a fetal position of its own accord, trying to calm the burning innards; my head felt like an iron band was tightening around it; my eyes were trying to roll out of their sockets and my mind stopped perceiving the surrounding world altogether, stuck on the sensations. Only the stubborn message kept floating in front of my face. Colored circles jumped around it, black dots were flying, strange images appeared and dissipated, but the message could not care less about the flashes that surrounded it or about my condition. It wanted a choice.

"NOO" – a rasp escaped my throat. I was unable to concentrate enough to push a button. So people in this game have obvious problems with numbers; their abilities are abysmal compared to vampires; perhaps my end in this game will not be enviable, but I will not regularly drink blood of living creatures. I'd rather die now than ever taste it again. This is not my thing.

You have rejected a race change.
Bonus received: your initial levels of physical and energy state are 25% of normal, rate of increase of the attributes is 25% of normal
Character adjustment is in progress

If I had thought that the fire burning me up from the inside was pain, I was grossly mistaken. The moment I mumbled my refusal, the flickering flame of a candle was replaced with the roaring fire of a smelter. I lost my hearing. My sight. My speech. I lost all feelings but THE PAIN. Screamed even though I could not talk. I pleaded with the shadows around me to kill me, even though I could not see. I heard the monotonous hum of one-dozens-hundreds-thousands of voices even though I was deaf. I lost my mind even though I kept thinking. I was the pain and the pain was me. At some point the blessed darkness took pity on my shattered mind and carried it into oblivion. Perhaps I was destined to die and never exist again, but staying in this hell was beyond what I could bear.

My consciousness returned, harsh and sudden, like the onset of winter for the snow removal services. At some point I realized that I was lying on the floor in a fetal position, shaking from the cold and the memory of the nightmare I had just gone through. I opened my eyes and saw a view worthy of the most illustrious impressionists: a bloodied floor covered with clumps of dirt, and Petrovich with his glassy eyes and torn-up throat. The digger, wedged between the table and the cabinet, rocking back and forth and mumbling something unintelligible and nonsensical. The underside of the table covered in congealed snot. A totally disgusting sight.

Quest received: "Road to the Citadel". Reach the headquarters for the forces of your class. Coordinates of the Citadel are indicated on your map.

The location map icon started blinking compellingly, informing me of new data available. However, new information was not useful at all: the map was still covered in dark fog, obscuring the map from me. The Citadel was marked on the map with a small flag, and if I figured out their scaling correctly the central base of the Paladins was somewhere on the other side of the world relative to where I was right now.

"I can't really figure it out — did you become a vampire or not?" — a derisive voice sounded, making me shift into a vertical position. I did not have the strength to stand, so I simply sat up, leaning my back against the wall of the trailer, and tried to look around. I was not able to accomplish the latter though: the amount of physical work required to sit up made me dizzy and breathless, as if I were an untrained runner having to cover a distance of a hundred meters in full battle rattle. In the midst of the multicolored sparks and fireworks in front of my eyes I practically saw a question come from my body: — *"What have I turned into if I am choking just from trying to sit?! This is what they call 25% of normal?"* An eternity went by before I could think clearly and finally was able to look around. And then my jaw practically dropped. In the door, wearing steel armor shining brightly in the light of moon and stars, there was a cat, standing there with his paws crossed on his chest and smiling sardonically. His sharp teeth were bared for all to see. More precisely, it was a man with a cat's head, paws and tail. As far as I recalled, felines were unable to stand on their hind paws so naturally, shoulder leaning against the doorframe.

"I will ask the question once again — did you become a vampire?" the cat repeated.

"Vanish!" I managed to squeak hoarsely. My thoughts were preparing to waltz again against the backdrop of multicolored circles, but I was suppressing the dizziness. I was able to anchor myself by a simple question: why was my mind perceiving a person who entered as a cat? Did my mind decide to follow the way of the digger who was still rocking back and forth and mumbling nonsensically?

"I will for sure. But later. So, are you a vampire?"

"No." Since the hallucination was not going to vanish, I decided to respond to it. Of course, it is not quite normal to talk to your imaginary companion, but I was not concerned with "normalcy" at the moment.

"But you did drink blood?"

"I did."

"Did you receive an offer to change your race?"

"I did."

"But you remained human. Why?"

"Salt is bad for you," I grumbled.

"Well, that's an option too," the cat chuckled. "Anyway, it's time to get you out of this pit; we'll figure out what to do with you at the Citadel. I hope you received the quest at least?"

"Yes."

"Well, at least something. Want to see something funny? Of course you do, you can't avoid it anyway. Look here! That's you!"

A mirror appeared in front of me – a huge one, hanging in the air unsupported. I should have been surprised by an object appearing out of nowhere, but this minor issue faded into the background. A head was staring at me from the mirror – ugly, bloodied, dried to the point of resembling a mummy – and in it were two bright blue eyes.

"Aren't you a beauty!" the cat commented sarcastically. "Even if someone on Earth were to remember you, they would definitely fail to recognize you now. Congratulations, brother Paladin! I have completely blotted you out of this world. My quest is complete! ... Wait.. Something is not right..."

"What do you mean by 'blotted out'?" I asked the contemplating cat with surprise, having temporarily forgotten my horrible appearance.

"It means that... Right! We have a living witness right here! I was starting to think that I had missed something, and here he is, rocking coolly right here."

Something like a green jedi light saber from Star Wars appeared in the cat's hands.

"O-Oomph!" the hallucination said matter-of-factly, as it moved its hand sharply. The sword went through the digger's body smoothly and without resistance; the cat then smiled contentedly. My breath caught from seeing how the neatly removed head of the person who had been so withdrawn into his own world rolled on the floor, so I missed the moment when a light level-up halo standard in many games started forming around the Paladin. The cat grinned mockingly and concluded:

"Dear Archibald, I congratulate my dear self on my new level of 352! You have been striving for this goal for a long time, blah-blah-blah, fanfare and the like. What's your name, by the way?"

"Wh-h-aat?" I stumbled through the question, as I was completely confused. All my attention was concentrated on the digger's head that had rolled up to the wall and stopped. The cat had just killed a person just to complete some quest! Just so! In passing! Because he wanted to get some blasted experience points!

"What's your name, pray tell?" Archibald repeated without concealing his mirth.

"Sergey." The shock of the digger's death was so huge that I forgot that I was surrounded by the game.

"For demons' sake, what 'Sergey'?! Stop clinging to your past life! Forget about it! Nothing links you to that previous world anymore! The Sergey that you used to be is dead! Got that?"

"How can nothing link me to it? I have a sister, mother, friends..." I stumbled seeing the scowling face of the cat — "WHAT?!"

"Every time a new player appears," the cat started to clarify, ignoring my attempts to stand up and grab him by the throat. This bastard killed my relatives! He is a dead man! I will destroy him even if I die trying! — "Head of class receives the quest for zeroization of the new recruit. He doesn't do the quests himself, his status is above working in the fields; so there's a lottery held among best players. Experience for kills, experience for quest completion, the loot – all goes to the lucky one. You were good loot, I have not seen such rich pickings in a long time. I can say for sure: you left lots of traces in your previous life. Normally the system generates a dozen or so targets, but in your case there were 32 NPCs defined as mandatory targets, 67 as recommended and 91 as desirable. I got them all! That's why, frankly speaking, I was a little late: one of my tasks was to pour some water down your throat after you spawned. But this way it worked out even better – I got two additional bodies for power leveling. The one that ran out of here ten minutes ago and this one. The System defined them as additional mandatory targets, so the experience... Quit thrashing! Get it, bro – you can't do anything to me right now. After they appear the recruits are weak and dystrophic. If you decide you want to settle a score, I'll be happy to accept your challenge. If you come back from the Academy, that is."

"You are a dead man!" I growled with hatred, abandoning my attempts to stand up. The cat was right: at this stage there was nothing I could do to that freak. There was only one thing to do: remember him and wait for the right moment to avenge every person he killed!

"Of course I am a dead man – what else could I be? Because a fearsome nasty battle hamster which has a 99% probability of giving up the ghost in the Academy without the right of respawn is threatening to take revenge on me! My poor tail trembles in fear!" — The cat chuckled, then continued in a graver tone, "Get used to it, brother: from now on you are a player. Everything that surrounded you before is just one of the game locations, and the people you considered to be independent creatures were merely NPCs controlled by the System. You think the 192 bodies I popped off will leave a blazing trail in the criminal reports? Ha! The System chose them as payment for converting you into a player; the system itself blotted... No, I really do enjoy the way you are looking at me! Hatred, determination, bloodthirstiness! Let's do this: I will not say anything now about the specifics of becoming a player. Pass through the Academy. Survive, learn, become stronger, survive again and then we'll see each other once more! My name is Archibald, a Catorian, level 352, Paladin, respawn point is Earth. If after the Academy you retain your itch for revenge, I am always at your service. By the way, someone formerly known as Sergey, you never introduced yourself."

"Yari," I growled angrily. "Remember this name,

you freak. I will it remind you in the final moments of your life! I am Yari! Non-initiated, human, level 1, Paladin, no respawn point assigned yet."

"Hu-uhh," Archibald drawled, scratching his head in a purely human gesture. Then he swept the supper of the now dead cemetery custodians off the table to the floor, settled in the cleaned space as if it were a throne, shook his head as if deep in thought and continued: "It looks like we still have to take a brief tour into the game. Otherwise you don't stand a chance of coming back from the Academy. Who will then take revenge on me? The game interface has a button for recording conversations; press it."

"Where is it?" I gave up after a minute of fruitless attempts to figure out the status bar. The icons available to me were player description, map, personal inventory, book of spells, list of quests – and not a single hint at recording conversations.

"I see," grinned the cat. "Have you ever played games before?"

"I have. A lot."

"Doesn't show though. You should be able to see the standard player status bar at the bottom of your field of vision. Do you see it?"

"I do. But it doesn't have means to record conversations."

"Don't hurry. You need to call up the status bar properties. Imagine that you are using a computer mouse. To activate the icons you were using the left button, now you need to be working with the right one. Surprise me, my future enemy. Beginner players master this task after just a couple..."

Archibald fell silent without clarifying: a couple of what? But I was not interested in these technicalities. Unless the cat was lying, the status bar is interactive. Which opens up a lot of possibilities for changing its settings and using it. Who said that it reacts only to two buttons? What if I had not a two-button, but a three-button mouse? Or a four-button one? Would the bar react differently to each button? As if confirming my words a rectangular semi-transparent box appeared in front of me: status bar properties. The panel contained twelve buttons, only two of which were available to me: descriptions and additional options. The rest were covered with a freakish looking icon showing a scowling skull with three red eyes.

"Judging from your joyful squeak" — Archibald continued, noticing my reaction — "you have discovered properties. Very good. As I already mentioned, it takes new players a couple of months. You will have to fiddle with the descriptions yourself; now open the additional options. There will be three options available to you: recording, calculator and system time. Drag recording to the main bar – you need to use this thing all the time."

"What for?" I could not help asking as I was performing the sequence suggested to me. The cat was not lying: at the first level only three options were available to me out of a huge list. The rest were locked by the same scary skull. "If this is a game, the system itself should keep the records."

"Did you turn on the recording?" Archibald responded with a question, waited for me to nod in confirmation and continued: "Remember, my future enemy, the game could not care less about you, about me or about all the players generally, perhaps with the exception of the Emperor. It never does anything on its own initiative. No recording, no conflict resolution, no constraints on using magic – the game does not control what it has created. Even more so – it would never create anything that would require its control. Players should be responsible for their fate themselves. If you want to revisit some points of the game, turn on the video. If you want to have remote access to trading, use the auctions. If you want something else, take care of it yourself. Don't rely on the system."

"The scary three-eyed skull covering most of the buttons: what is this? Or who is this?" I asked once Archibald fell silent.

"That's an unusual question from a former NPC to whom the prospect of immortality has opened. Is that the only thing that concerns you at the moment?"

"No, but you have already delighted me with the statement that you will only tell me the information necessary for survival in some Academy. What's the point of asking you something that you are not going to tell? The skull is obviously not part of the data that you are hiding."

"That's logical." Archibald nodded and started swinging his legs. "The skull is the emblem of the Emperor. Who is the only player with moderator powers. Do I need to tell you what powers those are? Once you reach a certain level the skulls will disappear. Now to the most important thing. Remember, Yari, information on your personal attributes is your most guarded secret. Never tell it to anyone, under any circumstances. Especially to warlocks. Particularly if the warlock is an elf. Have you ever read the Bible? Remember those guys – demons – mentioned there? They were extremely unlucky in disclosing personal data; they had, like, the worst luck ever. One of the elven warlocks, Solomon, destroyed their whole race practically single-handed. Acting through a front man whose name was not even retained in history, Solomon captured a minor demon, found out its name – Ornia – subdued it, and then through Ornia captured first the head of the demons – Baal – and then another 70 great princes from his clan. The captives were interrogated, chained, then forced to do the hardest labor; then, once Solomon was tired of dealing with them, the great demon princes together with the great hosts of their servants were imprisoned in a copper vessel and thrown into Chaos. If you are ever interested, you will find the details of this abominable affair in the grimoire "Solomon's Covenant".

"Why abominable?"

"Because humanity has never been framed so badly! Note the subtlety with which Solomon set it all up: he didn't capture a single demon himself. He acted either through a front man or through the demons themselves. What do you think, once the survivors of Baal's clan decided to get to the bottom of it and punish those at fault: who bore the brunt of their righteous ire?"

"People?" I put forth a guess.

"Exactly! The elves appeared innocent; Solomon gained so much experience points for destroying 72 princes that he was able to take his grinning ass to another location, and only people were left behind high and dry to face the enraged demons. Hello, Priest player Innocent III and the Inquisition he created, looking for any manifestation of demonism under the pretext of eradicating heresy! Hello, the slaughter known to everyone as the Black Death epidemic, which was, in fact, a demonic ritual that took, around the 1340s, about 60 million NPCs and one third of all players on Earth. Hello... oh, there were a lot of things going on in those times! Just the "Malleus Maleficarum" counts for quite something! The priests, under the pretext of fighting the demons, started to kill their own dark brothers — maleficars and witches, as the priests wanted to increase their own numbers! That's history, you can't get away from it. So, the maximum you can tell other entities about yourself is name and class. Level, respawn point, race, properties, specialty, other information — all that must be hidden. Otherwise you will follow the path of the demon princes.

"What do you mean by 'increase their numbers'? How can the number of priests increase at the expense of witches?"

"Well... Ok, I'll tell you that as well. At this time Earth houses the headquarters of 42 classes. As you understand, a class may include more than one race. So. There are several ways to become a player. The first and most standard one: every month for each class the System independently selects the most suitable person and converts him into a non-initiated player. The class members do a little purge – normally 3-4 people – and transport the recruit to the headquarters, from which he is then transported to the Academy. If the recruit complies with the game requirements and finishes the Academy, he returns and becomes a full-fledged player. As I mentioned, about one out of every hundred returns."

"Why?"

"Because if a player is killed he loses one level. Do you think the level 1 recruits have a lot to lose? Some classes developed a habit for power leveling their newbies before the Academy to level 3, the maximum allowed for non-initiated players, but it did not improve the survival rate. One out of a hundred. The other way to become a player is a kill. If the stars align the right way and an NPC kills a player, he will become a player himself. The killed player will return to respawn point and receive a quest 'Revenge'. The System does not like unplanned noobs so it tries to restore balance every way it can. If you return from the Academy you will have another enemy besides me. The third and currently most popular method is a player zeroization. The number of players is practically always stable. The newbies that come out of the Academy don't affect the stats much, and your case is just unique. So. If, for example, a Paladin completely wipes out a Priest, then Paladins get a chance to turn one of their minions into a player. The minion they gain that way will go to the Academy and will finish it with a 100% guarantee: the System does not allow initiated players to die. By the way, had you become a vampire, the Academy would have been an unpleasant memory for you. Because of the third way of becoming a player: in the old times classes slaughtered each other like pigs. Priests, together with us, killed Witches, Maleficars, Warlocks, Mages and other magical classes. In turn, we were killed by the Blades, Warriors and Assassins. It was quite a slaughter. Finally a peace treaty was made to stop the mayhem that reigned on Earth, so for 600 years now there has been an armed neutrality between the classes. Well, that's about all you need to know for now. You will learn the rest in the Academy. Oh yeah, one more thing! You already killed an NPC. Take this: that's your rightful loot."

Received: 1 Granis

"Granis is the monetary unit of the players," Archibald immediately explained. "It is used in all the worlds. Objects, mercenaries, services, auctions: everything operates on granis."

"If I am killed, will I lose the money?"

"Dude, first live to the point when this becomes relevant for you," the cat laughed. "You'll die in the Academy: what do you need extra knowledge for? I've taken too long with you anyway. Any more questions?"

"Yes. You said that personal information is the utmost secret. Then why did you reveal it to me?"

"So that you'd know who purged your family. Who killed your mom, your sister, your friends and neighbors. Your dog too! Who completely wiped you out from the world of the living. You want revenge, right?"

A dark veil of hatred flooded me again. If I only had the strength I would have jumped on the cat without a second thought.

"Remember that feeling, brother, once you come to. Hold on to it and don't let it fade. Then you'll have a chance to make it. See you soon!"

The last thing I remembered before fainting were the two cords of fog shooting from the cat's paws and snaking towards me.

CHAPTER TWO

DEPARTURE FOR THE ACADEMY

"TAKE THIS ONE, brother!" Archibald's voice came through the fog, filling my mind: returning me to the horrible nightmare called reality. " One more body for the Academy."

"What's wrong with him? Is he sick?" an unfamiliar voice asked tensely. I tried to open my eyes to refute the accusation of sickness but the body would not respond. No matter how much I tried I was unable to move a single muscle. The only thing available to me in my current state was the game interface, so I opened the map and stared at my current location with an angry grin. The Citadel. I had been delivered to the right place.

"Information on the purge overwhelmed him, so I had to stun him."

"What?!" The exclamation of surprise from the unknown interlocutor was so natural it became clear: Archibald had committed a serious violation. "It is prohibited to use magic on uninitiated players outside the Citadel! You are facing…"

"I know the rules, brother," Archibald interrupted. "Don't bother; I will report myself to the head of the Order!"

"Fine, brother, you may leave him. What stun did you use?"

"A complete one. With a mental block."

There was a long pause.

"The Head of the Order is expecting you," the Catorian's interlocutor said after a while, having gathered his thoughts. "As you leave, send a couple of recruits my way. It would do them good to see how to remove a full stun."

"But what's the point? If a miracle occurs and Yari returns from the Academy, why should we present a new player to the Mages? He sent Devir for respawn. That wacko already submitted the request to surrender the offender to him. It's much simpler to send this loser to the Academy stunned to guarantee that he kicks the bucket, and inform Devir of his sudden demise. It will be simpler for everyone."

"Is that why you broke the law and used magic?"

"Sharda, I have no faith in him. He had a great chance to save himself but he refused. Had he become a vampire and had Garbital to back him up, Devir would not have been able to do anything to him until the quest was voided. It would have only taken a year! But no, Yari decided to remain human! Besides, even as an NPC he was a no-name nobody! Average development stats, game addiction, asocial, no quests or hidden targets associated with him. Nothing at all! Had he perished in battle the System would have erased the memory of him in as little as ten years."

"You forget – he managed to send a mage to respawn."

"I looked into that case. If Devir had known Monstrichello's nature he would have won that battle. Without a scratch. But he realized too late that Monstrichello's immune to magic, and just as he was going to crush him with a tank Yari appeared with his machine gun. Not even him – just his torn-off limbs. The soldier, covered in shit and piss, was already dead by then. Do you think a player like that has any chance against one of the most promising headhunters?"

"Why do you think the head of our order would not speak for Yari? Or the head of the people?

"Sharda, do you believe in that yourself? Gerhard's already up to his ears in work; why would he need trouble with the mages? As for Bartos... That's not even funny. He couldn't care less about his race."

"I understand your turmoil, brother, but I will repeat the old truth – you need to have faith in the best. Who knows what is in store for this recruit? Maybe wiping him out would cause a war with the

Mages. That's good reason to give the kid a chance: why not?"

"Do whatever you want," Archibald said, but there was obvious disdain in his voice.

That tailed beast had already written me off and was going to get rid of me! I'll kill that bastard.

"If you want to get him up and running, you are welcome. They will be sent to the Academy in three hours. I am not going to teach him. If you want to bother with a future corpse, go ahead. I'm off to see the Head."

"Don't forget to send me the recruits," Sharda reminded him, and then my consciousness decided to take a break again...

"Does everyone understand the sequence?" The first thing I heard after returning from "the nowhere land" was Sharda's question. "If you try to remove a complete stun using the standard method your patient will become a vegetable. The body will awaken but the mind will remain blocked. So first we bring back the spirit and only then work with the body."

If I read Sharda's tone correctly, at this time I had the great honor of serving as a guinea pig used to teach young inexperienced neophytes. Forgetting that my body was not obeying me I clenched my fists and tried to open my eyes. I had no desire to serve as a museum exhibit. However, as soon as my eyes opened incredibly bright light hit them, as if a piece of directly aimed sunlight was set right in front of my face. I shut my eyes reflexively, turned away and pressed my palms to my face — the light was blinding even through closed eyelids.

"Had the mind not awakened," Sharda continued to explain, unperturbed, "our patient would not have made such a frightful face and tried to cover himself from the light. He would not have cared. Remember the main rule when using magic: after applying any ability you must check the result. Because even a harmless treatment can result in a horrible death if, for example, ulcer stitches in the stomach dissolve together with a blood clot. Anything can happen."

"Sir Shardaganbat, may I ask a question?" a male voice asked in an ingratiating manner, making it sound extremely unpleasant. "So it means that our abilities can misfire at any moment? Is this determined by something, or does the game itself determine the probability of failure?"

"That's a good question," responded Sharda, or Shardaganbat, as he had just been called. "When you learn your first spell or ability, your spell book will update. It will have the inscription with the ability's name, description, requirements for use; there will be a lot of things noted there. Also, it will have a column showing how many times you have used the ability. This is a basic parameter that determines the probability of success or failure when using the ability. So the more you train the lower is your chance of failure.

I moved my hands away carefully and opened my eyes. The room had brick walls and was small, more like a cell; besides me lying on a sort of a dais there were five other creatures. Some oddity looking like a huge upstanding monitor lizard with six limbs, of which four were legs. A pointy-eared youngster that looked like a human, but was most likely an elf. An old guy so emaciated it begged the question why his body was not falling apart in pieces. A gnome about a meter tall wearing steel armor and – this surprised me most of all – Fagov! Lance-corporal Fagov, damn him! The huge two-meter bruiser with the brains of a five-year-old kid! How did he get here?"

"What, did I look like a mummy too?" Fagov asked, unwittingly providing me with a couple of hints. First: the former lance-corporal was addressing the gnome, thus revealing who was the boss here. Second: he was not the one who had asked about the abilities. Third: Fagov is a Paladin just like I am!

"Yes," Sharda nodded turning towards the thug. "People players look like skeletons after the transformation. Now back to our question. Besides the frequency of use of the ability, there is another important thing: Energy. It is known by a variety of names: mana, magic points, internal reserve, fury, vigor, but the core meaning is the same: this is what constrains you. The more Energy you have, the more powerful and precise your spells will be, the lower the chance to make a mistake when using the ability, the stronger player you become. Never disclose this value to anyone. Your life will depend on this!"

"How can one increase it?" the elf-like guy asked, which showed that he had asked questions before.

"Now this is not a good question, recruit," Sharda frowned. "At this time you should be asking just one thing: how do we bring Yari here" – the

gnome casually waved his hand in my direction –
"back to normal. Paladins don't make distinctions
between people, elves, gnomes and other races. As
Paladins we see a brother and his problem that needs
to be resolved. So take this weakling and go off to the
medical office. In an hour I will be waiting for you in
classroom 45. All five of you. We'll be preparing to
leave for the Academy.

The gnome turned around and went out of the
room unhurriedly, leaving me alone with the four
future Paladins.

"I don't remember being carried around," the
old man rasped. His voice suited his appearance –
squeaky, shaky and barely audible.

"You s-s-simply looked less-s-s s-s-scary," the
walking lizard replied in a rumbling and somewhat
sibilant voice. "Yari does-s-s look like a s-s-skeleton.
Let's-s-s go, we sh-sh-shouldn't keep th-them waiting
for us-s-s."

"I think I've already seen this roadkill
somewhere," Fagov frowned, looking me over from top
to bottom.

I was looking at the alien and fascinating
creatures, but there was no mental excitement from
seeing these wonders. Nothing like "Wow, a talking
dinosaur!" or "OMG, an elf!" Even the amazing
presence of Fagov failed to dispel the sudden apathy
once I remembered Archibald's "motivating" words: *"If
you want to bother with a future corpse, go ahead."*
The gnome never objected to that, just underscored
that my death could be useful for the Paladins.
Neither the Catorian nor the gnome believed that I

would be able to stay in the game! They just wrote me off as scrap! What's the point of caring about someone who's about to kick the bucket? Bastards!

I regarded without interest as the monitor lizard grabbed me with cold slippery fingers and heaved me over his shoulder seemingly effortlessly, as if I were a sack of flour. I did not have the strength to lift my head and look around, so all that I could do was to stare at the lizard's grey mantle and the green tail sticking out from under it.

"What, another human?" a voice asked in surprise and I was dumped onto a couch. The white surroundings were blinding me, so I closed my eyes. "Why are there so many Paladins spawning this month?"

"I don't know," the elf responded. "Sir Shardaganbat ordered us to deliver Yari to you, to put him on his feet. We are to leave for the Academy in an hour and a half... Is that even realistic? Is it possible to put THAT on its feet?"

I noted to myself glumly that in addition to Archibald and Devir I had acquired one more candidate for a heart-to-heart: the elf. Amazing, but the fantasy writers in my world were not lying about the arrogance of these creatures. Just after a couple minutes of knowing him I already disliked the elf. I know that there are plenty of jerks among people, but this long-eared one definitely had it coming for "THAT".

"An hour and a half?" the healer grinned. "During that time you can treat anyone. And definitely put him on his feet if you know how to do it right."

Lightness and weightlessness washed over me. Pain and strain that felt like permanent companions receded, leaving merely a bitter memory. Such a drastic change forced me to open my eyes forgetting about the blinding light. But it was not there anymore. Only blue shining was emanating from the hands of another shorty. Looks like the local gnomes had some sort of fetish for steel armor: the doc was also covered in metal from head to toe.

"I remember! You're the crowbag from my platoon!" Fagov exclaimed joyfully. "Homie! You run for the Paladins too?

"Do you know him?" the old man frowned.

"Sure! He's the one that popped off the mage! With the machine gun right through the skull. Bam – his head just popped! But wait! You died too!"

"So Devir is your doing?" The doctor looked at me with interest. All I could do was nod in agreement.

"Now that makes it clear why there are so many Paladins. Chosen one, guest, minion, immune and fighter. A jolly crowd.

"Huh?" Fagov's face demonstrated such utter confusion that the gnome deigned to clarify.

"The guest is the reptilian who came to our Citadel in accordance with the agreement between Gerhard van Brast who is the Head of the Order of Paladins of Earth and Shlikandr de Zak who is the Head of the Order of Paladins of Versala, the reptilians' home planet. If I recall correctly, brother, your name is Sartal, a level 3 minion.

"That's-s-s right," the reptilian nodded making a funny swing with his tail.

"Immune — brother Monstrichello, level one. Was discovered during the area clean-up following Devir's silly attack. He is completely unaffected by magic. The System sometimes might spring a trick and create a unique one like that. Was recommended to become a player by the search team, and he chose Paladin class. Is that correct?"

"— Hehe! —Fagov's face broke into a moronic smile. "Always wanted to be a Pal! I ran for them in Warcraft! Once they offered, I – right at once! I'll be a tank!"

"Minion," the gnome continued to explain ignoring Monstrichello's words. Damn! What a name he picked! "brother Nartalim from Earth. Level 3 minion. Elf."

"There are elves on Earth?" I was unable to hold back an exclamation of surprise.

"They are much more numerous than people!" Nartalim snorted arrogantly, nodding to everyone present. "I am talking about players. Elves play the dominant role in ruling the Earth.

"What the hell?!" It was Fagov's turn to be surprised. "I've never seen no pointy-eared freaks in my TV!"

"Every day, you mor...," the elf squinted at the frowning doctor and corrected himself, brother Paladin. "You did see us every day!"

"The guilded youth!" It was a random guess on my part but from the elf's grinning face it became clear: I hit the nail on the head.

"True, Yari. We are the true rulers of Earth! We ...

"Let's leave Earth's affairs aside," the gnome butted in, stopping the discussion. "You chose Light, so follow it to the end. Next is the Chosen one. This month it's brother Dietrich. Human. Level one."

The old man bowed his head in greeting.

"And, finally, warrior. Yaropolk. The human who sent Devir for respawn, thus obtaining a ticket to our world. Full team for departure... Amazing. Every month the Citadel sends new recruits to the Academy. Normally just one, sometimes two and very rarely three. But five all at once... I have never seen that yet.

"Are you like, really from Earth?" Fagov continued to stare at Nartalim, stunned, ignoring the doctor's words. "Why didn't you tell us nothing before?"

"Yari, explain it to him," The elf did not bother to answer, turning away from Monstrichello. "It seems you figured it out."

"Do the explaining yourself, brother. You have all you need for that: a head, a mouth, a tongue. Or do you use them for something else?" — I quipped and immediately faced an intense stare from Nartalim. Damn him! The elf's rating with me went down another point even though that seemed impossible. He was used to get it all at his beck and call in his previous life, and now after becoming a player this bastard continued to treat everyone with disdain, issuing orders left and right."

"The boy forgot his place?" The elf's eyes were lighting up with anger.

"You have any complaints, golden? Monstrichello and I become players on our own, not because of daddy! While you are nothing without his money! You are a twit! Like hell you'll graduate from the Academy!" It was a random blow, but the elf's widened pupils told me that it struck home!

"An initiated player always graduates from the Academy, Yari, remember that," the doctor somehow appeared between the elf and me, stopping the squabble. For some reason the gnome was looking angrily at me, and not at the elf, as if I were the one that had gone too far. Among the present company there are only three initiated: Nartalim, Monstrichello and Sartal. Neither you nor Dietrich passed the initiation, so treat your senior brothers with respect!"

"Speaking of finishing the Academy," Nartalim blurted out spitefully from behind the doctor's back. "I will miss you!"

We walked to classroom forty five in complete silence. Nartalim felt like a winner, striding in the front with his head proudly raised. Amazing, but Monstrichello and Dietrich walked close to him holding back just a little. As if they were the entourage ready to jump to fulfill any whim of their ruler. It seemed like they had been together for a couple of days and the elf managed to subdue both the old man and the oversized kid. Sartal minced his steps behind the three but in a way that made it clear – he was not with that company. At the same time the lizard maintained some distance from me to show that he had no intention of joining me either. The reptilian was keeping to himself.

"You are early." Sharda grumbled, looking at our group sullenly. Classroom forty five turned out to be just a normal gym; around the perimeter there were racks with weapons, armor and unknown gadgets. Sharda himself, still wearing the same shining armor, stood in the middle of the gym holding a small hammer and breathing heavily. Apparently we had interrupted a training session. My eyes unwittingly widened in surprise: the gnome was holding Mjollnir the way they drew it at <u>Marvel</u>. The legendary hammer of Thor.

"Stay, guys, there is nothing else I could do with you now," the gnome waved acceptance at us as we tried to leave the gym. Miraculously, the hammer vanished from Sharda's hands as if it had never been there. Magic? I didn't think so. Most likely the hammer was replaced among his personal inventory. I ought to remember this for the future.

"Lesson number seven," the gnome continued busily, — "every player needs to have his own main artifact. A weapon, armor, a spinner, it does not matter. The important part is: one player — one artifact. Throughout your game, regardless of how it plays out, you will develop and upgrade your item improving its properties every time. If you want your weapon to curse with every blow – no problem. Add the "Drunken Master's Blow" and level it up to level 4. There's no limit on the number of properties for an artifact; however, the more properties you add the lower are the chances you'd get a really great item in the end. Because you have to work on each property in order for it to work well. Any questions?"

"Where can one learn about the properties?" I asked after a short pause. For some reason other

Paladins were just listening to Sharda silently, not making any attempts to figure things out in detail. As for me, it was enough to have to choose race and class without sufficient information. Regardless of my attitude to Archibald, I had to admit his words had been true. I should have agreed to become a vampire. Then I would have had a one hundred percent guarantee that I would get out of that strange Academy.

"The choice of artifact is complicated... What?" — as I was asking my question Sharda kept talking about the artifacts, but now stopped, looking at me angrily. The air around the gnome swirled lightly; Sharda himself started darkening and increasing in size like a balloon someone was blowing up. The gnome's changes and a heavy sigh from Dietrich conveyed the main idea to me — I should not have interrupted Sharda.

"Where can one learn about the properties of an artifact?" I repeated. It was too late to retreat, so at least it was worth working on the topic in detail before facing the likely punishment. "Since they are so important for a player, it should be an informed choice... the Temple of Knowledge, with all my respect to the name, provides so little information that after you read it the only question remains: 'What just happened?' with all of that: "The information you need is in this scroll. Study it." I imitated the old guy from the Temple of Knowledge.

"Have you already been there?" The gnome instantly "deflated", looking at me with interest from the bottom up. "What was your question?"

"Comparative characteristics of humans and vampires." Concealing the truth would be silly.

"Oh, that's interesting," the gnome drawled contemplatively, then looked at the elf. "Brother Nartalim, explain the gist of lesson number two to brother Yari."

"Why me?" The offspring of high society immediately rebelled. That was funny. I had always considered the guilded youth to belong to another civilization. Not just sons and daughters of rich parents. But visitors from another world. The majority of them couldn't care less about others' problems; for them the value of people was determined strictly by availability of money or connections. Having fun and partying even during the lean years, traveling in expensive cars and ignoring the laws, throwing money around and demanding that they be treated as royalty — everything pointed to the elite members being from another planet. The truth revealed now was much simpler — they were partying elves. The system never showed to common NPCs, such as Fagov, the old guy and I, the racial differences of the guilded youth. Why traumatize their minds yet again?

"Because I said so," an evil smile blossomed on Sharda's face. "Any questions?"

"In order to receive an answer to your question, an inquiry to the Temple of Knowledge must be phrased to be as clear and certain as possible. It's preferable to word it in such a way that it could be answered with a 'yes' or 'no'," the elf surrendered. Apparently, the words "Any questions?" from the gnome served as a trigger, after which democracy ended and was replaced by a brutal dictatorial regime.

"When a player enters the Temple of Knowledge," Nartalim continued, "a record with a counter appears for him. The counter increments with each visit to the Temple. Those players who have visited the Temple fewer than 100 times will receive the answer in the form of a paragraph or two with the maximum number of words not to exceed ...," the elf slowed down, trying to recall a specific number, and then Sharda came to his aid:

"Up to two hundred words. Given that you were interested in comparative attributes of two races the answer that was given to you would have to be as general as possible. Seems as though you received an answer, but in fact those tend to generate even more questions. As for the properties of artifacts, you can learn about those either in the Temple of Knowledge or in the Library of the Citadel, which houses all the knowledge accumulated by the Paladins of Earth. The Temple of Knowledge does not always open to seekers. Did I answer your question?" Sharda looked at me so eloquently that all I could do was nod in agreement.

"Excellent. Let's get back to the lesson at hand. As I mentioned, choosing an artifact is a complex process. You have to look within yourselves and understand what would suit you best. Who are you? Fighters? Creators? Healers? Craftsmen? The item should be chosen wisely depending on the direction you have selected for development. History knows lots of examples of stupid choices. For example, there was once a hunter Hermes. Whatever moved him to choose an artifact in the form of sandals and suit them for flight – nobody knows. No damage, no healing power, no concealment. Nothing at all except for speed and ability to fly. Until Hermes moved on to another world he worked for his more experienced colleagues as an unskilled worker, a gopher of sorts. He specialized in delivering wine and women."

"The messenger of the gods," I whispered in amazement. The world turned on its head yet again. The Greek gods and heroes were mere players! Hermes, Heracles, Zeus – all these creatures really did exist and at some point walked this location, until they were upgraded! Now I know that the Earth is not really a very popular place for power leveling. Following that logic, everything that I knew about mythology and religion was true! Dragons, mages, monsters, boogiemen under the bed! All that exists or existed in reality!

"There are certain constraints imposed on the choice of artifact," Sharda continued."It's only possible to select an object that is associated with your class. You cannot get magical mirrors, staffs nor other knick-knacks of cheap market tricksters. These trinkets are not even here," Sharda waved his hands around the class. "In this room we have everything Paladins are allowed to use as artifacts. Here we have just the blanks that will become artifacts after the trip to the Academy. Look, explore, feel, choose. Normally we allow the newbies half an hour but you arrived early so you have a full hour. Any questions?"

"What questions?" Monstrichello boomed and unceremoniously started for the racks with weapons and armor. "It's all clear! I'm a tank! "I need a shield!

Dietrich is a healer. He needs..."

"Brother Dietrich will make his own choice," Sharda said quietly but it made Fagov fall silent. I just wonder, what did the gnome do during those three days of training that even Monstrichello treats him with respect?

"Brother Monstrichello is right," Dietrich said in a grating voice. "At my age it's too late to swing a sword about. I'll become a healer to the extent that's possible in our class at all. Maybe it will work out. I think I'll take this banner."

"A sword!" Nartalim stated with determination as he pulled out of the stand a thin curved blade that looked like a saber. "I will name it 'Heart of Thunder'!" With its aid I will crush myriads of enemies, reach level 100 and set off for Zalta!"

"That's a worthy goal," the gnome nodded in approval. "Yaropolk, Sartal?"

"I chose my object a long time ago," the reptilian rumbled, then came up to the rack with armor and pulled out a steel breastplate. "S-s-steel armor is important for a Paladin. Unless-s-s he has-s-s it he is-s-s weak and helpless-s-s. Es-s-s-pecially agains-s-s-t the mages-s-s.

"The shield is the best armor for a Paladin!" Fagov immediately started defending his artifact as a child protecting his toy.

"Everyone has his own defenses, brother Monstrichello," the gnome reassured the thug. "Some like a shield, and some a breastplate. You need to treat the choice of your brother in arms with respect. Yari, do you need more time?"

"What is the point of the game?" I responded with a question. I did choose my class based on emotions without realizing what threats that would entail. I did not know the advantages and disadvantages of Paladins; their features, special attributes, ways for upgrading were all hidden from me. As a former semi-professional player I was quite frightened by that. With this approach to choice of character there would be only one word to describe a player: lamer! I do not want to be called that.

"The ceremony will be held in one hour," Sharda ignored my question and the hammer appeared in his hand again. "If by that point you fail to select an artifact, you will die. This time for good. It is prohibited to use help from your brothers in arms to make the choice. Only the player shall bear the responsibility for his choice."

"Why should we bother with him?" Nartalim dropped a phrase, staring at complex passes the gnome started to make with his hammer. Sharda continued his interrupted training session that looked more like a dance; the presence of young recruits did not bother him in the least. "Everyone knows he will not make it back from the Academy. We are just wasting time now."

I made a gesture to indicate to the elf where he could go with his suggestions and looked around. Once again I was thrown into a situation of compete uncertainty. The players who had already made their choice must be already familiar with the specifics of the class. Just the statement Dietrich made: *"to the extent that's possible in our class at all"* indicates that he had some minimal knowledge about Paladins. Which could not be said about me.

What should I choose?

In general future artifacts were divided into several categories: weapons, armor, clothes made of cloth, incomprehensible devices – probably accessories – banners and books.

I rejected the banners right away. Logic and observing other players making their choices told me that the main task of the banners would be to improve battle morale and other attributes of the players. Perhaps even heal them. Even though the banners looked rather attractive, I did not want to be a buffer.

I lingered at the shelves with armor looking at breastplates, hammers, gauntlets and other shining silvery metal parts. Polished to mirror shine, the armor seemed to call to choose one of them, but I kept going. Strictly speaking one needs artifact armor only in one case: if the player is likely to sustain damage either fighting other players or battling NPCs. I would try to avoid the former; for the latter ordinary armor should suffice.

Weapons... I spent more time there looking at different swords, morning stars, hammers and even clubs. I was always drawn to cold steel; a few times I even attended historical medieval reconstructionists' gatherings, watching people with several left hands trying to hit each other with a chunk of metal. With a heavy sigh I stepped away from the racks: one needs to know how to use the sharp and pointy objects and that requires practice. However, unless I find something better I will come back here. Weapons are a universal choice, Nartalim is right about that.

As for the clothes made of cloth at first I was not inspired. Shirts, cloaks, pants, hoods... of course, a player needs all of those, but making a personal artifact from something made of cloth... I was about to go to the next set of shelves when an ironic thought wandered into my head — to take a cloak and upgrade it to invisibility. I would be able to come upon enemies unnoticed and then... The skin on my back crawled as I was hit with another revelation: invisibility cloaks were real! Some player chose that seemingly useless cloth item, upgraded it to invisibility and made history! Practically every ethnicity has legends about invisibility cloaks and clever men who were able to gain some bonuses using them.

Only now did it dawn on me that with the right upgrades any object would be useful, depending on the player's chosen role. All that was left for me to do was to decide whom I wanted to be in that game? A tank? To run ahead with my shield proudly raised and crash into enemy lines? If someone were to suggest that to me during the first minutes of the game I would have agreed without a second thought. In all the games that I had happened to play I had been exactly that – a tank. But now I could tell for certain: never again! Sustaining damage, suffering pain clenching my teeth and hoping for healers' skill —Monstrichello can have it. Natural immunity to magic and an artifact shield will make him a good tank. What was left was a healer or a fighter. I needed to make a choice.

Actually, that was an interesting question: why was I thinking using standard concepts? Tank, healer, fighter... Role constraints in computer games were introduced only for one reason: to simplify writing of the code. Why should I treat as dogma a solution by some ancient developer? Players don't even have properties, so the difference between a tank, a healer and, for example, a dancer would be purely due to the skills of the player and his clothes, but not due to virtual strength, agility and intellect.

The decision on who I wanted to be in the game appeared immediately once I stopped following the standard model. My mind had been trying to work it out for some time, and now it presented a solution. Given that I had ended up in a world that had dragons, vampires, princesses and other bogeys, I would like to study it in every detail. Explore everything that could be explored. Study it and start trading in knowledge. Because it was clear already now: the most important thing in this game was not strength but information.

"I need information on an object from this hall that would be optimal as an artifact for the explorer of the world!" I stated to the air a question as specific as possible. Remembering in time Sharda's words that not everyone is allowed in the Temple of Knowledge, I added: "the player who initiated me did not tell me anything about the game!"

"Was that allowed?" Nartalim drawled in surprise

A message appeared in front of me:

Request is granted. Access to Temple of Knowledge is provided.

For the duration of study of information time for player Yari is suspended.

The hall with the racks full of future artifacts was replaced by the already familiar white room. The gray-haired man greeted me and pointed at the coffee table. I opened the character properties and grinned — a new parameter did in fact appear: number of visits to the Temple of Knowledge, which currently equaled two. Where there are two, there is a hundred. I opened the scroll and started reading the text:

Explorer of the game — a development direction for a player who chose the path of knowledge, discovering new lands (cartography), new monsters (monstrology), elixirs and potions (alchemy) and other areas of research <list of fields>. The most optimal artifact for world explorers from the hall of blanks of the Citadel of Paladins of Earth is the Book of Knowledge (accessory). Location of the Book of Knowledge in the hall of blanks of the Citadel of Paladins of Earth is shown in the figure <figure>.

Advantages of the Book of Knowledge as an artifact: accelerated replenishment of Energy; adaptive intellect of the Book enables it to read information from any source and systematically arrange it in accordance with the specified criteria. The Book of Knowledge can be upgraded to automate any areas of research <list of fields>. Drawbacks of the Book of Knowledge as an artifact: no player attack or defense properties.

"You received the necessary information," the old man reminded me of his presence as soon as I finished reading the scroll. "You need to select your artifact and complete study in the Academy. Remember: the doors of the Temple of Knowledge are always open for seekers."

"It didn't work? Loser!" Nartalim laughed as soon as I returned to the gym. For the players my disappearance and return went unnoticed. That gave me an interesting thought: the Temple of Knowledge could be used not only as a place where one receives information. I must think of a question that the system will consider compliant with the requirements and grant me a visit to the Temple, plucking me out of the world around me. For example, when I need to think about something thoroughly. That would be useful for the future.

The scroll with information stayed at the Temple, so I approached the rack with accessories guided by memory. I was not going to react to the elf's words. I would need to find out whether conflicts between players of the same class are allowed. Not now, but in a couple of years I will remind Nartalim of the way we first met.

Item is received: Book of Knowledge. Item type: personal artifact. To initiate the artifact visiting the Academy is required.

The Book of Knowledge turned out to be a thick A4 tome bound in smooth black leather. Despite its impressive size it weighed practically nothing. Rough yellow pages were empty, there was only an inscription on the flyleaf: *"Book of Knowledge* of *<undefined> Paladin Yaropolk"*. I automatically pressed the word in the parenthesis without thinking of whether it was allowed or not. I wanted to see what "undefined" meant. What would the choices be anyway? The System decided that my actions were within the game logic, so additional text appeared before me:

Allegiance options: Light; Darkness. To select allegiance initiation is required.

The number of questions grew in geometric progression: what does that mean: Paladin of Light or Darkness? What advantages are conferred by allegiance of one type or another? What does allegiance mean anyway? To whom or to what is it? To gods? Did it not become clear that gods were just high level players? Or was I mistaken? The questions appeared one after another, sometimes unrelated to each other, but there were no answers to them. I would have to find everything out for myself. Following a habit I had acquired back in the days of the computer games, I opened my small virtual shelf and placed the artifact on it. What else – drag it around in my hands all the time?

"Remember for the future, brother Yaropolk, you should not hide the Book of Knowledge in your personal inventory," Sharda addressed me. "The specific feature of the object you chose is that in needs to gather knowledge continuously. In inventory it will gather only dust. Don't forget that."

"You know how to us-s-se the inventory?" Sartal asked with interest; he had already put on his armor. Miraculously it fit the player, adjusting itself for the unusual reptilian body. "I was-s-s told that before the Academy it's-s-s imposs-s-s-ible."

"Why?" I frowned. "Can you not see the status bar?"

"Everyone can see it," Dietrich said as he approached us. "It's such an eyesore: useless and covers up some space."

"Strange... then how did you choose your names?" I remembered my first experience of interacting with the game interface, but the frowning faces of the reptilian and the old guy told me that my question was inappropriate.

"Recruits choose the names, but they are granted by their mentor," Sharda clarified, coming over to us. "The option of choice is provided only to those recruits who became a player via a kill. Enough talking – it's time to go! The ceremony for welcoming the Paladins will start in just a few minutes."

"Welcoming?" I was unable to refrain from asking.

"The Academy is located outside of time," Dietrich answered because Sharda started towards the door out of the gym without bothering to respond to me. "We were told at the first lesson that one can stay in the Academy even for all of eternity. For everyone else we will either instantly turn into Paladins, or no one will ever remember us again. The Academy will completely wipe the losers from memory."

"What is the Academy altogether?" I asked the old guy, finding a good topic for conversation."

"We weren't told much about it. It seems to be sort of huge obstacle course. Everywhere there it has teachers and training sites so the player chooses on his own how to level up. The number of teachers with whom you can study is unlimited – the important part is how to reach them. Because they are scattered throughout the site and as you can guess it's flippin' hard to figure out where the most useful ones are. In order to graduate from the Academy you need to complete ten mandatory lessons. There we will learn to use the main functions. It does not look complicated, but those ten are not located in the same place either. First you have to find them, and then survive trying to get to each one of them."

"Thank you!" I thanked the old man sincerely. Now I had at least some idea about the Academy. "Dietrich, where are you from?"

"From Germany."

"But we still understand each other," I noted with surprise

"There is only one language within the game, and all players speak it," Sharda who was walking ahead of us deigned to answer. "That was in lesson number one."

"I missed the lessons," I reminded the gnome.

"Preparation for the Academy starts three days before departure; the fact that you were clinging to your former life and were unwilling to become a player is your own problem. You cannot burden others with it." Sharda was not hesitating to hit the soft spot, reminding me how he felt about me. Neither he nor Archibald believed that I would return. Another wave of rage washed over me, but I did not let it take over. I should not succumb to emotions. Instead of getting mad at the gnome I started looking at the Citadel around. We were walking on a blue-green carpet covering the floor of a long and wide corridor. Every twenty steps we passed two doors set in front of each other. On both sides of each door statues of lions stood about a meter and a half tall. I was completely certain that in case of an unforeseen attack the statues would turn into formidable fighters. But on the whole there was nothing unusual or outstanding about the corridor. Nothing that would tell a random visitor who happened to find himself in the Citadel that he was in a fantasy game world and not, for example, in a hallway at Versailles.

Our goal was the twenty-first door. Sharda fiddled with the lock for some time, grumbling a few choice words about some Volson who had not oiled the lock in time. Finally, the obstacle was surmounted and we entered a small dim room lit up by blue light of a portal. There was no way THAT could be anything else.

"Put that on," Sharda ordered and only then did I see five suits of steel armor, practically identical to the one the gnome was wearing. "Keep your artifacts on. They will combine with the outfit."

The portal looked so incongruent to the customary world that I had a hard time tearing my gaze from it; then I went to the nearest heap of metal.

I picked up the helmet glumly and looked at the gnome sideways: there was no way I could put on all of that by myself. The ancient knights spent hours wriggling into their armor with the help of their squires, while we were allocated just a couple of minutes for the whole thing.

"Just start putting something on," Dietrich suggested to me; he was turning into a steel monster as I looked. "The elements will fit themselves in place."

Class suit of armor received

"Amazing," I whispered as soon as the last element of the armor fit in place. The moment I put my head through the opening of the breastplate it fit into the right location, adjusting itself to my anatomy. Turning into a steel colossus did not feel uncomfortable: the armor felt weightless and did not restrain movement. Had it not jingled when you knocked on it, you could think that you had put on a comfortable track suit. But the most amazing feature was a special holder for my book on the right thigh. Just as I touched it to the holder it attached to it as if it were part of the armor. And again, no constraint or discomfort. I was starting to like being a player.

"If you put on the helmet and lower the visor, you can go under water," Sharda said, noticing the stunned expressions of the five faces. New players were taught how to dress, but no one had mentioned that we would be given our own sets before going to the Academy.

"Before the irrepressible Yaropolk asks," Sharda added, looking at me with a grin, "only players can see the armor. As for NPCs, instead of the steel they will see whatever clothes are most appropriate for a given situation: formal dinner clothes, track suit, shorts, or even underwear. The System takes care of that. Remember situations when some celebrity constantly appears in public, wearing a different outfit every time? You think it's because they have vast wardrobes? Yea, right! It's just a common player who likes to be fawned over by NPCs. Newbies frequently go bonkers once they realize all the perks of the game. So a few words about the armor. The most important thing you must remember for the future: you may take it off only in the Sanctuaries. If you want to have sex, either do it wearing the armor – it will allow you to do that – or go to a Sanctuary. There are no other ways. Any player will be happy to send you for respawn as soon as he sees you without the class armor. Now put on the helmets and lift the visors, everyone. In the Academy you will learn how to make them invisible, but you are supposed to show up in full regalia for the ceremony."

"But where are the weapons?" Monstrichello asked. Packed into a steel suit of armor with his shield at the ready he was a frightening sight; however, the confused expression of a little child who did not receive the promised candy told it all.

"All you are allowed to bring to the Academy is your artifacts," Sharda explained. "No other weapons. "You will receive your sword after you return. This is true for the others, too, except for Nartalim. Enough talking. They are waiting for us!"

Passing through the portal was memorable. Despite my past game experience it's one thing when you place your character into the brilliant circle of light while you are sitting in a comfortable cozy armchair and it's an entirely different matter when you personally have to step into the lightnings and feel all the "pleasures" of the transition yourself. Sharda had never said anything about the operating principle of the portal, so it was unpleasant to feel a short stab of pain, as if someone had quickly pulled me in all directions and immediately compressed me back into my original shape. The pain was so intense that dark circles danced in front of my eyes for several moments. As soon as my vision returned back to normal I looked around and...

"What the hell...!" Monstrichello and Dietrich whispered at the same time, practically taking the words off the tip of my tongue. Nartalim scornfully snorted, as if he saw nothing unusual in the fact that we were transported to the stands of an enormous amphitheater. Having settled in a free seat the elf was looking with a bored expression at one of the several hovering screens broadcasting to the players in the upper rows what was going on in the arena. Even though it would be a stretch calling our places top rows: there were about fifty rows filled with players above us. On the other hand, there were a lot more rows below us and they were also filled with players. There were those who had tails, horns, wings, who were tall or short; the variety of game races was stunning. The only common feature among the players was that they were all humanoid: two legs, two arms, one head and walking upright. At least in the area of the stands visible to me.

A barely audible pop sounded from the right causing me to turn to look. In the few seats still available some red monsters in Paladins' armor had just appeared and I was barely able to keep my jaw from dropping once my brain compared the appearance of our new neighbors with the image stored in my memory. Orcs! They looked exactly like the orcs from "The Lord of the Rings" movie, only their skin was red!

"Shardaganbat, your recruit wants to tell us something?" one of the Paladin orcs growled. It dawned on me only then that I was staring at the orcs like a sheep staring at a new gate, and they did not like it.

"Grygz, friend, good to see you!" Sharda exclaimed gladly, standing between the orcs and myself seemingly inadvertently. — "Oh, I see you have two candidates this month? How did you get them?"

"Wiped out one long-eared monster, so we got a chance to turn a minion into a player," Grygz replied, looking at Nartalim with obvious meanness. "And you are still teaching people and elves?"

"Someone's got to do it," Sharda grinned. — "Why not me?"

"Oh here you are!" we heard a pleased male voice. "Sharda, you are damn hard to find!"

Gnome suddenly deflated, turned around and looked glumly at something behind my back. The change in the appearance of my mentor was so different from his normal cheerful appearance that I could not resist the urge to look at the new guest. If someone can intimidate Sharda that much, I should treat him with caution as well. Then later I will be able to .... Damn that!

A rather attractive smiling player wearing the loose robe of a mage was standing next to us. Grey streaks at the temples suited amazingly well to the deep black eyes making the mage potentially extremely attractive to any woman. The man's smile was so sincere that it would have made me feel that I liked that person, even though I didn't intend to, but for one thing. Those black eyes were the last thing I remembered from my previous life. The owner of these eyes calmly and without unneeded emotions had killed a squad of special force troopers; then his own death turned me into a player. And now Devir, who appeared in front of us accompanied by two other mages the same as himself, wanted to accomplish one of his quests: kill the insolent pest.

"Just try to attack him!" The gnome said glumly, but made no attempt to stand between Devir and myself. If the mage had decided to destroy me nothing would have stopped him.

"Sharda, I am not going to do anything with him myself!" laughed the mage. "Just think: would I be able to get any experience points from him? Why would I bother? I transferred the quest."

"WHAT?" the gnome exclaimed in amazement, but the mage was not listening to him any more. Turning to his companions Devir started describing the task:

"Target number one is Yaropolk, he is a priority. The one who manages to destroy him in the Academy will receive my personal favor. The main task is to prevent him from coming back. If Yaropolk graduates from the Academy, you would be all better off not coming back at all — I'll wipe you out myself. Target number two is that bear over there. You ought to be careful with him: he's immune to magic. He has already passed initiation, so my gratitude will be proportionate to the number of times he dies. If he returns from the Academy as a level one player, that would be excellent. Any questions?

"You don't dare sick your recruits on Paladins!" Grygz roared coming up to stand next to Sharda.

I have already dared, you atavism of the past," Devir smiled murderously. "I need to train and develop my recruits, and why should Paladins be treated better than other classes? Besides, all my actions are justified: as a mentor I have the right to share my quests with recruits. It's all within the rules of the Game. Or are you going to challenge my right to revenge?"

"Fight like a player!" Grygz continued, while Sharda stayed silent. "Give him time!" If you want to help your newbies develop, allow Yari to reach at least level three; then you can start your bullying. There is little honor in a first level player. If you are training new headhunters, prepare them for the fact that your prey can fight back."

There was a pause. Devir looked at Grygz in contemplation with eloquently raised eyebrows. Sharda kept looking at the mage glumly, without the slightest attempt to come to my defense, while the surrounding players watched with interest the free drama with a potential bloody outcome. Paladins against mages, and the mages were within their rights. Somehow I didn't like being the main character of this drama.

"Mentor, are those the weaklings someone is going to try and turn into headhunters?" A female voice asked, and another participant joined the drama. The Paladin orc at whom I had stared insolently for a long time turned out to be a female. I would have never guessed: the armor concealed all the sexual attributes, provided that race had them altogether. The femorc contemptuously looked Devir's companions over and snorted. The young mages returned the look but did not even move a muscle. Devir had trained his recruits even better than Sharda.

"Target number three — femorc Logir," Devir recovered and continued with the task description. "It's hard to admit it, but that relic is correct: you need to be tested in battle. You have been coddled for too long. You are allowed to attack all three after they complete training with five teachers. Until then do not interfere with them; moreover, you ought to help them. I will not be very pleased if they croak before the specified time."

"You have no right to attack Logir," Grygz grinned bloodthirstily. Now I failed to understand anything at all, because Grygz seemed pleased. There is a hunt announced against his student, and his mentor does not move an eyebrow; moreover, he radiates extreme pleasure and joy! Is he actually crazy?

"Why would Zagransh need good-for-nothings, who are unable to overcome hardships?" Devir smiled no less murderously. "It will be a pleasure to prove that she is not worthy the name of 'player'".

I will wipe you out, mage!" Logir shouted out defiantly, but to me it had too much flourish. Too elaborate. "But first I will wipe out those puppies of yours! Two mages... Phhh!"

"Two?" Devir frowned, then smiled. "Red-skinned wonder, from what kind of hole did you crawl out? "All the six hundred and three mage recruits will be hunting you, not just this pair. If you return from the Academy with bonus levels — good, you will have demonstrated that you have prospects as players. If you return at level one ... better not to. As for you:" Devir gave me a head-to-toe look — "aren't you an unlucky lad! If you had chosen mages, it could have all played out differently."

Devir turned around and quickly strode off.

"I'll be right back," the femorc dropped, rushing after the mages.

"You shouldn't've gotten into this," Sharda said, looking at Logir's retreating back. Devir is dangerous.

"I know," Grygz replied. "Logir wants to become a headhunter; Devir is the only mentor who agreed to train her. We have been discussing that with him for a while and he finally agreed. Logir will watch over Yaropolk so that he will not do something stupid and then would die when the mages need it. These are our arrangements. In addition I will be able to see how well she learned.

"So you are in cahoots with him?" Sharda frowned. "That's why; I thought it looked odd, because where would the old orc find the guts for that? I thought you were looking for an official excuse for a battle."

"Sharda, it's no secret to anyone that Yari is already a goner. If he's not wiped out in the Academy, after the ceremony Devir will not let him leave the Sanctuary. I have a chance to pull my daughter out of Zagransh and I am definitely going to use it. If this requires sacrificing a Paladin... oh well, that's his destiny.

"So this show with the five teachers..." Sharda started to say, but Grygz interrupted him:

"That was Devir's wish. He needs fighters, not baby-killers. They will help Yari to get to level 3 or 4 and then will start killing him."

The rosy aura of heroism that had colored the femorc for a few minutes now faded at once: Devir sent a snitch with me, by the way, providing me with very interesting information: players' relatives do not become players automatically. In any case they have to go the standard way: minion – recruit – Academy. Associations flooded my mind again: the gods of Ancient Greece and their children. The gods themselves, as was illustrated by Hermes, were players, but their offspring were only minions. Close to players, but still mortal NPCs. Only a few were able to attain the status of gods – that is, players. As far as

I recalled only Heracles was able to follow that path through to the end. Ok, I would remember that and take note. As for the femorc, I'll deal with my problems in the order in which they appear. It's just unpleasant to be reminded again that those from the game class you chose consider you merely a waste. Again.

"Does Logir know?" Sharda kept asking.

"Why would she? Her task is to watch Yaropolk and help him in everything. The mages will do the rest."

"I see. Do you know that Yaropolk can hear us?" Sharda asked with sudden mirth. "What do you think: will Logir be glad to find out about the role assigned to her if Yari were to tell her everything?"

"WHAT?!" Grygz looked at me, stricken, then at the grinning gnome and then at me again. "But I have cast the Curtain of silence!"

"There are three reasons for why he can hear us. First, he is a world explorer. Second, he is not initiated and has already been subjected to a full stun. You know very well what happens to players like that.

"And you said nothing!" the orc exclaimed in anger, leaning over the gnome.

"The third reason," the gnome continued, completely unfazed – he was not at all afraid of orc in the way he was of Devir – "I let him under the curtain myself. I was worried the first two reasons would not work. I know very well that Yaropolk will die in the Academy and that now is the last time I am seeing him. But it is he who is our brother, not the mage! It seems your love of your daughter has clouded your mind, since you have forgotten the basics of the class. We are Paladins! Our brother's problems are our problems! So if you betray one of us to the mages, you betray us all. I will report your actions to the management. Farewell, brother!"

Sharda pointedly turned to the screens, clearly indicating the conversation was over. The orc hanging over the gnome deflated as Sharda had in front of Devir a while ago. The orc even seemed to become practically the same height as the gnome; the weight of Sharda's words pressed him to the ground.

"Don't do this...," the orc finally groaned. "She is everything to me!"

"It's already done!" the gnome cut him off. "Gerhard van Brast has been informed of your actions. He will make the final decision after the ceremony of return, but in any case, expect Archibald to show up. That is not something that can be forgiven!"

"But he refused to teach her!" The orc roared, attracting the attention of those around us to the conversation. Apparently there was no silencing spell over us any more, as Paladins started to whisper, discussing what was going on.

"That's her problem." Sharda was adamant. "If the Catorian decided that she is not worthy, then it is so. He is rarely wrong."

"But he is sometimes!" the orc insisted.

"It happens." Sharda looked at me for some reason. "We'll find this out literally within half an hour."

"Teacher, I followed the mages and they did not notice me!" Logir returned, interrupting the strange conversation between the gnome and the orc. In the Academy they will be dead meat!"

"Excellent," Sharda praised her and added: "Logir, brother Yaropolk would like to tell you something".

Since only three stares zeroed in on me, the curtain of silence must have been replaced over us. The players outside could not hear us, and gradually lost interest in what was going on here; their attention shifted to the arena. It was then that banners were brought out to it: the welcome ceremony was beginning.

"So?" Logir asked, bewildered, a couple of seconds later. I was silent, shifting my eyes from Sharda to Grygz, cursing them both silently. What should I tell Logir now? That she had been used without her knowledge, so as to pull her out from some location? How will she react? Will she grin and say that she knew all along? Refuse to become a player? Attack her father or myself with her fists? Perform a ritual suicide? Who knows what orcs are liable to do? I definitely don't. But I know something else: a Paladin, whose image I had held high since childhood, would never tell. If I am destined to stay in the Academy, I should do it with my head unbowed.

"The way you move is very graceful," I said finally, having made my decision. The problem with the mages is my own problem. If Logir is supposed to protect me, then may it be so. "Would you give me a few lessons? Unfortunately before I became a player I did nothing of the sort. I would not want to be the bottom student dragging everyone back."

"Who is everyone?" frowned the femorc.

"She will help," Grygz was quick to answer, sighing with relief. "She has never tried herself out as a teacher, so this is quite a worthy challenge."

"Still, who are everyone?" Logir would not let it pass.

"There will be seven of you working together in the Academy." For some reason Sharda stared at me again. "Five of my recruits and two of Grygz's. The main task is for everyone to come back from the Academy, despite the mages. An additional task is to attain level seven."

"I will not work with an elf!" the femorc yelled immediately. Her scream never made it beyond the curtain of silence, so Nartalim did not even bother to protest or respond scornfully.

"Oh yes you will," Sharda's face broke into one of his murderous grins. "Paladins don't see elves, people or orcs. They see a brother and his problems. Any questions?"

"She will work as part of a team," Grygz summed it up. "Even with the long-eared beast. Got that?"

The last question was addressed to Logir. For a while the orc and his daughter played the game of "crush your opponent by your charisma", then the girl surrendered. Grygz was obviously stronger.

"Our team will include seven intelligent beings, and our main goal is for everyone to come back," she repeated in a lackluster voice.

"Excellent!" Sharda even rubbed his hands, enjoying his victory over the orcs. "In this case, let's get back to the others. The ceremony is already underway."

In fact, by that time the ceremony of bringing out the banners was complete. As soon as the last banner was in place, a blue-skinned creature took the floor.

"Welcome to the welcoming ceremony!"

"It's the viceroy of the Emperor!" Logir, who was standing next to me, whispered. Of course, an orc's whisper sounded like a thunderous rumble, but I didn't mind enduring it for the sake of information. "He is the third highest ranking person in the Game, after the Emperor and his Counselor. My mentor said it's the viceroy who decides at what location in the Academy a player will appear."

"Are we not all going to be transported to the same place?" I frowned. I did not want to lose my freshly acquired team.

"No, of course not!" The femorc looked at me as if I were crazy. "Did they not tell you about the principles of going through the Academy?"

"Quiet!" Sharda hushed us. "Show some respect to the viceroy! You will have plenty of time to talk later. All seven of you will be sent to the same place because you are a team!"

Silence fell over the arena as new players hung onto the viceroy's words.

"Today is one of those rare days when we are sending over thirty two thousand recruits to the Academy; one thousand and forty two of them have already passed the class initiation! We have not seen that in eight hundred years! We have every chance to set a record and within one month receive twelve hundred players! I am calling on non-initiated players! Fight and struggle! Fight each other tooth and claw, but return from the Academy! For a new record we need fifty nine non-initiated players to return, and we believe that you will be the ones!

I did a quick mental calculation. The ratio of 58 to 31,000 yielded an overwhelming result of 0.2 percent! The viceroy is hoping that at least two recruits from every thousand would come back from the Academy! Unless my calculation was off, those who came up with the Game have obvious problems with rationality.

"I bet ten Granis that the record will stand," I heard Sharda whisper.

"Go find another fool!" an unfamiliar voice responded, but I did not look back: my attention was fully occupied with the theatrical show that now started on the arena. The viceroy had already left the dais, and actors began showing complicated skits using magic without hesitation. Once a fire-breathing dragon appeared in the arena and was immediately overcome by the conjured knight – without fear and beyond reproach – even the arrogant elf's jaw dropped in amazement, and he never bothered to pick it up. The rest were not even worth mentioning: players in all the stands, with the exception, perhaps, of smirking mentors, were still as wax figures in Madame Tussaud's museum.

The dance the actors performed was

enthralling. I was never a connoisseur, but now I could easily see when the actors presented various emotions: pain, despair, hope, faith, betrayal. The scenes followed each other continuously, and at some point I felt tears flowing down my cheeks from being overcome by "joy".

"Good luck to the players!" the viceroy's voice boomed as soon as the actors stopped in elaborate poses. Tears were still standing in my eyes, but I was able to gather my strength to look at my neighbors. Everyone was crying: Logir, Dietrich, Sartal, Monstrichello, an orc who had not yet been introduced to us, and even Nartalim! I shifted my eyes to Sharda, looking at his recruits with a smirk.

"Prove that Archibald can be wrong too!" The gnome suddenly said to me. "Return from the Academy. We'll figure out what to do with Devir!"

Before I had a chance to make any response everything around me drowned in complete darkness lit only with a snow-white message:

Welcome to the Academy

CHAPTER THREE

INITIAL KNOWLEDGE

"**W**AKE UP!" I heard a rough voice, followed by a ruthless kick to the stomach. I felt no pain because of the armor, but it was unexpected and unpleasant, so I opened my eyes prepared to show my indignation. But that was impossible! I was able to open my eyes, intending to voice all the thoughts I had – mostly very expressive curses. But my intentions remained just intentions: someone's hands were covering my mouth. I was pressed tightly to the ground by three players wearing mages' robes; another two were looming overhead.

"Quit wriggling!" one of the mages growled as soon as I realized my situation and tried to struggle free. Accompanying his words with another kick to the stomach, which was again blocked by the armor, he bent down right to my face: "Listen here, you dead meat! You got a choice – to croak calmly without trouble, or with pain and emotions. If you follow our instructions, we'll kill you without extra torture. If you try kicking, I'll send you for such a respawn you'll curse the day when you became a player. Nod if you got me.

"So you want to do it the hard way," the mage continued bloodthirstily, failing to extract any reaction from me. Frankly speaking, I was not being heroic – I was scared! After I realized who had surrounded me and held me down I was so frightened, I didn't even understand what they were saying to me. There was just one thought in my head: 'Help!' and it flooded my entire consciousness.

"Let's drag him over to the teacher," my captor ordered and stepped aside.

"What do we do with these?" His partner asked, pointing somewhere next to me. "They will sleep for another hour at least. The mentor said the Pals never give any potions to their recruits."

"What do you mean, 'what do we do?'" the lead mage sneered. "Devir told us clearly what to do with all the Paladins."

The mages laughed, and before they lifted and carried me off somewhere I heard six stifled death-rattles. One did not need to be a prophet to realize that our entire team had just been sent for respawn. Another wave of chilling fear rushed through me: Dietrich and the nameless orc were non-initiated level one players; there will be no respawn for them. Neither will there be one for me! They will just strangle me and forget my name! The only reason I was still alive, albeit temporarily, was Devir's order!

I was saved from further descent into panic as literally a minute later I was thrown to the ground like a sack of grain. The impact of the ground made sparks dance in front of my eyes; however, that helped me keep conscious and drove away the fear. Devir ordered the mages to help me level up till I reach the fifth teacher; so until then they would not do anything to me. I needed to develop as much as possible, level up and figure out a way to escape. For this I needed a clear mind without fear and a feeling of inferiority. There will be time to be scared later, after I return from the Academy. Not "if" but "when", besides.

I heard a calm, drawling, and somewhat old voice next to me:

"Welcome, recruit, now I will teach you to use the artifact you have chosen. Stand up and hark to my wisdom!"

Learning progress: You have reached teacher 1 of 10

"You were told: stand up!" Another rude shout from a mage, and a kick, this time on the head. The sparks reached a new level: now they turned into full-blown fireworks, so when I came to I was already upright. Two mages were holding me under my arms so that I would stand upright in front of the teacher. He looked exactly like the old man from the Temple of Knowledge.

"Present your artifact," the old man addressed me. He could not care less about what was going on, as if nothing unusual was happening. So what if a group of mages is holding a Paladin, kicking him periodically? That's the Paladin's problem. What if they are into erotic games like that? Once you interfere, they'll blame you for something ...

"Did you hear?" The mage who had never said his name started again, but I decided not to provoke a new fit of rage. I needed to show my kidnappers that I was broken and ready to follow any order from them. Until I reach level two I cannot afford to die, or else I'll end up like Dietrich. So I'll play along with the mages for now, and then we'll see.

I detached the book and held it out to the teacher.

"Book of Knowledge?" for the first time the old man's face showed some emotion.

"I will be an explorer," I mumbled, making an exaggerated move to hunch my head into my shoulders, as if expecting a blow. Let the mages gloat. A chorus of loud laughter from the five players and a weakening of their grip showed that I had chosen the right tactic: they did not perceive me as a serious opponent anymore. The mages surely must be betting among themselves whether I had already soiled my pants. Because what else are those Paladins good for...?

"That's a worthy choice," the old man ignored the mirth of the mages. "Do you want to transfer to the book all the knowledge you have gained since you became a player until now, or to start from a blank page?"

"Transfer," I managed to blurt out before the mage had time to bark: "From a blank page! No damned need to hang around here!"

Artifact is activated

The world around me changed again, leaving me one on one with the old man in the midst of a rather strange forest. Oaks in there neighbored tall pines, poplars grew next to palms and birches next to cacti as if nature had decided to completely ignore the logic and biological features of tree growth. As far as I recalled from school, tall pines would obscure the sunshine, so deciduous trees would not be able to grow next to them – they would become lanky and weak. But local nature could not be bothered with that: it decided to create a melee of trees, and did so by the right of the strongest. Anyone who is unhappy is welcome to submit a written application on company letterhead signed by the director. In other words: not at all.

Automatically I noted there were several trees not familiar to me, and then:

Book of Knowledge received +1 Experience

"This is precisely how your artifact develops," the teacher's voice distracted me from studying a new line in my character properties. I was surprised to discover that section kept extending. That line was not there before. "Book of Knowledge can do a lot, but it is just a medium for your memory and attention. If you did not notice something, failed to see it, did not pay attention or ignored it, don't expect for a note to show up in the book. The book will receive additional experience only when you consciously pay attention to something or reach the right conclusions. As an explorer you will have to continuously study the surrounding world, otherwise your development will come to a halt. Being an explorer is simple and hard at the same time."

"Are there any consequences if development stops?" I frowned. "Will the book start degrading?"

"No, once the knowledge is in the book it stays there forever. There is a different problem: a player's artifact must develop continuously; moderators keep a very close eye on that. As soon as development stops, the player is no longer interesting for the Game. For that reason many choose battle artifacts: it is easier to receive experience with them."

"So then the player who chooses the Book of Knowledge as his artifact is doomed for sure?" I frowned even more. "Knowledge is finite. Sooner or later there will be nothing left for me to explore."

"We are all mortal," the old guy noted philosophically, shrugging his shoulders. "The Game will take everyone."

"The Game... What is it, anyway?" I immediately asked the question that had been bothering me for a long time. "How did it appear? Who created it? What was there before?"

"You are asking these questions of the wrong rational being," the old man's face showed some emotion for the second time in our entire conversation. "My functions include only training in the use of the artifact and assistance in selecting its first attribute. Nothing else."

"The wrong one...," I drawled, looking at the smiling teacher. "Whom should I ask these questions?"

"The one who has the knowledge and can share it." The old man was obviously amused.

A sudden guess flashed through my mind:

"Is there someone in the Academy who knows the answers to my question about the Game and is capable of sharing this knowledge?"

"Of course." His smile grew wider. "This is the place for receiving knowledge. It has all sorts of things!"

"Where would one find this being?" Getting information from him was like pulling teeth.

"In the Academy – where else?"

"Where in the Academy is that being located and what is the shortest road to it?" I asked in the most detailed way, following the principles used for working with the Temple of Knowledge.

"That is the wrong question, recruit, so our conversation is over." The smile instantly faded and the old man again turned into a statue without emotions. "Are you ready to transfer the information you received earlier into the book?"

"I am ready," I drawled with displeasure, scolding myself internally. Who would try to find out the information so obviously?

"Remember everything you want to transfer

into the book," the old man clarified; after that the Book of Knowledge burst from its holder on my thigh and flew into the air, hovering right in front of my eyes.

Artifact update process initiated

The Book changed. The pages that had been empty were now partially filled with text and pictures. The moment I fixed my eyes on some area in the book it would mysteriously zoom in, enabling me to read the text. At this time the book was showing a detailed report of my meeting with the first teacher: the old man's picture, a full record of the conversation, a panoramic view of our surroundings, including the names of trees and plants. Some of the plants had question marks floating over them, indicating that I had no information about the object at this time. In effect, the Book of Knowledge turned out to be sort of a video recording device that registered everything that I looked at. Stop. I had the video activated! Why would I need to remember things when I could just watch the record again?

"That's an interesting solution," the old man drawled as soon as the Book of Knowledge occupied its place at my thigh. Thanks to Archibald, my video recording had been activated ever since we met and now, once I pushed the "Video record" a thin white thread seemingly made of thick white fog formed between the icon and the Book of Knowledge. After a few moments it disappeared, and so did the "Video record" icon from the status bar. The unpleasant part was that now "Video record" did not show at all when I opened the properties. It simply was not there! I was about to get upset when new messages appeared before me:

Video recording integrated with artifact
Book of Knowledge received +1 Experience

"Now that all your player knowledge is in the Book, you need to select the initial artifact trait," the old man continued as soon as I was able to tear myself away from the updated artifact. Pictures of Archibald, Sharda and our entire former team occupied places of honor there. However, it took time getting to them: the Book had no navigation, search, or table of contents. In order to find information you needed, you had to leaf through the book page by page, looking at the contents. Basically, the Book of Knowledge was like a huge Wikipedia, with each page dedicated to one specific subject. For example, "Academy Teacher No. 3", "Archibald", or "New player welcome ceremony"; the pages had references to each other, sort of like hyperlinks. Actually, that's how I was able to find Sharda and other Paladins I knew. Including Dietrich, whose page said: "Killed in the Academy".

"Do the traits include the possibility for information structuring and search?" was the first thing I asked the old man. It would be totally stupid to be a world explorer and not have immediate access to the notes in the Book.

"Could you explain what you mean?" The old

man came out of the 'statue' mode again and regarded me with interest. Since I had the page on him still hovering in front of me, I could see information updated in real time. A new line appeared in the Book:

"Academy Teacher No. 3 is favorable towards recruits who seek information. Never ask him direct questions on how to do things. The method to use is indirect hints and a circuitous approach."

"There are two points. The first thing is: upon looking at any object at a mental command I would like to have in front of me all the information about it available in the Book of Knowledge. The second thing: even if there is no object available, but I have a clear understanding of who or what is the subject, at a mental command I would like to have all that information as well.

"Is my understanding correct that you need to search?" the teacher clarified, and mischief danced in his eyes. That was an amazing combination — an outwardly calm old man with eyes dancing with mischief.

"Not just search," I began cautiously. "Intelligent perception and comparison with available information, structuring the available information, table of contents and, of course, the search itself."

"In effect, you need context search with mental control?" the old man clarified again. "Catalog capability, tags, table of contents, index, navigation and other things: it includes all that. Also, comparison of outside world objects and information in the Book. This trait is actually called 'Context search'. Do you want to add this?"

"I would like to verify what is the path for upgrading this trait." I remembered in time that in the Game everything develops. Including artifact properties.

"At level one, which you will receive now, search and comparison will be available," the teacher started explaining. "The second level will have navigation and an alphabetical index. The fifth: table of contents. The tenth will provide tags. At level fifteen there will be a capability for downloading information. Further upgrades will depend on the development path that will be chosen at level fifteen, so I will not describe that now. Do you want to add this?"

"Yes, let's," I nodded, and messages flashed in front of my eyes, informing me of the addition of the new trait.

"Actually, this completes your training with me. This is all I have for you. Move on to other teachers and may luck be with you!"

"Wait!" I yelled and the surroundings that were starting to dissipate became firm again.

"Is something unclear about the artifact?" the teacher was surprised.

"No, it's fine," I already checked out the semitransparent pop-up window with information. The search worked like clockwork. "I have a different question: after we return to the Academy, will we be in the exact same place or is it possible to alter the point of return? Even if it were just by a couple of meters?"

"Where do you think we are right now?" The teacher raised an eyebrow in a question.

"In an extratemporal subspace of the Academy," I ventured a guess. "You need to instruct thirty two thousand recruits. Even if you spend a minute per person, that training would take twenty two days without sleeping and eating. But you spent about twenty minutes with me just now. Therefore, we are in a temporal pocket, and hardly a moment will have passed in the Academy."

"You answered your own question," the teacher cornered me. "No matter where you go within this world, which is limited by this small clearing, you will still return to the same point in space and time from where you left to train with me. You will not be able to escape from the mages this way.

"So you did see all that?"

"Do I look like I'm blind? The mage recruits, prior to arriving at the academy, took a 'Mihonarium' potion which enabled them to wake up immediately; they organized themselves and, while everyone else was still asleep, dragged you over to me. People do that frequently.

"And you are going to do nothing about it?"

"What for? Sooner or later you will die – you have arrived at that thought yourself. Why should it not happen sooner? You will serve to provide experience to your peers. In the Game nothing is wasted. If that was the only question for which you stopped me, I have to leave you now. As you rightly noticed, there are thirty two thousand new recruits waiting for me."

The space around me shifted and in a couple of moments rearranged itself into the Academy and the mages holding my arms.

"Your artifact is activated and the information has been transferred," said the teacher. — "There is nothing else I can teach you!"

You receive +1000 Experience
New level attained
You receive +1 Energy level

"Excellent!" The leader of the five mages replied with satisfaction to the teacher's statement. "Four more teachers and then we'll finish him off. Let's clean up everything here!"

I was finally able to take a good look at what the Academy actually was. There was a huge area littered with players, as if they were bodies in an enormous battlefield. The heaving chest and nervously twitching tip of the tail of a reptilian lying next to us made it clear that he was just sleeping. Apparently, the players would be waking in succession so as to avoid a crush around the teacher; but now there were only six players on their feet: myself and the five mages: three humans, an elf and some strange winged creature. I could not see the murdered Paladins from my team. Most likely they would be at a respawn point; I didn't know how long this process took. I hoped Logir would be able to find me and fulfill the task posed by Sharda. I did not have much hope for the others. At the opposite side of the clearing by the sleeping players there was a steel and stone jungle – a jumble of stone boulders, twisted steel rails, wooden studs and hell only knows what else. As if at some point a tall multistory building had been standing here and then, due to some catastrophe, it collapsed into pieces, baring all its internal works and not quite falling to the ground. From where we were standing it was possible to see two passages into this crazy three-dimensional labyrinth.

"Every one of them?" the elf said, confused. "Olzar, but there are a couple of hundred of them here! Devir said nothing about the other players, and the Pals will respawn only after an hour."

Book of Knowledge received +1 Experience

"Every single one!" sharply said Olzar, the lead of the mage recruits. "Each player you leave alive is a potential enemy. Besides, don't forget – there may be not just first levels here, so we'll get experience points. Wipe them all out!"

"What do we do with him?" A mage nodded in my direction.

"He won't go anywhere, right?" Olzar smirked bloodthirstily bending over the nearest player. "We already broke him. You wouldn't mind standing here, right, little Paladin?"

Knowing what was expected of me, I quickly nodded, and even gasped when the player Olzar strangled vanished as if he had never existed. Even the grass was not crushed. Like myself, Olzar had no weapons, so he had to have killed the player with his bare hands.

"I bet a granis that I'll get a level 2!" the mage of unknown race yelled merrily, rushing to the players on the ground. The mages who had been holding my arms were not far behind joining Olzar and the rest; almost immediately I heard one of them shout with joy:

"Yes! This one is level two! Crap! Olzar, did they show you how to turn off these messages in front of your eyes? It's OK now, but later there will be more and more of them!"

"Look at the character properties," the leader responded angrily, moving on to the next player. Judging from his mood he was getting just first levels. "The options will open when you click on the name. Enough: stop distracting me!"

The mages set to work diligently while I was gradually moving, step by step, towards the labyrinth of stone and steel, remembering to startle after each joyful shout. Attacking five level 3 players would be pointless: they would overpower me and tie me up even without their abilities. The teacher near whom we were did not provide training on spells and ways for working with them, so the mages had to kill the recumbent players using only their hands, by strangling them. Struggling with the players who immediately woke up required their complete concentration, so for a while they forgot about me. Besides, really, to where could I escape from them? There were only two roads leading away from this area, and they were certainly controlled by groups of other mages. That meant I could not use the conventional paths available to everyone else.

"Hey, where's the Paladin?!" a stunned exclamation from Olzar was music to my ears. It took me about ten minutes of moving step by a cautious step to reach the border of the steel-and-rock labyrinth, another moment to make sure that all the mages were occupied with their opponents, after which I crouched behind the nearest boulder. My heart was racing like crazy, I was gasping noisily, but I was in no hurry to get up and run ahead full tilt. A year of service as a trooper combined with clashes with real fighters that Sintsov arranged periodically had been drilled into me: I started thinking. I slowly crawled into the jungle for a couple of meters, then, making sure to keep some boulders between me and the clearing, started climbing upwards. My body was shaking from an adrenaline rush, so I had to control my every movement. Falling down headlong would take just one wrong move. The image that I was trying to create would lead them to believe I was frightened and weak, so the mages should be supposing now that I must be running as fast as I could into the heart of the maze. Some messed up headhunters indeed! If I were to be testing them I would be throwing them out on their ears for incompetence!

"Sirin, Belket?"

"He's gone!" voices replied from right and left. I was correct: mages controlled the passages. That meant there were not five of them in this team but seven. They were not completely clueless after all.

"Did he try to go straight through?" There was even more confusion in Olzar's voice now. "Who can recall – where was he standing?"

"Here somewhere, I think!" someone replied. "You said he was done in?"

"I did! That's what Devir said!"

"Damn it! Where are we going to catch him now?"

"Jerk... let's run to the respawn point! Yari is level two, it's impossible to survive in the jungle, so in a couple of hours he'll show up there. Let's go."

"We are not going to finish off the rest?"

"Let them live, we'll get them later. The most important thing is to be there first, otherwise we'll have to fight tooth and claw for it. Every team wants to get a reward from Devir."

"What, are we not going to follow him into the jungle? He could be standing right at the edge laughing at us!" one of the mages asked in surprise. I clenched my fists helplessly – who made that smart-ass open his mouth?! I so wanted to strangle him!

"Into the jungle?" It was not even Olzar who laughed but the other mages. "Dude, only after you! What, did you miss all the lectures?"

"I didn't, but we still ought to check!"

"I already checked!" A new voice I had not heard previously replied from practically underneath me! I clung to the steel beam on which I was lying and held still. The eighth mage! How many are there all together?! "There's no Pal and no tracks. Looks like this idiot is just running headlong at full speed. Olzar, why in hell didn't you guard him?"

"What are you doing here?" Olzar was taken aback. I would give a lot for a glance at the new arrival but moving was out of the question. The slightest noise could betray me.

"Watching over you, morons! There were no Paladins at our spawn point, so after the training we rushed to the nearest teacher, which was here; and you are doing hell knows what!"

"Yari is ours! We found him first!"

"Just because you spawned at the same site with him does not mean you have already won. To lose a first level player! This is complete nonsense!"

"He's already level two, we went through the training," since Olzar was the one who answered every time it seemed the status of the new mage was much higher than his own. There was a possibility he was one of that pair that showed up together with Devir during the welcome ceremony. The one that behaved like he was the center of the universe. There was nothing else that could explain his tone.

Book of Knowledge received +1 Experience

I guessed right?! Judging from the new message that appeared, the capabilities of the Book of Knowledge were much broader than I had supposed. Using some attributes unknown to me, maybe voice, smell or body movement patterns, or maybe something else, the book identified the player and, since I had guessed correctly who it could be, counted it as a correct answer. Immediately I brought up in front of me the page with information I had available for the guy and was barely able to hold back a sigh of disappointment: without my help the artifact was unable to determine which one of Devir's companions was standing underneath me right now. Both portraits were shown with an exclamation point before them. So it was one of the two. No name, no description, nothing. Just a note that this was one of Devir's companions and probably a student of his.

"What are you standing here for?! You expect me to finish off the bodies for you?"

"But..."

"All three respawn points have been under control since the very first minutes, so Yari will not get away. Strangle the rest. The fewer non-mages there are left among the non-initiated, the better!"

For thirty minutes I sat on the steel beam listening to death-rattles. This time there was no elation, the mages were just doing the work. The number of concurrent sounds told me that another group had shown up at the clearing. That meant the second spawn point of the players and, consequently, the second teacher, were not that far. I definitely could not go there. When yet another message appeared notifying me of experience received by the artifact I had enough and followed Olzar's advice: changed the settings and removed notifications of experience received, damage and other stats leaving just the most important ones: updates or receiving quests, general information and global information messages. I could see everything else in the properties, while constantly staring at *Book of Knowledge received +1 Experience* was not very tempting. If I live to see something "constant" anyway…

I sat on the beam for about an hour. The mages had cleared the field of the players who never woke up, then left about twenty minutes ago. Gradually new players started appearing, making it in groups to the current teacher and learning the principles of functioning of their artifacts, but I kept sitting in the same place, unable to move. The adrenaline dissolved, leaving apathy in its wake: the mages' hunt was not just an empty threat. No matter where I could try to go now, only one thing would be there for me: groups of mages waiting for me to approach the teachers.

Panic and depression were creeping up on me, so I used the tried and true method for retaining an adequate perception of reality: I started thinking. I already knew that there was only one way to leave the Academy: completing training with ten teachers. The main question that would determine all my further existence was – are those ten specified and fixed or not? If the answer is yes, I could as well jump down head first, respawn, lose a level and surrender to the mages. It would make no sense to try and do anything further. But if one needed to train with any ten teachers, 'ten' being the key word, I had a chance. The Academy was full of teachers, the trick was to find them. If I were to stay away from the main passages, I might survive. There was nothing else left for me. Now it was necessary to understand why the mages were so afraid of the labyrinth. Even though calling this mess of stones, reinforced concrete structures, steel beams, rods, wire and wooden boards a "labyrinth" or a "jungle" would definitely be a stretch. "Obstacle course" would be more accurate. I looked down, swallowed and instinctively clung to the beam again. As I was trying to hide I had climbed about five meters up. It does not seem too high, but still quite a ways to fall.

The beam on which I was sitting turned sharply a meter above me and leaned towards one of the passages. I stopped grabbing convulsively everything that came to hand and started climbing upward: I needed to see for myself how and where the second teacher was situated. If I were to move along the tops, did I have to constantly look down or could teachers be waiting above ground? If the latter were true, then I would not even get down to the ground; I'd turn into Tarzan!

"Derv, there is another teacher in the clearing right ahead!" I heard from below the excited whispering of a player just as I climbed the beam and settled on it with a sigh of relief, trying to get my breath back.

"Would you be quiet!" Someone hissed angrily in response. "Is the field clear?"

"No, there are three mages there. They are standing next to the teacher waiting for someone."

"Mages…" there was so much hatred in Derv's voice that I had a hard time refraining from coming down to hug the comrade who shared my hatred of the mages. That wasn't why I had spent so much time climbing up. "We are leaving. There's nothing for us here."

"But... why? You saw for yourself that at the last teacher's location they didn't bother anyone... except for Paladins... But we are Rogues!"

"Listen, I've had enough of you! You want to be killed – go alone! At the last teacher's they didn't bother people 'cause there were too many players of other classes. And here there's no one other than themselves, so they'll send us for respawn for sure. The two of us can't harm them!

"But then what should we do? We are already... Did you hear that?!"

Not only Derv heard THAT, but I did as well. Besides, unlike the rogues, I could very well see the source of the low throaty roar: a few meters below a huge black panther appeared out of nothing – that's the only way I could describe it. The black tail was whipping her heaving sides frantically. All the panther's attention was on those standing below: the rogues.

"We must get out of here!" was all Derv had time to shout, then the panther roared menacingly and rushed down like black lightning. There were two screams of agony, then a few moments of silence followed by remote yells: "What was that?" and "Get to the paths, everybody! They are safe!" The players found out with surprise about a new condition: in the Academy not only other players are a source of danger, but also the creatures of the Academy itself. I was sure that the panther was not the only local creature; there must be others.

It took me half an hour to calm down the shaking and then make myself move on. The latter took a lot longer: my fear of wild animals was much stronger than fear of other players. After I finally forced myself to crawl for a few meters pretending as well as I could to be the 'invisible man', I saw a "⇑" symbol in front of me. Dusty and partially hidden by stones, the symbol seemed to try very hard to stay unnoticed. Had I not been crawling along the beam with my nose to its surface, I would 99% guarantee that I would have missed it.

My progress slowed down again. I discarded the possibility that the symbol indicated the direction towards the nearest teacher right away: the nearest teacher was standing a dozen meters away in the direction opposite to that shown by the symbol. And no one would be creating symbols special for me: Archibald's words that the system couldn't care less about any of the players were etched deep in my mind. Particularly given the latest events. So, the arrow must be pointing at something else. But at what?

As could be expected, the system did not welcome me with open arms hurrying to explain what was going on. I made sure that the Book of Knowledge recorded the appropriate line and the map... I got that sinking feeling – how could I forget that in this world I could record my location? Just because the information about the world around me was continuously recorded by the Book of Knowledge even without my active participation did not mean the map would necessarily follow suit. A semi-transparent window popped up in front of me and I barely contained a sigh of relief: the map did update automatically. The Academy was a huge rectangular site obscured by dark fog; only a tiny colored spot showed on the bottom right: the field where I first appeared here. At least in this the Game was similar to the games I was used to: all the available Academy space was shown to the player from the start. Had the map had no boundaries it would have been impossible to estimate one's progress in exploring its territory. However, the map header "0.0001% of Academy territory explored" was grounds for optimism. Everything is possible within the Game; the main thing is to avoid players and animals. However, I was quickly able to see the drawbacks of the map: when I zoomed in on my current location, the map offered me a rather funny 3D picture showing the path I covered. What was above or below this path was unclear: the map properties did not record the areas that I had not seen. So if I were to try and explore the entire 100% of Academy territory I'd have to try extra hard.

I made it to the entrance within the obstacle course uneventfully; either the panther did not notice me or the two rogues were enough for it. Constantly jumping from the steel beams to the stones and back, eventually I found myself above a passage two meters wide and three deep. There was a path covered in yellow sand leading within. The stones and steel structures stopped miraculously at the entrance, forming the elaborate corridor Diablo players like so much. Over ten minutes that I observed the path, four teams of ten players each went under it; there were neither mages nor Paladins among them. Most of the players were carrying weapons; it seemed like they did not concern themselves too much with the choice of artifacts. "The shiny and pointy blades are all we need." When I come back – not "if" but definitely "when" – I must make sure to find out why bladed weapons are preferable to projectile ones or, say, something energy-based. I would have thought that the players would be running around with blasters, pulse cannons and other sci-fi equipment rather than swords, bows and similar antiques. However, they did not. So I would definitely have to look into that in detail.

I had no desire to initiate contact with the unknown player teams; so I waited till yet another group went by, then followed them cautiously along the steel beams above the path. With each passing minute I became more convinced that the seemingly chaotic structure of the obstacle course in fact followed a strict algorithm. For example, the steel beams served as guides along which one was supposed to move; the symbols "⇐", "⇒" and "⇑", located at the beginning and end of each beam, suggested movement somewhere toward the center of the Academy, serving as road signs. Stone boulders and pieces of wood served as guards or handrails, or were purely decorative without any meaning. The road above ground was not easy: you had to continuously climb up and down, leap from one beam to another or make a hard choice when the beam split and its ends led in opposite directions. In those cases I clenched my fists, as I was very intrigued by the goal indicated by the arrows but still kept moving above the path.

The teacher was more important now...

It took me an hour to reach the second teacher. He was located in the middle of a small clearing, about twenty meters in diameter. It was surrounded by the steel and stone jungle, but it stopped miraculously, the same way it did for the paths, forming a clear space. The positive findings were that there were three paths leading away from the clearing to subsequent teachers, so it would be much easier to find them; the negative: there were ten mages standing next to the teacher, acting as gatekeepers. About twenty players of other classes accepted this rule, forming a line. The mages thoroughly searched each subsequent player, then let him through to the teacher and started searching the next. They paid particular attention to fat players. As if they could be hiding someone within. Me, for example.

No one was eager to challenge the mages' insolence, perceiving their total control as a normal turn of events. I spent about ten minutes on the beam trying to figure out a way to get to the teacher, but in vain. The mages were very thorough in their search and were not distracted for a moment. Feeling that I would not be able to gain anything there, I started to crawl back cautiously when I heard the metal clattering right below me and a loud scream turning into a gurgle. Someone was drowning in their own blood. Was there another panther?

My curiosity was stronger than my instinct for self-preservation, and I crawled to the clearing once again. After all, what could threaten me at this height?

"Quick, get help!" someone shouted, and immediately two mages dashed out of the clearing. I was about to wonder why there were only two, as three paths led out of it, when I heard beneath me more clatter and the familiar, practically welcome, booming voice of Monstrichello:

"I'll crush dem freaks! Where are they?"

The space around the eight mages suddenly and miraculously emptied: players of other classes decided not to join the skirmish between Paladins and mages. The area directly below me was obscured by boulders, so I had to impatiently bite my lips to keep from yelling from joy and rushing down. Monstrichello could be alone and even he would not have a chance against eight mages. And if I were to join him it would not improve his chances: I had never had to consciously kill a sentient being, so I would not be much help. The events at the cemetery trailer did not really count, as I had literally run amok.

"Let's work as we did before," Nartalim joined Monstrichello, and it was the first time when I was glad to hear the elf. Even despite his contempt for everything alive in his voice.

"Maybe we could make an agreement?" one of the mages stepped forward and then the four Paladins stepped into the fighting space. Powerful Monstrichello, holding the shield in front of him and acting as a breakwater. Nartalim, playing with his sword, following right behind the tank. Sartal, his armor-covered tail whipping in irritation. And Logir holding a weighty hammer. Neither Dietrich, nor the orc whose name I never knew were among them. Two out of four Paladins who had chosen weapons as artifacts, together with Monstrichello's protection, were quite capable of standing up to the mages, even if there eight of those.

"There's nothing for us to agree about," Monstrichello roared, but Nartalim held him back:

"Wait. Let's try." Just as I supposed, the elf had become the leader of the team. "You give us free access to the teachers, this one and all the subsequent ones; we stop hunting you. Yaropolk's fate is of no interest to us, you can do whatever you want with him. I have no intention to return from the Academy as a level one player because of just one twit.

"It's a reasonable demand. Is this the view of your entire team?"

"This is my view and therefore everyone's," Nartalim said curtly and, to my great surprise, the other Paladins said nothing. Even Logir! My team just turned me in!

"Let's wait for Dangard, he will confirm our arrangement," the mage exhaled with obvious relief, as if he really did not want to do battle. Which was understandable: there is not much one can do with fists against weapons.

"Who's that jerk?" Monstrichello asked with all the political correctness he ever had.

"One of Devir's students," the mage started explaining. He and Ahean were appointed the leads for passing through the Academy and fulfilling the teacher's tasks. He should be close to here, so we won't have to wait long. Oh, there he is!"

The clearing was quickly filling with mages. The Paladins, who crowded together and stood back to back, were surrounded, but no one touched them: the sword and the hammer cooled the belligerence of the players. Even if a crush were to begin, Nartalim and Logir would then likely send at least several players to respawn, and I was not sure that the mages had already passed initiation. Nobody wanted to sacrifice a level and become one step closer to being wiped out. Finally, Dangard appeared in one of the passages, and the Book of Knowledge started vibrating markedly — one of the two Devir's companions was recognized.

"Where's Yaropolk? Having exchanged a few words with the mages who were guarding the teacher, Dangard leisurely approached the Paladins. His movements, voice and demeanor conveyed such confidence and strength that it made you feel worthless against your will. I shook my head, dispelling the illusion. I could not get rid of the feeling that the mage had a way of influencing others' minds, suppressing his opponent's will.

"I have no idea," Nartalim stepped forward. "When we respawned he was not there anymore."

The mage stared at the Paladins for some time as if they were funny animals in a zoo, then his stare returned to the elf.

"We need to talk privately. Follow me."

In the same relaxed and slow gait of a mafia boss, Dangard strode by the Paladins to the edge of the clearing. The spot the mage selected for the conversation was just a dozen meters to the right, and

I felt an irresistible itch in my backside to listen in on them. Knowing that I was doing something unforgivably stupid, I carefully started along the edge of the clearing to the coveted spot. I needed to be in a strategic location before Dangard hobbled to the edge of the clearing. Once I slipped on the beam and was barely able to avoid falling, grabbing at a boulder at the last moment, bloodying my fingers. There was not much noise, but I still froze listening to the sounds from the clearing – had the players gotten alarmed? Everything was quiet, so I moved on.

"Elf, we have no issues with you," I heard Dangard's muffled voice, and stopped again. It would not make any sense to keep going – I could hear everything very well from where I was.

"Just with me?"

"I would say with the lizard as well. The femorc and the wardrobe boy will leave the Academy at the first level. That is not subject for discussion.

"Pff!" Nartalim snorted with disdain. "I couldn't care less – do whatever you want with them. If no one interferes with me going through with the teachers, those two are yours."

"I am glad we understand each other. At the next teacher my fighters will deal with that pair. Now about Yaropolk: I need him. Really need him."

"Listen, I really don't know where he is. We came to at a respawn point, he was not there and..."

"I already heard that," the mage cut the elf off. "If you run into Yari, just send him for respawn, immediately and without asking unneeded questions. Make that clear to the others."

"He is not dead yet?" Nartalim asked in surprise.

"Now let's talk about you," Dangard ignored the Paladin's question. "As I mentioned, we have no issues with you, so no one will bother you much."

"Much?" Nartalim asked, when the mage fell ominously silent.

"They might catch you by accident – it happens, you know. To guarantee protection you need to buy it. I think the price of one granis is quite adequate. One privilege of protection – one granis."

"What?! A whole granis?!"

I frowned. I was losing the idea again – this time of the process of price determination within the Game. I received my granis after I killed Petrovich, an ordinary NPC, of which there were hordes on Earth. So then, two Petroviches would yield two granis. Then three, four and up to seven billion; as far as I recalled that was the population of Earth. So why was Nartalim so surprised?

"Are you objecting? I should count you together with the other two?" Dangard clarified derisively, openly mocking the elf.

"I don't have a granis," the Paladin was practically weeping. I frowned: Nartalim cracked! The selfish elf – a member of the guilded youth – broke down during this conversation with the mage! This is impossible!

"You are initiated," the mage continued to sneer. "Let's make a deal, and after you graduate from the Academy you will repay the debt to me.. I am not even going to charge you interest."

"A... deal?"

"Call the Game to witness that two days after you leave the Academy you will hand me a granis. Voluntarily, and without me having to remind you. That will be enough."

"But..."

"Enough! Either you hand me a granis, or I am sending you for respawn right now! Five. Four. Three..."

"Two days after I leave the Academy I will give a granis to Dangard," the elf practically shouted. "Voluntarily and without being reminded. Is that it? Are you happy now?! Am I now free to go?!"

"Now you are free. Completely and utterly." There was an electric crackle, a stifled rasp from Nartalim, an indignant yell from Monstrichello, a tussle and rattle of steel, several more electric crackles, and then I heard the quiet and contemplative voice of Dangard:

"Where do they make these morons? Promising something without specifying conditions... Paladins..."

I clung close to the beam. The electric crackle made it clear: the mages had reached the teacher who trained in the use of abilities. Now one could expect anything from the players: an electric kick, a burst of fire, a water tornado and other magic tricks aimed at killing enemy troops. Now attempting a one-on-one fight would be dangerous for me: I am not immune to magic like Monstrichello.

"The Paladins have been killed, we lost seven," I heard quick steps and then some player smartly reported the current situation to Dangard.

"What about Yari?"

"Nothing. He did not appear at any of the respawn points; we are controlling all the nearest teachers, he was not seen there either. Dangard, why did you take that Pal aside? I had even thought we were actually going to make an agreement with them."

"I bilked him out of a granis, I need to work on my artifact after all. I put him off his guard, subdued his will and forced him to make a promise to the Game.

"Come on! An entire granis?"

"I don't like traitors. Since it's impossible to punish them any other way in the Academy, I'll make them feel the pain by taking their money."

"Cool... what are we going to do about Yari?"

"Look for him – what else? This Pal turned out to be smarter than Devir thought. In any case, he will soon croak without food. We'll wait. Are you done with all of the local teachers?"

"No, I just came up to the fifth when Hendy came running screaming like mad about the Paladins. So I had to drop everything and rush here."

"That's right, the quest is the priority. Let's go, we need to finish training..."

The mages left the edge of the clearing, leaving me to my new chunk of information: it's necessary to eat something in the game, or else you will die. By my estimate I had been a player for a little longer than a day; however, I was still not feeling any hunger. I was neither hungry nor thirsty; moreover, I had not thought of it until now. I assessed my condition and frowned: my body felt no discomfort. Despite spending a day without external nourishment, my body was not screaming that things were dire and I needed to go and eat a piece of bark right away. Meanwhile the mages were certain that soon I would starve and then die. Why were they so convinced that they were right?

There was no benefit I could get from the current teacher, so I carefully continued moving. All the nearest training points were controlled by the mages, therefore, it would be pointless to attempt to go there either. Seeing no other option I decided to move into the depths of the Academy, following the arrows. They should lead me somewhere after all, right? The most important thing would be to not encounter local animals...

The first signs of exhaustion started appearing two hours later: my Energy level dropped to 40 units and refused to come up to its original level even after I stopped to rest. Moreover, during the thirty minutes of rest the Energy level dropped by another two units, which enabled the Book of Knowledge to make the appropriate entry: players in the Academy are doomed for continuous respawn. If one were to suppose that there is no food in this jungle of stone and steel (forget about the panther and whatever other living things for now), then sooner or later my Energy level would drop to zero and the mages at the respawn point will have their day, catching me with their greedy paws. By the way, it meant that a non-initiated player would not be able to stay in the Academy forever: sooner or later he would run out of levels and die for good.

I did not feel any discomfort from the loss of Energy other than minor weakness and shortness of breath, but those could be attributed to having to constantly play Tarzan. Moving along the beams, constantly moving up and down, was not easy. I realized that staying in one place would mean certain death, and kept moving. Even if I were to be sent for respawn, at least I would die fighting rather than hiding under some stone. One thing pleased me: as I was moving along the beams I did not encounter any local fauna, as if the intertwined and multi-level steel bands were a safe route. While I have Energy, I should use that to the fullest. There will always be time to die.

"Suppose you manage to creep by the guards and reach open space," a slightly hoarse voice out of nowhere made me freeze, despite an extremely uncomfortable position (I was hanging in the air trying to hook my feet onto the nearest beam). "But will you like what you find there?"

Completing a trick that would be practically impossible for an ordinary person, pulling myself up and jumping onto a beam, I turned around. No one there.

"A quick one, aren't you," the invisible one mocked. The voice came from everywhere at once, so it was hard to figure out where the old man could be. I had no doubts the hoarse voice belonged to an old guy; it was quite similar to the voice of the first teacher.

"My greetings!" I said, looking tensely into the jumble of steel and stone. Could I be so lucky as to find a hidden teacher? "Would you allow me to partake of your wisdom, teacher?"

"Not just quick, but also a smartie-pants." The voice did not become one iota less sarcastic. "He wants to learn, doesn't he? Wants to partake of wisdom. You, dearie, should first figure out how to get to me, before trying to partake of whatever you can reach."

I was thinking of asking the old guy where he was located, but my memory immediately brought up the conversation with my first teacher. We had conversed quite well, but as soon as I attempted to ask about location of the source of knowledge, the conversation died at once. Something was telling me that I was dealing with the same thing here.

"Getting to a place is not the problem," I started cautiously. "What guards do you mean?"

"Guards?" I could hear surprise in the voice of my invisible interlocutor. "That's a sudden question. A funny one. And not an ordinary one..."

"So what about the guards?" I said just in case, as the voice fell silent for an entire minute. "How can one sneak by them? Anyway, who are they? Are they panthers?"

"What do panthers have to do with it?" The voice returned.

"I saw one of the panthers kill two rogues..."

"Pffff! He saw! Do you at least understand what you saw? How can there be a panther in the Academy?"

"There really was one!" I insisted. "It's true, I did not get to see how it killed the rogues, but I did see the panther with my own eyes! I even have a picture of it in my Book of Knowledge!"

"Right, because of such sloppy explorers we get wild tales about the Academy. We don't have any panthers here! Not a single one at all! You saw an ordinary level 5 player, a druid who has passed initiation and specializes in transformation. An ordinary headhunter!"

"So then who are the guards?" I was taken aback.

"Oh yeah: the guards, right?" The sarcastic note slipped back into the old guy's voice. "OK, take a look. Here's a prominent representative!"

There was a reinforced concrete slab not too far from me; it created a convenient path and led away from the steel beam. Had it not been for my decision to strictly follow the arrows, I would have been unlikely to find any reasonable objections against walking on that slab. It looked really good and led to quite an interesting passage in the stone boulders. I frowned, thinking the voice was mocking me again, but then the slab started moving. There was no vibration, no cracks, no dust; in literally a moment the slab moved to a vertical position, somehow fitting through the top layers of the labyrinth; a huge red eye was staring at me, shining with a blood-tinged light right from the middle of the slab. The concrete slab was alive! Thin tentacles appeared at the edges of the monster and rushed towards me.

All that was so unexpected that I swayed back, slipped and almost crashed down; at the last moment I held on to the beam, skinning both my palms. The tentacles were just a touch too short to reach me, barely over a meter remained. From fear I shut my eyes, pulled my body up to the beam and hugged it with both my arms and legs, as if it were my closest relative whom I never wished to let go. Fear washed over me in waves, pushing me to abandon the beam and fall down, but I struggled. I did not know what for, but I still resisted.

Suddenly everything stopped and the fear subsided as if it never was there.

"While you are holding on to the guiding line, the guards won't do anything to you," I heard the old man's voice again, and dared open my eyes. The tentacles disappeared and so did the monster. There was nothing except the concrete slab leading to the mysterious passage. Just for some reason looking at that passage made cold rush down your spine.

"A guard can assume any shape," the voice continued, as soon as I was sitting on the beam again. "It can be a slab, a stone, a branch. The only thing it cannot be is the guiding line. If you were to stop touching it for over ten seconds, they will start a hunt for you.

"Another one?" I smiled bitterly. "Seems like too many hunts for just a single me."

"That's why I decided to talk to you. I don't really like what the mages are doing: with each killing the number of trainees diminishes further. This needs to be stopped."

"Then why are killings allowed in the Academy altogether?"

"Life is so complicated! You need to win the right to be a player, even if you are fighting against an opponent who is bound to be stronger, and who took

---

a banned potion."

"Mihonarium?" I exhibited my knowledge.

"Yes." I could hear bitterness in his voice. "The players were supposed to wake up gradually, so as not to interfere with each other's exploration of the Academy, but the mages spoiled it all. I don't like it, so I want to spoil things for them, too. So that's why I need you. In four hours you will die ..."

"WHAT?!" I was unable to contain my emotions.

"Practically everyone dies in the Academy. This is normal. Unless a player brought some food with him, every twelve hours he will respawn. The Academy was created to complete training with the teachers, not to hang around here all your life. If you want to survive you will have to work hard for it. First of all, you have to return to the team with which you came here."

"They betrayed me to the mages!"

"Not all of them: just the elf." The voice was resolute. "Alone, you will not get out of the forest, even the guiding line will not help you. In this area of the Academy there are just five common and three hidden teachers; that will not be enough to go all the way back. You will have to go into open space."

"So this is not an obstacle course around me, but a forest?" I frowned, thinking of the old man's words. It was hard to admit it but he was right: with Monstrichello and Logir with her hammer by my side, we could fight the mages off. The Paladins did that before. If we were to forget about the elf's betrayal and make use of his saber, my chances of reaching the teacher for class attributes would only increase. The question remained, however: was I ready to meet the Paladins who were willing to sell me out to the mages?

"Would you help me reach the hidden teachers?" I could not but ask, thinking I would decide on rejoining my team later. "It would feel a lot less nervous meeting the mages with four levels under my belt."

"Why do you think that each teacher would give you a whole level?" The voice was surprised. "At level one you need to train with one teacher to get an extra level. At level two it will already take two teachers. At level three it will be three and so on. If one goes quickly through all the teachers the player comes back from the Academy with level four and rosy thoughts. Not more than that."

"But the hidden teachers can teach me things to improve the odds of survival and help to stop the genocide of players begun by the mages!" I would not give up. "I am not likely to have much fighting success with my bare hands against lightning bolts!"

"Not only a quick and smart one, but also slippery as an eel," the voice was once again sporting snide notes. "Going to fight, indeed... Forget that word! You are an explorer! Your only weapon is hanging onto your leg and sponging up information right now. Use it. No need to lug around swords, cudgels and other metal scrap. You are the knowledge warrior!"

"Yeah, right. History knows heaps of those," I grumbled mulishly. "Giordano Bruno, for example. His knowledge didn't really help him to avoid being burnt at the stake."

"You are confused, Paladin. What happens among NPCs should not concern you. Even if they were to blow up the planet the players would move to another game world and keep developing there. Lose the habit of being mortal. If you want to become a real player, you need to reject the world of your past. The Game does not start a large-scale purge so that the players would then reflect on times past. You need to keep going forward constantly!"

"How did it come about anyway, this blasted Game!" Sad memories of my lost family overwhelmed me again, and, upset, I cursed mightily. I never asked anyone to turn me into a player! Had it not been for Devir, I would have returned to my family without a problem and lived the rest of my life peacefully, not having to worry about being hunted down.

"Just like any other game: it was created."

"By the Emperor?" I ventured a guess. "The mysterious three-eyed moderator?"

"The Emperor monitors compliance with the main laws, but after all he is also an ordinary player, even though a very high level one. The Game was created by specific individuals for a specific purpose, and currently it fulfils all its tasks. If you want to find out more about it, find me. I am not even going to hide: I am located at the very center of the Academy, on the island, in the third tower. If you crave knowledge: welcome to my abode. Goodbye for now; the time left till your respawn is melting away unstoppably. I agree that you need help; your map will constantly show the current location of your team and — alright! — one of the hidden teachers. He will teach you a lot. Hold on to the guiding line, stop the mages and find me — I have a lot to tell you, explorer."

The map has been updated

CHAPTER FOUR

GENOCIDE

I T TOOK ME about an hour to reach the point marked on the map. At the beginning of the way I was seeing a guard practically in every stone, so I tried to avoid touching things if I didn't need to. But when I almost lost my balance, I stopped caring, and continued on my way grabbing on to everything I could, taking care to make sure that at any given time some part of my body was touching the guiding line. Actually, speaking of body parts... a rather long time had passed since I became a player, but I still had no urge at all to visit the bathroom. I knew that I was losing precious time and looked like an insecure little boy, but I still couldn't resist it: I pulled down my steel chausses and looked at what the Game had endowed me with in terms of my male equipment. I could not contain a satisfied chuckle once I made sure that everything I had before had stayed with me. Based on a visual inspection my everything looked healthy and — again, I couldn't help checking! — after several quick strokes it reacted the way it was supposed to: I had an erection. With a heavy sigh I rid myself of the temptation, then dressed and kept moving. The guards of the forest of stone and steel were not the kind of audience I would want to regale with the sight of masturbation, even though it would have been really great to relax right now. As soon I as squirmed out of trouble I would definitely find a woman for a night. Sex is the best method of stress relief.

The first thing I realized once I saw the teacher was: it would have been impossible to find him on my own. If you had not known that there was a grey-haired old man in this particular spot, it would have been extremely hard to find him in the middle of a jumble of reinforced concrete. It took me several minutes to orient myself and locate a barely noticeable steel beam a meter below me, disappearing under a huge stone. Having carefully climbed down and made my way along the new guiding line, I ended up nose to nose with an old man covered with dust, sitting in the lotus position. The only sign indicating that he was still alive were two blue eyes in his motionless face, watching my approach intently.

"Welcome, recruit, I will be training you. Now harken to my wisdom!"

Learning progress: You have reached teacher 2 of 10

"You will have to choose what I am going to teach you," the old man continued in a hoarse voice, as dust fell away from his face at every word. Apparently, this teacher had not talked to any players for some time.

"What options do I have?" I asked with trepidation. Had I finally got lucky, after all?

"I can replace any of the ten mandatory teachers. But only one. It is within my power to teach you how to use either the artifact, game interface, defense, attack or secondary class abilities, specialty, craft, attributes, class outfits, or teach you the basics of the Game. Choose what is most interesting to you at this point. I would like to remind you that you need to choose one thing only.

I took a few deep breaths, fighting a strong desire to study the attack capabilities, so I could go beat the mages. As the unknown voice had said, knowledge was my weapon, so that's what I needed to increase to the max. Choosing my words carefully so as not to give the teacher a reason to pick on something, I started questioning:

"Before the Academy I didn't have a chance to go through the initial training, so it's hard for me to choose an area of training based just on names... If you were to give me the names of all ten training units, the choice would be more rational and logical. As of now I am being overwhelmed by over-the-top entropy."

"There is nothing forbidden about this information." The teacher did not put on airs. "Your artifact is already activated, so you know very well what you can learn in this unit.

"In the game interface unit you will learn to open and close virtual windows and use buttons; you will receive clarifications on all the functions of the game interface and the ways to update it.

"In the unit of class abilities you will learn one of the three paths for development of the Paladin and learn to use various class abilities.

"The specialty unit will enable you to choose the path for your development regardless of the Artifact you have chosen.

"The crafts unit provides technical specialty basics. You will be able to improve your equipment, make elixirs and other things of that nature.

"The attributes unit will teach you the specifics of working with attributes, and clarify what they are and how they are different, for example, from class abilities.

"The unit of class outfits provides information on how you can upgrade class armor, how to work with your inventory and how to expand it.

"And, finally, Game basics unit will give you an understanding of the overall principles of the Game, starting from the Auction to the development and political framework. What would you like to learn?"

"What is the 'development path'?" I frowned in bewilderment, not understanding the purpose of specialty in the least. "What does it mean – 'regardless of the Artifact you have chosen'?"

"If this is what you would like to know, you would need to learn the use of specialty. Is this your choice?"

Lately so many unpleasant and unexpected things had happened to me that it took me an enormous effort to stop myself from socking the old guy one in the kisser. Is it so difficult to answer a question? Is it really necessary to make a problem out of everything I ask? What kind of stupid approach is that?"

"Yes, I would like to learn how to use specialty," I said, trying to calm down and looking over the list of training units once again. I would learn the class abilities later – they are not crucial now; all the rest, with the exception, perhaps, of the general basic principles of the Game, were not particularly important for me at the moment. However, I did not want to use the entire teacher to learn the rules for using the Auction, while the specialty issue really bothered me. What did it mean: "path of development"?

Process of specialty choice has been activated.

The space around me changed, turning into the clearing I had seen previously, surrounded by the strange forest. Even though I was sure that this clearing was completely identical to the one I had already seen, I still looked around the entire space that I could see, fixing my eye on the small details: the reddish leaves of the trees, the grass that looked like blue plantain leaves, and noticing the sun was not visible even though the weather was generally clear. The Book of Knowledge needed to be leveled up all the time.

"Specialty is the cornerstone of the player's development," the teacher started explaining as soon as I finished exploring the area. "In essence, it's the way the player uses his game skills, his profession. Through a symbiotic relationship with the Artifact or independent action, the specialty maximizes the player's necessary qualities that would enable him to express himself to the fullest in his chosen profession."

"...?" my face so vividly conveyed all the understanding I had of what was being said to me that the old man grinned, and suddenly asked:

"Tell me, Paladin, how do you see yourself in this game?"

"...?" — another vivid reaction.

"What attracts you the most? Fights with other players? Battles with NPCs? Politics? Dungeons? Searching for treasures? Exploring the world? Something else?"

"I was planning to explore..."

"What for?"

"Any information has a price: I was thinking of selling it," I gradually relaxed, taking an active part in the dialogue. At least now I could understand what the teacher was talking about and what his question was.

"A price?" The old man was surprised. "Since when does something available through a simple query have a price?"

"Not everyone has access to the Temple of Knowledge," I quipped, having figured out what the old guy meant.

"Nonsense! It's accessible to everyone! Moreover, the more you ask for help, the easier it is to enter the Temple. I heard you – you were planning to sell information. To whom? Those players, who, as you put it, don't have access to the Temple of Knowledge, won't be able to pay you. They simply don't have the money!" While those who would be willing to open their purses and pay their granis for information are unlikely to buy information about the Game on the side. It's much simpler and more beneficial to fly over to the Temple of Knowledge and find everything out there.

"What do you mean – 'don't have the money'?" I was quite stunned, as this turn of events was totally unexpected to me. "Do players have money problems?"

"Are you planning to charge NPC money for information?" The old man was even more surprised.

"Well, actually, that was my initial plan," I said slowly, trying to figure out what to do. My plan for a carefree existence was creaking under my feet, because if the old guy was right, no one would care a crap for the information that was currently accumulating in my Book of Knowledge.

"It's a rather stupid plan, I would like to point out, but it's up to you. If you decide to concentrate exclusively on relations with the NPC, I am not going to try and talk you out of it. That's exactly why I asked what you like most of all. I would like to recommend selecting as a specialty some wonderful occupations such as "Speaker" or "Inventor". They will combine very well with the Book of Knowledge and will enable you to become a popular and famous person."

"Wait, so specialty is a profession that would have within the game world?" I ventured to guess.

"Not quite. What you are going to do in the world will depend on the creative profession that you choose. It sounds similar, but there is a global fundamental distinction. Specialty is the direction for the player's development and application. For example, a "Speaker" could be anyone: a boxer, a street sweeper, or jobless. The specialty will manifest itself in his personal attitude to various phenomena of the game world. In this example, the boxer will, at each win or defeat, regale the public with wonderful public statements that come from the depths of his being. The sweeper will, with each sweep of his broom, speak such philosophical statements that he will acquire followers. I think you understand the point. That would not be the player's main profession, but the direction of development that he had chosen."

"Can players be street sweepers?" I was surprised.

"Why not? It's a profession. There is payment in the same granis for cleaning territories as for completing dungeons or killing other players. Not all the players like chasing each other or NPCs. Some like it quiet. Have you never noticed that some of those grey-haired, huge, bearded sweepers are very nice, communicative people with their own set of views on life, their own philosophy? That regardless of their social status one wants to talk to them, feel their attention? NPCs have even made up a special word for that: "charisma"; but now you know why that actually happens. It's just that someone chose the "Speaker" specialty. By the way, I do wish that to you as well, if you decide to sell knowledge. Who knows – you might be able to convince someone to buy some from you.

"Does this mean that being a world explorer does not pay?" I said with disappointment.

"Not at all; being an explorer not only pays; it's one of the most well-paid player development paths. The question is simply how to use the knowledge you acquire. It's unlikely that you'd be able to sell it to players, although nothing is impossible."

"I'm all ears," my breath caught from this news, but the old guy returned to his previous line:

"That's why I asked you about your preferences in the game. You need to decide here and now what it is that you want to do; then I will be able to provide you recommendations on the specialty most suitable for you and your Artifact. Or, if you have already made a choice prior to entering the Academy, you may simply name it."

"It's hard for me to choose a single thing," I admitted some time later. "Everything that was listed, with the exception, perhaps, of fighting other players, interests me. Politics, exploration, searching for treasures, and many other things. Is there some generalized specialty for a world explorer?"

"Why not...? There is everything here. Without a large variety of options, but it does exist. As I already said, the main task of the explorer is to find a way to use the information he has acquired. The more of it there is, the more experienced, educated and wise the explorer becomes. That's why the specialty "Judge" suits them like no one else. The explorer accumulates knowledge of an object or event, then delivers a verdict: "guilty" or "not guilty", and assigns punishment in case of a "guilty" verdict. Then it would depend on circumstances: the sentence may be passed on to headhunters, may be executed by the Judge himself if he deems it necessary, may be deferred, etc."

"I don't want to be constantly judging people," I grumbled, astonished. Of all things that was something that I really didn't need for sure.

"You are once again confusing specialty and profession. This is just a direction for development. For example, you became a member of a team that performed a dungeon raid. You completed the dungeon, acquired some loot, and now it's time to divide it up. The raid leader proposes that everything be divided equally, but the Book of Knowledge immediately tells you that the girlfriend of the raid leader did not take part in any of the battles with the monsters, and that she was away from the team, so she does not deserve a share equal to everyone else's. If you have the attribute "Context search" and you have leveled it up to level 15, you make this information available to all the raid participants, and then a joint decision is made regarding the fairness of dividing the loot. If needed, you could even call on the Game to help you, but I would definitely not advise that you do that. That would have consequences. Being a Judge does not mean sitting on a chair and listening to the arguments of the parties. Being a

Judge means exploring the world actively and recording its downfalls."

"You are describing this specialty in such rosy terms that it immediately begs the question: what's the catch? Now it all looks too good to be true."

"There is a drawback." The teacher was not going to deny it. "There is always one. The Judge has to be objective."

"...?"

"The Judge has no friends or enemies; he has only truth that he must follow. If his friend — a player or an NPC, it doesn't matter — breaks a law, the Judge must deliver a verdict. Regardless of whether he wants to or not."

"But there is much room for abuse." For some reason arrangements for corruption appeared in my mind at once. We are such strange creatures after all: instead of rejoicing and thinking of the bright side, we immediately start looking for ways to circumvent the law.

"It's possible; frequently that is what Judges do. But it's not so simple. Any verdict is checked by the moderator — the Emperor. The Game provides to him all information concerning the event, and if the moderator decides that the Judge was not objective, the moderator will send a headhunter after him."

"So all he does is check verdicts?" I was surprised. "Or are there just a couple of players who are Judges? How come the Emperor has so much time on his hands?"

"Actually, Judges are not numerous; in each game world there are probably not be more than a hundred, and they belong to different classes. As for the time for review... Yaropolk, you need to stop being used to your former life. In the Game time is not uniform. Will a single second pass in the main world while you are training at the Academy? No. It's the same with verdicts. The Emperor can spend a hundred years to review all the verdicts delivered in a day, but it will not be noticeable in the main game world.

"So who controls the Emperor? Who can guarantee that he reviews verdicts properly and correctly?"

"The Game itself does that. Its creators wanted to eradicate in all players a craving to break the law, but there were only enough system resources for the Emperor. Thus, he is the most pure and righteous creature in the entire Game, and his every word is the law. If the Emperor decides that the verdict was delivered improperly, the Judge will lose one level: headhunters will send him for respawn."

"And if the verdict is correct?"

"You get a bonus. You will know what it is after the very first verdict."

"But one could still manipulate." For some reason various schemes occurred to me of how one could get around the rules. "Keep sitting at the lower levels so that it would be easier to level up; then, even if you are sent for respawn it won't be a major problem."

"It's a good thought but you are not the first one to whom it has occurred. A Judge has the right to deliver one hundred wrong verdicts. Once he makes the hundredth wrong decision, he will be wiped out, as someone who has not lived up to expectations. If he has any levels left by then, that is."

"Fine." I thought for a while, then requested a clarification: "Is my understanding correct that a player whose specialty is "Judge" can actually be doing whatever, even herding cows, but if someone breaks a law in front of him, the Judge must study the issue from beginning to end and deliver a verdict?"

"In general that's correct, but there is one thing: the Judge doesn't have to study the issue in detail; he may deliver his verdict guided purely according to his experience and attitude to events. The Emperor will later decide whether the Judge was correct or not."

"But I don't have to choose this specialty, right?"

"You don't. I have told you about the specialty most suitable for the development path you have chosen. You can choose any other one and it will be immediately assigned to you. If that is the case I am waiting for you to name the specialty. What will your choice be, Paladin?"

"I think I will ask you a few more questions. Is a Judge always obligated to deliver a verdict? With respect to any violation that occurs in front of him?"

"Yes – this is the drawback of this specialty. However, each misdeed has a certain period of limitation for action. If during this period the Judge does not have enough time to investigate the case event, the case will be closed and the perpetrator will be deemed not guilty.

"But this is..." I started saying, but the old man interrupted me:

"Let's not state the obvious out loud."

"How many cases can a Judge have open concurrently?" It seemed to me that I had found a decent loophole. If I don't feel like investigating something, I could just blow it off.

"Ten. If the Judge runs up against a necessity to deliver an eleventh verdict, he would have to deliver it here and now, based purely on his attitude to what's going on. So it's not recommended to accumulate unfinished cases: you risk losing a level."

"And would I have to deliver verdicts for everyone? Both players and NPCs?"

"No; whatever NPCs do is determined by the algorithms of the Game. A Judge would be working only with players and minions. Nobody else. You don't have to pay any attention to whatever NPCs might do – the Game itself will take care of it."

"How many Judges are there on Earth?" I made a last-ditch attempt to postpone the obvious choice. It was shameful to admit, but the mere thought that I would be able to hold players and minions responsible for their misdeeds was so attractive that, really, there was no other choice.

"Thirty-two."

"And how many have been wiped out already?"

"Three thousand two hundred and seventeen." The teacher shocked me. "For some reason Judges on Earth are not very much in favor of following the main requirement of this specialty: being objective. What is your choice, Paladin?"

"I agree with the suggested choice," I finally decided. "I accept the specialty "Judge"!"

Specialty has been selected
Character adjustment in progress

Fireworks exploded in front of my eyes, and I lost consciousness from unbearable pain.

"How did you get info on this teacher?" Through the darkness of faint I heard a voice sounding more like a growl. Knowing very well that time was working against me, I tried to open my eyes, though unsuccessfully. My brain was overwhelmed by a chorus of a thousand voices combined with the crescendo of a symphony orchestra. Grabbing my head with my palms, I began moaning and rolling around on the ground trying to make all that noise subside. It was quite hard for me at the moment to perceive the surrounding reality in an adequate way.

"Should I just send you for respawn to put you out of your misery?" The growling voice was kindness itself, but it was that phrase that enabled me to switch from feeling the pain to perceiving the reality around me. The hum was still there, but it faded into the background, which enabled me to do the incredible: open my eyes and look around. Three things drew my attention immediately. First: the teacher sitting in the lotus position, having completed his mission for training me. Second: a huge panther looking at me, her head tilted in contemplation. Third: the game interface has changed. The third thing was so unusual that it pushed even the panther into the background.

In the left top corner of my field of vision a verdict counter appeared; under it there was a line "Case No. 'None' ", and another line "Case investigation". Based on the fact that currently it said "0%", it was supposed to indicate the depth of my "delving" into the situation. The status bar showed an additional icon; pressing on it showed a list of active cases, of which there were none at the moment. But the most fascinating thing was something else: in the top center there was an unusual icon: a shining semicircle with a futuristic arrow, resembling a speedometer. At the moment the arrow pointed strictly upward, without leaning to either of the sides, which were a bright light on the right and total darkness on the left. My mischievous hands (well, eyes, really, in this case) immediately clicked on the mysterious speedometer.

Allegiance has been activated. Current value: "Neutral"

"Hey, Paladin! Hello! Anyone home?" The panther roared in a human voice, distracting me from studying the game interface.

"Bagheera, " I drawled with a smile for some reason, focusing my eyes on the panther. "'We be of one blood, ye and...'"

"You really are a twit, rather than a creature 'of one blood'," the panther cut me off and then – I actually had to rub my eyes in surprise – turned into a girl.

"I repeat the question: how did you get information about this teacher?"

Unlike the throaty growl of the panther, in human form the girl had an amazingly charming voice. A strange patchwork outfit could probably be called a sort of a dress if it were not for parts made of chainmail and metal plates. However, even this incredible outfit could not conceal how tiny the girl was. On her feet the former panther wore not elegant green booties intended to underscore her graceful shape, but two heavy boots, looking more like army boots. But her face was the most amazing of all. I had not seen such so well formed, charming and attractive a face in my entire life. At first glance the girl looked human: twenty two or three years old. Two bright sapphires – for some reason looking cold as the arctic at the moment – were watching my every move; her long chestnut hair was drawn into a simple pony tail, so as not to interfere with her movements. This shapeshifter, or, as the Book of Knowledge helpfully suggested, druid, was not wearing any headdress that I could see.

"One of the local teachers shared it," I told her honestly, understanding that quarrelling with the panther at the moment would be impolitic.

"What teacher?" Her cold eyes showed some interest.

"As far as I understood, the chief one at the Academy." I decided to inflate my value. If she was the very girl who had sent the two rogues for respawn, she would not have much trouble doing the same to me. I needed to interest her. "He got in touch with me from a remote location and provided the coordinates for this very yogi."

"How do I reach him?" The druid kept asking. I looked at my Energy level and sighed sadly: there were just ten units left. In a couple of hours I would end up having to face the mages.

"He is not in the forest; he is sitting in some other place. If you want, we can set out to reach him together."

"Pf!" the druid snorted contemptuously."Why in hell do I need you? To distract guards while I run away?"

"Why do you run away from the guards?" I was surprised. "Don't you know..."

"Don't I know what?" Despite being pint-sized, the girl practically loomed over me as soon as I fell silent, biting my tongue. Why should I share important information? "There is a way to pass by the guards?!"

"Of course there is. Or how would I have gotten here? Since I have no weapons."

"I see that... What's the way to do it?" I nearly jumped with joy once I figured out that the druid did not know about the guiding beams. I could turn that to my advantage!"

"No, it doesn't work that way. I am offering a partnership. I share information, you help me get away from the mages."

"No partnerships and no agreements." The girl grew suspicious. "From whom do you want to get away?"

"From mages. In an hour, or two at best, my Energy will drop down to zero and I will be sent for respawn. Mages are waiting for me at all three respawn points. I need help."

"So you are the one they are hunting?" The druid was interested. "What would prevent me from turning you in to them?"

"Information." I shrugged my shoulders indifferently, even though I had a sinking feeling inside. "The mages don't have it, or else they would have rushed after me into this forest. Since you don't run on the ground, additional knowledge about the guards would be useful to you."

"How did you gain it?"

"I am an explorer of the world. I had to figure out how the local monsters work. Have they ever caught you?"

"Twice." The girl cringed. "And another forty times I got away. For some reason they would just stop the chase. Oh! Do you know why?"

"I do," I confirmed, once again barely able to contain my joy. The panther rushing to get away from the guards must have managed to touch the guiding line, and the chase after her would stop. Even now the girl was standing touching just one foot to the beam.

"So, to sum it up — you will share information on how to avoid the guards; in exchange you want me to help you to get away from the respawn point where you will end up going in an hour since you don't have any food with you. Right?"

"As if you have some," I mumbled grumpily,

looked at the druid and drawled in amazement: "Oh really? From where?!"

"I was taught to use inventory prior to the Academy," the druid said proudly. "You can't bring food here directly – only stored in your inventory."

"Would you share it?" I said too quickly, and immediately scolded myself silently. I should not show how much I need to replenish my Energy.

"No, it doesn't work that way," the girl mocked me. "How can one avoid the guards?"

We tried to stare each other down for about a minute. Neither one of us wanted to surrender first, as there were no guarantees that the other would keep his word. Since she refused to enter into an official agreement, one would have to rely on the other's word only.

"Yaropolk." I didn't know what else to do, and stretched out my hand, introducing myself. Time was money, and in my case time was life. I couldn't afford to waste it. "Paladin. You may call me Yari for short."

"Dolgunata, a druid." The girl hesitated for a moment, then returned my handshake. Despite the fact that I was wearing armor and the druid's hands were covered with thick leather gloves, the feeling of close contact with her graceful hand was unforgettable. "Nata for short."

"There are eight teachers in total in this forest." I decided to give up some information to establish a partnership. "Five are open and available to everyone, and three are hidden. You can see here one of the hidden ones. I don't know where the other two are."

"What about the guards?"

"You need to be touching the guiding line..." I told her about the steel beams, without mentioning the symbols, however. That was not part of our unwritten agreement.

"What did you mean by the 'chief teacher'?", Nata kept asking, making my face darken. The girl was in no hurry to keep her part of the bargain.

"Food," I reminded her, but was immediately put in my place:

"We have no agreement and you are not in a position to bargain. I am waiting."

Good luck to you in the Academy," I grumbled, then turned away and walked off. Dolgunata clearly demonstrated the main principle of the game: sink your opponents at every turn, while taking advantage of them to the max. I hoped for the girl's sensibility and waited for her to call me, but she did not. Before jumping onto the main steel beam, I turned around — the girl lost all interest in me, involved in talking to the teacher.

Bitch!

Despite the fact that after meeting the druid my mood was right through the floor, I moved towards the Paladins. We needed to join forces. The map showed that my team was staying in place, not trying to move anywhere. Having spent fifteen minutes to get to another clearing while remembering to touch the steel beam, I peeked out from behind a stone boulder and assessed the situation from four meters above ground. It was, to put it mildly, not to the advantage of the Paladins...

In front of me I saw a wide clearing with a huge

three-meter stone on it, all covered with mysterious runes; they were emitting an evil green light. As I watched, a small ball of sun-bright light appeared at the bottom of the stone; it quickly grew and turned into a cursing player. Someone was extremely unhappy at being sent to respawn. This was a respawn point! There was only one path leading to the clearing; now it was blocked by a crowd of mages. A lightning bolt flew from the hands of one of them, hitting the newly respawned player right in the head. There was an electric crack, a scream of pain, a corpse on the ground that disappeared at once and the raucous laughter of the raving players. It horrified me even to think what kind of person would enjoy killing! The mages needed to see a psychiatrist right away, and beg him for a lobotomy. There would be no other way to cure them at this point.

On the other end of the clearing, keeping the respawn stone between themselves and the mages, was my team. Behind Monstrichello, whose face was drawn and glum, there were Logir, Nartalim, Sartal and three more Paladins whom I did not know. Apparently also victims of the mayhem created by the mages. Despite an impressive company, the Paladins were not in a hurry to fight the mages for the right to leave the clearing, while the mages were in no hurry to finish them off. This was a stalemate which the mages broke up periodically by killing respawned players. During the ten minutes while I was sitting there trying to figure out a rescue plan, ten players were killed that way.

"Bastards!" A guttural roar from my side was

so unexpected that I nearly tumbled into the clearing from my vantage point. The panther twitched her tail frantically a couple of times and turned into a girl.

"Eat!" she ordered, handing me a green patty. "This will fully restore your Energy."

"Why?" I could not help asking, while nevertheless chewing the patty thoroughly. It had no taste, no smell, the texture felt like plasticine, but the growing Energy bar was making me euphoric. I gained an additional 12 hours of life!

"I needed to check if you were saying the truth. That's number one. Number two – I needed to understand how far you would be willing to go to save yourself. Creeps and sellout scum should be eliminated. Number three – I need information.

"How did you find the location of the previous teacher?" Despite her help, my attitude to the druid was guarded. The anger had subsided, but an unpleasant aftertaste remained.

"I was running away from a monster when I heard your scream. It was too long and full of suffering for a guard victim, so I ventured to look, particularly since the guard was not chasing me anymore. You were squirming on the ground in front of the teacher, so I decided to question you first, and then kill. You know the rest."

"Kill?"

"Never mind. What are you planning to do?"

"Even if I were to join the Paladins, there is no way we could fight through the line of mages. I would take them to the forest to the hidden teacher, then we would make a circle. There is a limited number of mages, so they are all distributed among various teachers and respawn points. We would catch small groups and kill them. Want to join us"?

"If you kill the mages, what next?" Dolgunata ignored me.

"We would train with all the teachers in this forest, then we'd go looking for the rest. There are five more somewhere else. If we keep together, we'll be able to survive."

"Reasonable. What can you offer for my help?"

"Information."

"I am not ready to risk levels for knowledge that will be of no use in the main world."

"In that case... what would you say about a granis?" I remembered the currency in my possession. If Dangard was so happy about getting a granis out of the elf, maybe the druid would also like that price.

"Are you initiated?" Nata's eyes narrowed.

"I am not."

"Then it's not an option. If you were to be killed for good, you wouldn't make it out of here. Who would give me my granis then?"

"You will get a granis here and now if you help us," I said, but the girl's astonished look told me that I have no idea about the game currency.

"But you are not initiated! How did you get it?"

"It doesn't matter," I replied cryptically, trying to hide my own confusion. I received mine from Archibald, as a reward for the NPC I killed. Can it be that prior to entering the Academy recruits never killed anyone? Somehow I had a hard time believing that. So why was Nata surprised? "Agreed?"

"What do you want from me?"

"Call the Game to witness that you will help me and most of these 'pretty boys'," – I nodded towards the Paladins huddling together – pass through ten teachers and finish the Academy successfully. As payment for this I will now give you a granis; the only thing is, I've never done this, so the transfer may take more than one attempt. But I guarantee that I will give it to you. If it is possible at all in the Academy."

"No agreements," after a rather prolonged staring match the druid forced through her lips. "Either you give me the granis and I help you, or we part ways."

"Thank you for the food," I said with regret. Staying in the company of this charming beauty was nice, but it did not help me get closer to my final goal. Given that at least four of the Paladins huddling beneath had weapons as artifacts, even if Dolgunata's claws were to help us, it wouldn't be crucial. "If I tell you where the chief teacher is, will you give me a couple more patties?"

"One," the girl reacted quickly. "My reserves are also limited."

The exchange was completed without an agreement, as if Nata had some kind of a hangup about that. Casting a parting glance at the clearing, the druid turned into a panther and left me. She was weird... beautiful but weird ...

"You are so pissing me off!" Another electric crack and scream, and the guffaws of the mages were heard from the clearing. Someone else was unlucky. By the way, that's a thought! Why should we only help Paladins? My experience of talking to Dolgunata demonstrated that other classes may include players who were, even though weird, still sane enough. And that a granis is quite a valuable thing in the game world. If we managed to get away from the mages, why shouldn't we propose to other classes that they join our team? Many players, especially non-initiated ones, would readily give up everything they have in order to stay alive. We should use this!

It took me half an hour to circle the clearing and carefully climb down: the guiding beams wound and twisted in a complicated pattern, so frequently I had to move away from the respawn point rather than risk being caught by a guard. Holding onto an overhead beam with my hand, I reached practically the edge of the stone forest when I heard the Paladins talking:

" I have two hours worth of Energy left," said an unfamiliar voice. Must have been one of the Paladins who had newly joined the group.

"Same crap here," Logir responded to him, and then I finally peeked out from behind the stone.

"Let's kill all dem freaks!" Monstrichello rumbled, causing a howl of laughter from the side of the mages. It would be hard not to hear the tank's roar.

"What killing: it's my last level," a lanky Paladin said despondently, then whispered with a hysterical note in his voice: "I don't want to die!"

I was just starting to try to figure out how to call the Paladins without attracting the attention of the mages, when I heard a wild and horrible roar coming from behind me. A large cat dashed by me like black lightning, and behind her... she was followed by flying steel. Dolgunata had encountered a flying monster that looked like the nightmare of a person taking heavy drugs: a jumble of steel rods partially covered in black fog; it had three bright red eyes. The creature glided, breaking every law of physics, periodically emitting wild screams. My breath caught. I froze like a statue, and just noted from the corner of my eye that my hand was still clutching the guiding beam. It should not go after me...

"What kind of nonsense with a tail is that?" I heard surprised shouts from the mages, after which I felt better. The flying monster stopped oppressing my mind and turned itself into a detail of the forest, looking so much like an integral part of a nearby wall of reinforced concrete that even though one knew the nasty thing was there, it was impossible to see it on the stone.

"Quiet – I am one of us!" Nata growled quietly, so as not to draw the attention of the mages; her tail twitched nervously. The Paladins had regrouped; they managed to place Monstrichello, who was covering himself with the shield, between themselves, the mages and the druid. "If you want to live, follow me."

"Who are you?" Nartalim piped up at once. "Why should we listen to you?"

"Because you'll just die here!" The panther shot back, and, making sure the flying monster left her alone, in one jump landed in the clearing in the stone forest. Follow me! I am with Yari!"

"But there are monsters there!" the lanky

Paladin whined, but for Logir my name served as sufficient reason to believe the panther. Slowly, so as not to provoke the mages to action, she approached the panther, swallowed nervously and looked inside the stone jungle. She lingered, then swallowed and made a step towards the forest. Only now did I realize that I could clearly see the invisible line that separated the safe clearing from the horrors of the reinforced concrete chaos, and that just now Logir crossed that line, starting a ten-second timer. If during that time she did not touch a guiding line, a monster would appear.

"Here, quick!" I stepped from behind a neighboring stone. "Grab onto this block!"

"Why?" The femorc frowned, but then Nata came to my aid:

"Do what he says, or else a guard will appear!"

"Fine! But I don't understand...," Logir didn't have to be asked twice; in just a couple of moments she was standing next to me. "Are you alive?"

"That's a stupid question," I grumbled. "No, I've been dead for a freaking year, and now you are talking to a ghost."

"Logir, are you OK in there?" we heard Nartalim shout, and I had to show him by gestures that shouting was not optimal. I was right, as then we heard the mages yelling from the far side of the clearing:

"Hey, Pals, who's that pussy running around with you there? Where are you hiding the femorc?"

I slanted my eye at Dolgunata, who had indifferently put her head on the steel beam and closed her eyes. By her entire appearance the panther was showing that she was resting, and nothing going on around concerned her in the least. But her heaving sides indicated that just a few minutes ago the druid had had to run for her life. The main question remained: why did she return?

"Logir, your task is to get all the Pals here, into the forest." I looked into the dark eyes of the femorc. "If you hold on to this beam, the guards will not come. By moving through the forest we can cover all the teachers without running into mages."

"Yari, I…"

"Let's talk about it later, about why and how you were going to turn me in to the mages, ok?" I cut the femorc off. "Now the most important thing is to get you all out of the clearing. If the mages try to follow us the guards will make short work of them. Are you with me?"

"Your own people wanted to betray you?" Dolgunata said with surprise as soon as Logir returned to the clearing and started to explain something to the Paladins, constantly pointing in our direction. "Then why are you helping them?"

"Why did you come back, by the way?" I ignored the druid's question. "We decided for sure that there wouldn't be any agreements between us."

"There won't be," the panther agreed, turning into a person. "But you did not tell me all the info on the guiding lines! You wanted to send me to respawn? After I shared food with you?!"

"What?!" Even though I was taken aback by this unexpected accusation I could not allow her to blame me for such nonsense. "I told you everything I knew! Instead of saying thank you and sharing food you made that idiotic test and now you are accusing me?! Are you flippin' crazy?"

"Now I am crazy?!" Dolgunata was not holding back. "Fine, then explain why the beam onto which you are holding is a guiding one, and this one is not?" The girl pointed at a piece of steel sticking out from some reinforced concrete. "What's the difference?"

"What do you mean, what's the difference?" I frowned. They are different... even the color..."

"Like crap they are different! There is no difference between these two pieces! But for some reason you are holding onto that one! I nearly got killed because of you!"

"Wait..." my anger at the girl suddenly left me. I was shifting my eyes between the two different pieces of metal and became more confused by the minute. In fact, if one were to disregard the color, there was no difference at all between the two pieces of steel: They were the same size, the same shape and even the same length! But still I knew very clearly that the greenish color of the guiding beams meant safety while everything else meant death. Since the guards were, well, on their guard.

"Onto what are supposed to hold here?" I was drawn out of my deep reverie by a booming voice. I focused my eyes and frowned — the Paladin who approached us was a catorian. It immediately brought up an unpleasant memory of Archibald, but I tried to stuff it deep down again. Whoever this Pal was, it was not his fault that Archibald was a jerk.

"We'll wait for you!" The mages rough laughter was heard from the clearing, and the remaining Paladins showed up following the catorian.

"Hold on to this beam, now!" I ordered them and started towards the forest. "Those who are not touching the beam will be eaten by a guard in ten seconds!"

"Homey!" Monstrichello beamed, as he, totally unembarrassed, wrapped me in a hug. "They told us they wiped you out!"

"Here, here, I am alive!" I extracted myself from the tank's embrace as Dolgunata snorted, and prepared to move on. "Come on, there is a teacher ahead.

"You think this will save you?" Nartalim snorted contemptuously, but he put his hand on the beam nonetheless. "The mages won't let you out of the Academy alive."

"Most important is that they should let you out, pretty boy," I retorted with open anger. "I suppose Sharda will be glad to hear that one of the Paladins betrayed the order!"

"You'll never prove anything, you goner! Monster, send him for respawn, will you? If we turn him in to the mages, they won't bother us!"

"But..." Monstrichello lingered. "But he's, like, helping us..."

"What helping? This is a trick!"

Case received: Nartalim's Betrayal (Slots available for: 9 more cases)

Description: Reasons have arisen to suspect that

Nartalim, level one Paladin, betrayed the foundations of his class

Task: Investigate the case and deliver your verdict on it

Case investigation: 64%

Period of limitation of action: 3 months

The recently added interface changed, filling with newly received data. The inscription appeared, the status bar filled in, but the starkest change was that above the head of Nartalim, the suspect in the case, a bright yellow number "64" appeared, reflecting either my progress on the case investigation or the extent of the elf's guilt as the system saw it.

"Monster, I don't get it – why are you stalling?! Kill him!"

Case investigation: "Nartalim's Betrayal": 65%

"Nartalim!" I said, and my voice was full of hatred. If the elf had not tried to dig his heels in, I would have postponed delivering the verdict until the return from the Academy. Probably by then he would have corrected his behavior and realized how wrong he had been; then we would have found a way to resolve the issue peacefully. But since the elf decided to stand in my way, so be it! Case investigation at 65 seemed sufficient for me to make my decision. Even if it were based on emotions for the most part! "I pronounce you guilty of betrayal and attempted murder of a Paladin, and I sentence you to..."

"You sentence me?" Nartalim, laughed

168

interrupting me. "Who the hell are you, to sentence me? Have you gone completely bonkers?"

Please verify your status

If there were not a laughing elf standing in front of me, I would have given more thought to the message that appeared. But the sight of a contemptuous sneer on Nartalim's lips left me with just one desire – to wipe that smirk off of his face, so I growled through my teeth:

"Who am I? I am a Judge! And I sentence you to be stripped of your initiation and die! You are not worthy of being a Paladin! You are not worthy of graduating from the Academy! This sentence is final and not subject to appeal!"

Status is verified
Verdict is confirmed
Verdict is deemed: harsh
Case No. 1 "Nartalim's Betrayal" is closed. The task is assigned to the nearest Headhunters
Reward allocated to Headhunter:1 granis

"What the...?!" I heard three surprised voices at once: Nartalim's, Logir's and Dolgunata's, but I was concerned with something else at the moment. The arrow on my virtual speedometer moved to the dark side and "1" appeared over it. I grinned: the Emperor confirmed my verdict as just, but excessively harsh, and changed some parameter towards the dark side. Kindness is not my thing. Following a sudden guess, I opened the properties window and confirmed that I was right: from now on I was "Yaropolk, Paladin of Darkness".

"Yari: are you raving mad?" Nartalim roared wildly, when for a few seconds mysterious red light flashed around him. "Return it back the way it was! I'll complain to my dad, he'll bury you! We paid for the initiation!"

"Yari, I can't...," Logir whispered, giving me a stunned look. "I am not ready... This is cruel..."

"I'll do it!" Dolgunata dropped, turning into the panther. Nartalim screamed like a stuck pig, drew his sword and tried to run it through the panther that dashed towards him, but Nata was too quick for an inexperienced swordsman. Claws flashed, we heard a stifled rasp and there was one less player in the Academy. Nartalim could be blotted from memory.

"Down them!" the catorian screamed, attacking Dolgunata. A member of his class had just been killed in front of him, so the offender should not go unpunished. Following his emotions rather than his mind, the catorian made a decision and started acting in accordance with his own understanding of justice. A true Paladin!

"FREEZE!" My shout was probably heard even by the mages at the respawn point, but I couldn't care less. "Anyone who as much as twitches I'll wipe out to hell!"

I had no idea what stopped the catorian – my scream, Dolgunata's scowl or some personal system messages, but he did freeze just a few steps before reaching Nata.

"Listen here!" I continued to roar, pouring out all the rage and anger accumulated over recent events. "Nartalim wanted to turn us all in to the mages. I personally heard his conversation with Dangard who is a leader among them. It's harsh, but he got what he deserved! There will be no traitors among the Paladins! Now we shall move to a teacher, complete the training with him. If someone is unhappy about something, you are welcome to return to the clearing where the mages are waiting. They will welcome you with open arms. Any questions?"

I looked at the remaining group, frowning. Logir and the lanky Paladin looked down; from Sartal's appearance it was impossible to understand what he was up to, even though the tip of the lizard's tail was twitching nervously. Monstrichello was shifting his eyes from one player to another in bewilderment, not knowing what to do and whom he should beat up. The catorian was staring daggers at me. It was only the third of the newly-joined Paladins, who looked like some sort of gnome or maybe leprechaun – hell knows – who was staring at the landscape vacantly, as if all this had nothing to do with him.

"If there are no questions, let's move on. Our objective is to reach the teacher."

"What good would that do?" the catorian said in a forced tone. "Soon our Energy will run out and we'll respawn anyway."

"What's your level?" I turned around but faced six pairs of eyes looking sown. Nobody was in a hurry to share personal information. With a deep sigh, trying to calm down, I clarified: "Guys, if you are at the first level, the training will level you up to two. This will help the non-initiated players survive the respawn. There are no mages at the location of the teacher to whom I am leading you. It's quite possible that each leveling up fully replenishes Energy. If you want to survive and pass through the Academy, you'll have to trust me and tell me about yourself a little more than is strictly speaking the norm."

After this statement everyone responded, making me curse thoroughly and with feeling. By now everyone was at level one; all three of the Paladins who joined the team had not passed initiation and had ten units of Energy each. Two hours tops. We needed to hurry.

"Did you not forget something, Judge?" Dolgunata asked as soon as we reached our goal. The Paladins immediately rushed to the teacher, saving themselves from the final death, so for a few minutes Nata and I were left alone.

"Like you'd let anyone forget anything." I tried to relieve the situation, but the druid's eyes told me that I had failed. The anger at the elf drained away, and, while we walked towards the hidden teacher in complete silence, I had been turning the situation over and over in my mind trying to justify my verdict. It was confirmed to me that it was fair, but I could not get rid of the thought that my punishment of the elf was excessively cruel. Judging from the looks they cast in my direction, the Paladins thought the same. Not understanding very well how to give Nata her granis, I opened the list of delivered verdicts and highlighted the only line present there at the moment. A button immediately appeared in front of me saying "Complete task"; clicking on it materialized a brown coin in my hand. Granis.

"Your reward." I handed the coin to the druid. Thank you for accepting my assignment!"

"Was this necessary?" Dolgunata's eyes turned into two cold splinters of blue ice. "He had a weapon; passing through the Academy with him would have been easier."

"It was." I confirmed sadly. "If not now, he would have shown his true self later. And if he had done it during a battle with the mages, we would have all been in deep..."

"The Energy is filling up!" The joyful cry of the lanky Paladin who completed the training cut off my thought.

"I get what you're saying," Nata lingered a moment, then took the coin. So: a Judge?"

"So: a Headhunter?" I answered a question with a question. "I would have never thought..."

"That's the idea," Nata grinned. "Who would suspect a Headhunter in a lovely maiden? Particularly if she can do this: "nya!" ..."

The world became still. Somewhere far away there were the merry shouts of the Paladins who completed their training, but that was completely irrelevant: a creature of divine beauty appeared next to me. I did not dare breathe lest I startle her somehow. The huge blue eyes of the goddess charmed, enthralled and made you forget the whole world. Tilting her head slightly and shifting her feet slightly, as if she were shy and not daring to do something, the goddess looked at me from under her lowered eyelashes, said another magical "nya!" of hers and smiled. Now not only did the world become still; time itself stopped! Losing my cool, I rushed towards the goddess and embraced her, wishing only one thing – to cover her lovely face with kisses. The goddess avoided my embrace deftly, while still allowing me to retain some hope. Once she was bored with the struggle, she grabbed my head, bent to my ear and breathed into it noisily a few times, making my body tremble with languor and longing for delight; then she said:

"You get close to your victim, make it lose its head and surrender to you; then you carefully run a dagger through its eye socket and turn it three times. Once to kill it, twice – for pleasure." The magic of the moment disappeared in an instant and my awareness returned in a snap, but the druid held my head with a hand of steel, preventing me from moving. How could a delicate girl be so strong? Turning from an unearthly goddess into an ice queen in a split second, she added bloodthirstily: "No armor could save them! That's how a real Headhunter should be."

"What was that?!" I exhaled noisily as soon as the druid released my head, and I took a few steps back. "You invaded my brain!"

"Ph! Like I need your brain!" Dolgunata snorted. "You are a Judge; I a Headhunter. You have the right to Judge, I have the right to execute."

"What you did had little resemblance to punishment for the guilty," I grumbled, looking at the girl in a completely different way. A beauty who was not too hard to get along with, and moving with certainty from the category of an "acquaintance" to "close acquaintance" or even "friend" suddenly showed her true face and put a sign "deadly dangerous!" all over herself. Judging by what happened to me, Dolgunata used some kind of tricky ability the Headhunters had. Devir's student had been able to suppress Nartalim's will in a similar manner. Now the druid had just showed me that mental attacks in the game were as real as physical ones. I urgently needed protection from such influence.

"It happens," Dolgunata shrugged her shoulders calmly, refusing to get further into the topic.

"Since you are a hunter, you must have a mentor." A close look at the druid activated the Book of Knowledge, bringing up a separate page of everything I knew about the girl. There was abysmally little information, so I decided to clarify the most important part: "Is Devir your mentor?"

"What difference does it make to you?" Dolgunata frowned. "Even if he were, what does it matter?"

"It matters a lot. Devir wants to destroy me. It is on his orders that the mages are wreaking chaos in the Academy. If he is your mentor, I suggest that we part right away. I don't want to kill you."

"You haven't grown yourself a killing tool for that." Dolgunata thought for a moment, then added: "I have nothing to do with Devir. The rest is not important: you already know way too much about me.

We are done with questions: there is little time." Nata turned to the training Paladins and shouted: "Hey, Pals, are you done?"

Having agreed in advance that the Paladins would ask the hidden teacher to train them in anything they wanted except activation of artifacts and use of interface, we started on to the point where we had appeared in the Academy. The Paladins from my team had never been allowed to train with the first teacher; this lapse needed to be corrected. In additional, I wanted to test the battle worthiness of the team to see if we could fight against the mages.

"There are seven in the clearing," whispered Teart, whom I had sent scouting – a leprechaun Paladin from the world called Karval. Teart was just about the only Paladin in Karval; he even had to look for a mentor in a different world. Paladins were extremely unpopular among the small, red-bearded sly humanoids known in our world from Irish fairy tales. Once you imagined Teart wearing a green hat, it immediately made you want to grab him by the lapels and demand your pot of gold. However, shaking a treasure out of the leprechaun would have to be postponed, because Teart had a truly unique gift in the Academy: like myself, he could see the guiding line. Unfortunately, trying to find out why he could see the right beams did not yield any results: the leprechaun simply did not understand what I wanted from him. The beam was green and that was it, and the fact that others could not see it was their own problem. They needed to open their eyes then.

"There are three more at each pass," I added,

trying to organize the available information, but it wasn't working out too well for me. I was not a fighter. As soon as I realized that, I immediately tried to transfer the responsibility for making a decision from my poor head on to the entire team. If someone were to be wrong, at least let all of us be that "someone": "What shall we do?"

"Dat's no thinking deal!" Monstrichello was in his usual style. "Let's kill dem freaks!"

"Not so fast, my tank-headed friend," Logir cooled the bruiser's urge, which made him drop his gaze and fall silent. The only reason my jaw did not drop was because I was wearing a helmet: Monstrichello submitted to the femorc! Logir put her hand on the giant's arm and suddenly addressed the druid: "Dolgunata, what would you advise?"

"We shouldn't come out to the clearing right away: the risk is too high," the druid started explaining, completely unabashed, as if she had expected to be asked. "The optimal move would be to test ourselves on a small troop, when we would have an opportunity to retreat into the forest right away. One option would be to clear one of the passes."

"That's what we'll do! Yari, lead us to the right pass." Imperceptibly to the rest, the femorc took the lead in our team. Of course: she is the daughter of a well-known Paladin! It's not as though anyone protested; on the contrary, no one wanted to assume the responsibility, but the fact itself amused me: while the Paladins trundled from the respawn point to the teacher, no one had any doubts as to who was the leader. The one who saved all the rest was the leader.

But as soon as you showed people a visible light at the end of the tunnel at once there would appear alphas, omegas and other letters of the Greek alphabet trying to bend everyone else to their bidding.

I did not bother to fight for the leadership of the team: that wasn't what I needed. It would be impossible to turn me into a prince on a white horse leading his brave warriors forward onto enemy lines. I would prefer to live a quiet and orderly life somewhere in a house in the country, surrounded by beautiful women. Knowing that the mages stood between me and my ideal house from a dream, I decided to follow Logir and her orders until they contradicted my moral principles. Nodding in agreement, I led the team towards a passage away from the clearing. Tough luck for the three mages guarding it: they would be our guinea pigs.

"Monster, you go first." We stopped a couple of meters above the pass and Logir started to work out the tactics of the impending battle. "Let's do it the way we did before, but instead of Nartalima we'll use the panther... You're with us, right?" The femorc stopped briefly, as before this moment she had not given any thought to the reasons why on earth the druid should be helping us.

"I am," Nata grinned, for some reason looking at me. "What will Yari be doing?"

"He doesn't have any weapons, so nothing."

"So he won't get experience points for killing then?"

"Oh, that's what you are talking about... No, let him stand to the side for now. He is an explorer, not a warrior. So let him explore whatever is around. No need for him to be underfoot down there. Let's set out!"

The Paladins started climbing down, but Dolgunata still looked at me, not taking any action. I had to nod to her indicating that I agreed with Logir's decision. Without saying a word Nata followed the others. The hunt for the mages began.

"Hey, what the hell?!" I heard a wild scream from below, followed by electricity cracking, several dull clunks and death rattles. I tried to see what was going on, but a jumble of boulders and beams obscured my view. Thus, all that was left for me was to fidget, waiting for the results of the first foray. There were no Paladins seen. The waiting was becoming unbearable and I started thinking about climbing down when Monstrichello's booming roar came from the clearing:

"All the way! Mages are bitches!"

Having no idea whatsoever as to what was going on, I rushed along the guiding beams to the edge of the clearing to evaluate the situation and decide whether it was time to panic or everything was going according to plan. I was there at the finale: a group of twenty mages was raining fire and lightning on Monstrichello, who was moving towards them, completely ignoring the chaos wreaked all around him. The rest of the Paladins huddled together right at the entrance to the clearing, making no attempts to come closer to the battle. Monstrichello had come practically up to the mages when they suddenly started falling on the ground one after another, blinking and then disappearing as if they were being sent to respawn. I frowned, trying to understand what was going on; then a sudden insight made the whole puzzle fit together: each time one used an ability it ate up the Energy! Sharda had mentioned it before! The logic of the Paladins' actions became clear at once: in the Academy the level of Energy governs respawning, Monstrichello is not affected by magic, and the mages had become used to being able to resolve everything with a single lightning bolt; so, it was necessary to deprive the mages of Energy. It wouldn't matter how many mages come out against Monstrichello: one, two or a hundred! Having become used to the power of magic the players became weak. Good thinking for the Paladins... But they could have warned me: I was worried!

"Regroup!" Logir commanded as soon as the last mage disappeared. Paladins led by the femorc stepped into the clearing, lined up behind Monstrichello in an attack formation and started moving towards the crowd of scared players who had moved to the edge of the clearing to stay out of the way.

"Let us complete training with the teacher!" I heard the voice of one of the players. "Your battle with the mages doesn't have anything to do with us!"

"Consider that it's not your day!" Logir was adamant. "Onward!"

Today was truly a day for unpleasant discoveries! The Paladins, without a declaration of war and without obvious reasons attacked the players, who only wanted one thing: to train with that damned teacher! Monstrichello's shield, the Paladins' weapons and Dolgunata's claws dealt death right and left, sending players to respawn in droves. My jaw dropped: what were the Paladins doing?! Even the mages did not allow themselves such excesses! Panic broke out, the players were crushing each other trying to get away from the deadly and, apparently, crazy Paladins.

"Everybody stop!" I screamed wildly, climbing down to the clearing along the boulders. It registered in my mind that I had let go of the guiding line and in ten seconds the guards would start hunting me, but in my soul I didn't give a damn. The Paladins needed to be stopped! Crashing into the clearing as I lost my balance in the end, I jumped to my feet right away and screamed again: "Stop that!"

"Yari?" The Paladins slowed down, obviously not expecting that I would appear.

"What the hell are you doing?!" Without slowing down I ran at the team, still shouting. Perhaps it was a surge of intolerance of injustice that I received, together with my chosen specialty. It was silly, of course, but I couldn't do anything to stop myself. I did not like what my partners were doing. I simply had to stop all of that. "Did you forget how the mages cornered you at the respawn point? Forgot that feeling when you can only wait for respawn? What makes you better than the mages now? These players are not at fault for wanting to live!"

"Yari, calm down." Logir tried to reason with me. "We don't need additional problems..."

"What problems?" That only aggravated me

further. "What are you talking about? What can the players do to you, when they are scared to the point of fainting? Interfere with your training? But it only takes a moment!"

"You get experience points for each killed player who is above level one." Dolgunata came out from behind Monstrichello's back. The pause enabled most of the players to get away from the clearing; some stayed at the pass waiting for the outcome of the situation. "Experience points mean levels. Levels mean replenished Energy and not going for respawn. Would you be willing to sacrifice yourself or us for the sake of some players you don't even know?"

"You have all gone raving mad!" I whispered in astonishment, realizing that the Paladins were killing other players on purpose.

"We don't have time nor desire to sort them," Dolgunata cut me off. "It is not a threat to initiated level one players; as for non-initiated ones... This is the Academy, people die here sometimes. It's time for you to get used to it."

"I'll add you to the team," Logir offered. "You'll get experience points, together with all of us."

Request received for adding player to team

"No!" I said icily, pressing the "Reject" button." By killing players in the Academy you are not breaking any game laws or rules. But you are breaking another law, no less important: the law of humanity. Being a player does not mean you have to be a freak. There is no truth in what you are doing..."

Do you wish to initiate a case "Improper Behavior of the Paladins"?

"Yes!" Whatever that means! By killing other players, the Paladins are behaving in a manner unworthy of their class!

"Ok: no is fine." Logir shrugged her shoulders indifferently. "My task is to finish the Academy with as high a level as possible. You helped us believe in ourselves and showed us the right way to kill the mages. For that I thank you. But I will not let you stand in my way. If you are not with us, you are against us. Farewell, Yari! It's a pity we couldn't pass through it together."

Before I had a chance to do anything or object, Logir's heavy hammer came down on my head; my consciousness shattered into a million tiny shards, and darkness came over me.

CHAPTER FIVE

STUDYING

"SO HOW LONG are you going to lounge here?" Dolgunata's scornful voice trickled through the darkness, returning me to reality. Once I opened my eyes, I saw a fascinating view: against the background of the blue sky of the Academy was the tilted dark head of a blue-eyed panther with her tongue lolling out; her whole face showed so much sarcasm that I could not contain myself and grumbled:

"Bugger off, you imp!"

"What, is he, like, alive for real?" I heard Monstrichello asking from somewhere off to the side.

"Of course he is alive, as if that could harm him." The panther looked off to the right. "Sometimes it's useful to wear a tin bucket on your head. Saves you from obsessed femorcs."

"He's a dead man anyway! Even if it is not I, someone else will destroy him!" There was so much open hatred in Logir's voice that I was cut to the quick. Ignoring the thunderous bells sounding in my head that started as soon as I tried to lift it, I sat up and glanced around from under my brows. We were in the same clearing with the teacher where the femorc had attacked me. Other than the familiar group of seven players and the teacher the clearing was empty: either the Paladins finished everyone off, or everyone had run away. For some reason I wanted to believe it was the second option. Monstrichello was standing a couple of steps away from me, holding Logir in his huge paws; the other Paladins were standing behind them with guilty looks, staring down. Only the panther was pleased: to the extent that she was just about jumping around impatiently. As soon as I frowned, wondering what was going on, since the panther's actions were completely outside of the logic of the situation at hand, the messages that appeared in front of me made it clear:

Case initiated: "Improper Behavior of the Paladins" (Slots available for: 9 more cases)

Description: You consider that players Logir, Sartal, Monstrichello, Teart, Refor and Dirion behave in a manner unworthy of the name of Paladin by having initiated a genocide of players of other classes. In addition, with the connivance of the other team members, Logir attempted to send for respawn a comrade in arms.

Task: Investigate this case and deliver a verdict
Case investigation: Not applicable; the case was initiated by the Judge himself
Period of limitation of action: None

The panther was eager to receive her next granis.

"Why?" I asked hoarsely, fighting the headache. The femorc's hammer blow was really strong. Suppressing an impulse to sentence everyone and everything to life in some kind of forsaken prison with regular cruel respawns, I decided to figure out what was going on. I needed to understand why representatives of my class had turned out to be such villains. It would be useful for life after the Academy.

"Go to hell! Logir practically spat out. "I am not going to explain myself to some scum! If you want to play judge, go right ahead!"

My brows crawled up in bewilderment. Logir, who was an initiated trained Paladin, the daughter of a mentor, a creature that one could readily consider an experienced and reasonable player, was behaving like ... I couldn't even figure out what to call it ... some totally messed up freak!

"What happened here?" I asked Dolgunata, understanding that I wouldn't be able to get any useful information from the femorc. There should be someone who retained at least some sanity.

"Nothing much." The druid became human, adjusted her hair and shrugged her shoulders. "The great commander showed his true self at the first available opportunity. You shouldn't have sentenced

Nartalim to death."

"I don't get it ..." I was confused.

"Our red-skinned beauty had fallen head over heels for the long-eared one. From what I understood from the conversations, they were just starting to hit it off when you appeared and sentenced the elf to death."

"Shut up!" Logir tried to wriggle out of Monstrichello's grip, but in vain: the thug was holding her tight.

"Did it not seem strange to you that a headhunter refused a granis when a task appeared?" Nata continued, ignoring the femorc's yells. "A sane, reasonable, logical hunter lost it when the object of her adoration was destroyed. That's the reason for not wanting to add you to the team for receiving experience, that's the cause of her anger and her urge to destroy the entire world, and the attempt to kill you as well. I figured out right away what her idea was, so I was able to push you away, and the hammer strike was just a glancing blow rather than a direct one. That's why you just took a nap rather than going for respawn. Of course, the helmet helped to some extent, too. So, it's a classic case when emotions overpower reason. You think she ever contemplated what she would do after the Academy with a past like that? Ha! There is a great justification for doing stuff like that: "Well, I am only a girl!" Since you are the Judge, go ahead and judge! That was an assassination attempt on you: things like that should not be left unpunished."

"Why were you killing innocent players together

with the Paladins?" Dolgunata's speech unsettled me so much that I grabbed at every chance to postpone delivering the verdict.

"Do I look like a philanthropist?" the druid snorted. "Logir ordered us to kill everyone, the Paladins followed, why should I drag behind? To lose experience? That's a mug's game! I repeat: judge!"

"Don't push me!" I snubbed the druid. "Until I understand Logir's motives, there will not be any judging done. A wrong verdict would cost me too much."

"Is there something still unclear to you?" Dolgunata was surprised. "She wanted to kill you; I prevented her and saved your ass. The reason is simple: you sentenced the elf. What other motives do you need?"

I ignored Nata's statement and came up close to the femorc. My emotions screamed that Dolgunata was right, I should finish up with the current case and sentence Logir to death and all other Paladins to respawn, or at least fine them, but my logic resisted, calling on my reason and pointing out obvious contradictions. The main one was Logir's last words before she attacked me: she wanted to send me to respawn not because I had destroyed the elf, but because I was an obstacle in her way to graduating from the Academy!

That could not be right! Something here was not adding up. But what was it?

I found the description of the events that had occurred in the Book of Knowledge on the page "Logir attacking Yaropolk in the Academy". By the way, by now the Artifact had leveled up to 488 points, filling half of the status bar of its experience. If it continued at this rate, I would have a chance to develop a new attribute or enhance the "Context search" within literally a couple of hours. I had been receiving information as a constant flow; maybe it would be even better that I had not been going through proper training before coming to the Academy.

"How soon are you going to be done?" Dolgunata asked again impatiently, distracting me from studying events. She was so impatient to get some granises! Trying to resist the provocation on the part of the druid, I decided to review the video of the attack. I did need to understand why Logir had gone mad!

"...you get experience points for each killed player who is above level one..."

The Game decided that I needed to see the events not from the moment when Logir attacked, but from Dolgunata's speech as she was trying to explain the behavior of the Paladins. By the way, there was one more thing I found strange: I would never have thought that someone like Sartal would be so bloodthirsty. While the druid was explaining to me the reasons for genocide of the players, the reptilian and catorian together, bare-handed, were tearing into pieces some short hapless victim in a cloth outfit. Fiddling with the video settings and zooming closer to the Paladins made me frown: I had little understanding of the physiology of other races, but it was enough to understand that both the reptilian and the catorian were not themselves. They were mad. I refocused on Monstrichello's face and my frown deepened: the bruiser's eyes were glassed over. He was standing next to us, but didn't see anything. I looked at the faces of all the team members and realized that only two retained an adequate perception of the world around them: the leprechaun and Dolgunata.

This confused me further. Only two of the team members remained sane; the other five turned into monsters, extremely cruelly destroying innocent players. A sudden idea made me look through the Book of Knowledge, trying to find the video on the Paladins' appearance in the teacher's clearing. The video was taken from an inconvenient vantage point, as I had been trying to hold on to the guiding line, but what I saw was enough to determine that the leprechaun did not take part in the battle. Unwillingly, he dragged behind the Paladins, shaking his head sadly; the other members of the group were out of their minds. Dolgunata was really going at it. While the Paladins hung close to Monstrichello, the panther crashed into the thick of the players and dealt chaos, death, panic. Nata's sharp claws cut the players down in droves, not leaving them a single chance to escape. At the same time the first video had shown that the druid was quite aware of what she was doing, unlike the others...

"You carefully run a dagger through its eye socket and turn it three times. Once to kill it, twice – for pleasure."

Nata's words flashed through my mind, making me view the situation differently.

"Monster, why did you guys start killing the players?" I asked the tank who was holding Logir.

"Duh... there weren't no more o'dem mages, and our guys showed up and it was, like, no stopping..." Monstrichello rumbled."

"Sartal, why did you start killing?" Understanding that it was hopeless to expect an intelligent answer from the tank, I addressed the reptilian. It had always seemed to me that he was a reasonable player.

"The experience, the levels," Sartal started, then faltered, fell silent for a little while, then hissed: "They all jus-s-st looked at us-s-s being cut down-s-s and no one would help u-s-ss! If we had joined forces-s-s-s, the mages-s-s would not have done anyth-th-thing to anyone. But they allowed them to kill us-s-s!"

"Teart?" I turned towards the leprechaun, because the reptilian suddenly froze and his eyes glazed over, as if he was remembering all the offences inflicted on him by other players "You did not take part in the battle. Why?"

"Because it's stupid and unproductive. I hate battles. I tried to get the rest to see reason, but... you can see what came out of it."

"Are you done?" Dolgunata came up to me, casually putting her hand on my shoulder. "Yari, we don't have much time. Energy in the Academy does not replenish itself... Deliver the verdict and then the two of us can continue together.

"Fine," I agreed, thinking in surprise why the thought even occurred to me to try to investigate. Everything was crystal clear: the Paladins are guilty;

they need to be judged and punished! Because that's the wish of...

Of whom? Was it my wish? Or someone else's?

The desire to make a judgment here and now dissipated. I looked at Dolgunata, who raised a brow quizzically; noted her beauty one more time, squeezed my eyes, gathering my strength, and then said, addressing the skies:

"I need additional information to deliver a verdict! I need a description and examples of use of headhunters' ability to suppress the will of other beings!"

Dolgunata's eyes widened in surprise; she was about to start saying something when the long-awaited message appeared before my eyes:

Request is granted. Access to Temple of Knowledge is provided.

"Welcome to the Temple of Knowledge, young Judge," the old man said, opening his arms in greeting. "Before you study the information, the request for providing which has been granted as justified, please explain the logic of your query. We are interested in your line of thinking."

"We?"

"First warning, young Judge," the old man cut me off, smiling. "Two more and you will be banned from the Temple of Knowledge for a year. Why did you decide to learn more about the specialty of headhunters? Is Logir's betrayal not a sufficiently grave reason for delivering a verdict?"

"I am starting to get the impression that there was no betrayal," I replied in a dead voice, becoming more and more convinced that my conclusions were right. After all, being a judge is not easy, particularly when a case concerns people who are close to you or have become so. "The Paladins' actions defied logic. They did not correspond to the psychological pattern of the team that I had observed, so I started to dig. Reviewing the video only confirmed my suspicions: it was as if the Paladins were affected by something that made all their base feelings come out. I recalled the moment when the druid suppressed my mind, leaving only animal lust and passion; therefore I requested additional information. I need to know the capabilities of hunters who suppress other beings' will."

"We heard you... a coincidence... Well, that too has a place in our life. Description of the specialty is waiting for you." The old man pointed to the coffee table, losing interest in me.

Suppressor: specialty, available to players who choose "Headhunter" as their development path. A most popular specialty for Headhunters. Players of this specialty bring out their victims' basest desires and feelings, enhance them, remove moral and physiological constraints, take control and make the victim perform the actions Headhunters need. Limitations: initial levels require physical contact with the victim; advanced skills enable remote application. It's impossible to force the victim to perform actions that are not its secret or internal desire. Number of simultaneously controlled beings: unlimited;

determined by the level of specialty development. Active suppression of the victim's will lowers Energy level by 20 units; maintaining control over victim requires 5 Energy units per minute per victim.

Example: Headhunter's victim hides in safe location. Victim is known to love flowers. Headhunter specializing as "suppressor" places flowers around the victim's refuge, then influences the victim forcing it to express its love of flowers. Victim without high moral integrity will be forced to leave safety to look for flowers.

Suppression can be avoided by: use of amulets (probability of suppression is determined by amulet strength and suppression level); absence of secret and internal desires; high moral integrity. This is not a magical ability.

"What for?!" I heard Dolgunata's exclamation of surprise, then she stopped, having met my gaze. The Game returned me to the Academy precisely at the same moment as I was stating my request for information, so the others did not notice my absence. But Dolgunata did. One glance was enough for the druid to understand: I knew everything.

"What are you gonna do, Judge?" the druid smirked, taking a few steps back and quickly chewing an Energy-replenishing patty.

"First – I close the case that I initiated, "Improper Behavior of the Paladins" due to absence of elements of crime in their actions." I didn't know from where so much ice appeared in my voice, but right now all the penguins of the Antarctic would have become my avid fans. The smile started fading from the druid's face and she took two more quick steps back as if apprehensive either of me or of my verdict.

"Second – Monstrichello, let Logir go, she is not guilty."

"You know where you may go, you and your orders? You are a dead man!" The femorc exploded as soon as she was freed, but it did not stop me. Ignoring the hammer that appeared in Logir's hands, I came right up to her, put my hand her shoulder and continued in the same arctic voice: "Logir, I understand your attitude towards me. Just like you, I am familiar with the pain of losing someone close. But you are a headhunter! You don't have the right to allow emotions to govern you. Otherwise the Game will shut you down. No one forced Nartalim to become a traitor – that was the choice he made himself. But you have been forced. In order to resist the influence you must accept the loss and let him go. If you want to get back at me for Nartalim, I am at your service, but after the Academy. At this time it's not even as though only I need you – the whole team needs you. You're trying to leave Zagransh; do you really want to be stuck there forever? There's no such thing as an impulsive Paladin..."

"I..." the moment I mentioned Logir's homeland, the femorc's eyes cleared. There was no more fury and hatred in them: on the contrary, there was confusion and worry. Logir was able to overcome the druid's influence: her secret attraction to Nartalim was no longer secret; strong negative emotions for her former place of residence completed the process of freeing her by pushing the druid out of her mind. Confirming my thought, the femorc whispered: "Yari... I didn't..."

"Sartal, Monstrichello, Refor and Dirion!" Stopping Logir, I started working on freeing the minds of the remaining Paladins. Thanks to Sartal I knew the secret pain of the team: inaction of the other players. So that's what I'd have to work with. "I know the feeling of helplessness that you experienced. Sometimes it seems that the whole world is against you, and instead of helping, other players pass you by, pretending thoroughly that they haven't noticed your pain. You need to overcome this, grow stronger and move on. The Game is cruel. No one will ever come to your aid unless there's a worthwhile reward for it: get used to it. The only creatures in the game from whom you might receive help for free are your class brothers. But you must be worthy of the name of Paladins! Right now I am only seeing a herd of sheep who have followed the sweet words of the druid and now do her bidding! Wake up! If you want to be players – don't be like sheep!"

"You're a sh-sh-sheep yours-s-self!" Sartal grumbled, returning to his normal state. Once again I had ended up having to talk a lot to find the right influence point, but the result was achieved: the druid's influence dissipated. "We are worth-th-thy Paladins-s-s!

"What the fuck!" rumbled Monstrichello, looking around in amazement. "What, we, like, for real whacked dem all dead? Why in hell?"

"Dolgunata." Finally, I turned around to the

culprit of the whole scene. The druid had recollected herself, and was looking at me with a smirk, awaiting my further actions, but not worried for her life. Neither I nor anyone else from our group would be able to send her to respawn singlehanded, and we were very far from being a united team at this point. I knew that and so did she, so she was simply waiting to see what would happen next. The current situation amused her. "Go away. Just go away. Our ways part from now on."

"So simply?" the druid asked mockingly, suddenly standing next to me. "Without all of the 'I sentence you to disqualification for life' or wishes of horrid punishments? Will you really let me go, darling?"

The world stopped yet again. The most desirable, wonderful and sweet girl in the word was there right next to me. I needed to love her, kiss her, adore and admire her, not send her away! How did I have the heart to tell her "go away"? Don't I understand that if we part now I will lose here forever? Just like my mother and sister?

Suddenly the image of smirking Archibald flashed through my mind, and all of Dolgunata's charm faded. The druid was still just as desirable and attractive, but I had regained my ability to think!

"It seems like I also need to bring to light all my secret desires." It was hard to talk, my tongue twisted, wanting only to praise the druid, but I was adamant. I needed to go through this! "Dolgunata, I admit that you are attractive, beautiful and desirable. I admit that I wish to an incredible extent to have sex with you. To hold you in my arms and never let go until the end of my life. You are my ideal... But I am not an animal! I will not allow you play on my lust and obscure my mind. You are dangerous. You are ruthless. You are a cripple. Not physically, but morally. You don't have principles, you don't have boundaries, for the sake of granises you were ready to frame my entire team... Our ways part here. Good luck in the Academy."

"Amazing – the kids have come to their senses," Dolgunata drawled, shifting her gaze from one Paladin to another. I didn't even need to turn around to be able to say with conviction that Monstrichello was standing right behind me, ready to cover me with the shield at any moment; at my sides there were Logir and Refor with their weapons at ready. The Paladins had united. Each of us would be helpless and weak against the druid on our own, but together we were a force that even she would have to reckon with.

Closing the case "Improper Behavior of the Paladins" is confirmed

"I admit that I went a little too far with the control thing, but no one wanted to attack the players," Dolgunata smiled affably, spreading her arms. "Why should we lose out on the experience points? We didn't come to the Academy in order to think of some moral principles. The Game is cruel – I shouldn't be the one telling you about it. I agree, I did want to get rid of the femorc. You could see my point here – it's not often that you work next to a judge who hands out granises left and right. Easy riches blinded me, and I... I am at fault, I can't deny it, but after all nothing happened! Everyone is alive and well. Moreover..."

Dolgunata spoke beautifully and compellingly. If one were to listen to the druid, it was she who fell prey to the circumstances; moreover, we were the ones who forced her to commit all the wrongdoings of which we were accusing her. But in truth she was the white and fluffy one, poor, innocent and defenseless, even though, for some reason, we failed to see that! I smiled sadly: it would be interesting to see Dolgunata's suppression level right now. Does she really not need to touch the players for it at this stage? And how many Energy replenishing patties does she actually have?

"Team! Listen to my command!" I shouted, distracting the Paladins from Dolgunata's charming words. Enough suppressors for us. I still needed to sort it out with Logir – what did she choose as her specialty? I can't afford a potential hypnotist hang out freely in the team. "Dolgunata is our enemy! Kill her!"

The hammer and the saber came down on the druid's head at once, as if Logir and Refor had trained together for years to achieve blow synchronicity. Dolgunata only had time to open her eyes wide in surprise; then her body glimmered and winked out of existence, leaving barely trampled grass behind. I turned around and looked at the Paladins.

"Dolgunata will respawn in an hour; she will do everything she can to avenge her respawn. She is a clever and dangerous adversary; compared to her all the local mages are silly toddlers. So! Get going NOW! Rest will wait! Logir, gimme an invite..."

Functionally becoming part of a team didn't bring me any dividends; in the top right corner a small tab appeared with the Paladins portraits – that was it. Clicking on a portrait opened information on the player, but there was nothing that I didn't already know. Maybe just the levels: killing the players brought Monstrichello to level 5 and the others to 4. With my level 2 I looked like a kid next to them. There was no other information available — nothing on Energy level, age, or specialty. The Game concealed personal information most thoroughly, and only the players themselves had the right to disclose it.

Training to use the artifacts took just a few moments, so once the last Paladin had left the teacher, I commanded, remembering my sergeant from the boot camp:

"Ready? We need to get to the next teacher! Monster first, followed by Logir and Refor – I'll take the rear. Onward! On the double!" Our sergeant had a hallmark phrase that would have suited the current situation very well: "If you want it done well, do it yourself or hire some Mexicans. There are no Mexicans here, so "On the double!" I needed to finish the Academy at all costs. I wanted to survive. So going under Logir's rule would be silly and pointless; I remembered where the group ended up under her command. I had no management skills myself; however, I would rather make mistakes and take personal responsibility for my own mistakes than later kick myself for my partners' mistakes. You end up having to do everything yourself. No one tried to contest my right to command, even Logir. Paladins took off and ran to the next teacher who would train them in using the game interface. But literally a minute later I heard an excited shout from Monstrichello:

"Kill dem freaks! All the Way!"

We ran into some mages.

The procedure for destroying the enemy we had worked out at the previous teacher's site worked like a charm this time as well. Out of twenty players in dark robes who ran to the clearing from all the nearby passages only three had the brains to control their Energy use: those we had to finish off ourselves. The rest sent themselves to respawn without us having to give them as much as a kick to send them on their way. By the way, the outcome of the battle showed me Dolgunata's point of view. As soon as the first mage had sent himself to respawn, the system gladly and pleasantly awarded me 200 experience points. Once for each body. 17 retarded overgrown lemmings – that was the kindest name the mages deserved – had lifted me to unprecedented heights: 3rd level, 103 Energy units. Once I saw that I had less than a hundred experience points to attain level 4, I nearly rushed off to strangle the three mages who were, stunned, looking at their hands, at us, and then at the nearest pass. Once we took just one step forward, two players streaked away, howling like mad, apparently deciding that their own skins were worth more than the potential reward. However, not everyone ran off...

Unstoppable as death itself Monstrichello

moved towards the remaining mage. Being slow must have been a personal problem of this particular player, and we would be solving it for him now... But as soon as Monster lifted his shield for the final blow, the mage crashed to the ground and broke out bawling, trying to cover his head with his hands:

"Noooo! Don't! Please don't! It's my last life and I am not initiated! Please don't kill me!"

The kid, selected by the Game as a mage, was seventeen at most. Lanky like our Dirion, with fair hair that was knotted, with bright green eyes filled with primal terror, trying to protect himself with his hands against Monstrichello's shield, the mage was a pitiful sight. Instead of the necessary anger and hatred, the only feelings he aroused were disgust and fear of touching something nasty. Our thug froze, looming over the whimpering player and looked at me, confused. Despite his limited intelligence, Monstrichello didn't want to mar his shield with that creature.

"Have you killed any Paladins?" I asked once the thrill of the battle subsided.

"Don't kill me! Please don't!" All the young mage was capable of at the moment was to beg and spread spit and snot on his face. This was no way for any constructive dialogue, let alone interrogation.

"Shut up!" Monstrichello got it right: we were not going to kill the kid, so using the old tried and true method he made the mage shut his trap. Or howl from pain, actually: not every player could withstand a kick in the stomach with a steel boot. The blow threw the mage a ways to the side; he whimpered but at least stopped begging for mercy. Perhaps he also understood that we were not going to kill him right away. Or maybe he just went bonkers from fear.

"Guys, get on with the training," I pointed at the old guy looking into space with a distant air; then I turned around to face the kid, who was now quiet: "Can you talk?"

"Ye-ea-ah..." the creature whined, flattening himself on the ground in some semblance of a bow and making me curse internally. Until now it had seemed to me that there was no way one could fall any lower, but the mage had outdone himself. Now I felt disgusted even to look in his direction. I knew that fear of death sometimes turned some people into something like animals, but still, shouldn't there be a border below which your pride – or education, or self-respect – wouldn't let you fall? There must be! But apparently this very mage had nothing of the sort, or else it was so low that I felt nauseated even trying to contemplate it!

"Show me your personal information," I ordered him, overcoming my disgust; but the mage shook his head, talking a mile a minute:

"I don't know how to do it! The elders ordered me to stand here and wait till the Paladins appear, and they expressly forbade me to come up to the teacher! They said they would allow me to train with him only after twelve hours following my arrival into the Academy."

"Stop! Who are the elders?"

"Initiated players and their minions. Not all mages are hunting after you; some were just told as a fact that the Paladins are evil. Those who were chosen by the Game itself, the mages don't count as part of their circle. Please don't kill me, please! I don't want to die!"

The mage became hysterical again, so I nodded to Monstrichello, who administered another mind-clearing kick, sending the player flying. Taking several deep breaths to get more oxygen in my blood and clear my brain, I looked at the sniveling mage and realized with finality: I would not be able to kill him. It's not an enemy, it's a piece of crap that one feels disgusted to step into. Let others kill him, or maybe the Game itself. With this approach, even if he goes through the training with this teacher, this kid won't survive. But it's his problem anyway.

"How much time do you have till respawn?" I came over to the mage still sprawled on the ground. "If we let you train, you'll up a level and replenish your Energy. You'll get another twelve hours of life. But I want to be certain that you won't betray us and won't attack at a time convenient for you."

"Never! I'll never betray you or attack! I don't want to kill! I just want to survive! I don't remember how much time has passed! I only have twelve Energy! How long will that last? Please don't kill me, I beg you! I have nothing against Paladins, mages, and generally any living creatures! I just want to live!"

"When they gathered you all, did they tell you why the mages should hunt the Paladins?" As soon as my decision about what to do with this kid at my feet formed in my head, I breathed easier. As if a burden had rolled off my shoulders. While the remaining

Paladins finished training with the teacher, I started gathering additional information. There's never too much of that.

"N-no!" The mage's eyes once again filled with tears. "We were just ordered to kill Paladins at the first opportunity and follow all orders from Dangard and Ahean. They are personal students of one of the mentors."

"Yari, we're done." Teart came up to me. "Did you already train here as well?"

"Not yet," I looked at the mage one last time before blotting him from my memory for good. "Don't touch him; he's a goner anyway."

"Don't leave me here!" The kid screamed once it dawned on him that we were not planning to take him with us. "Please don't chase me away! I beg you! I don't want to die! Don't abandon me!"

"Shut the hell up!" roared Monstrichello, sending the mage flying yet again. Crashing on the ground like a broken doll and lying still, the black-robed player, however, did not disappear. Monstrichello had just knocked him out.

"Welcome, recruit, I will now teach you to use the game interface. Stand up and harken to my wisdom!"

Learning progress: You have reached teacher 3 of 10

"I don't have anything to teach you, young recruit," the teacher delivered the "good" news to me as soon as the training clearing filled the world around us. "You have excellently figured out, without my help, how to command the game interface; you have learned not only how to open and close windows, but also to bring up properties. The visit to me was simply a formality for you. I am sorry."

"Oh really?!" I was taken aback clearly not expecting this turn of events. "It's not possible that there could not be something else that I could learn about the game interface. Hidden buttons that appear only at certain times under specific conditions, properties that are not shown under the standard configuration, an option to adjust the interface for my own needs... There must be something!"

"There is all that you have listed and more," the old man smiled. "But it's not part of the Academy study program. Develop your Artifact, add a property to its Interface configuration, and you will attain additional possibilities for control. Including information on them. There are no other ways to learn about it."

"I see..," I drawled unhappily. "May I ask a question on an unrelated topic?"

"You may try," the old man was slow to respond. "If it doesn't concern your future training, perhaps you'll get an answer."

"I think it doesn't. One of the teachers with whom I trained told me that in case I deliver a correct verdict I will receive a bonus. I did deliver a verdict; it was acknowledged as justified even though harsh, but I didn't get any bonus from that. The question is – did they lie to me or is there something obvious that I am failing to see?"

"It's the latter," the old man's smile grew wider still. "You were awarded a bonus for the correct verdict, it's just that you have not had a chance to use it yet. It is quite rare to have a judgment case in the Academy. Normally, even if cases arise here, they are postponed till graduation. But you not only delivered the verdict, you also ensured execution of the sentence as you stated it in the vicinity of a Headhunter. That kind of thing is rare in the Academy; so you were awarded a bonus which you confirmed.

"Status?" I guessed what he was talking about.

"Yes, status. From now on you are a Judge, whether you want it or not."

"And?.." I was looking at the old man with interest. "What does that give me?"

"What do you think? What is initiation?"

"Confirmation of race or class," I frowned, as we were now talking of a very sensitive topic for me.

"Not quite. Initiation, first of all, is a confirmation. It does not matter of what. Class. Race. Chosen path for development..."

"So by confirming my status,.." I stood completely still, fearing to voice my thought.

"You became an initiated player," the teacher confirmed my guess. "Speaking in the players' terms, your chances to complete the Academy have improved significantly. That was the bonus awarded to you for delivering an impartial verdict."

"Improved?" I was surprised. "Is there no guarantee that an initiated player will definitely return?"

"In theory, that's true. One of the Paladins, Nartalim, as far as I recall, believed that as well, it seems to me. Where is he now?"

"He deserved that." The mere memory of the elf made my chest tighten with anger.

"Did he really?" The old man raised one eyebrow demonstratively. "You delivered a verdict that Nartalim betrayed his class. But tell me, Judge, are you the head of the class? Are you the one to determine what is allowed and what is not for Paladins?"

"No," I was taken aback at first, but immediately returned to thinking that my decision was right: "My verdict was correct. The Emperor confirmed that.

"No one is arguing that you were right," the old man shook his head as if he was unable to get through to me. "But you sentenced to death a player who could have been of use to the class in the future. The Paladins have several game worlds that by the standards of your world can only be described as "Hell". Despite all the horrors, those worlds are very popular: some extremely rare minerals are mined there. You could have sentenced Nartalim to a life in a world like that as a disobedient Paladin. He could have added value even as he was punished. But you decided to cut his life short... No one argues: the verdict was correct. The questions arise with respect to the harshness of the punishment. Did Nartalim deserve that? That's a good question to which only you would be able to provide an answer."

"No!" The old man's words could not breach my

attitude to the elf. "Nartalim's punishment was commensurate to his deeds. Death was the only appropriate punishment. One can get out of Hell."

That's why you became a Dark one," the old man said sadly, sighing heavily. "With this approach it would be hard for you to return to the Light."

"If the Light is turning the other cheek when anyone slaps you on the right one, then I choose Darkness. Evil must be punished; any slack would only make it stronger. This should not be allowed!"

"It will be hard for you in your world with this approach to judgment. There is nothing else I can teach you. Farewell, Paladin..."

"Onward!" I commanded hoarsely as soon as the space around me turned into a clearing in the midst of reinforced concrete jungle. Despite attaining level 4, talking to the teacher left its mark: my mood was totally ruined, even though I was still convinced that I had been right: Nartalim had not deserved any other sentence.

"What shall we do with the mage?" Logir asked for instructions.

"Drag him to the teacher and wake him up. Let's give the kid a chance, let him learn. If we meet him later in battle, we can kill him, but no need to finish him off now. We are not mages."

We reached the next teacher without having to fight. No one attacked us, no one set up ambushes or other traps. As if all at once the mages in the Academy had decided that their plan to destroy the Paladins had failed and it would be better not to mess with us. But I had a more likely version of events: the two mages who had managed to get away had warned the others of our tactics, and the mages had decided to give us one teacher while they developed some more sophisticated ways to battle us. I couldn't believe that they would just let us go like that.

The clearing with the teacher was overflowing with players of different classes, but at first glance there were no mages nor Paladins among them. As we approached, we could hear the hum of an overcrowded space, but as soon as we stepped into the clearing, everything became quiet. The players tensed, not knowing what to expect of the newly emerged team. Imperceptibly and sort of instantly an open space formed between us and the teacher. They were letting us through, preferring not to mess with us; however, we were in no hurry to run headlong towards the teacher. The mages had taught us to be careful. The barely audible voice of the teacher floated from the other side of the clearing:

"Welcome, recruit, I will teach you the attack capabilities of your class ..."

"There are about a hundred players here," Logir whispered. "This teacher trains recruits in attack capabilities. If they attack us they'd crush us without bothering to ask what our name was."

"I agree." I was in complete agreement with the femorc's opinion. "Going in directly is dangerous. Let's retreat. We'll get to the teacher through the forest. We'll come out behind him, and then train. It's always better to have a safe space behind your back."

"We'd lose time..." Refor started, but I cut the catorian off:

"It's better to lose half an hour than to run into a respawn. Does anyone here know the class outfits? Who are the players here?

"Hunters, druids, rogues, warlocks, necromancers, warriors," Logir started listing. "I'm sure there are more, but I can't see from here."

"Retreat! We'll move through the forest. I don't really trust anyone other than our class. By the way, that's one more reason we have to go around: does anyone see any Paladins? So there... Teart, look for the guiding beam..."

Half an hour later I cursed heartily for what seemed like a hundredth time, in my mind remembering unkindly myself, my own decision, and the players who crowded the clearing with the teacher. The guiding line was so winding and sometimes was so high above the ground that time streamed like sand through our fingers. There were a few times when I wanted to abandon it all and return to the clearing. At those moments the precaution seemed excessive; however, I squashed those defeatist thoughts at once and pointed out the new correct beam to the group. Dolgunata had shown me that not only mages were worthy of respect in the Academy; that meant that among a hundred players there'd be at least one ringleader, and then a massive melee would begin.

"Yari, come here!" I heard Teart's surprised voice from somewhere to the side. Since he, like I, had the ability to see the right way, the leprechaun was moving on the outside of the team, studying the area around. Following the interface use training, I made everyone turn on their video recording so that after they returned to the normal world we would have more comprehensive information about the Academy. Maybe now the Temple of Knowledge was capable of providing any player with any available information about the Game, but it was much more efficient to train the minions when you had a manual on hand, rather than in some other piece of virtual space. So that was exactly the manual I was going to prepare. One has to cover one's living expenses after all.

"What've you got?" It took me a few minutes to figure out, using the map, where Teart was, and then reach him holding on to the beams.

"I've got some weird shit here," the leprechaun mumbled in bewilderment, pointing at a small pile that looked as if it were post-construction trash."This crap keeps coming back."

"What keeps coming back?" I wasn't sure I understood Teart. "The trash?"

"Don't look at the trash," the leprechaun said curtly, irritated. "Look at what's underneath!"

Under Teart's unfaltering stare I moved the pile of trash with my foot, but still found nothing. I looked at the Paladin in bewilderment, but he was just making impatient gestures to demand that I should keep moving the trash. I cursed the one hundredth and first time, set my foot on the guiding beam to ensure that I would avoid issues with the guards, then shoved the entire pile aside. If Teart was sure there was something under it ... What was that?

Under the trash there was a small rectangular inscription with text written in a language I did not know. The text had a caption, or at least it would be logical to suppose that the few words at the top of the rest of the text served as a caption for whatever was concealed by the unknown symbols. Part of the text was written in bolder font than the rest, as if someone wanted to attract attention to its most important parts.

"What do you think this is?"

"Well, it's some kind of shit all right." I agreed with the leprechaun's initial assessment. "How did you find it?"

"Well...," Teart was hesitant, so I had to press him:

"If you have some information regarding the Academy, we all need it to survive!"

"No, I have nothing," the leprechaun finally ventured. "It's just that I was going to become a Searcher, so I, like, prowl around everywhere.

"A Searcher?" I frowned. "Did you mean to say, an Explorer of the world?"

"No. As the teacher told me, a Searcher is someone who discovers new worlds, new knowledge, and such like. A Searcher is something that fits my soul. Searching for treasures, troves, secret shelters... I am a leprechaun, it's our fate to look for treasures."

"So the pot of gold is not a myth?" I grinned, but as Teart's face tensed I figured that I had hit on a topic that was sensitive for him. "Never mind. So, you found a pile of trash, and it seemed suspicious to you, so you disturbed it and found this inscription?"

"Not this one," leprechaun exhaled with relief, seeing the conversation had moved away from his pot of gold. What a naïve one! I would need to get him talking and figure out what in those fairy tales is truth and what is fiction. But that will come later. "This is already the third pile, and under each of them there were their own inscriptions. I can tell right away that they are different. The principle is the same: header and then text, parts of which were highlighted, but the symbols were different.

"Did you photograph the previous inscriptions?"

"I recorded them on video, just as you advised. Wait, I'll give the record to you," the leprechaun's eyes glazed over as he started to fiddle with the internal settings."

"In the Academy you can't...," I started saying, but a system message that appeared in front of me demonstrated that I was completely ignorant of all the subtleties of the Game:

Player Teart is offering you a trade. Accept?

"It works!" The leprechaun rejoiced. Information exchange in my current world was set up in the manner classic for all computer games: a panel divided into two halves, with several buttons. As soon as an icon for video file appeared on Teart's side, one of the buttons on my side became active: "Accept". As soon as I pressed it, the Book of Knowledge beeped, signaling receipt of new portion of information. So it seems that exchange of material objects that one can hold in one's hand is performed in the normal way for the real world: from hand to hand; and exchange of intangible items such as video, through a separate set of functions. That's convenient! But immediately it brings about other questions – why is downloading information from the Book of Knowledge for other players only available at level 15 of the "Context search" attribute? Can I not simply download it in a way similar to what Teart did? By the way, what did he do?

"The teacher showed how to download the video," leprechaun explained as soon as I peppered him with questions. "I knew you were an Explorer; I wanted to do something nice for you. There is a problem, however; I can't upload someone else's videos, and downloading my own only works for events that have occurred during the past 24 hours. After that the Game transfers them somewhere into remote backups, and downloading to other players becomes impossible. Did you receive everything?"

"It seems so," I found the right notes in the Book and compared the three pictures. They were in fact different as if someone was using the same principle to describe various objects, phenomena or rules... RECIPES! I felt as though hit by lightning: these must have been recipes for professions!

"But this is wonderful!" the leprechaun said gladly, as soon as I shared my guess. He even started rubbing his hands, anticipating some loot. "If we get out of the Academy, what if it turns out that there is something worthwhile among those recipes? Now, in the beginning, they are quite likely to be commonly accessible, but the deeper we advance..."

"Partnership? I proposed immediately. "You will

travel around the forest, working on the path for development that you selected; we'll be at the bottom organizing access to the teachers. Once we finish the Academy, we'll share equally all the profits from the recipes."

"This doesn't seem to be a very equal partnership." Teart grinned. "I'd be working, risking an encounter with the guards, while you'd be strolling down there along convenient passages, and then we share the profits half and half? 90:10, in my view, would be the best proportion."

"Why do you say it's not equal?" I was actually thinking that leprechaun was right: at this stage of negotiations my position looked extremely weak. But I did have something to offer him! "In exchange I could share some information. For example, how to obtain initiation within the Academy. Interested?"

Judging by how round the leprechaun's eyes became, he was more than simply interested.

"I would like to point out right away," I continued, to make sure there were no unnecessary questions, "that I was going to tell this to you, Refor and Dirion in any case. You are not initiated. I learnt this from the previous teacher, and there never seemed to have been a chance to talk. Once we are done with the upcoming teacher and find a decent site, I'll tell you the ropes then.

"Em... Then I don't understand the point of your offer."

"That's what I'm saying: I'll share information with you. Various bits of information, not just about initiation. Besides, you need a device to record the recipes you find. You have mentioned yourself that after 24 hours the video is transferred into some long-term storage and it is not clear whether it's possible to call it up from there or not. Downloading information is one of the properties of my artifact, so there'll be no problem with that."

"80:20," the stubborn leprechaun wasn't going to give up." What will I do with information about the Academy in the general world?"

This red-bearded one was no fool!

"Not just about the Academy. For example, do you know how to gain access to the Temple of Knowledge? Since you are a Searcher, this information would be useful for you.

Before they finish the Academy recruits cannot enter ...," Teart started, but faltered, seeing my smile.

"Three times!" I announced, anticipating his question. "Of which one time was already in the Academy, before I chased away Dolgunata. I understood the principle based on which you would be let in there. I could share it. This has nothing to do with class – that was my own research. Interested?"

"Damn you! 70:30! Yari, you are doing exactly nothing to obtain the recipes! I have to do it all, you are just acting as a storage facility! Have you no shame?!"

"Fine, 70:30." I agreed to the leprechaun's conditions. "Then let's agree that it will apply to everything that you find in the Academy and offer for sale. Recipes, symbols, pictures and other trash. Agreed?"

"Are you sure you're a Judge?" Teart looked at

me with interest as soon as the Game confirmed our agreement. We did not even have to say any extra words: saying "I agree" by both parties generated a line in the book stating the conditions of the deal. Something suggested to me that breaking this agreement would not be a beneficial thing to do altogether. The Game would not forget it. Even though if fact it couldn't care less. It would be more correct to say that the Judge would not forgive it. Particularly such an interested Judge as myself.

"It's just that you seem so much like a profiteer! Just like my uncle ... Oh, what the heck is this now?"

"What are you talking about now?" I frowned, since the leprechaun's eyes suddenly glazed over.

"It's offering to me that I should confirm some kind of status, I have no clue what that is and what I am supposed to confirm," Teart said, confused and surprised." Do you know what it's talking about?"

"Freeze!" I ordered, forcing myself to breathe calmly. "Don't click on anything and listen carefully!"

It took me a few minutes to describe to the leprechaun in detail the principle for turning into an initiated player. It turned out that Teart had selected trade as his specialty. In his own world that was pretty much the only thing everyone did, so it would be silly to expect a different specialty from a treasure-hunter. Our bargaining triggered the initiation process, and as soon as the Game determined that Teart had achieved conditions beneficial for himself, suggested that he confirm his trader status. Which is what the leprechaun joyfully did.

"What took you so long? Where's the leprechaun?" Logir started questioning as soon as I came back to the group. Teart set off looking for more trash piles.

"He is fine. Guys, we are going to take an unplanned break. It's time we have a talk and get to know each other better."

"It can't be done after the training session?" Logir growled impatiently. "You've said yourself that the mages will become used to our tactics and then it will be harder to survive. It wouldn't matter to Monster, Sartal or myself – we'll make it somehow – but the four of you would be as good as dead."

"The two of us, by now," I quipped – and could not suppress a smile, seeing their long faces – "Teart and I have become initiated players. That's why we need to take a break here and now. It's time to protect ourselves."

Skinny silent Dirion, who tried to be quiet as a lamb, had chosen a breastplate as an artifact; the first property he added was additional protection against magic. Dirion came from a world called Viels, where humans were an extremely unpopular race. Viels was ruled by elves. Dirion learnt about the Game only when an elf Paladin showed up at his door and literally dragged him off for training, killing all his family in passing. He was trained by the book, and so back at the Citadel Dirion had decided to become a keeper working at the library. Knowledge in and of itself did not interest Dirion; he was attracted to the quiet and regular life within the library behind the Citadel walls. As a specialty the teacher had suggested "Librarian", so Dirion gladly agreed. That was a rare coincidence of the specialty and chosen path for development.

Sartal, a reptilian, came from the world named Versal. Sartal's father was one of the Paladins' minions, but had never made it to the full initiation to become a player. Sartal was luckier: the Paladins killed an Assassin, and that enabled them to turn a minion into a player. Sartal's father was the lucky one, but he transferred the privilege to his son. Sartal completed full training for a minion, choosing being a fighter as his path of development. There were skirmishes between classes pretty much continuously; the fighters would be the ones to end up in the front lines first. To Sartal it seemed interesting, exciting and agitating; he even chose the specialty to fit: melee fighter. Now, that he had seen death and horrors firsthand, the erstwhile confidence of his choice had faded.

The homeland for Refor, who was a catorian, was a desert inhospitable world called Bubastis. After saying the name of the world Refor stared quizzically at me and Monstrichello, as if the name was supposed to tell us something; however, the dumb expression plainly revealed on our faces saddened the catorian. As it turned out, Bubastis was a city in ancient Egypt; it had been named after the felines. Catorians had set up pretty decent relations with the ancient Egyptians and even ruled them for a while. Bast, who was the goddess of joy, merriment and love, female beauty, fertility and the hearth, and was depicted as a cat or woman with a feline head, was no more than an ordinary catorian player. After yet another war between the players, catorians cut off all relations with Earth; therefore the locals only remembered them as gods. As for Refor himself, in his own tribe he had been a long-lived respected old man. Having survived all his wives and even children, the catorian had been going to die in peace, when he was suddenly selected by the Game as a Paladin. As he had been involved in wine-making his entire life, Refor planned to not give up his favorite occupation in the Game; hence, he had chosen crafts as the path of development. He had not received a specialty yet: at the hidden teacher's location he trained in defensive capabilities; however, he was planning to take something that would have to do with production. The catorian's artifact was a saber, because in the catorian's opinion a cutting weapon was the most suitable for cutting back vines. And in addition it turned out to be useful in the Academy as well.

As for Logir, everything turned out to be not as simple as I had thought at first. The femorc had been sent off to the Academy as a headhunter, but the more familiar she became with her future occupation, the less she was enthralled with it. Killing players because the Game desired it turned out to be an unbearable burden for Logir; that was confirmed by the situation with Nartalim. Headhunters were not supposed to have attachments. The Game would always force you to choose between your feelings and your duty; the femorc failed that test. Despite her race, Logir since childhood had been enchanted with elves, who were, in essence, blood enemies of her race. At Zagransh, which was the femorc's home world, there were no living elves any more even among the NPCs; for that reason meeting Nartalim was a joy for the girl. Then when the elf began to allow her to admire him, showing more attention to Logir than to others, the girl completely lost her head. But then I came and ruined everything... In her mind Logir understood that it would never have worked out between Nartalim and herself, but at the bottom of her heart she was still mad at me. A headhunter was not supposed to feel those emotions, so Logir was confused and couldn't figure out her place within the Game. She didn't even select a specialty after training in the general principles of the Game. It looked like I'd have to talk to her again – this time one on one – without unwanted ears around.

As for Monstrichello, I knew much more about him than he did himself, except perhaps his specialty and artifact properties. Here Monster surprised me by how well-thought-out his choice was. As he was immune to all magic, Monstrichello added to his shield additional protection against non-magical damage: poison, cold and inertia. As for his specialty, Monstrichello became a crusader, a Paladin without fear and beyond reproach, who hurries to help the dispossessed and those who have lost the roof over their heads. According to the pleased wardrobe-boy, this specialty fit like no other with his desire to be a tank.

Then it was my turn to tell the team about myself, Teart and the method of achieving initiation. Dirion and Refor listened practically glued to the spot:

an ephemeral chance to pass through the Academy and leave with the team was turning into a real possibility to stay alive and unscathed right before their eyes. That immediately brought up the question of how to make the game inquire about the status of these two, but I already had an answer to that. Dirion wanted to become a Librarian and Refor a Craftsman. So what would fit really well for both? The players frowned, not understanding where I was going with that, so I had to tell them about the recipes and my agreement with Teart. One player could keep the recipes, and the other study them.

We had to take another break and lead the group to the recipe found by Teart.

"Oh! What are you doing here?" the leprechaun exclaimed in surprise as he literally fell on top of us, but then stopped, seeing funny faces of the Paladins shining with joy, and asked excitedly: "Did it work for them too? We'll all return home?!"

In response there were joyful screams, hugs, thanks, assurances of eternal friendship and other corny stuff that eats up time worse than computer games. Only Dirion was able to receive initiation, since Refor had not yet selected a specialty, but at least we understood the algorithm for making a true player out of the catorian. We just needed to find a teacher who would teach him his specialty. As a result, by the time we reached the teacher of attack capabilities, all the players we had killed earlier, as well as the mages and Dolgunata, should have respawned already. I needed no crystal ball to state with certainty that the only thing they would want was righteous revenge. So we needed to be careful.

"Damn that!" Monstrichello whispered, surveying the clearing from the height of four meters. "What, dey're gonna kill us for real? Damn bastards!"

The clearing was still crowded with players. The Book of Knowledge obligingly pointed out that these were the same players who had been here an hour ago. Only now there were mages among them, interrogating those present. We could not hear every word, but the overall concept was clear: the mages, using the universally understood curse language, expressed interest as to why the players had not attacked us immediately once we appeared in the pass. Because that's precisely what their arrangement had been!

"Beautiful picture, isn't it?" A voice came from behind us, that I had both dreamed of and dreaded hearing.

I had known that Dolgunata would find us sooner or later, but hadn't counted on it happening so fast. Were we really so predictable?

"If I were to just push you down into the clearing, the player named Yaropolk would be blotted out of the Game forever. You owe me, Paladin! And I came to recover my debt!"

"You have problems with seeing reality?" I quipped, taking a few steps towards Monstrichello. In case a skirmish started he would cover me. "If anyone here owes something to someone, then you owe me."

"What do you think will happen if half of you were to be sent to a respawn point?" Dolgunata was obviously in the mood for only hearing herself. The panther's tail whipped her sides angrily, her claws were out, and the entire appearance of the dark cat indicated that she was ready to attack us at any moment. Dangerous, scary, and crazy — I was not sure that we'd be able to contain her. Last time the surprise factor had worked in our favor, while now we were completely within the druid's power. "Half of you will survive, you're too hard to kill but still I'd be able to take a few with me. I am not afraid of respawn. While you're together, you're strong, but as soon as you become separated the fairy tale called "Paladins" will be over. Shall we dance?"

"Monster, catch her on your shield!" Understanding that it was pointless to talk any further, I started organizing people. Instead of cutting us down one by one, the druid wanted to talk and show how tough she was. Too bad for her! We weren't sons of blanks either! "Logir on the right, Refor on the left, the rest get behind the tank. Want to dance?" I addressed the last question to the druid. "No problem. Ladies' choice dance, the ladies invite the gentlemen!"

No lightning rod would have been able to stop the black lightning that rushed towards us. Dolgunata's leap was so powerful and fast, that Monstrichello, Logir and Refor flew in different directions like bowling pins. I wanted to yell to the thrown players "Quick, to the beam!" but Dolgunata flew through the air and with all her mass – which was significant – crashed into me, toppling me to the ground, knocking the wind out of me, and then plopped on top of me with her full weight. The panther must have weighed a couple of hundred kilos, so I could neither move nor even breathe!

"Just try to move – and he'll die!" Dolgunata roared.

"He's initiated, stupid!" Logir returned and that calmed me down somewhat. The players were able to get on their feet and return to the lifeline beam within ten seconds. At least the guards weren't going to show up.

"It's impossible to pass initiation within the Academy!" Dolgunata snorted. "What he mistook for initiation was no more than confirmation of specialty and path for development. As soon as Yari is dropped to level 1, the Game will offer him a choice: either lose confirmation and respawn once more, or die forever with his head proudly raised, clutching his development path. The result will be the same: the mages will wait for him to respawn and then kill him. What –you think no one has ever before thought that it would be possible to pass initiation within the Academy? You think you're unique? If it were so simple, at least half of the thirty thousand players would've come back to the main world. So stand still and be quiet, and I'll do the talking."

"You're already talking," I rasped, by some miracle drawing a bit of air. There was not much discomfort from not breathing, thanks to the Game; however, the mechanics of making sounds stayed the same: it required air. Which I didn't have.

"You can't imagine, Yari, what pleasure it would be to gouge out your eyes," the panther growled bloodthirstily, her claw screeching on my armor. "But you owe me, so first I'll collect my debt!"

"I owe you nothing!" I rasped with the last bits of air, but then was crushed to the beam with finality.

"Listen to me carefully," Dolgunata addressed the Paladins. "The mages issued an ultimatum to practically all the players: either they or the Paladins. It's not hard to guess what everyone chose: you have seen that at the clearing. Now each teacher's location as well as each respawn point is controlled not only by mages, but by ordinary players, too. Everyone wants experience and granises. Yes, for your heads the mages promised a reward of whole granises! That's why I am here. That's not a good idea, Logir. I will still have enough time to kill him.

"What do you want?" the femorc asked.

"To receive my due."

"I don't understand you ..."

"Yari promised me a granis if I help you all to complete the Academy. I want to receive it."

"What in hell do you think you are?" I thought that I had run out of air, however, the druid's claim must have forced me to locate some extra reserves and express my resentment.

"Don't you dare move!" The druid shuffled on top of me, finding a more comfortable position. "I am not done yet ... What the...! Meow!"

It was not comfortable, lying underneath the panther's huge body. Knowing very well that I had no weapons, Dolgunata did not bother to restrain my hands believing that I would not be able to do any harm or damage. On the one hand she was right; on the other, the panther had such a cute, furry and soft belly which had, contrary to all rules of feline anatomy, just two nipples, that I could not but pet it. My hands sank in the warm soft fur of her belly, and my palms covered the delicate nipples, one in each hand. Perhaps I am a pervert, but I really liked petting the druid's belly; however, the pleasure was not mutual. Dolgunata soared into the air, having pushed off with all four paws and her tail to boot. The entire area must have shuddered from a wild and indignant scream, and then the panther's huge body crashed back down. Only now she had protracted her long claws as she landed right in the middle of my chest. A brief flash of pain was replaced with the soft lull of the dark that yanked me out of the claws of the enraged cat. The last thing I remembered was the druid's attempts to shred me into small bits. Apparently, the girl didn't like my caresses. Could she be frigid?

> *You were killed and sent to a respawn point*
> *You lost one level*
> *Your current level: 3*

"Dirion, grab him and drag him off! Yari, come on, wake up! Don't be so slow!"

Logir's voice tore the blanket of darkness, yanking me from a state of complete calmness. Feeling that I was being pushed to the ground and dragged somewhere, I tried to protest. Couldn't they see I was enjoying it? Why tilt and roll me so? However, as soon as I opened my eyes, consciousness returned in a snap, accompanied by yet another system message:

You receive +100 Experience

"Monster, retreat!" I heard the next command from Logir. Dirion, grumbling something highly obscene under his breath, was dragging me towards the forest from where Teart was waving at him. From the other side of the respawn clearing I could hear elaborate cursing, the rattle of metal and players screaming; so I pushed my hands off the ground, jumped to my feet and took a look around to take a final assessment of the situation. Chaos reigned at the only entrance to the respawn clearing. Having learnt to use their attack capabilities, players of all classes were pushing forward, trying to enter the clearing and kill the Paladins who had forgotten their place. However, they were impeded by an insurmountable mountain – a two-meter giant with a shield. Standing in the center of a huge ball of fire, lightning, ice and who knows what else, Monstrichello actively wielded his artifact as if it were a club, toppling the players who attacked him. At the sides of our tank, it was a familiar sight by now to see Logir and Refor, shearing a level off the dropping players, but behind them... Dolgunata was standing behind Monstrichello, waiting for an opportune moment; after she found one, she jumped over the tank's shield into the thick of the players and turned into a whirlwind. After just a few seconds the druid went back, accompanied by information on receiving new experience, only to repeat her leap a moment later. Experience points flowed like a river, but the crush of the players wanting to kill us never thinned. Everyone wanted those damn granises.

"I'll be fine from here! Run to Teart!" I told Dirion who was still trying to get me to the concrete forest; then I turned to the femorc and shouted: "Logir, I'm fine! Get out!"

Dolgunata was the first to run by me, giving me a very telling look. As I didn't want to end up in the forefront, I ran after the panther, and then, from the edge of the forest, I watched how properly and carefully the Paladins retreated, making sure to keep their backs to the forest at all times.

"Retreat! We need to get out, guys!" Teart commanded, pointing out the guiding beam to Dolgunata and Dirion. Players rushed into the clearing; some of them were still crowding the Paladins, while some rushed towards us, hoping to get rid of us in a hurry. I frowned: did the mages scare everyone so much that they just turned into such a herd? Once I climbed a few meters up, there were wild screams of horror and pain filling the surroundings. The players ran into the forest for more than ten seconds, immediately attracting the guards. We didn't need to fear a chase from that quarter.

"Yari, pleas-s-se try not to attack her at onc-c-ce," Sartal warned me as soon as I climbed up. Dolgunata in her panther shape was sitting, looking aloof and studying her paws, as if it were not she who had sent me to respawn barely an hour ago. "First we need to make sure we get Logir here. She'll explain it all to you."

"Explain what?" I was taken aback. Does Logir

really know why in hell this mad cat was trying to frame us all? She killed me!"

"My dearie," Dolgunata deigned to talk to me, displaying a scowl of huge sharp teeth. "After what you did, as a decent Paladin, you only had two options: either take me as a wife or die. Let's consider that I made the choice for you. I'll tell you here and now – you do something like that again and nothing will save you. I'll bury you alive!"

"I am not your dearie," anger at the druid demanded an outlet, so I attacked her with reproaches. "You call me that again, I'll bury you myself! Now..."

"Guys, why don't you settle it between you two after we get the others out of there, Teart interrupted us. "I'm not sure that Monstrichello's immortal. You'll figure it out with the druid later..."

The operation for the safe extraction of Monstrichello, Logir and Refor took us most of an hour. For most of that time we were looking for a place where the guiding beam would come as close to the clearing as possible while not being the only beam in the area. It was clear to everyone: the players would rush after us into the forest and see the Paladins grab onto a beam. It was pointless to hope that mass madness would overcome each and every player; someone was certain to connect the dots and also grab the beam. We needed to make sure that their beam would be the wrong one.

We were able to accomplish what we intended, even though in the process we nearly lost Sartal, who was not careful, poked out from behind cover, and was hit by a lightning straight in the chest. However, either the charge was weak or the reptilian's artifact had upgraded to such a level that it fully absorbed the hit. Sartal got off easy with just a burnt spot on his armor and an angry shout from Logir, who ordered the reptilian not to stick his tail where he shouldn't. Once the guards came to our aid by killing players one after another, it became clear: we were able to get away.

"Now that we are relatively safe, maybe you'll tell me what's going on!" I turned towards the team as soon as we put some distance between ourselves and the respawn point. Nodding towards Dolgunata, I added: "Why is she alive and with us?"

"I'd be interested to know that as well," said Teart, stepping up next to me. "Why were we supposed to risk ourselves? I admit, it was very nice to reach level five, but was it worth killing Yari?"

"You don't know what's going on either?" I was surprised.

"I do wish! I came to the meeting point and saw everyone discussing the major plan for saving you. But why you needed to be saved was about as clear as mud. You'd demonstrated that you were a sensible being and were unlikely to get yourself into so much trouble that you couldn't get out of it. Hence, you died in some kind of a weird way. But no one said what happened. From snippets of conversation I figured out it was the druid that put you under. But for what, how and why no one would say. And I'm curious!"

"We have an agreement." After a noticeable pause, Logir took on the brunt of it. "We're helping each other to pass through the Academy."

"Congratulations," I said testily, "but this doesn't answer a single question I asked.

"We... it's a condition of the agreement..." Logir said uncertainly, when Dolgunata came to her aid:

"According to the conditions of the agreement they can't tell you anything, or else the Game'll wipe them out. Either we all continue together, or else no one goes anywhere. I will not allow anything else.

"Even so? What are you going to do, kill us?"

"If I have to, yes." Dolgunata showed no emotions at all, as if she never doubted her superiority. "I'll keep sending you for respawn time after time until we reach agreement. We'll keep going together."

"Logir?" I looked at the femorc in confusion. Even despite her red skin I could see the blush of embarrassment. As if the femorc found the druid's words unpleasant but could do nothing about it. I shifted my eyes to the rest: "Guys, what's up with you?"

"Don't look at me, I've got nothing to do with this," the leprechaun responded in a voice as bewildered as mine.

"You have no choice." Dolgunata continued with her line. "Without me you've no chance of surviving. You know nothing about the Academy. You think the forest is the main obstacle?"

"As if you've got any more information," I quipped, trying to figure out what to do. The druid, using the right of strength, was trying to play boss, and six Paladins had to put up with that. Personally, I was unhappy with that approach.

"The territory of the Academy is a regular rectangle with spawn points for players in each corner. Along the perimeter of the Academy there is a two-kilometer reinforced concrete forest with passages, and five teachers in the vicinity of each corner. Then there is a wasteland followed by a desert; in the center of it there is a lake; in that there is an island where the head of the Academy is located. Between the forest and the wasteland there's a labyrinth with traps; it's only possible to pass through that as a group. I know how to avoid some of the traps. The rest we'll explore once we get there. This is just a small part of what I know about the Academy. If we agree on the temporary truce, I'll tell you everything I know.

"Temporary truce?" I frowned.

"For the duration of our stay in the Academy. As soon as we return to the main world, I'll destroy you. I'll tear you to pieces for what you've done! But for now we need each other. Or, actually, I need you, and if you don't need me it's your personal problem. The next time we'll pull you off the respawn grounds after you die two or three times, to make you more agreeable. You don't have a choice, Yaropolk. By the way, neither do you, Teart – stop hiding behind Yari's back thinking you can get away. I am faster anyway."

"So you want to share information about the Academy?" I laughed in the druid's face. "You want to buy us for data that's completely useless in the main world? I'd thought you were a sane player."

I tried to keep independent and calm, while

working on analyzing the situation in something like supercomputer mode. What was going on? Why did Dolgunata behave as if she were fully in control of the situation? Why was it that the Dolgunata whom I had met in the very beginning and the Dolgunata who was standing in front of me now behaved like two different people? Why had she changed so dramatically? But most of all, I was perplexed by the Paladins' indifference to the way the druid threatened me. It seemed that the Paladins had come to realize that we were all brothers and that we need to stand fast to protect each other; yet again it turns out that they're ready to betray me just to stay alive. What could Dolgunata have promised them to gain their unconditional support? Granises? That sounded like total nonsense.

"But what else do you want?" The druid said in surprise. "Money? Then I'd like to remind you, in case you've forgotten, that it's you who owes me a granis for help. Whether you need it or not I don't really care. I want to get it and I'll get it from you. From you or from your body. By the way, here's another tidbit of information for your development: after the final death of a player, all his granises stay on Earth. So they'll be mine in any case. And forget about your initiation – it won't save you. Are we done? May I turn back into a good girl?"

"You must have also forgotten – without Teart and myself you won't be able to follow the guiding lines. Go ahead, kill me. We'll respawn and squirm out of it somehow. While you'd have to trundle from here through the entire forest to the nearest path, and it's not guaranteed that even with your speed you'd be able to avoid the guards. And all of you would be just dead meat," I looked at the Paladins. "Guys, don't you see that she's just using you?"

"Yari, just say yes. Believe me, Dolgunata doesn't wish us ill." Logir spoke as if forced. "She just wants to finish the Academy, as we do. No one is using anybody."

"Oh, really?" I looked in the druid's mocking eyes, making my final decision. "You need my help? No problem, I'll help. We'll go through the Academy together. Pony up three granises. That's my condition."

"Why not ten?" The druid laughed. "Or a whole hundred at once ..."

"Teart, have you found any new pictures?" I turned to the leprechaun, ignoring the druid.

"Yeah, I got a couple," Teart followed our rules and sent me the trade. After a pause the leprechaun added: "Yari, I side with them. Somehow I want to live more than I want to show my attitude. If Dolgunata can help us pass through the labyrinth and provides information about the Academy, let her be the lead! Maybe the girl has some kind of hangup about leadership. Hungry childhood, wooden toys nailed to the floor, all that; so now she's trying to force everyone to kowtow to her. I don't see anything horrible about letting her be in charge."

"Let her be in charge, I have nothing against it," I shrugged my shoulders, amazed at myself. Where did I get so much courage and certainty that I could do no wrong? "It's just that nothing comes free.

Besides information I want three granises, and either I'll get them or she can go f..."

"I warned you." Dolgunata instantly turned into the panther and leaped towards me. "We'll see how you sing when you run out of lives ..."

There was a brief flash of pain followed by another system message:

You were killed and sent to a respawn point
You lost one level
Your current level: 4

Waking up after the second respawn was like a bright light turning on in a dark room: suddenly everything appeared out of nothing, including my awareness of myself in the said everything. I appeared next to the respawn stone, and just a few moments later another player appeared next to me. Then another. And another. And more... the clearing was filling with players of various types; they were trying to spot Paladins within the host of appearing creatures, so the decision on what to do next came together with someone's shout "Paladin! Get him, guys!" Using Dolgunata's tactic, I leaped straight from the spot crushing into a reptilian who had just appeared next to me. The player, who hadn't expected my maneuver, crashed to the ground, and together we rolled on the ground right under the feet of the crowd that was running towards us. I was working on pure instinct: if you want to survive, run straight into the thick of it. Next to me strange black lightnings were flying, along with arrows and other stuff. Once an axe whistled by; however, all of that did much more damage to the others around me than it did to me.

"What in hell are you doing?" rasped the reptilian crushed under me, and I found no better answer than to whack his head on the steel boot of one of the players. The reptilian went limp and I made another somersault, using my victim as a shield.

"Where is he?!" I kept rolling on the ground creating a bigger and bigger pile-up. In their rush to kill me first, the players hindered each other, fell on the ground, tripped their neighbors; some of them even started killing their competitors, as I guessed from surprised and indignant screams. At some point I realized that the reptilian I was using as a shield had disappeared; either he had got loose in the crush, or he'd fulfilled his mission and protected me against a deadly blow. Whatever! I kept rolling, out of the corner of my eye tracking the final goal of my wild maneuvers: the edge of the forest.

Freeze, all of you! Or he's gonna get away!" I knew that voice. The Book of Knowledge immediately confirmed: the screamer was Dangard, a student of Devir, so I redoubled my efforts. "There he is! Hit him!"

A stone boulder that was suddenly right in front of me shattered to smithereens; sharp shards drummed on my armor. I reached the edge! Without slowing down I jumped onto all fours and, like a monkey, took off in running leaps into the forest, rolling over in a random direction after each leap. I needed to put my chasers off target; lightning bolts and icicles that were missing me left and right confirmed that I had chosen the right tactic.

"Don't let him escape!" Dangard's shout was so close that I nearly lost my rhythm. After yet another leap I jumped over to crouch behind some boulder and raised my head for the first time, to look around and find a guiding line — I had just a few seconds left before the guards would become active.

"I ain't going into that forest!" I heard an "encouraging" yelp from behind — it gave me a couple of seconds of lead. And then I saw the greenish light. The guiding beam was just a couple of meters ahead. "The monsters!"

I was running forward, not looking at the path, periodically touching the saving beam. My intuition warned me against trying to climb up right now; there was simply no time for that. Making sure to dodge and weave, jumping behind the boulders that kept appearing in my way, I cursed myself for being stupid and naïve. Was the first time not enough to make it clear the only person you could trust in this game was yourself? No one else! Dolgunata had again found some inner fears of the Paladins, forcing them to submit. Made some kind of agreement to boot, blasted alley cat! Why in hell did she stick to us anyway? What, do you have to sacrifice someone in the labyrinth in order to pass through? There was nothing else to explain her actions.

"You'll still die! You can't pass through the labyrinth! I heard Dangard's scream right behind my back; then he choked and went silent. The mage had encountered a guard. Only then did I stop, calming my madly beating heart and stilling my desire to rush on. I was practically soaking in adrenaline, so I released my emotions by screaming at the skies: "Basaastaaards! I'll blast y'all to hell!" I was shaking so hard that I nearly let go of the beam. Only a guard's red eye that opened barely a meter away reminded me that I wasn't in a safe place.

It took me about five minutes to calm down. Trying to find something that would enable my brain to stop and switch to something else, shifting it from the "panic" mode to the mode of conscious actions, I started looking around trying to find anything unusual. Anything that differed from the background, anything that I could study. I was able to do that. Even twice.

The first thing that caught my eye was the frame of the team, showing that the Paladins and Dolgunata were alive and well, having received an extra level during the past hour. At this point I was at the lowest mark, with my level at 4. Teart had the 6th, Dirion and Sartal the 7th, Logir and Refor the 8th, Monstrichello the 9th and Dolgunata – I could barely believe my eyes – level 12. The druid was over 10 already! As soon as the level of adrenaline in my blood dropped to acceptable values, I did something important: left the group. I'd had enough fighting together! Because of the gift from the head of the Academy I could easily see the current location of the Paladins: they were even now going around the respawn clearing and moving in my direction, while I had no intention of showing them my location on the map.

I scowled — the druid just wouldn't settle

down! One needn't be a Nostradamus to predict the future: Teart would lead the Paladins along safe paths toward me, Dolgunata would again give me an ultimatum, I would not take that well and be sent to respawn again. I had no intention of submitting to the druid. Did I really need that? Not likely!

The second thing that caught my eye and prevented me from immediately climbing up along the guiding beam was a strange yellowish glow that came from a pile of trash that was sitting right on the ground. I was taken aback at first, trying to understand the logic behind the glow, and then the Book of Knowledge came to my aid. A marker appeared above the pile: "97% match", and when I mentally clicked on it I saw the entry on the recipe found by Teart. So, once you see an object, in this case a pile of trash hiding the recipe or something else you were seeking, it then would begin analyzing everything you saw and highlight similarities that it discovers? Wishing to check my guess, I ran up to the pile and brushed it aside. I smiled, seeing that there was in fact a recipe under it. Now looking for objects to generate future profits would become a lot easier; I only need to do one small thing: survive and complete this blasted Academy. The first step toward that was simple and clear: I needed to keep away from my former team.

Constantly checking the map for the location of the Paladins moving towards me as they apparently decided to check out the spot where I was before leaving the team, I moved towards the teacher for attack capabilities. My escape from the respawn point gave me an interesting tactic that I wanted to test at once: a lightning-fast attack and then a retreat, just as rapid. The training itself is instantaneous, the teacher is standing at the edge of the clearing near the forest; even if he were monitored all the time, players' concentration would not be perfect. They are not elite fighters who have been training for many years! In the majority of cases these are tired players, intimidated by the mages and hoping to survive. Where would they get lightning-fast reactions? They would most likely linger, giving me a few seconds, and I should take advantage of that. Because now it's time to work on my own development.

The clearing with the teacher was still full of people. Clustering into groups, the players whispered among themselves, lounged on the sand, fought – I was not sure if they were serious or just sparring in jest, to check what they had learned. The players were doing whatever one could imagine, but were definitely not guarding the teacher. The only ones who maintained some sort of concentration were the mages I knew from my time entering the Academy: Olzar and his team. They were the ones that had caught me, taken me to the first training and then lost me. Trying to make as little noise as possible, I moved directly behind the teacher's back and listened to the conversation of the mages.

"... only 2 levels left. It's a day of life. What then, just kicking the bucket?"

"Dangard ordered us to control this teacher, so that's what we'll do." Olzar was adamant. "It's better to croak here than to return to Devir. You've seen yourself what he'll do to everyone should the Paladins return. So we need to hold on."

Oh, wow! Devir held a show of an execution in front of all the mages in the Academy? Someone was killed only to demonstrate what's in store for those who return? Devir is obviously totally psycho!

"Olzar, but we are not initiated. There's the labyrinth ahead – we'll just freakin' die in there, and that'll be the end of us. I don't understand why we're hanging out here! For the life of me I don't!"

"I don't myself, either... Dangard said that for those who know the rules the labyrinth would not be dangerous. But only he and Ahean know the rules. And who the hell knows in which corner of the Academy he spawned. So we'll wait for Dangard."

"He knows the rules, right! Ha! If he'd known the Academy as well as he says he does, he'd never have gotten himself caught by a monster. And now it looks like it's the Paladins who are better prepared. They know the rules for moving around the forest. And that's despite the fact that they drew the lot to be the sacrifice!"

Lots? Sacrifice? The Book of Knowledge sucked up information like a sponge, and I even forgot for a while why I came there. It's not often that it becomes possible to listen in on such a frank conversation about the root cause of all your problems.

"Yeah, they do," Olzar confirmed, but immediately added wryly, "but what good will it be to them? So they know how to wander around the forest: so what? All the teachers are blocked off and we control all the respawn points. Once Dangard respawns he'll tell us what happened between him and the Paladin and why they didn't just pop him off right away. Perhaps they used the magic again, and that huge prick absorbed it all. Sooner or later they'll just run out of Energy and will have to get down on the ground. So that's not the worst. I'm much more scared of the wastelands. Like really scared. From what I heard it looks like it's some sort of real trash place! They say that... Damn! Have you gone completely bonkers there, you cross-eyed freaks?!"

Three arrows, one after another, stuck in the ground next to Olzar's foot; they came from the players who were fighting each other. The arrows vanished practically at once, showing that they had been a creation of one of the game capabilities; a group of dog-headed hunters froze in place like they were statues. Apparently, knowing how to use the attack capabilities is one thing, and practice in using them is quite another, and some players had obvious problems in that respect.

"Do you understand that you could've hit us, you morons?" Olzar kept screaming, slowly approaching the hunters. — "This is the Game! Here, if it were to as much as touch me..."

The entire group of the mages moved after Olzar, willing to punish the hapless hunters, and I saw that I'd never find a better moment to get my training. If it weren't now, it would be never. I was sitting three meters above ground, so I took a deep breath, banishing fear, and jumped towards the teacher. There was no time to climb down in comfort.

Hitting the ground almost knocked me out, but

I used what remained of my consciousness to leap over the distance separating me from the teacher, and blurted with one breath:

"I want to partake of your wisdom and learn to use the attack capabilities of my class!"

Learning progress: You have reached teacher 4 of 10

"You are impatient and harsh, recruit," the old man grinned as soon as the space around us changed. "It's an uncomfortable feeling when I am not even allowed to say my words of welcome ..."

"You know very well why I had to do this," I responded, plopping on the grass. My ankle hurt and standing on it was too much for me. Apparently, I wouldn't make a stellar traceur.

"I know, and that's why I allowed you to become lost outside of time. We aren't particularly happy with what the mages are doing."

"Fate chose the Paladins as a sacrifice," I said, venturing a guess. "So that's why they're trying as hard as they can."

"Fate always selects someone as a sacrifice, but that's no reason for everyone to follow it blindly!" the old man responded. "Everyone's supposed to have their own head on their shoulders! Besides, who appointed the mages as executioners? The Viceroy? For some reason I have grave doubts about that."

"Whatever for is it necessary to choose someone to sacrifice at all?" I grumbled, pulling off my steel boot. My ankle was swollen as if I'd twisted it.

That's something I needed like a hole in the head!

"I'm not authorized to discuss the decisions of the founders," the old guy cut me off. "Use healing – with damage like this training is questionable."

"I don't have healing," I grumbled, but then, remembering what Dietrich had said when he selected a banner as his artifact, I added: "Can Paladins heal?"

"Why not?" The old man was surprised. "Anyone can heal, even hunters or assassins. Healing is not even related to abilities. Don't you know that?"

I shook my head in response, and immediately sighed in relief: I was able to find a position in which my limb didn't hurt. Perhaps to an onlooker it would appear funny, but the absence of burning pain was more important to me. The old man fell silent for a minute, thinking of something, then apparently decided that a brief overview of the players' physiology would not exceed his level of authority.

"From the standpoint of physiology players are not that different from NPCs. No 'life bars', 'health levels' and other bling. We are whole and indivisible. That's why any player can heal if he has pills or potions in his inventory. Yes, those preparations have the same effect on players as on NPCs; healing a common cold with high level magic is silly and inefficient. The only class that has the ability for initial level magic healing is priests. But even they can't heal other players – only themselves. I think I'll repeat that: it's only possible to heal other players magically if you use high level magic which is accessible only to highly specialized players if theirs is the right artifact. Everyone else is healed in the same

---

way as NPCs: with medicine. The main difference between players and NPCs is in the personal or class resilience. Untrained people such as you, if they fall down from a height of three meters, twist their ankles, break ribs and generally feel quite uncomfortable. On the other hand, even an untrained vampire would not notice a small jump like this even if he were to drop down head first."

"So, if a player loses a leg it can't be reattached?" I frowned. "It's unlikely to grow back from chewing pills."

"You forget about respawn, during which the player's body would be completely renewed. However, if someone would rather not lose a level, then yes, he'll end up limping for the rest of his life. Remember Hephaestus. Anyway, you are talking about an extreme case when respawn would in fact be necessary. But in everyday practice all players' ailments can be easily cured with the elves' ointment. Elves have advanced far in healing that can practically bring both NPCs and players back from the dead Some even call it magic, even though in fact it's just a well designed marketing campaign and use of the water of life. I'd thought you had a vial with you."

"From where?"

"Well, you did get some food somewhere. Are you ready for training?"

I moved my foot and the pain that seemed to have subdued returned with a vengeance. I had to shake my head, sighing heavily. It seemed I'd end up sitting here for a while...

"It's a pity... Ok, we'll wait. We aren't

constrained for time."

"Perhaps we could talk on neutral topics to pass the time," I ventured. "For example, I would like to know: do you live in the Academy all the time or only come here periodically in order to teach?"

"How would we know then what's going on in the outside world?" The old man grinned, accepting my offer of conversation. "Teaching is an obligation imposed by the Game, that we have to fulfill once per month. During the rest of the time we just lead our own lives. The only constraint is the appearance. By agreeing to teach we change and lose our original appearance forever. What you see is the projection of your understanding of what a mentor is supposed to look like – in other words, a creature that possesses knowledge; you are welcome to think of any other appropriate title. We look different to each race. The funny part is that if anyone at all were to believe that the wisest creatures were babies, to him we would in fact look like them. With pacifiers, in diapers, and broccoli puree on our faces. But at the subconscious level for some reason everyone believes that old people are the source of knowledge. As for wisdom, in fact a narrow specialized area of it, a sort of street smarts could be something that old people have. But knowledge... Doesn't it occur to anyone that the physiology of all living creatures is such that the aging brain deteriorates and loses some of its functions? Old men don't become more clever or wiser, they just become older. That's why all long-lived players strive to keep their age at the threshold of physical aging; not everyone has the Book of

Knowledge. By the way, that's a very good choice for a Judge; combined with a good choice of abilities it will enable you to make more informed and balanced decisions."

"Speaking of Judges," I latched onto the topic that bothered me. "Does the Game have some set of rules, after breaking which the player is considered a criminal? How does one understand, for example, that a player who killed another player is not a criminal, but an ardent representative of his class? How does the Game determine when it is necessary to open a case and when it's not?"

"There's no rule," the old man smiled. "That's why it's hard being a Judge. You are the prosecutor, the council and the judge at the same time. As soon as a Judge learns about some events that clash with his personal understanding of what is right, the Game will either generate the assignment itself, in case of past precedents, or propose that you initiate the case yourself. In case of the latter there's significantly less time to deliver a correct verdict, but a successful verdict lands a much higher bonus. Based on his own understanding of what's right and fair, the Judge delivers his verdict, which will then be approved or rejected by the Emperor. No one said that it's easy to be a Judge, but the bonuses you receive outweigh all the drawbacks.

"Bonuses for a successful verdict depend on what the judge needs at that given moment?" I showed off my brilliance by guessing. "I was afraid to die irrevocably, so I was granted initiation as a bonus?"

"That's right. Your chances of successful graduation from the Academy have increased," the "old man" confirmed.

"But later I received information that this initiation is fake. That it's just an additional level that can also disappear."

"Not quite. Dolgunata — we are talking about the druid, correct? — is both right and wrong at the same time. It is true that as soon as you are dropped to level one the system will offer you a choice: either a final death in an initiated state, which would be stupid, or respawn with loss of initiation. In case of the latter, respawn time will increase from one hour to three, thus misleading your enemies regarding the finality of your death. Those waiting at the respawn point would leave, thinking that your death was final. Let's make it clear though – this works only within the Academy. In the main world there wouldn't be a choice like that. The final death would be final."

"Let's get back to verdicts and cases. Now the mages are engaging in total lawlessness; they kill other players, prevent them from learning... My very soul rebels against it, but I did not receive any suggestions that I should open a case. At the same time, as soon as the Paladins knocked me out there was a case generated right away. Where's the catch?"

"That within your heart you are certain that the mages are correct," the old man surprised me, "while the Paladins' action was out of line with your understanding of the core essence of the class. If you want to open a case against the mages, you'd have to believe that they are at fault, collect irrefutable proof and deliver the verdict. But you can't do that because you understand: the mages aren't doing anything that would go outside the overall framework of the Game. It's unpleasant, it's not nice, but it's normal and common."

"The Chancellor doesn't like it."

"There're lots of things he doesn't like, so that's not a good indicator. For example, he'd prefer for us to always stay in the Academy, the way he does, but it doesn't mean we should blindly fulfill his wishes. One needs to keep one's own head about one's shoulders. Or heads, if we are talking about Derantians."

"So that means that you are ordinary players?" I was surprised. "Not minions or NPCs..."

"That's enough questions, you've upgraded your Book of Knowledge quite well," the teacher cut me off. "Let me know when you're ready for training."

It took me about ten hours to be able to step on my foot more or less painlessly. I'd never thought that the trite saying "time drags its feet" had a right to exist. I, as a true child of modern technology, was always short on time. Sometimes you'd sit down to play a computer game for ten minutes, and somehow lose half a day... Or you might decide, around eight o'clock at night, to watch a single episode of a new interesting show, and then at six o'clock in the morning, red-eyed, you suddenly realize that you have to get up in just one hour. And then that one hour of sleep was enough for you! Moreover, there was some time left to think about the actions of all the characters and your attitude towards all of that! It's a pity this approach cannot be used when some part of you is hurting.

"I'm ready!" I shouted happily as soon as my foot was able to fit into the steel boot. In addition, a short jog to the edge of the clearing and back did not cause me pain, just some minor discomfort which was easily bearable. For the time of my recuperation the teacher tuned out, completely ignoring my questions, so I was left to my own devices. For ten hours. By the way, I found out one more interesting thing: I didn't feel sleepy in the Academy. Not at all. I spent about three hours with my eyes closed, diligently counting sheep, but to no avail. "So what about the attack abilities?"

Acquired Ability: Templar's blow.

Description: you strike a crushing blow with a weapon enhanced by your word.

Use: before the blow you need to state out loud or silently to yourself the activating key phrase: "I am the Templar's blow". Critical hit chance: 15%. Critical hit is defined as striking a vital body part. Cost: 25 Energy.

In case of damage to a vital body part: gamers are sent for respawn, NPCs are killed, dungeon bosses and quest participants sustain damage that is calculated by the Game on a case by case basis.

In case of damage to a non-vital body part: gamers and NPCs can continue battle; NPCs, in addition, suffer a state of shock for a duration of 10 seconds; dungeon bosses and quest participants sustain damage that is calculated by the Game on a case by case basis.

"The book of spells that are available to you has a new entry now," the old man continued as soon as I finished reading the system messages. "Open the book."

After a slight confusion associated with searching for the right icon there was a book in front of my eyes, previously empty. Now its virgin whiteness was marred with the black blot of a table providing a more detailed description of the acquired ability: rollback, radius and range, number of targets and other stats that were currently of no interest to me. This blow required a weapon to be used, whereas I had none. So there was no benefit at all from learning of this ability.

"With each use the chance of a critical hit and armor ignore will increase," the teacher continued, "up to 50%. The more frequently you use this ability, the more effective it'll become. Oh! The Energy cost will also diminish with each use until it reaches 3 units. That's not bad for a professional fighter."

"Only I'm not a fighter," I grumbled, closing the description. "What else is there in the attack arsenal?"

"Nothing," the teacher smiled, but my frowning face hinted to him that he needed to explain: "There's nothing within the Academy. There are about a hundred different attack abilities available to Paladins, but you will learn about them in the main world. For the Academy a simple blow is enough. It's a pity you don't have weapons with you. You could have trained now. Several years of training to use the ability and bring it to the top level available in the Academy would've helped you survive."

"Several years?" I frowned, considering the already trained players from a different angle. What if the mages who were hunting us decided to spend some of the eternity to level up? When I was together with Monstrichello, he absorbed all the available magic. An entire thirty lightning bolts from one player. Now I don't have Monster with me, and it would be stupid and unprofessional to hope that each player I encounter would only be able to deal three or four blows using the ability. I need to be ready to the fact that I will run into dangerous opponents.

"These trees serve as dummies for the training of your ability," the old man gestured toward the trees. "Time has no power over this place, and Energy doesn't run out. So, train and develop. The whole world is open to you. And remember: the Game is a very multidimensional thing. You never know when you will win some or lose some. Tell me when you're ready to return to the Academy. Meanwhile: farewell, Judge. It was fun talking to you."

The teacher settled in the lotus position and fell silent. It seemed he even stopped breathing, diving in the depths of his consciousness. My foot still hurt, so I suppressed the urge to return, deciding instead to take advantage of the teacher's hospitality and fully recuperate. Once I returned I'd have to show wonders of agility and speed, and it's easier to do that when you are in peak form.

Time slowed down again. Once I was bored sitting in one place and randomly leaf through the Book of Knowledge, refreshing the forgotten bits of my short stint as a player, I started studying the clearing.

Its width, types of trees and bushes, depth of forest to the impenetrable black wall that was hard and cold to the touch, the variety of grass cover and complete absence of animals. I was interested in everything that could up the progress of the Book's development by another unit. By now its experience level had reached 923 out of 1000; in the near future that would bring it up to level two, thus upping the "Context Search" property by a whole unit. Search would activate and it would make using the artifact easier by an order of magnitude.

Tired of twiddling my thumbs, I even tried to use the newly received attack capability by hitting a tree with my hand. Can't hands be called weapons? Masters like Chuck Norris and Bruce Lee would not only confirm that, they would forever beat that axiom into the stupid and naïve heads of the common herd. However, reality showed that I still had a long way to go to get the level of Bruce Lee. I would hit a tree, but the activating key phrase wouldn't work. My hands weren't weapons like those of the famous master from Hong Kong. By the way, that was an interesting thought: was Bruce Lee a player? He was lightning-fast, he did things that were impossible even for trained fighters, and passed on from this life – in our case into another game world – while he was still quite young. As if he leveled up on Earth and moved on to conquer new heights. I should find that out once I return to the main world.

Having practically decided to go back, I still thought to perform one more experiment. In accordance with the game rules each player had a personal artifact, enhancing his abilities depending on his chosen path of development. The artifact could be a weapon, armor, clothing, an accessory, a banner or a book. Paladins are not capable of casting lightning or ice shards, so those of us who chose weapons as artifacts are extremely valuable allies. Before the druid made Logir and Refor lose their minds, I was really safe with them.

But there were three points that bothered me. Number one, Monstrichello used his shield to topple players onto the ground, knock them out, injure them in other ways, and generally tried at all times to use his artifact not only for its original purpose of protection, but also for attack. Number two: Dolgunata. I had no idea what she had chosen as an artifact, but as a panther she used her claws and teeth with perfect skill, sending players to respawn in droves. Number three: I had a massive blunt object at hand; just one blow with that could knock someone out.

So, the question of the day was – is it possible to use the Book of Knowledge as the favorite weapon of schoolkids whapping each other over the heads? Pacifism, of course, is a fine thing, nonresistance to evil by force and all that, but you can't do good without using your fists, as wise people say. So I needed to understand whether I'd be able to fight back in the future.

First of all I tested the Book of Knowledge for strength. A weak, medium, and, finally, strong full swing blow on a tree didn't result in any problems with the functioning of the artifact. The Book still sucked up knowledge like a sponge, and the appearance of the artifact stayed unchanged: it developed no dents or scratches. So the crucial moment came. I grabbed the Book with both hands for a more comfortable grip, aimed, said in my mind: *"I am the Templar's blow"* and with all my might whacked on the thinnest tree I could find in the vicinity: I was worried about the Book. What if something were to happen to it?

BAM!

New artifact property discovered: "Weapon". Would you like to activate it?

The clash of the Book enhanced by the attack ability and the tree resulted in such an impressive light and noise show that for a few moments I was unable to see anything around me as the stars danced in front of my eyes. If it weren't for the system message that ignored all the effects of temporary confusion, I could easily have lost my position in space – so unexpected, loud and bright was the explosion. Shaking my head, I pushed the "activate" button without hesitation.

Artifact property "Weapon" has been activated; current level: 0

In order to use the property "Weapon" outside of the testing range of the Academy you need to bring its level up to 1 (current artifact development experience: 924 of 1000)

Artifact has been modified

As soon as the stars cleared out of my eyes, I shook my head again, chasing the phantoms away. My A4 size Book of Knowledge, which had been sitting so conveniently on my right thigh, had disappeared! Now, instead of it, on my right glove some strange device was located, sporting spikes; only under the influence of some hard drugs would anyone call that a book. Having become several times smaller than the previous version of the artifact, the thing was an odd kind of a hand weapon; one of its halves was attached to the back side of the glove, and the other to the forearm. The part that was attached to the glove sported additional spikes that had not been there before. Apparently so my words would carry more weight.

I clenched and unclenched my fist, checking for the freedom of movement of my hand, but there was none: the renewed Book sat there as if glued on without causing any discomfort. It took me several minutes to figure out the principle of attaching the book and shifting it from battle to transport mode: the holster on my thigh changed as well. From now on in order to attach the artifact to my hand and use it as a powerful knuckleduster, it was enough to put my hand on the Book and make a twisting motion. Having returned the Book to my hand, I made sure that the counter in the spell book, showing the use of the ability, has increased by one, and grinned. The moment I returned to the Academy, the Book would stop being a weapon, at least until I received the remaining 76 artifact experience points. However, there was a subtle point! I could actively use the weapon here, at the test range, thus upping the counter of using "The Templar's Blow" and, as soon as I increased the "Weapon" property to at least one, I'd be able to fight back. The teacher mentioned something about several years of training? Not a problem – let's see how long my patience would last... or the trees...

CHAPTER SIX

TESTING THE KNOWLEDGE

"I am the Templar's blow". BAM!
"I am the Templar's blow". BAM!
"I am...

I AM NOT here anymore!

For the thousandth, or maybe ten-thousandth time, I dropped on the ground exhausted. That was the consequence of those unpleasant "20% of normal" physical parameters for the human race. While in the Academy I had not encountered problems in this respect as there was no serious physical strain, as soon as I attempted any serious effort, my body started drowning in lactic acid. I tried to resist to the last, bashing madly at the trees, but the result was always the same: falling on the ground. There was one positive moment though: while at first I was exhausted literally after five minutes, now, after six months of training, I managed to hang on for half an hour.

"It's a good day today, isn't it?" As I was lying on the ground, I gathered just enough strength to address the teacher. During the entire time I was trying to improve myself, he didn't make a single movement nor said a single word, even though I tried to talk to him with a determination worthy of a better cause. Back when I was still an NPC I'd watched the movie "Castaway" about a guy who ended up on an uninhabited island. A modern Robinson Crusoe, may he rot in hell. In order to preserve at least some of his sanity the character there made himself a "friend" from the materials he had on hand, and talked to it all the time. He knew that socialization was an important part of our lives. That's why one of the worst punishments is a single cell and complete isolation. Even death is not so fearsome as the lack of a chance to socialize, or at least see another living being. Many go mad. Whether that applied to players or not, I didn't know, but to protect myself just in case I kept talking to the old guy. I told him about my attitude to mages, Paladins, other players, weather, trees, the fact that I didn't want to hit those damned trees; I told him fairy tales, anecdotes, jokes, entries from the Book of Knowledge... I talked about everything, just to avoid keeping silent. But the old man never responded; he couldn't care less about my attempts to stay human.

By the way, after half a year my anger and ire with the Paladins faded, leaving just sadness and regret behind. Having fallen under Dolgunata's influence, my former comrades-in-arms could not be considered independent fighting units. From then on they were simply druid's satellites; and throughout my six months of training I kept thinking about the same problem: should I once again rid them of her? Risk myself for the sake of others? Or would it be better to leave things as they were, moving on alone? Both options had pros and cons; so I was in no hurry to return to the Academy, madly hitting the trees, doing push-ups and squats and telling the teacher stories. Before I saved or refused to save anyone else I needed to understand myself. What was it that I needed personally?

"In fact, it's quite an ordinary day," came the raspy response that made me lie completely still staring at the blue sky. It's not so scary talking to yourself in an empty house; it's scary to hear someone else answer! I turned my head slowly and saw the teacher's grinning face.

"Today it's precisely six months since you came to the training range, so I need to explain to you the conditions of extending your stay here," the old man clarified as I was rolling to my side. I had no strength even to sit up.

"Are there any conditions?" I was able to groan, crashing onto my back again. I wasn't able to roll over.

"Of course! Players are way too devious to just

---

let them be. They'll figure out a way to live forever and use it until the Emperor himself comes after them. We really don't need him showing up here, so listen carefully, I'm not going to repeat myself. From now on each day will cost you one Energy unit, which, as you understand, won't replenish itself. If you have food or elixirs, that won't affect you at all: eat, drink and train on. Your friend spent two years here this way before she decided that she'd had enough of scratching the trees.

"So a hit with the claws is her attack ability and not just a physical trait of the druids?" I was surprised.

"A trait that enables you to inflict damage, ignoring steel armor? Solitude obviously wasn't that good for you," said the old man sarcastically. "Your thinking ability has deteriorated. Anyway, I did inform you, I have nothing else to do here. Let me know when you're ready to go back."

"Wait!" I barely had time to scream. "I have a question about the attack capability that I wasn't able to figure out myself. Would you help me?"

"I'm listening," the old man, who had practically turned into a statue, revived again.

"During six months I have leveled up the properties 'Critical hit chance' from 15 to 28 percent and 'Armor ignore' from 15 to 16 percent. Does that mean that, say, approximately with every third blow I could kill my opponent even if I were to hit him on the leg? This seems to be some mega-killer blow that completely ignores the opponent's levels. Then why do we need 'Armor ignore'? What does that ignore with such a high critical hit chance? Or does that mean that it works for normal, non-critical hits? So, I'm confused and I need a clarification on how this works."

"Better late than never, right?" the teacher smiled. "I was surprised the last time, wondering if you were so upset by the absence of conventional weapons that your ability to think logically had completely shut down. Clarification: besides the attack abilities each player also learns defensive ones that provide him with one of several types of protection. The class armor, even the plate type, is never used for protection: its function is different. What it is, you'll learn from the appropriate teacher. The players receive most of their protection from those very defense abilities which can absorb, deflect or block the hits. So even if your hit is a critical one, it doesn't mean that you'll instantly kill the other player. First of all you need to penetrate his armor. I hope you noticed that armor ignore increased only by 1% after six months? This is one of the most important parameters for players who decide to become fighters or hunters. If you can't pierce the armor, all your critical damage will do is lower the opponent's Energy a little. However, if the stars are right and you are able to ignore your opponent's armor while making a critical hit, no one will be able to survive that, regardless of his level. Even the Emperor would be sent for respawn."

"And the defense abilities must have some kind of an opposite property, like 'block armor ignore', right?" I guessed.

"It's nice to see that you are regaining your ability for logical thinking. What you are talking about is called 'Armor resistance' and yes, this parameter determines the extent to which you can ignore the other."

"Does this mean then that two players who are at the same level and equally developed wouldn't be able to inflict any damage on each other? Is that reasonable?" I frowned.

"You aren't quite right. The damage lowers the level of Energy, and the stronger the hit is the more Energy it shaves off. In case of a battle of matched opponents, the most important thing becomes the agility with which the player manages to avoid blows, the strategy of using Energy-restoring elixirs and the number of those available.

"By strategy you mean using the elixirs not when your Energy is at half-bar, but closer to the bottom?" I guessed again. "And thus risking missing a critical hit that would drop it down to zero?"

"A standard elixir would restore Energy to 100%," the teacher confirmed my guess. A player's store isn't infinite, so the more frequently he uses his elixirs, the more he has left in store. It's elementary."

"Elementary..." I smirked. "It's classic: money is strength."

"Is that not an axiom? It's always harder when you're sick and poor. Have I satisfied your curiosity?"

"Not quite," I glanced at the progress of my artifact, and barely contained the urge to jump up, grab the teacher by the lapels and shake him, demanding that he tell me something else. I had just

14 points till the next level, so I urgently needed to have the teacher talk about the topics I hadn't raised before. "How many Energy-restoring elixirs would I be able to buy with one granis, and is such a purchase possible here, at the Academy training range? Or within the Academy in general?"

"You have a granis too?" The man was obviously taken aback.

"What do you mean – 'too'? Has someone... Dolgunata?!"

"It's practically unreal to earn a granis before the Academy; the Game monitors that very thoroughly. It's possible to trade one for some services or jewels, but even so just in order for the Game itself to transfer that granis as payment for initiation or upgrade from an NPC to a minion. Not more. I don't know of other ways to receive a granis before the Academy, so much more surprising it is to find not one, but two recruits with granis. Where did you get it?"

"I'll offer you a trade," I immediately figured out a way to turn it to my advantage. "I tell you how we managed that and you tell me how to activate my defense."

"You want me to teach you the defense abilities?" From a sweet old grandpa the teacher turned into a frowning old coot, but I was beyond stopping at that point.

"Not teach, just tell me how to activate it and what to do with it. You *do* want to know how two granises appeared in the Academy?"

"You cannot have a granis! It's prohibited!" The

teacher even jumped to his feet.

"Offer me a trade," I grinned, in my mind thanking Teart who taught me this. "I'll show you what I have and what I don't."

<Hidden> is offering you a trade. Accept?

The Game carefully concealed the teacher's real name, but it was impossible to miss the word "dartirian" in the window that popped up. So then, the teachers are players as well? That's an interesting point. In this case, what criteria are used to select them? Also, this means that I at least know the race of this teacher. If I set this as a goal for myself, I could find this creature in the main world.

Book of Knowledge has reached a new level. You need to increase the level of the artifact properties: "Context search" (1), "Weapon" (1), <Choose value from the list >

By an incredible strain of will I looked away from the words *"Choose value from the list"* and clicked on "Weapon". Despite an overwhelming urge to fiddle with the list of available artifact properties, I realized: without a hefty argument represented by a weapon there was nothing I could achieve in the Academy. While if I were to get into it and investigate, I'd be more than likely to find something useful that would prevent me from using the available properties upgrade unit for "Weapon". I noted another interesting and pleasant thing: the artifact experience bar updated and now showed the current value as "2 out of 1000". So it looked like with each new artifact level – which is not, by the way, shown anywhere directly – I gain an opportunity to raise the level of one of the properties; and the number of necessary experience points needed to reach the next level stays the same at 1000 points. Given the fast rate at which the Book of Knowledge absorbs information, leveling up at the initial stages shouldn't be a problem.

As for the "Weapon" property, at level one it increased the "Armor ignore" parameter for all attack capabilities by 1%. At level 2 this quality would increase already by 2%, at level 5 by 3%, at level 10 by 4% and at level 15 by 5%. However, it was unclear as to whether these values would add up or replace one another. If they added up, receiving an additional +15% to "Armor ignore" looked like a very promising development.

"Why the defense?" the teacher, who had been frozen in righteous shock, recovered his senses. "I could tell you how to use secondary abilities, provide information about the Game, teach you to customize your armor. Why are you interested specifically in defense?

"Are there any restrictions associated with it?" I was surprised; this whole exchange convinced me even more that this particular training unit was exactly what I needed right now. If they didn't want to provide it to me, it meant there was something valuable about it.

"There are only thirteen teachers in the whole Academy who teach defense. There are two hidden teachers in each of the four Academy training sectors, four teachers in the wasteland – they are also assigned to their own sector – and, finally, the Chancellor himself. Learning this unit at the initial stage of training provides a recruit too much of an advantage over the others. Particularly if he has items that replenish Energy. I cannot tell you how to use defense abilities."

"Well, if you can't, then you can't." I was not going to give up. "I've already visited one hidden teacher in our sector, so now's the time to visit the other. I'll trade the information on granises for the coordinates of the hidden teachers of our sector. This information isn't secret, right?"

"Only the Chancellor can..."

"What does the Chancellor have to do with it?" I cut the old man off. "You yourself train recruits prior to sending them to the Academy when you aren't teaching here, right?" I was fishing for more information and the teacher's widened eyes told me that I had guessed correctly. "Don't you want to give your future recruits an additional chance to survive? I am not asking you to teach me anything, I'm just asking for the location coordinates of the hidden teachers of our sector."

"All of them?"

"Why all? Just two. I know: if I ask for the location of one teacher, you'll send me to the one I've already visited. So – two. By the way, how many elixirs can one buy for a granis and where can one do it? Do you have them? Or is there some special place?"

"I don't have elixirs," the old man was so slow to answer that I started worrying that I'd pushed too hard. "You can buy them from the trader. Now I understand why we have one in the Academy. I'd been wracking my brain over that."

"There's a trader in the Academy as well?!" I exclaimed in surprise. "Where is he?!"

"I'll tell you the location coordinates for a hidden teacher whom you haven't visited yet, and the trader. That'll make two, just as you asked", the old man smiled. "Once you buy the elixirs, come back for training – you'll up your "Armor ignore" by another percent."

"Umm... Is it allowed to return?" I didn't expect that.

"Why not? No one prohibits you from coming back to a teacher and going over the training again if you missed something the first time. Or the second time. Everyone learns at a different pace. Sometimes you see such knuckleheads, it makes you wonder how they managed to survive that long. Are you satisfied with the trade?"

As soon as the system message appeared informing me of the map updates, I opened the Book of Knowledge and read verbatim the entries on obtaining granises. Both of the one received by Dolgunata, and the one that I received from Archibald. As I was relaying the information, I came up with a tentative idea as to how I obtained my granis, and the Book of Knowledge instantly reacted, adding the corresponding entry. The three diggers who extracted me from the grave had not been included by the Game in the mandatory wipe-out list. Once these NPCs had decided that I was a zombie, the Game added them to the list of those to be destroyed and offered a reward to all the nearest headhunters. I killed one of the NPCs, so Archibald gave me the granis received from the system; he must have received the message that one ought to share. Before I had a chance to talk to the catorian, this version seemed the most plausible to me; the Book of Knowledge confirmed that.

"Interesting..." the teacher drawled meaningfully once I finished talking. "Being a Judge is not for everyone, there are generally few of them in the Game, but to arrange for several additional NPCs at the time of a player's spawn and then immediately pop them off... That's an interesting thought; I need to work on that some more. Let me know once you're ready to go back to the Academy."

"Right now's fine," I decided, attaching the Book of Knowledge to my hand. If it was possible to come back here, first I needed to visit the local store. "Another question, by the way: besides the teachers, hidden teachers, the Chancellor and the trader, is there anyone else in the Academy?"

"Of course," the old man smiled. "The Academy isn't that different from the main world; you just need to look at it from the right angle. There's a lot to be found here, you just need to know where to look. Good luck to you, Paladin..."

"What the...?" I heard a surprised yell as soon as the space around me transformed from the training range into a clearing filled with players in the midst of the reinforced concrete jungle. "Freeze!"

I had been planning the moment of my return to the Academy for the entire six months, every time I was lying on the ground completely exhausted. I had complete and detailed information on what was going on around the teacher, what the mages were doing, along with other players, what their distance was from me, who was picking their nose, how deep, and where they were looking while doing so. Unfortunately, they were all looking in my direction: falling down from a height of three meters didn't go unnoticed. As for advantages, no one was throwing objects or lightnings at me. The players were too shocked by my unexpected tumble. That's what I'd have to make use of.

"I am the Templar's blow"! I shouted at a dead run, socking the face of the mage that was standing between me and the forest that would be my refuge. Of course, I could have made it even without the blow, but I really longed to test in practice the results of my six month training. No one had made the mage stay in place – he could have run off towards the sloppy hunters as everyone else did. But, since he decided to show vigilance and continued to guard the teacher, that was his problem.

You receive +200 Experience

A hit on the head proved fatal for the mage. Amazingly, besides information on receiving experience, there were no other messages. For example, that was the first player I had killed; surely there should've been some special achievement for that. If those exist in this game at all! Besides, for some reason I received as much experience for killing someone on my own as I did as a team member. That was strange...

"Stop!" Someone screamed again, and only now a lightning hit the boulder behind which I dove. I was lucky there wasn't a single headhunter among the so-called guards here: those were much quicker to react to changes. Having climbed to a safe height and left a couple hundred meters between the clearing and myself, I sat down on the guiding beam and started studying the updated map. I needed to figure out what would be closer – the teacher or the trader, remembering to avoid running into the Paladins. I already had a plan for what to do with them – I just needed to prepare.

The trader was closer.

I'll probably never figure out the principle by which the hidden creatures are placed within the Academy. I reached the location I needed, but there was nobody there. I climbed down. Nobody. Climbed all the way to the top. Still nobody. And only once I climbed down yet again and in a futile rage hit the reinforced concrete with my fist, it turned out that nothing was simple in this Game. The concrete block turned out to be a portal.

"Greetings, recruit!" I heard the joyful voice as soon as the swirls of the portal faded. I was standing in a small cave lit by a few dim torches. All of the cave walls were covered with cabinets, but getting to them wouldn't be easy: there was a counter between myself and the cabinets. And a smiling leprechaun standing behind it. "Oh! You have granises as well! Decided to buy something for yourself?"

"I did," I confirmed, looking at the content of the cabinets. The Book of Knowledge huffed and puffed, soaking up new information, while I was trying to figure out the purpose of the skulls, sticks, vials and other surprising items more suitable for an alchemist's shop than a trader within the Academy. On the other hand, what do I know about the traders in the Game? Maybe it's those objects that are the main goal for half the players, while I'm so naïve that I know nothing about it. Remembering the fall, I decided to kill two birds with one stone: "I need an Energy restoring potion and elves' ointment."

"That I have." The leprechaun rubbed his hands, anticipating a sale. "I'll tell you right out: there's no trade in goods in the Academy. You'll have to buy it at the price I name, or not buy it at all."

"So how many elixirs can I buy with a granis?" I tensed. In the absence of a working anti-monopoly agency the leprechaun could set the price so high that afterwards I'd be in debt to him for half a lifetime.

"Three hundred vials," the trader stunned me with his answer. "The price is the same for Energy or ointment. I can see, though, that you've got no place to put them. The initial inventory space fits only thirty elixirs. I can offer you advice: buy an inventory expander, to extend it by three times at least, and then one hundred and twenty elixirs. A hundred for Energy and twenty for health. They'll fit right in. Deal?"

"That's for one granis?" I drawled in astonishment. Actually, I'd thought to be able to buy maybe ten or at most fifteen elixirs, but I couldn't even hope to receive such a generous proposal. But the leprechaun thought differently, considering my rhetorical question to be an ironic one.

"Nothing more would fit in the inventory, but I could add some with that... I don't know, everything takes space in the inventory though... Do you want fewer elixirs instead?"

"How about information?" I found a solution at once and gestured around the store. "For example, what are all those things for?"

"Oh! Information! I get it!" The leprechaun rolled his eyes indicating that all the granis in the Game wouldn't be enough to learn the secrets of the little pot shards, empty glass bulbs and frog legs.

"In addition, I need to know the language in which all the recipes are written that can be found in the Academy," I finished, ignoring the theatrical antics of the trader. By his behavior the leprechaun indicated that information was not one of the fixed price items, so now he was trying to figure out how much he could charge for selling it to me. Wasn't he a naïve one! I had been a computer gamer for longer than he had lived! I had had dealings with hundreds of greedy goblins and tight-fisted gnomes! Even though I dealt with them in virtual worlds, practice showed that very many things there were similar to my current reality. Why not take advantage of that?

"Ahem," coughed the leprechaun who hadn't expected a new demand. "Recipes?"

"Sure," I confirmed. "It'll take a while to reach the crafts teacher; meanwhile I need to know here and now what I'm finding. What if it's some kind of nonsense?"

The bargaining started in earnest. The leprechaun wrung his hands and repeated that I was not just robbing him, but depriving his brain of the last crumbs of knowledge, and then the half-witted creature would end up as a single father for twenty little hungry kids, as his wife would certainly abandon him, but I was adamant. I needed information in order to develop and if the trader could provide it I did need to pump him dry. Finally we agreed that he would tell me about applications for all the goods he carried and decipher the recipes that I already had. The trader refused outright to teach me the language in which the recipes were written. Well, not exactly outright, but he demanded a whole granis for it, which was not possible in my case.

"What, do I need to put them there by hand?" I said in surprise after we made our agreement and the leprechaun gave me 100 bottles with blue liquid and 20 with red along with three shimmering pieces of wood. As soon as I touched one of the pieces, my small inventory shelf appeared before my eyes; one edge was shimmering. I touched the new board to the shimmering part and it bound at once; I received the informational message about increased inventory space. The remaining two boards followed the first one, but the elixir bottles refused to jump into the inventory on their own. I had to load all of them in manually:

"Isn't there a more convenient method?"

"No," the trader shook his head. "Only by hand. So, what are those recipes you have there?"

"That just doesn't make sense," I grumbled as I finished with the vials. "The recipes I can only open in the Book of Knowledge. Will you be able to see them there? Oh, and one more thing! If we hadn't agreed, you would have to give me some change, right? How much would that change have been?"

I didn't ask him directly about money denominations in the Game — the trader could've thought that I was trying to get more information out of him. So a neutral question about the change was quite appropriate.

"Let me think..." the leprechaun said slowly, turning pensive for a moment. "120 elixirs and three inventory space units come to 0.9 granis, so I'd've given you ten gold coins for change. And then it would've been your problem where to put them. You could've stuffed them in your boots, I suppose.

"You use gold in the Game?" I was unable to refrain from asking, and the leprechaun's face drooped:

"Oh, you didn't know? Oooo...," the trader's face turned into such a funny grimace that I couldn't help smiling.

"Is it normal gold or something special?"

"Gold game coins." The leprechaun was so upset he looked really pitiful. "Here, there's your information. Nothing much, just general initial recipes, you can buy them from any teacher. As for gold, we use it to pay the NPCs. One game coin is worth two kilos of gold, so then granis, as you can easily guess, is two hundred kilos. It's amazing what the NPCs are willing to do in order to become even minions."

"We? So you're also a player?"

"Emm... So I've fulfilled my part of the agreement; I sold you the vials; you've received the information on recipes and everything I have for sale here. Thanks for visiting my store." The trader suddenly began bustling about. "Once you get more granises, come again. The portal lets through only players who have granises. See you soon!"

Before I had a chance to say anything in response, the cave faded and threw me out back to the Academy. Annoyed, I kicked the former portal which had now turned into an ordinary stone. At some point I'd have to learn to keep my mouth shut if I wanted to receive information. Maybe there're some courses for that? For example, "Special skills: fishing for information" or "Interrogation: Theory and Practice". I'd need something to help me understand what was going on a little better.

Actually!

The thought that appeared was so unusual for me – for what I used to be – that I almost forgot to touch a guiding line. Only when the nearby boulder moved it reminded me that I was surrounded by a dangerous forest full of monsters. One of the teachers had called me a follower of Darkness, telling me with regret that some "Light" was closed for me. If so, why was I behaving like a follower of the Light? I needed information and I knew a rather effective method for obtaining it; I just needed to receive my ability for defense. That's what I needed to do right away!

"Welcome, recruit, I will be training you. Now harken to my wisdom!"

Learning progress: You have reached teacher 5 of 10

With the defense abilities everything was even simpler than with the attack ones. Only one defense was taught in the Academy; it was charmingly called "Energy armor". The ability required 20 Energy for activation and 1 Energy unit per minute to maintain it. Not really a cheap deal for those who had no elixirs or food. It was simple to upgrade the defense as well: you needed to activate and maintain the armor for 5 minutes; then the Game added +1 to its use. Over the free six months of training that I spent in the test range I was able to reduce the activation cost to 18 Energy and increase "Armor resistance" from 15 to 16 percent. That was all I was able to achieve; nor was I successful in getting the teacher to talk. Either the teachers communicated with each other, or I ran into a particularly reserved and withdrawn representative of the profession, but he would say nothing beyond the standard phrases. Could it be a feature specific to hidden teachers? Talking less and doing more?

In any case, I decided to implement the plan I had developed during the half a year of training. I needed information and I was going to get it.

"Paladin!" A player shouted as soon as I stepped out into the clearing with the teacher. In my sector there were two more teachers available in the open, and one hidden teacher; by now I'd abandoned all hope of finding the latter. However, I was not going to neglect the training: I needed to be prepared before arriving at the Labyrinth, whatever that was. I looked over the clearing, spotted the mages among other players there, and slowly, inexorably like fate, moved towards them. My knees were shaking, my chest was tight with fear, my hands were trembling, but I clenched my teeth, made a poker face and walked on, holding my head high. I needed to test everything I learned, and the only way I could see for it was a good fight with the players.

"Stop right there," the mage ordered, but seeing that his words had no effect he screamed hysterically: "Kill him!"

"I am the Templar's blow"! I answered, dealing a straight blow to the warrior who rushed at me. The player was one of those select few who'd chosen a weapon for an artifact, so I didn't bother dodging his blow, taking it on my energy armor. I understood very well all the risks I was taking – whatever protection I had it would not have withstood a simultaneous hit from a hundred players. That's why I chose the furthest clearing from the attack abilities teacher. The number of players capable of enhanced attack should be minimal here.

Silence fell over the clearing when the warrior who attacked me dissolved in the air like fog in the gust of wind. Enhanced hit on the head proved fatal for the player while he in turn only took 1 Energy unit off of me. That's what it took to block the sword. What saddened me most was the amount of experience received: a mere 10 points. Apparently, the player who attacked me had been at level 1, and if he hadn't been initiated that mean that I had just completely killed a living being. What did I feel? Regret? Sadness? Remorse? Phh! The warrior knew what he was getting into trying to stuff me with steel, so it was his own fault. I am the truth!

There were no volunteers among the rest of the players to repeat the feat; practically immediately a wide path formed between me and the mages. A few more arrows hit on my shield, but they petered out fairly soon: the players made a collective decision to give me to the four mages. If they needed a Paladin, they'd have to take him themselves.

"Die, you bastard!" The leader of the local mages shouted with such hatred it sounded as if I'd killed all his kin, having maimed and raped them first. Four lightning bolts hissed off the mages hands, and impotently licked my protective shell. The A-hour had struck; that was the moment I feared the most; however, the reality proved not so terrifying. 10 Energy for each lightning, and neither of them was able to penetrate my "Enhanced defense". I allowed the mages to strike again, then took another Energy elixir and, finally, rushed toward the mages. Now it was my turn to attack.

"I am the Templar's blow"!

Six months of training and destroying the trees hadn't been in vain: I needed to use my attack ability only once. The mages didn't have an active defense, so my precise blows of the spiked knuckleduster reduced their heads to a bloody pulp: the mages had no skills for close combat. The physiology of players and NPCs were the same, and the appearance of a piece of steel inside the brain never made anyone better off. One after another my opponents dissipated, sent to respawn; however, my plans were a bit more extensive than a simple massacre. Dolgunata had taught me that in the game it was possible not only to be killed but also to be knocked out. So I used my spikes to crush both legs of the local mage leader so that he wouldn't run off. Then I took off my artifact and socked him one in the eye to put the guy to sleep.

"Bleagh!" I whirled sharply, hearing an unfamiliar sound. The statues, pale as sheets, that used to be players, froze in righteous terror from the sight. Some particularly impressionable ones who hadn't expected such a bloody payback were retching where they stood. However, no one hurried to help the mage sprawled in the middle of a bloody puddle. My opponents had leaked a fair amount of blood, but I took it in stride. They had wanted to kill me. I killed them as I fought back. I would never have thought that I could be so bloodthirsty and untouched by the pain of others. Perhaps the world, after all, managed to kill the naïve and humane Yaropolk, who had come to the Academy wanting to conquer the world, and it would take me a long time now figuring out who had appeared in his place.

"Any more volunteers to stop me from training?" I growled, addressing the "statues". There was silence. Recruits who'd become players just a few days ago were still not used to the realities of the

Game. Not everyone had had a chance to think all the events through. It took me a year, so now I looked a lot more mature than the rest of the present company. "Guys, work on your own development! Stop listening to the mages! If you don't train with the teachers, you'll simply croak without reaching the next level!"

The statues revived and startled to grumble something in response, but I wasn't listening to them. Grabbing the mage who was still unconscious I dragged him towards the teacher. Before I worked on obtaining information I still needed to train.

Welcome, recruit, I am going to teach you your specialty presently. Now harken to my wisdom!

Learning progress: You have reached teacher 6 of 10

You have already completed specialty training; this teacher does not count

Learning progress: You have reached teacher 5 of 10

"Why do you need the mage, recruit?" the teacher asked as soon as the space around us turned into the training range.

"He's my source of knowledge," I scowled bloodthirstily. "I never had a chance for decent training prior to the Academy; this gap needs to be filled. The recruit I selected is quite suitable for this."

"I don't like what you're planning to do with him," the old man sighed. By inflicting pain on someone you consciously drive yourself into

Darkness."

"Darkness. Light. Aren't those two names for the same thing?" I wasn't going to give up. "What is meant by 'allegiance to Light'? What is meant by 'allegiance to Darkness'? Following some rules and traditions? But they don't exist!"

"You're mistaken!" my musings had affected the old man. "The Game defines clearly what is Light and what is Darkness! What the Light ones can do and what the Dark ones can do! I'd like you to know that ever would a single Dark one be able to enter the gate of Vargolag! A unicorn would never accept a Dark one – never!! Never will a single Dark one touch the hand of the great Iurm!"

"You have some problems with the Dark ones?" I guessed after hearing 'never' a few times too many.

"Dark ones killed all my kin!" The old man tried to retain control, but it was obvious that he was shaking with rage. "They shouldn't exist!"

"You still never told me what's the difference between Light and Darkness!" I wasn't going to surrender. Just because the old guy had trouble communicating with the Dark ones didn't mean that it was a bad path. It was simply different.

"My duty is to teach you a specialty, Paladin." The teacher seemed to have regained self-control and turned into a block of ice. "If you want to find out about the difference between the Light and Dark development paths, talk to the Chancellor. He'd be glad to reduce you to dust, Dark one!"

There was a pause. The old man was standing with his head raised high, showing with his entire appearance that there was no way I could extract from him any additional information I needed so much. All that was left to me was to sigh heavily and say, suppressing my pride:

"I've got nothing else to do here ..."

Having come back to the Academy, and seeing that the players in the clearing still hadn't regained their composure, I dragged the unconscious mage further into the forest. I needed to justify being called "Dark"...

"Noooo!" the mage's wild scream could probably have been heard throughout the entire sector. He was trying to crawl away, but his broken arms and legs prevented him. It was funny: his emotions didn't affect me! There was a half-maimed living being lying right in front of me, and all that concerned me was when the mage was finally going to talk! I perceived the torture not as something outstanding, but rather like a normal game process. Once I killed the mage (and there was no doubt that I'd kill him), he would respawn safe and sound again. What I had been able to find out from him by now was his level: level three.

"Arius, do understand: you have no choice," I repeated one more time. "Until you tell me everything I want to know, I won't let you go."

"Go to hell, you!" The mage had blurted out, overcoming the pain and attempting to attack me with lightning yet again. But not so easy! Knowing very well that the player could have used the key phrase several times, draining his own Energy and going for respawn, I had broken both his arms. And legs, just in case. Moreover, I had done it so carefully that even though he didn't have a single unbroken bone, Arius did not bleed to death: the artifact allowed me to retract the spikes. Besides, after some training sessions I had learned to extend them at will, instantly or slowly. Certainly, that did not add any pleasant sensations to my subject: no one would enjoy sharp three-inch spikes piercing his flesh slowly and inexorably like an approaching train, ignoring any obstacles.

"Oh well, to hell with hell," I sighed, extending the spikes to pierce the mage's shoulder. It was horrible even to imagine what this player must feel right now; personally, I wouldn't have been able to hold on for so long. To prevent the mage from escaping, I periodically applied some ointment to the pierced area to stop him from bleeding. That was an expensive method, but I saw no other choice — I needed information! Another scream of pain echoed through the forest and the mage fainted. He was lucky this time.

"Enjoying yourself?" Dolgunata's appearance was so unexpected that my heart jumped in my chest. I constantly monitored the Paladins' movement on the map, but couldn't see the druid's location. I had supposed she was with them and had forgotten that the panther could use her speed to outrun the guards. Apparently, I'd have to pay for being careless. "Decided to take your anger out on this poor soul?"

"This 'poor soul' was trying to kill me," I shot back, jumping to my feet and activating my protection. The druid should've killed me outright: she might not get another chance. "Now it's time for payback."

"You could've just killed him. Why all this bother?"

"I need information. He refuses to talk, so I have to extract it. Did you want something?"

"You owe me," the druid started her same old song.

"It's too late, beautiful. I've visited the trader. Shall we dance?"

"How did you...", Dolgunata tensed, but a moment later shifted from a panther into a person. "Listen, I'm fed up playing those games. Let's talk?"

"Oh, we've graduated to an urge to talk," I quipped, extending the artifact spikes and extracting an Energy elixir from the inventory. Dolgunata is not a mage — you have to be careful with her. "Don't you think it's too late?"

"It's never too late to talk," the druid returned, sighed, and then blurted out, practically gluing me to the spot: "For the past seven years I've been Archibald's personal student. He sent me with this particular group of recruits so that I could help you graduate from the Academy. Whatever you did affected him; he even broke the rules casting a complete stun on you. I think that's the reason you can see the guiding line. Teart also was hit with a full mental block before he reached the Academy. In this way you're similar and, I think, that's why both of you can see the way. There's no other way to explain it. Archibald gave me clear instructions: to provoke you constantly, thus making you develop. He considers that's the only way you'll survive. You should agree:

he was right and I was able to needle you above and beyond normal. You've covered practically all the teachers within the sector; the next quest is the Labyrinth. It's impossible to complete it alone. I propose that we cooperate until the end of the Academy. I need to complete my teacher's assignment; you and the Paladins need to survive. I lost my head when you... touched me, and so sent you to respawn. I had to tell everything to the team, hoping that I wouldn't have to tell you anything. I supposed that you'd be scared of death and would start playing nice. It's my mistake: I'm ready to accept punishment, but only after we return. What do you say to that?"

"Why didn't you explain everything from the start?" I frowned. I had never expected any help from the catorian; so Dolgunata's story was that much more surprising.

"It's Archibald's condition. If I had been able to help you pass through the Academy without telling you anything about myself, my reward would've been a lot higher than what I can count on at this stage. That was the reason why I didn't want to enter into any agreements with you until now. I could've betrayed myself in some way.

"So in addition to all of that you get a reward?"

"Naturally."

"Why did you decide to be so frank now?"

"Because the mages have figured out how to fight Monstrichello. The Paladins barely got out alive from the last teacher. Alone they won't make it to the Labyrinth."

"Why, all of a sudden, such affection for our class?"

"Have you read Saint-Exupéry? I do agree with what the Fox said about those things."

"You become responsible forever for what you've tamed..." I drawled, but immediately it dawned on me: "How much were you promised for each Paladin?"

"A granis per non-initiated head," Dolgunata responded defiantly. "You protest against your brethren surviving?"

"Far from it. I support that entirely. After the next teacher I was going to rid them of you, supposing that you had taken them under your control again. But you didn't – right?"

"After I was sent to respawn I didn't use my abilities on Paladins – I swear by the Game!" Dolgunata said and for a few seconds a light glow shimmered around her. The druid was telling the truth.

" ..."

"It's simpler than trying to prove something to you," she said in response to my silent question. "You never said... shall we continue together?"

"No!" I answered after thinking a while. "Our paths part from now on."

"WHAT?!" Dolgunata was astonished to the extent of being unable to hide her emotions.

"What you heard. I now know how much a granis is worth, so I realize that you're vitally interested in making sure that Teart, Refor and Dirion graduate from the Academy. There's no point in taking them away from you. It's your problem now. Logir, Sartal and Monster are already initiated, so they aren't in danger. So they'll kick the bucket a couple of times: big deal... They are no one to me. So you say the mages figured out a way to fight the tank? I've been down there and seen the mages fight. They can't put up a good fight against you. Take the Paladins around to the remaining teachers, make sure they get the training. I'll give you the location of another hidden one – make sure everyone learns defense, I don't need to tell you how important this is. That'll help you survive. But we'll go down different roads. You can report to Archibald that you didn't just fulfill your task, but have overdone it: now I don't believe anyone. Did you really think I'd trust a creature who wanted to frame my entire team, and who killed me twice? That I'd trust you just because of a connection to Archibald – a freak, whose tail I look forward to breaking as soon as I get out of the Academy?"

I told Dolgunata the hidden teacher's coordinates; after that we stared daggers at each other for about a minute. Neither I nor Nata wanted to look down first, like two teenagers fighting to establish who's tougher. Finally, the druid gave up, dropping her gaze, but only to immediately look at me, not with the eyes of a teenage girl, but an experienced and cunning woman. The change was so drastic that for a moment I was taken aback.

"The boy has grown up. The boy has become a man," Dolgunata drawled in such a languid voice that I felt as if everything inside me was melting, and my libido hit the stratosphere. She was trying to control me again! What a bitch!

"Stop that!" I growled with the remains of my sense, trying to push Nata out of my head. It seemed like I was starting to succeed when the druid used her trump card: suddenly moving very close to me...

"Stop what?"

"I am ...." I had no other choice but to kill Dolgunata. The druid was dangerous. But for some reason my thoughts were moving so slowly that I only managed to push out two words before Nata practically finished me off:

"Stop this?"

The druid's green dress opened, revealing the girl's perfect form. My world toppled, and all my troubles floated away. How could a being so perfect be evil? Had I really wanted to hit her just a moment ago? That was unforgivable of me! I was saddened to note that she had underwear on that concealed the beauty's breasts. Size B, my favorite. Not huge tits like a cow's and not little lumps like those of flat-chested skinny girls. This breast would fit in my hand just right, allowing me to enjoy its tenderness and sweet softness and ...

"You're weak and helpless, Paladin," Dolgunata whispered, bending down to my face. I jerked forward, trying to kiss the goddess who had descended to me from the sky, but she easily moved back, not allowing to touch her velvet lips. "You'd never compare to my teacher! Learn, risk the Labyrinth on your own; once you understand that you are just a no-name nobody, I might agree to help. But I warn you outright: if you want me to help you'd have to crawl to me on your knees! I opened to you, offered you a helping hand, but you pushed me away. Too bad for you. Until we meet again, Paladin. I don't know what the teacher saw in you..."

You were killed and sent to a respawn point
You lost one level
Your current level: 4

"Paladin!" The players scream, to which I was becoming accustomed, informed me that I was at the respawn point again. "Catch him!"

"I am the Templar's blow"!

I was using up Energy elixirs at the express rate. The players were trying to get to me from all sides, but unlike the last time, I wasn't attempting to run away. On the contrary, I openly rejoiced at being in the center of a huge crowd of players wanting to kill me. At the previous site it was enough for me to kill a warrior and the players had parted, letting me pass; but here, at the respawn point, no one was in the mood to retreat. In my current state I actually needed that, since I needed to vent my emotions on someone. Dolgunata had yet again shown me my place, demonstrating that even six months of leveling up my defenses was no guarantee of safety. She'd made me lose my concentration, and then the protective shell had dissipated as if it had never been there. So the local players were out of luck: I was angry.

"Regroup!" I heard Dangard's order and for a few moments I was left alone. Another empty vial was set on the shelf and I turned towards the mages. Socking in the face the rogue who rushed towards me, I moved on, fatal like an avalanche, towards the leader of the "Say no to Paladins" movement. Instead of catching me by my arms and legs, pressing me to the ground and finishing me off, so I wouldn't be able to get up, the players were trying to be the first to hit me, getting in each other's way and enabling me to collect my bloody harvest. Just five minutes of this melee not only restored my level 5, but actually brought me up to level 7. I looked at the mages who clustered together, and immediately a funny plan occurred to me, as brilliant as it was original. There was nothing left for me other than to start implementing it immediately.

"Hi! Shall we talk?" I said, stopping within just a few steps of the mages. One half of me wanted to tear and crush everything within reach, but the other half, including my consciousness, stifled that urge, and worked on extracting maximum advantage from the current situation. Information! I needed information, and Dangard was the only player who possessed it. The Book of Knowledge, working like a live video relay, showed me that a crowd of fifteen players gathered around my back, but was in no rush to attack. The players still couldn't figure out how it was possible that an ordinary Paladin, not even armed with a sword, had been able to send to respawn over fifty bodies while not sustaining any visible damage. If they'd only known that this battle had cost me half of my store of elixirs, they probably wouldn't have stopped …

"Let's talk," to my surprise, Dangard turned out to be quite a sensible player, who adequately saw his chances for victory. At this point he saw none, so he was trying to stall for time: the runners must have already gone off to the neighboring clearings; soon reinforcements would arrive. "Did you find a hidden teacher somewhere and learned defense?"

"It wasn't only that," I saw no reason to hide the obvious along with the fact that I was still holding an elixir in my hand. The teacher was right: at the initial level the defense really did make a player invincible. I needed to use this fact to the max.

"I see. But sooner or later you'll run out of elixirs – you understand that, right?"

"Right."

"And you understand that we have no choice: either we destroy you, or Devir will destroy all of us."

"I know that as well."

"In that case I don't understand what we could talk about."

I need information about the Academy. What, where, how and why. You have it. The point of my offer is simple: you share information with me, I stop hunting you and let you through to the Labyrinth at a level higher than one. Otherwise I'll just trap you all here and will keep you here until the majority are dead. You are the only initiated mage in our sector, right? I'll make it so that you'll have to keep going by your lonesome. I don't care what Devir will do to you later – I care what I'll do to you now!"

"I am the Templar's blow"!

It would've been pointless waiting for a

response. The mages weren't ready for this dialogue now. Dangard's pose, expressions and body language indicated that he wasn't taking my threats seriously; so I did what the druid had taught me: attacked first. The mages were sent to respawn without even as much as throwing a lightning at me; or it was possible that by then they didn't have enough Energy to do it. Seven blows, seven slowly disappearing corpses.

"Everyone's free to go!" I turned towards the remaining players. They never dared attack me, deciding to wait for the outcome of the showdown between Dangard and myself. I checked the map and pointed towards the center of the Academy: "The Labyrinth is there! The longer you are cooling your heels here the less time you have. Or does someone have a secret wish to get back at me? I'll count to ten and then kill everyone who remains in the clearing. One. Two..."

There were no stupid ones, and for a while I was completely alone. Amazing, but Dolgunata had been able to wake in me something that I hadn't even known was there. Anger. Thirst for killing. The impulse to crush and stomp. During the hour several groups of mages ran into the respawn clearing and I sent them to take a rest and respawn without much ado. . I had only forty two vials of elixir left, but I wasn't going to give up and abandon my plan. I needed information!

Taking a position close to the point where players appeared, I extended the spikes to their maximum length and started training on precise hits to the head. Players appeared one after another; yet during the first three hours I decided not to bother sorting them, simply sending everyone to respawn. My actions were the same as the genocide started by the mages; the Chancellor would certainly not like that, but at this point I didn't care anymore. Light is not my thing.

"I agree, damn you!" Dangard yelled, appearing in the Academy after the third respawn in a row. During the three hours of non-stop fighting I had managed to reach level 10, and was starting to seriously contemplate totally wiping out all the one hundred and twenty seven players who were caught in the respawn mill. I let no one escape – neither the mages, nor other class players who were caught in this crush accidentally. Everyone got it bad.

"You'll get the information! Stop this!"

"You forgot to add that until the end of the Labyrinth the mages and your local minions will forget about the Paladins."

"Fine. Game is the witness — we won't touch the Paladins until the wastelands!" Amazing, but Dangard had broken down too fast. Either his level had dropped too low and he realized that dropping it further meant major problems, or he completely hadn't expected such cruelty from a non-initiated player. By all accounts I should've run off to a dark corner and sat there trying not to attract attention, but I didn't like playing according to the pre-established standards any more. I stepped aside, allowing the next mage to appear, and looking at Dangard all the while. He was supposed to signal that there was no need to attack me, that we'd reached an agreement.

There was no attack.

"What do you want to know?" It took Dangard about ten minutes to recover and collect his thoughts. During that time most of the players respawned and decided that the respawn point wasn't the best place to hang around. Only the mages stayed at the clearing; they couldn't figure out what had happened and why their leader was suddenly talking with their main intended victim.

"Everything you know about the Academy. Teachers, hidden teachers, traders, tricksters, crapsters, completing the Labyrinth... I need exhaustive information."

"I'll figure out a way to get through your defenses," Dangard growled with hatred, looking me straight in the eye. For a moment I felt a weak urge to take off my armor and embrace my brother, who by some fluke had turned out to be a mage, but I only grinned, and the temptation passed at once. Compared to Dolgunata, Dangard was nowhere close to being able to control other players well. Had the druid's influence on us been at the same level, perhaps I would still be among the Paladins. By the way, by now they must have made it rather far from the territory discovered by me. They must be approaching the mysterious Labyrinth.

"The Academy is divided into four large sectors," Dangard started, as he realized that the attempt to take me under control had failed. "Each of the sectors ..."

Listening to Dangard, I clenched my fists in

impotent rage, understanding that I had simply missed out on a certain part of training in the Academy. Why were there hidden teachers in the Academy? They didn't teach you anything special, just enabled you to select the sequence of training, and in essence didn't affect your return to the main world? Dangard explained what my mistake was: if one were to refuse the training and offered wisdom, the teacher wouldn't count. Instead the recruit would receive additional information on the current Labyrinth setup and the key to one of the tests that had to be passed there. The Labyrinth was the only part that always changed from one batch of students to another, and so it was impossible to prepare for it outside the Academy, only inside it. In addition, it was set up in such a tricky way that refusing to train would make the process of passing through the Labyrinth much easier: if you were to find all the hidden teachers in the sector and refuse to train with them, you could collect three keys from the four tests. And the final nail in the coffin of my hopes was the caveat that only one recruit in each team was able to use the keys; he could take up to ten players with him. So, if two players on the same team were to turn down the training, only one of them would be able to deactivate the test; all the other group members' keys would be destroyed. Now it became clear what Dolgunata had meant by saying that she knew how to complete part of the Labyrinth. She had become a key master! I was unable to hold back a curse: in a bout of kindness and desire to save my "brothers" in class I had presented to Dolgunata the location of the second hidden teacher! Now half of the Labyrinth would be practically easy as pie for her! Where was Dangard a couple of hours ago?!

The mage didn't have much information regarding the wastelands, only a generic notion: the wasteland inhabitants were divided into Light and Dark ones, diligently killing the opposite factions. The point of completion was that one had to choose one's side while in the Labyrinth, and use assistance from allies in the wastelands. Dangard did not refuse to explain what was Light and Darkness; he just didn't have a lot of information about it himself. Everything turned out both simple and complicated at the same time. First of all, all players in the Academy were supposed to form an allegiance with their "hue"; there was no place for neutral ones. If a player were unable to take a side, the Game would wipe him out. Once the recruit returned to the main world, the top scale disappeared and the selected side would be the player's side to the end. What was the effect of this, Dangard didn't know. He knew one thing only: it was important to be "Light", for Devir wouldn't teach the "Dark" ones, even though he wouldn't kill them either. I looked at my scale and frowned: the arrow rested almost halfway down the dark die. If I were to continue with my atrocities, it would reach the end, and then I'd receive the first level of Darkness. Like everything else in the Game, players' allegiance leveled up as well. What benefits that would give me, or from what it would protect me, nobody knew.

Book of Knowledge reached a new level. You

need to increase the level of the artifact properties: "Context search" (1), "Weapon"(1), <Choose value from the list >

After I was alone again I decided against testing fate, and returned to the forest. While working on the available properties I'd become vulnerable. Agreement is one thing, but someone among the players might decide that it wasn't made with him personally, and send me for a spin. So I climbed up, made sure the Paladins were still as far off as before, and opened the list of the available artifact properties. Improving the Book of Knowledge or attack capabilities seemed excessive to me at the moment. The battle with the players had demonstrated what I was lacking. I had issues with availability of free Energy; before investing in something I needed to make sure that issue was resolved.

CHAPTER SEVEN

PARTNER

I APPROACHED the last of the generally available teachers in the reinforced concrete forest with a clear understanding of what I wanted from this life and from the Game specifically. I'd spent about three hours working to figure out the artifact properties and selecting the ones most suitable for the current situation and future game; at the same time I contemplated the strategy of my further actions. I even tried to gain access to the Temple of Knowledge a few times, but to no avail: the Game must have considered that my need for new knowledge wasn't vital. So I had to study the list on my own, and in the end selected the three properties the description and use of which seemed the most understandable: "Acceleration", "Protection" and "Thoroughness".

"Acceleration" reduced the cooldown time for all abilities and increased the rate of Energy restore. It was a somewhat marginal quality for now, given that Energy doesn't replenish within the Academy, but given the inevitable return to the main world that quality looked quite advantageous. The only thing that concerned me was a rather narrow applicability of this property: it would be useful only to fighters and defenders, but not, really, for a world explorer.

"Protection" enhanced "Armor resistance" and reduced the amount of Energy needed to block a blow; that would be extremely useful both within the Academy and beyond. In time the other players' probability of dealing a critical hit would increase, and I needed to be ready for that. The drawbacks of this quality were that it did not affect Energy at all and required a continuously activated energy shield.

"Thoroughness" reduced the amount of Energy drawn by the use of all abilities by a certain value; it was also useful to players who had chosen a creative path by mysteriously lowering the rate of "low quality results". Given that I'd been unable to discover any properties that directly increased the level of Energy, this one would have to do.

As before, the description of each property was only available to level 15, so, having thought out all the pros and cons, I decided on "Protection". Here in the forest I was a tough and hard to kill player. But by the wastelands the mages would have studied defense and it wouldn't be beer and skittles any more for me. I needed to protect myself.

"Welcome, recruit, I will tell you about the

basics of the Game. Harken to my wisdom!"

Learning progress: You have reached teacher 6 of 10

"How interesting, a practically darkened recruit!" The teacher said with surprise as soon as the world around us turned into a training range. "That's rare for the initial stage of training!"

"Would you stop pointing that out to me already?!" I lost my temper. "Would someone finally explain to me what's the difference between Light and Darkness?!"

"You need to revise your behavior; a Judge shouldn't be so emotional," the old man said coldly. "What's good for a berserk isn't acceptable for others. Especially for you."

"I lost my temper, I admit," I agreed. "But I am so often reproached about Darkness without any explanation that I couldn't contain myself any longer."

"You broke down, that's a fact," the teacher confirmed. "But it didn't happen just now. The emotional breakdown started immediately after respawn; you still can't come to your senses. Explain: why did you need that massacre? You could have easily avoided it and preserved a huge stock of elixirs."

"I needed the levels."

"Do you even believe that yourself? You killed seven players to the final death and brought another twenty recruits to level one. Was that worth your levels?"

"Yes," I had no doubt that I was right. "I was not the first to unbury the hatchet of war, so it's not up to me to bury it. They wanted to kill me – I fought back. So you say I killed someone? That means there was no place for them in the Game!"

"Stop!" The teacher said suddenly. "Record your current emotions. Describe them! What do you feel?"

"Indignation," I decided to follow the teacher's advice and listen to the emotions roiling in my chest. "Yearning for justice. Desire to set things in order and eliminate injustice."

"Actually, that's why you turned Dark," the old man smiled. "Judges are rarely Light anyway."

"I still don't understand anything," I honestly confessed to the teacher.

"In the Game the difference between Light and Darkness is minimal, strange as it may sound. The difference is in how the player replenishes his Energy. What is Darkness? It is absence of Light. What is Light? It is radiance from any source. Actually, that's the difference. Light makes it possible to replenish Energy using external sources: holy relics, artifacts, symbols of faith and other similar objects. Darkness replenishes Energy directly from the surrounding world, pulling it out of emotions and everything that is not a material object. You have to remember: as soon as Light appears, Darkness disappears; that's why an ordinary Dark one cannot enter the places that you are used to calling churches: for the majority of dark players the amount of Energy spent is equal to the amount of Energy received; so if you take away the source, it will result in practically instant respawn or death. The same thing is true with respect to the sources themselves. For example, the closer you place a Christian cross to a witch, the weaker she becomes, up to dying. As you understand, both Light and Dark players can be good or evil; the difference is just in the way they restore Energy.

"Then why do they loath each other so?" I answered in surprise. "If the difference is so insignificant?"

"You weren't listening carefully. The Light ones replenish Energy from physical sources, and the Dark ones from emotions. But what do you do if in the environment around you there aren't enough emotions?"

"Take an elixir."

"That's an option, but we'll discuss that later. Suppose you have no elixirs. What would you do?"

"I'd need to generate emotions," I guessed.

"That's right! Do I need to explain further or will you guess yourself why the Dark ones aren't well liked?"

"Generating emotions...," I was rolling the thought around in my brain until a sudden epiphany froze me to the spot. "Torture. Inflicting pain. Killing their kin..."

"Artifacts of many Dark players have an "Accumulator" property which enables them to store additional Energy," the teacher continued sadly, picking up at the point where my thought trailed off. "No need to frown; this property is not available in the Academy. It's much simpler to fill the surrounding space with emotions of pain and despair than with joy and happiness. Questing for Energy, some Dark ones don't care about NPCs, minions or even other players, sometimes destroying entire game worlds just to top their 'storage battery'."

"You are speaking with such regret as if you're also a Dark one and those examples are not to your liking."

"I am the only teacher in the Academy who has the right to show his true face. You're right — I am also Dark, just as you. I'm known under different names: Father Frost, Santa Claus, Joulupukki and hundreds of other names. The overall point is to bring emotions to the worlds. Positive emotions. This is how I can save my Dark brothers to some extent and prevent them from turning into animals who are only capable of inflicting torture."

Yet another layer of the Game was revealed to me. While I was an NPC I always wondered why most of the religions call on their flocks to be modest, peaceful, obedient, following the traditions and certain dogmas. It's because a crowd of like-minded people have no emotions! They would, like robots, follow the instructions without generating Energy! And since there's no Energy, the Dark ones would feel uncomfortable. They would either turn into various "Vlad the Impaler" types, or simply leave the uncomfortable game world forever. That's why one of the teachers mentioned that I wouldn't feel comfortable on Earth: it's inundated with the Light ones!

"Wait... it's clear about the Dark ones, but

where do the sources of Light receive their energy? If they continuously dispense Energy, then sooner or later they must dissipate."

"Or recharge," the teacher smiled. "That's exactly the point the Light ones very much dislike to discuss. Sources of Light recharge all the time by drawing Energy from those very same emotions. Only the Light ones use different words for that: Inquisition, crusade, jihad, prayer, voluntary attainment of nirvana. The Light ones came up with a million ways to replenish the sources of Light, covering cruelty with pretty words. This is, in fact, the full answer to your previous question as to why there's a war between the Light and Dark ones. Simply because it's a war for Energy sources! The Light ones have learned to gather it from the living, and the Dark ones, most of the time, are used to simply killing everyone. Conflict of interest – it's elementary. Besides, we shouldn't forget that it's the Light ones who make the elixirs!"

"What does this have to do with anything?"

"Think. Now you know the nature of Energy replenishment for both Dark and Light players. So why do the elixirs work for both?"

"Because it contains both a source and emotions," I stated the obvious, but from the teacher's look it became clear that it was just the beginning of the train of thought. "So the elixir is made from something wondrous, which has both a physical body and an emotional one... Wait... It's..."

"The only ones who have both are living creatures." The teacher confirmed my guess. "Sentient living creatures. NPCs. The exchange rate is quite democratic: one elixir takes one NPC, who is processed in his entirety. As I mentioned, the Light ones have a monopoly on that; in the process they also recharge their sources. Since the NPCs are going to die anyway, why let them do it quickly and painlessly? They can be useful instead."

"But that's horrible!" I said, stunned.

"It's the Game." The old man shrugged his shoulders. "You weren't concerned about killing mobs in computer games? Imagine that you're playing using full virtual reality immersion."

"But why am I turning Dark?" I whispered, impressed by what I had just heard.

"Finally you become interested in what's happening to you personally! Remember what I asked you in the very beginning: what you felt as you were killing other recruits. You didn't say "regret", "conscience", "guilt". You named "indignation", "yearning for justice", "desire to set things in order". That's where the answer lies. First of all, you needed to become Dark. You did that by killing the elf. You were fully aware of your actions, rejecting the "Thou shalt not kill" that had been drilled into you since childhood. A murder was accomplished on your instructions; however, your subconscious, shaped by your upbringing, realized that this was Evil. Actually, that's how the allegiance is chosen in the Academy: the attitude of the subconscious towards the actions you commit. This cannot be changed. After that it becomes simpler: you committed actions your subconsciousness perceived as "bad" while your mind was telling you that it was "right". Each discrepancy like this shifts the scale further and will continue to do so – you aren't planning to give up killing, right?"

"So if someone has been told since childhood that killing is good, he'll become Light? And with each killing will accumulate more and more Light?"

"You're getting the idea. Yes. And another thing I need to tell you: the Light ones have one clear advantage: if they have a source, it's hard to kill them. While the Dark ones can be unsettled if you throw a source of Light at them. Keep this in mind and be careful. If you have no more questions about allegiance, I'll tell you now about other special features of the Game."

"Wait. I have two questions. The first one is: is it possible to level up the allegiance? In other words, does it have its own levels? Second: why would the Chancellor kill a Dark player?"

"You already know the answer to the first one: just as with any other phenomenon in the Game, allegiance has its own levels. It's unlikely that you'd receive the first one while still in the Academy, but should this happen you'd be able to use the feature of Dark players: absorb emotions from your surroundings to replenish your Energy. As for the second question: our Chancellor is a unique being, I wouldn't state it with any degree of certainty. Maybe he will and maybe he won't, it would all depend on his mood at that particular moment. But in general, well, he isn't particularly fond of the Dark ones. There's more Light than Dark in him by now."

"What's unique about him?"

"He is a Dark vampire." The teacher though for a very long time before answering. "Constant struggle of Light and Darkness can drive one mad, so the Viceroy shut him in the Academy forever. The Chancellor cannot leave it."

"Emm... But aren't vampires Dar... Blood! Vampires have a source of energy: it's blood! They are Light by default!" Today was the day for revelations. "But wait: how did he become Dark?"

"It's the upbringing," the teacher grinned. "It's all in the upbringing. By the way, I'm looking at your logs... Don't worry, that's an option only available to teachers, and then only in the Academy... You could have become a vampire. With your attitude to killing things you would've become one more Chancellor and would have been unlikely to survive after the Academy. The Game doesn't need freaks. If that's all you have, let me complete your training. I still have a lot to tell you..."

Book of Knowledge has reached a new level. You need to increase the level of the artifact properties: "Context search" (1), "Weapon" (1), "Protection" (1) <Choose value from the list>

"Those who select the path of knowledge have certain advantages," the teacher smiled when at the same time as the upgrade message appeared for the Book of Knowledge I was returned to the Academy. "Good luck in the Game, Dark one, and remember: a Judge should not yield to emotions! Dark players cannot use their own emotions, so why feed a potential enemy?"

I fully agreed with the teacher's statement; I increased "Protection" by another point and looked glumly at the players crowding around me. There were a few mages among them. No one was in a hurry to attack: Dangard's order had already been made known at all the locations. I walked straight through the crowd of players, keeping my face carefully blank. I had some unfinished business in the forest, and nobody present could interfere with that. Why should I jump from stone to stone like a monkey? There would be time to do that later.

Two years of training, a year each at the ranges for attack and defense abilities, brought my stock of elixirs down to 38; however, the result of voluntary solitude was worth it. I was able not only to enhance my attack and defense; I was able to organize all the knowledge I received from the trader, Dangard and the teacher. I was also able to finalize my attitude towards the Game and my place within it. What had guided me before? Emotions, impulses, desires, standards of conduct, wishes of the group – completely not thinking about the most important thing: what will the benefit be to me personally? Players enter and leave the Game alone, so first and foremost one needs to think about one's precious self. Which is something I had not been doing at all previously. As an example, the story with Dolgunata kept coming to mind: I gave her the location of the hidden teacher, and what I received in exchange was respawn. This kind of thing should not be repeated. As for the druid herself, I could not touch her within the Academy. She should lead the Paladins through. I was not thinking from the standpoint of love for the class, but rather from the standpoint that Sharda wouldn't let me in the Citadel's library if he should learn that I hadn't helped my "brothers". The gnome did have some kind of hang-up about that. However, letting Nata off the hook completely wouldn't do either: if I were to indulge in such folly as forgiveness, I'd stop respecting myself. The druid had to be punished; the only question was: in what way? During the training I'd been unable to come up with a clear answer. Only one thing was certain: I was in for a good fight with the panther, so I trained thoroughly not only in my abilities but also in agility, training my body, which was not at all used to physical strain. The funny part was that the emotional toll of the first six months of the first bout of training was much harder than now. At that time I had no goal or understanding of what I was doing. While now I knew very clearly why I was mutilating the trees or repeating rolls and push-ups. The Game doesn't like the weak. If I wanted to survive I'd have to tear at each and everyone with my teeth... After all, I wasn't Dark for nothing...

"Come on sweet, show up already!" I whispered, holding my hand above the guiding line. Following the training I didn't immediately rush to the Labyrinth, as might have been expected; rather, I decided to test the skills I had acquired in real combat. The recruits now served as cannon fodder for me; they weren't fit for fighting back and so there was no way to test my strength and defense ability with them. But I knew who would be a worthy opponent for me: forest guards. The fact that it was possible to run away from them meant they were relatively slow. If that was true, why not attempt to fight one of them? At worst, it'd cost me a few elixirs, one level and an hour of my time. Nothing irrevocable. However, if everything were to come out as planned, I'd gain a lot more.

My legs trembled in fear and the hand I was holding out dropped onto the guiding line by the force of inertia. The guard snuck up on me, if this term was applicable to him, from behind; had I not taken the precautions, I wouldn't have even known what killed me. I turned around and the Book of Knowledge helpfully highlighted in red a boulder that hadn't been there previously. I took a few deep breaths, sending some oxygen through my body to get rid of the induced fear, attached the artifact to my hand and, making sure to touch the beam, approached the stilled guard.

Test number one: testing attack abilities.

An hour later the guard started blinking and then disappeared, leaving nothing behind: no crumbles, no experience, no loot and no satisfaction. I used "Templar's Blow" a couple of times, but did not observe any visible effect; so I decided against wasting Energy, using just "un-enhanced" blows. This chunk of stone apparently couldn't care less what was hitting it. Once two more guards departed to rest in eternal peace bringing me nothing except fatigue, I declared test number one completed: it was not possible to level up using guards in stasis.

Test number two: testing defense abilities.

You were killed and sent to a respawn point
You lost one level
Your current level: 9

It didn't work. Having waited for the guard and made him still, I expected to fight a frontal attack, but the blow came from behind. The stone highlighted by the Book didn't even stir, while a beam that had been in that place to begin with turned into a horrible monster and, despite my so-called upgraded defense, killed me with one blow – just piecing me straight trough. Test number two was a failure as well.

Morally preparing myself to the last foray into the forest, I wandered from one teacher to another; I couldn't help noticing how few players were left here. While at first everything was overcrowded with players getting in each other's way, now each clearing had at most two or three players scared of their own shadow and hesitating to approach the teacher. There were no more mages, Paladins, or organized groups: apparently, they've all gone to the Labyrinth. There was only one path leading to it, but again I forced myself to retreat. I had an unfinished task, and couldn't afford to move on until I fully studied and resolved this issue. I needed to understand where the arrows on the guiding beams led...

Three hours later they led me to a rather wide clearing located about four meters above the ground. In the center there was a two-meter crater whose jagged edges indicated its unnatural origin. There was someone sitting next to the crater, thinking; at a first glance at its figure I associated him with the Predator. The creature that was unable to destroy the future Governor of California. However, after I looked a little more carefully, the similarity faded somewhat. The player was a biped sentient orthograde being with very well developed muscles, over six feet tall – even though I could be wrong on that since he was sitting. He had strong legs and something like sandals on his feet, and wore knee guards made of some strange bluish material that looked like metal and dragon skin at the same time. Above that was a strange skirt-like piece of clothing with a wide belt that had a blue crystal instead of a clasp. His torso was criss-crossed with ribbons the same color as the belt; the shoulders were covered with guards in the shape of the skulls of some unknown animals with the same bright blue crystals for eyes. On top the player wore a cloak reaching the ground. A meter-long double-pointed staff was attached behind the right shoulder. All that glory was crowned with a dog's head that looked very much like a terrestrial Doberman, and made one think of Anubis. I wondered what kind of a strange race that was?

"I can sense you!" The stranger shouted without moving. "Come out and we'll talk."

I stood still for some time thinking he was addressing someone else, and expecting another player to come out into the clearing; however, there was no one hurrying to step out from behind the stones. Activating my defenses, as I had no idea what to expect of this player, I stopped at the edge of the clearing looking for a guiding line. There was none.

"It's safe here. Come off the Way."

"Who are you? What are you doing here?" It must've sounded rather rude, but I wasn't going to believe the word of some random guy. Stepping into the clearing and holding my hand over the guiding beam, I was prepared to drop if a guard were to show up, but after ten seconds none appeared. The stranger wasn't lying, after all: it was in fact safe within the clearing. I walked around the center disfigured by the explosion, keeping it between myself and the recruit, and stopped a few steps away from the crater.

"Zangar, a necromancer. Here because of a dorn. But was too late. Someone else came first. Sense the right of first claim."

The necromancer spoke in short phrases, pausing between his sentences. It gave me the feeling that the dog-headed player only had enough ram memory for 3-4 words, after which he hit stack overflow and froze up. Zangar was calm, as if he didn't need to worry about his safety. The conclusion was obvious: the player was sure of his strength. Either he was actually strong, or he had some additional information not accessible to common players. There was no other explanation that I could see.

"Yaropolk, Paladin," I introduced myself in turn, thought and realized that in fact I had nothing to lose, so I asked point blank: :What's a dorn?"

"..."

"I was led here by the arrows on the beams,

which you called the Way. I have no clue what a dorn is, the right of first claim or what all that was needed for. I wasn't looking for anything specific purposefully, just exploring the Academy. I plan to become an explorer, so any information is valuable."

Truth is a mighty weapon. Had I tried to wriggle and spin tales that I already knew everything but wanted to check my information just in case, Zangar might have kept silent. But having heard my frank admission, the dog-headed one folded his ears in a funny way and stared at me for some time trying to figure out if I was lying or not. Then he said:

"Dorn's a hidden teacher. Mechanism. Teaches all abilities. Even closed because of level. Right of first claim – prerogative of finder. Possible to blow up mechanism. Earn experience. Receive artifact enhancer. Someone better than me. He made it first."

"What's an artifact enhancer? I've never heard of this thing either. What does it do, increase the level of the artifact?"

"Three levels plus," confirmed Zangar. "The one who finds a dorn becomes strong. Like a monster in the Academy. Unstoppable."

A guess flashed through my head as to who could've used the "right of first claim". Who could attain an inexplicable number of levels even having died several times? It was amazing we were even able to kill her! Perhaps, Nata hadn't expected a double blow with weapons. But that wasn't the most interesting part. I was puzzled by something else: did that mean that I was purposely misled from the true way and not allowed to find the dorn?

"Did you come here using the arrows?" I verified with Zangar just in case, received a positive answer, inhaled a chestful of air and shouted with all my might: addressing the air, not worried that a strange player was standing next to me:

"Chancellor! I need explanations! You favored other players!"

"So what?" a thunderous voice replied, as it seemed, coming from every stone. "It's my Academy, and I'll do whatever I want!"

"This is wrong!" I wouldn't give up. "You are caring about other players, considering the mages' actions wrongful, but you act worse than them!"

"Then convict me, Dark one!" There was so much open malice in that voice that I shuddered. Apparently, the Chancellor really disliked everyone who differed from Light ones. "Show your Judge's skills and deliver a verdict that I was wrong!"

"There'll be a time when I'll do just that," I growled in response. The Game did not open a case, so apparently the Chancellor's actions fully fit within the established law and order. Moreover, my internal sense of injustice didn't raise its head either, refusing to initiate anything. My subconscious was in agreement: that one hidden teacher had now been replaced by another.

"If that's all, I am waiting for you and your silent companion in my tower!" The Chancellor ordered. "I'll have to decide what to do with you!"

"What does the necromancer have to do with it? We aren't even on the same team!" I was taken aback. "He was just sitting here ..."

"That's your problem, Dark one! Since you considered him worthy of hearing our dialogue, now you are responsible for him!" the Chancellor cut me off, then continued in a completely different tone, changing from irate to interested and addressing Zangar: "Besides, I'd like to know why Levard's minion turned out to be a non-initiated player. How long have you studied, Light one?"

"A lot," Zangar responded mysteriously, retaining his calm. The necromancer was Light? That was something new... "Levard gave me a task. What waits beyond the wasteland. Clarified requirements. Gave me choice. I decided to take risk."

"Funny. For a cynocephalian you talk too much."

"Many years a guest. Elves. Gandrys. Sires. Learned language. Became a player – the skill was retained."

"Come to me with this careless recruit and you will receive what you are seeking!" the Chancellor stated pompously and the sounds of the surrounding world returned. As it turned out, while the Chancellor spoke even the wind and remote cries had died down.

Quest received: "Visit" Reach the Chancellor of the Academy as part of the group; minimum group membership: necromancer cynocephalian Zangar and Paladin human Yaropolk. Coordinates of the Chancellor's Tower are marked on your map

"There are no quests in Academy!" Zangar stated , after staring into the air in front of him for a few moments. "That's what my teacher said."

"So, he was wrong. Gimme the group invite, Light one. Now this is truly weird. A Light necromancer."

"Is your world unique?" Zangar was surprised. "Necromancers always Light. Our force is the dead."

"Why not emotions?"

"Dead have no emotions."

"But those around do. When around the dead. Especially when close to them. Crap!" I even started cursing as I realized that I was talking like the necromancer. Apparently it's true that "one fool makes many".

"Extra weakness. If no one around? World is Light? To die? It's easier for Light ones."

"Possibly. What do you have to say about the quest? Shall we form a group?"

"I wait for Way seeker!" The necromancer said mysteriously. "Came here by arrows. Can't see Way. If you see – let's go. I need to get to Chancellor."

"What for?" I couldn't refrain from the question. "If we're to continue together I'll need information on to expect in the wastelands and beyond."

"That's not equal exchange," Zangar objected stubbornly."From me – information. From you – nothing. Unequal. I'll join group. That I need. Ready to sign agreement. We need good group. But information is personal. What do you offer in exchange?"

"Have you visited hidden teachers?" I needed additional knowledge as badly as air, and it was necessary to make sure that my imposed partner visits the teachers. That would increase our overall chance of survival.

"Their coordinates keep changing..." said Zangar. "Teacher didn't name them... You know where teachers are?"

"That's right," I beamed a smile at him. "You share information about the Academy, I take you to the hidden teachers. You'll become the keymaster."

"Having one key makes no sense. There are always two passages. We can enter but can never leave."

"I'll give you two keys." The necromancer had some kind of additional knowledge about the keys, so it was a matter of honor to get him to talk. "But I need full information on what you know about the Academy. Only then will we be able to finish our quest."

"Question. Do you see the Way? Not just the arrows, but the Way itself? That is important for me to make decision."

"Yes," I confirmed. "I was subjected to full stun prior to the Academy, so the Game highlights the safe way through the forest in green for me.

"What does stun to do with that?" The necromancer was surprised. "It's not related. The Way not accessible to all. So I look for explorer."

"Stop!" I guessed. "Only explorers or searchers can see the path? Then you are in luck: an explorer of the world is standing before you. I can see the Way."

"Then we can agree. We need agreement. That we're partners."

"I have an idea," a guess flashed through my

head and I decided to implement it immediately. I filled my lungs with air and shouted, addressing the Game as I had addressed the Chancellor earlier: "Game! We need to enter into a standard agreement between myself and Zangar on partnership and exchanging information! We shall not attack each other, shall support and help each other in every way until we leave the Academy, since it's so important for the Chancellor that we visit him. I will take Zangar to the hidden teachers; in exchange he'll tell me, in as much detail as possible, the information he has about the Academy. If he forgets something it shall be not counted as breach of agreement provided that the forgettance is inadvertent."

"I will tell if possible," Zangar added. "Some topics forbidden. Not everything I can tell."

Request is accepted, the agreement is prepared

A huge sheet of text appeared in front of me; in quite simple layman's terms it listed all the main points of our agreement. As for the last clause, I included it so as not to make myself judge Zangar later, should he suddenly remember something extra.

"Non-initiated players have advantage," Zangar started telling me as soon as the text of the agreement received both our signatures, turned green and then disappeared. Now we were full-fledged partners. Even a special icon appeared in my panel. I'll need to enter into an agreement like that with Teart as well; a notebook is no place for storing agreements. "Chancellor gifts them."

As it turned out, some advanced minions enter the Academy without initiation on purpose, so as to receive an opportunity to meet the Chancellor. He would meet only with non-initiated ones, rewarding them with gifts for their determination, faith in themselves and taking a conscious risk. Zangar's teacher received as a gift a soul catcher that was able to capture the souls of players and NPCs up to level 200. In addition, the catcher was an energy source in itself, which made Levard one of the strongest players in his world. If Zangar were to have a similar gadget, even with a lower capture capacity, he'd become a very well respected necromancer. The Chancellor strictly prohibited Levard from telling anyone the principle behind receiving the bonus; however, the clever teacher was able to find a loophole and, using the dead, made the information available to his student without breaking the prohibition.

Cynocephalian Zangar, who turned out to be a level 5 player, just hmmed, seeing my 9th. I decided against upsetting my new partner by telling him that once I was at level 10. What if he developed depression; particularly since Zangar had thought for a while before sharing information on the chosen path of development, specialty and artifact. Since we were partners we both needed to understand what we were capable of. The necromancer had decided to become an Exorcist: a player who travels between the worlds and destroys the dead that have become undead. Wild vampires, shapeshifters, ghosts, other undead – the scope of work for a potential Exorcist covered a lot and they were paid quite well, which was also important. As a profession that would be the best match with his path of development: the Game had suggested "Draftsman". A special feature of necromancers' work was that they needed to draw icons quickly, surely and with certainty; thus, the choice was obvious. Zangar had selected his artifact in the same way I had, using the Temple of Knowledge. Showing me his pike, the necromancer called it Necrospike almost with love, to the extent that he had emotions. It was a stabbing weapon and a necromancy enhancer, all in one. As an attack capability, necromancers received a curse, "Touch of Death"; to activate it they had to draw an activation icon in the air. For quite a while Zangar refused to try the curse on me; however, I was able to convince him that it was necessary to try both his blow strength and my defense, because all sorts of adversaries could be awaiting us.

The necromancer sighed, quickly waved his pike a few times... the air between us darkened, densed, turned into a skull of fog and crashed into my defense. A second went by, and another, and a third...

"Stop now!" I shouted at the cynocephalian, replenishing my Energy with an elixir. The protection was cracking up, eating up the Energy at an express rate. Necromancers were dependent on the drafting, that's where their weakness lay. However, as soon as they cast a curse, they could just maintain it! Zangar pointed his pike at me that was emitting the fog and now observed, with as much interest as I had, the results of his attack. Normally, it took less energy to continue using an ability than to activate it, so Zangar was a formidable opponent for any player, even one with defense capacities.

"You have elixirs," the cynocephalian noted, stopping his attack. "You didn't say. Is that partner-like? It has to do with Academy."

"I didn't tell you much yet about myself and my place in the Academy," I shot back. "You know that the Paladins have been chosen as a sacrifice, right?"

Now I knew what the selection of a sacrifice class was. Just before the recruits were sent to the Academy, the Viceroy cast lots to select a class. Killing its members would bring triple experience points for other recruits. That class was assigned to be a sacrifice class. As a bonus, practically all members of the sacrifice class were sent to one sector. Myself and my former team had been unlucky in that: we were thrown to a place where Paladins were rare as hen's teeth.

Zangar nodded in affirmation, which made it easier for me to tell about the mages, the players they hired, the elixirs, my agreement with Dangard on doing the Labyrinth and lots of other things. I had to warn my partner regarding my enemies, as well as telling him about my capabilities: I didn't leave out Dolgunata either, and told him my ideas as to who could've found the dorn. Before encountering me the druid had purposefully been running around the forest for some reason; it was quite possible that she had run into the clearance and destroyed the mechanism.

After we were done exchanging information I took Zangara to the hidden teachers. After refusing the training both times the necromancer received two massive brass keys that looked like they came from some treasure story. One key opened the entrance, the other – the exit. Thus, Dolgunata's certainty that she'd be able to go through half of the tests in the Labyrinth was premature. With two keys it was possible to pass one test, not more. My partner turned out to be a silent sort, so through most of the way we kept silent without bothering each other with questions. Even though I was sorely tempted to ask him about necromancers, as the class in itself was very intriguing and mysterious to me. Given that Zangar was a minion, his desire to become a necromancer was a conscious one, and I really wanted to understand the reason for his actions. Fiddling with dead bodies and zombies is not for everyone.

"The Labyrinth," cynocephalian said as soon as we stepped out of the forest. The change in our surroundings was drastic. I even had to squint at the bright sun that joyfully illuminated the 50-meter border between the sections of the Academy. A wide abyss, the bottom of which was obscured by roiling fog, separated the reinforced concrete jungle and a huge wall about 20 meters high. Across this abyss a road led to the Labyrinth, paved with stones and rimmed with high curbs to protect careless players from falling. The wall sported a wooden double door; right at that moment a group of players was passing through them. As soon as the last group participant disappeared into the depths of the Labyrinth, the doors shut with a resounding clang, as if informing the Labyrinth dwellers that new victims had arrived.

"That's not where we need to go," Zangar said as soon as I stepped onto the bridge. "We need to skip first test. It screens out majority."

"But you said that nobody knows what the tests are. That they change constantly."

"Tests change. Essence the same. First one hardest. Need to go around. Lead: the Way is here. There is passage there! One hundred meters."

The necromancer pointed away from the Labyrinth, to the border between the forest and the abyss.

"From our side?" I was surprised, yet found the guiding beam and went deeper into the forest. Sometimes it's so nice to have information! The forest was so close to the drop-off, that we had to go in deeper, it would've been impossible to pass along the edge. The Book of Knowledge gave us a boon: it marked on the map the approximate final point of our journey; after reaching it we ended up in a relatively clear area, which was an opening criss-crossed with guiding beams. Their presence enabled us to come up to the very edge of the abyss without worrying about the guards.

"Now what?" I was tired of looking at the practically vertical wall, so I shifted my gaze to Zangar. "There's no more road."

"Trust me, Paladin. I am partner. Not enemy. Give me your hand."

Silently, I extended my hand to the necromancer, while trying to convince myself in my mind that the Game wouldn't allow the necromancer to breach the agreement and push me down. Besides, it would make no sense for him to do so.

"Most important – don't be afraid. Just trust," the cynocephalian repeated like a mantra, grabbed my hand for a more comfortable grip and pushed me beyond the edge of the abyss. My feed stopped sensing support, and my chest contracted. I wasn't afraid of respawn, I was just really scared of heights. The one thing that was positive in all that? Apparently, cynocephalians are very strong creatures capable of holding up a person wearing steel armor with one hand.

"At count of three." My partner started rocking me, preparing to throw me over the ledge. "One, Two..."

"Mo-o-otherfu.....!!" I screamed at the top of my lungs when Zangar released me into free flight. That was something I definitely didn't expect! All my short life started flashing before my eyes. Just as I got to elementary school, I plopped on a hard surface, shaking all the images out of my head. Opening my eyes I had shut in fear, I shut them right back: I was sitting on nothing but air!

"It's the road of trust!" Zangar landed heavily next to me. "It's not possible to tell. Only possible to show. Feel trust. You passed test. You trust me."

I opened my eyes again. The necromancer was, in some unfathomable way, sitting right on the air without any visible discomfort. Overcoming my fear, I raised myself – at first on all fours, and then standing up. Even the short flight wasn't so terrifying as standing on something invisible!"

"We go there," now Zangar was pointing at the opposite side of the abyss where the Labyrinth was located. "Follow me. Follow every footstep."

The necromancer slowly moved forward as if he could see where he was going. I stood still – couldn't force myself take a single step. I was scared to no end! I cursed myself in every way, calling myself names like "weakling" and "coward girl", but my internal motivators refused to work. My body seized up and refused to move on.

"I help." Zangar returned and threw me over his shoulder, like a sack of flour. "I trained: you – no. Hard if no training. Teacher warned me."

I didn't even have the strength of a cynocephalian. I grabbed him hard, hanging on like a hungry tick, and it would have been a truly heroic deed for me just to unclench my fists. The entire world contracted for me to the sight of the skull on my partner's back; I was hanging on the fangs of it with both my hands. When Zangar set me on my feet again it took me quite an effort to unclench my cramped and pale upper limbs. I would never have thought that I suffered from acrophobia! I was a paratrooper after all; I even got to skydive once! I wondered – was that the last trick my body just played, or should I prepare myself for more surprises like that? What else did I not know about myself?

Gradually I felt better. Zangar was doing his own thing, letting me regain my composure. The cynocephalian did not try to slap my cheeks or shake me back to normal – it was as if he knew that I just needed to be alone for a while. Once I regained my ability to perceive the outside world I realized that we were standing on a small ledge on the wall of the abyss, and within just a couple of meters of us there was a big door about two meters wide.

"Passage!" It was as if the necromancer felt that I could control myself again. "We skip first test. Say when ready."

"It's fine, I'm okay now. How do you know about the passage?"

"My teacher told. He's great player! He'll be Viceroy soon! Test in one year. Let's go."

All I could do was be surprised at the encounter my fates had arranged. I noted to myself that I needed to ask Zangar thoroughly about life outside the Academy. Once I got a chance, that is.

The group needs a key to continue
2 keys detected within group
Need confirmation of permission to use key

Three system messages appeared in front of my eyes as soon as Zangar touched the door. With a soft whispering sound it opened, presenting a dimly lit corridor of gray stone.

"Go first. You see the Way." Zangar moved to the side. "There are traps there."

"How are the traps related to seeing the Way?"

"They aren't." My partner sighed heavily and added: "You afraid of heights. I don't feel well in dungeon. Bad concentration. Afraid to hurt group."

The door closed with a barely audible sound as soon as we stepped into the corridor. I took a couple of steps into the corridor and then returned to the door. For some reason I briefly forgot that I needed to explore everything and my life depended on it. The inner side the door had no handles, buttons or openings. As soon as I touched the door, the familiar system message appeared before my eyes:

The group needs a key to continue
1 key detected within group
Need confirmation of permission to use key

I indicated by gestures to Zangar that we didn't need to activate anything, stepped away from the door, lowered myself down on all fours and slowly crawled forward, studying every stone thoroughly. An outside observer might've thought this move stupid; however, I recalled a movie where a similar invisible road existed, the same as the one along which the necromancer carried me just a few minutes ago. Indiana Jones, and I couldn't remember which part. If one were to juxtapose that movie with Zangar's warning about the traps, we had to use special care moving forward.

It was the attention to detail that enabled me to see a slab that seemed incongruous to the passage cut through the rock. It was set right in the middle of the corridor. It was just under a meter wide and placed in such a way that avoiding stepping on it was practically impossible. The Book of Knowledge immediately highlighted the slab in red, indicating danger. I was about to jump over the possible trap when something caught my eye: there was a small round hole in the wall, right above the slab. It was quite hard to notice in the dim half-light of the corridor. The hole had an identical counterpart on the other side. Thirst for knowledge overpowered common sense. Having explored both walls and ceiling around me to find any extra unexpected holes, I stretched out my arm and carefully pressed down the slab.

Phphpht! Phphpht! Phphpht!

Three lightnings flashed in front of me at such speed that only the Book of Knowledge helped me figure out what had happened. Each wall had three counterpart openings. From the holes on one wall, steel arrows with barbed arrowheads were shot, flying into the openings in the other wall. One arrow was shot at the level of feet, the second about waist-high and the third close to chest height. That's why I hadn't noticed the top two sets of openings: I was mostly crawling around close to the floor. Repeated pressing on the slab activated the arrow again, as if the trap mechanism had an unlimited supply. I put my hand next to the hole and sighed with relief when nothing happened. Apparently, this trap did not have photo sensors, so nothing pierced my hand. But this was just the very first trap! An initial level one! Just to show sloppy players what was in store for them... More than likely there would be not only photo sensors, but other interesting things as well. Bracing myself, I aimed for a point beyond the slab and took a running jump across the dangerous area. It didn't work out as gracefully as I planned, but the main goal was achieved — I avoided being killed.

"Zangar!" I called the necromancer. "There's a

trap here. Be careful."

"Thanks." My partner jumped over the slab and joined me. "I see problem. Speed is low. We could run out of food."

"I agree with you on that one," I stood up from my knees and leaned against the wall. Only the Chancellor knows how many traps are set further down the road. If I were to spend 30 minutes for each, that'd be a very long road indeed. "How did your teacher pass through this corridor?"

"I don't have information."

"Was he alone?" I was getting another crazy idea.

"He found partner. They came out together. Why question?"

"So, listen. I don't want to move at a snail's pace. You can see yourself: that's slow. Do you have any objections against adding another player to our group?

"No. More is easier. Where we find new one?"

"Excellent! So here's the setup: if I die, you should go out of the corridor and wait for us at the entrance. But only in case of 'if! Then use the second key. I'll find a new player, take him to the hidden teachers, he'll get his two keys; then I'll come back and we'll go through the corridor anew."

"The idea is clear but I have questions. Why would you die? Why 'if'?"

"Because I'm the one that has the protection. If you had it, you'd be the one who could die."

"The idea stopped being understandable," the necromancer laid his ears back.

"There's nothing to understand." I activated the defense, put on my artifact just in case, took an elixir in my spare hand, looked again at Zangar, who never figured any of this out, then screamed: "Leeeroooooooy!" – it resounded throughout the corridor – and rushed in.

Enhanced defense was my only possibility of success. The idea was simple: if we were to study the passage to find the traps at the rate we were moving, we'd be stuck there for a very long time. Therefore, one needed to activate them all, preferably at the same time; well, at least as quickly as possible. Nothing else occurred to me besides activating them with my own body, and I rushed ahead before common sense had a chance to kick in and put a stop to it. I was bit by arrows, stakes popped out from the ground, fire tired to burn through my shield. Once the walls moved in trying to crush me, yet the protection held. Or, rather, another vial I downed restored my Energy before it crashed to zero. I tumbled out into a huge room, tripped over a thin string line which was supposed to have cut my feet off, and practically smashed my face on the stones. The Energy bar leveled out at 32 and stopped twitching, indicating that the troubles were over. Getting up to my feet, I looked back along the corridor and could not contain a surprised whistle: by now the Book of Knowledge had already digested all the information it received and now highlighted both the traps and the safe path. A narrow green passage framed by everything else lay in front of me!

"You are alive!" I heard Zangar's almost

surprised shout from somewhere far away. "The frame says so. Will you come back for me?"

"Wait! I shouted in response, looking around the room. "I'll be back soon!"

The corridor had led me into a huge cave hewn in the rock; one couldn't really call it a room. Lit by a few magic lights, the cave was mostly drowning in darkness; however, one couldn't miss the small pedestal, about a meter high, that looked like a dais in the very center. And a thick open book resting on it.

I blew off an ample layer of dust and sadly stared at the unfamiliar letters: the open page was written in a language I didn't know. Making sure that my artifact photographed the page well, I leafed through the entire book cover to cover, but was unable to find anything I could understand. Except for a picture showing three humanoids wearing loose hooded clothes and standing around a shining ball, their hands up in the air as if they were casting a spell. That was the only graphic in the book. Despite its significant size, the book had just twenty pages: the sheets were made of wooden boards.

It would've been incredibly silly to leave the book in its place, but I was really uncertain about trying to take it with me, given the kind of place this was. I was practically sure the book would have some kind of spring under it that would activate a clever trap, so that the entire cave would collapse. That was the reason I never looked at the cover: the risk was too high. There was nothing else interesting in the cave; the next thirty minutes were taken up helping

Zangar avoid all the traps in the corridor.

"You studied this?" The necromancer immediately figured out the situation, seeing, just as I had, the dais with the book first.

"I don't understand the language," I sighed. "I recorded everything, but right now this all looks like Greek to me. Just a jumble of strange symbols.

"Cynocephalians' language is complex. Not many know it. My teacher wrote book. Left here. Told me of it. I can read. You interested?"

"So this is not a creation of the Labyrinth?" I said gladly, heading towards the pedestal. "Then we need to expropriate it and then..."

"Stop!" Zangar yelled. "No taking the book! There's a trap under it! Teacher took old book. Left his own! Thus he avoided the trap. You have a book? What do you give in exchange?"

"What was in the book he took out of here?" I immediately peppered him with questions. "Have you seen it? What is it about?"

"No, I never saw. Teacher protects it. In it there's power. There's knowledge. It will help become a Keeper. Not allowed to talk about it. Forbidden."

"Fine, but what's this book about?" I said slowly in dismay. If Zangar's teacher was planning to become one of the big wigs of the Game, it would be pointless to hope for his goodwill and permission to at least study the item he stole.

"Process of Game creation. Teacher obsessed with this topic. He studies. Researches. Seeks. What he found he wrote down. The book's five hundred years old. So long it's been here. Teacher wrote it when he was recruit. Then found new knowledge. It's not here. That's old. You interested?"

"Go on, read already!" I ordered, burning up with curiosity, but caught myself in time and added: "When you read – read it in the original language and then translate at once. Additional knowledge wouldn't hurt me."

Zangar agreed and started moving his finger along the symbols, reading them out loud in a strange guttural tongue; then he explained the meaning. As a result the Book of Knowledge helped me read the last page without the necromancer's aid.

The main idea of the book was that about four thousand years ago three powerful beings, whose names were unknown, came to realize that the world's setup needed to be changed. They created the Game: a sentient mechanism, into which they placed certain algorithms and transferred all their power and strength. The process of creation was what the picture showed. Those beings died, and the Game itself then developed the rules and laws which it had to follow. The mechanism randomly selected a limited number of beings from all the variety of the worlds available and turned them into players. The rest were taken under full control by the Game and forced to do whatever it deemed necessary. The difference between an NPC and a player was that the latter had a "soul" image – a copy of consciousness, knowledge and experience that the Game transferred to respawn point in case of death. A respawn point was, in effect, a 3D printer that printed a vessel into which the "soul" would then be placed and live there. NPCs had "souls" as well, but after each death the Game wouldn't restore them; it would wipe out the memory and place those "souls" into new bodies: the children. That was the basis of all the various theories concerning reincarnation. Seeking to reduce the load on its resources, the Game chose the Emperor for itself, granted extremely broad powers to him and altered him, adjusting for its needs. The Emperor was a player, but only in terms of the presence of the "soul" that persisted. In essence, however, he was a part of the mechanism that was an inalienable part of the Game with a certain personal will.

"Teacher continued research. Always studies. He learnt name," Zangar added as soon as the book was finished. "Name of one of Creators. It was human. A woman. All worlds know her. Madonna."

"That's not possible," I frowned. "That woman lived two thousand years ago. But definitely not four!"

"Time flows vary. Somewhere faster. Somewhere slower. Problem of the Game. Not enough resources. Your world is slow."

"Wait. So, some three guys created artificial intelligence, conferred enormous powers to it, forced the whole world to do its bidding, and after that quietly died, leaving the players to deal on their own with that creation?"

"All correct. The three were strong. All-powerful. Decided to start all anew. Decided not to kill. Created a machine."

"Which does the killing for them. As far as I understand, only about one percent of living creatures are players! The rest are NPCs, who simply weren't so lucky as to be chosen! Based on that logic, the quantity of NPCs is always stable: their souls are copied from one body to another. Then how can one explain, for example, the birth rate boom in my world? There, the number of people is increasing exponentially!"

"No contradiction. The Dark ones destroyed several worlds. The worlds are not there, NPCs are not there. Their souls return. Overpopulation is everywhere now. Soon new worlds will be made. Will take most of NPCs. There'll be war. In all worlds. Preparation is underway now. They make NPCs mean. To like blood. To like destruction. Less load for worlds. Easier for players."

"It's a mad world order we've got," I whispered in astonishment. "The Game does whatever it wants! What if it decides that the creatures are imperfect and need to be destroyed? Who would stop it?"

"I have no knowledge. Teacher studies, not I. Talk to him. He likes explorers. We need to move. Door is ahead."

"Wait a minute," I still couldn't get over the knowledge I just received. I'd already decided that the Game had existed forever, that it had predated all that there was, and now it turned out that it was just a cool-looking chain leashing all the creatures. How had Zangar's teacher found that out? Most likely not from standard open sources! Perhaps from the book that had been here before? I looked at the wooden book again, at the necromancer, who had already opened the door at the other end of the cave, and then I asked yet another question:

"What was in the book that lay here?"

"You repeat yourself, partner. I have to repeat also. Not allowed to talk about it. Forbidden."

"I'll start from a different angle. How did your teacher find this passage?

"He is great player. His partner is great researcher. They found together. Chance encounter."

"Great, let's try to unravel this topic. The passage through which we just arrived. Who said that it's the only one? What if there are other passages? That would enable you to skip not only the first level of the Labyrinth, but also all the rest? Why did we rush in at once? We need to return and explore it in detail."

"Only one key left. Entrance door is closed. We can open one door. Entrance to here, exit from here. No choice."

"There's always a choice." I wouldn't give up. "We can add another player to the group, take him to the hidden teachers and get a new keymaster. Don't you want to check it out? What if I am right and there's one more cave? And in it there's the book about which you wouldn't tell me anything? What do you think – which will please your teacher more – that you return from the Academy, or that you'll return from the Academy with the book?"

"With the book better," I didn't have to convince Zangar of the obvious. "Not clear how to return. Not possible to jump up. Invisible bridge creates fear. It checks confidence. I won't be able to return."

"So, my fear of heights was induced?" I exhaled

with relief. "Fine, then I have another suggestion outright. We can return through respawn. We'll just walk into one of the traps."

"High risk. Could end up in Labyrinth. It has a stone too. Will be unpleasant."

"I agree, it's risky," I couldn't deny the necromancer was pragmatic. "But I don't see another way to return. I wouldn't want to jump into the abyss. What if that kind of death was final? Besides, if we were to come back within the Labyrinth, no one can prevent us from coming back into the forest. What if we had forgotten to do something there?"

"I agree with the last argument," Zangar surrendered. "It's possible to return. It's not forbidden. Let's find trap. We'll respawn."

"Why go anywhere?" I grinned. "There's a trap right next to us! We wouldn't want to leave such a rarity behind, right?"

With those words I lifted the book from the pedestal and placed it in my inventory. Zangar just grinned, and then a powerful jet of fire burnt first him and then myself to ashes. Painful, but that's the deal. I needed to verify my guess.

"We were lucky," Zangar said as soon as the system stated that I had only 8 levels available now. We returned to one of the respawn points near the forest, as if the Game did not count us among those who had entered the Labyrinth. "Whom shall we take as new partner?"

"There's not much point in looking on purpose, we can take anyone. Let's take him! I pointed at a player crouching in the shadows, cast a more thorough look at him and added, barely able to contain my surprise: "Mage, do you want to stay alive?"

I was nailed by the scared and haunted stare of the desperate player. The very same kid who had pleaded that I not kill him was sitting under the respawn stone, fearing even to breathe.

"He's weak and helpless. Bad partner," Zangar assessed the mage who'd curled up in a fetal position.

"I am afraid we are unlikely to find anyone else right now." The respawn clearing was unusually empty. While before there were always players here, now just the three of us decorated the landscape with our presence. I drew in some air, remembering my army past, and shouted practically into the mage's ear, making him jump: "Boot camp! Wake up! Ready! Front!! Recruit: name?!"

"...," the mage, cross-eyed, tried to mumble something, but I was beyond stopping at that point.

"Check mumbling! Answer clearly, concisely, no stuttering! Name!"

"M-marinar," the kid jumped to his feet and even stood at attention, as if he was actually familiar with the army way of talking.

"Marinar. Level!?"

"First!"

"Your world!?"

"Varnax!"

"Chosen development!?"

"Production and creation!"

"Specialty!?"

"Alchemist!"

"Artifact!?"

"Pulverizer!"

"Why did they leave you here!?"

"Weak and helpless were left behind to die!"

"How much Energy you have left!?"

"Ten units!"

"Do you want to live!?"

"Yes!"

"I can't hear you!"

"YES!!!"

"Are you ready to follow all my orders, instructions and commands in order to finish the Academy and come out of here alive!?"

"YES!!!"

"Game! My request is to create an agreement with player Marinar. We'll be partners until completion of the Academy. We'll get him out of here alive."

Request is accepted, the agreement is prepared

"Sign it," I said calmly now, as soon as the kid's eyes glazed. He was reviewing the text.

"Alchemist is valuable in Game," Zangar piped up. "In wastelands we teach him. The profession teacher is there. Ingredients are there. No recipes. In Academy Alchemist is useless."

"We'll see," I said with meaning, re-evaluating Marinar. Among the recipes I'd found, two had to do with alchemy. Minor potions for agility and, most importantly, Energy replenishment. If we drag the mage to a professions teacher and provide him with the ingredients, he'd be a very useful team member.

"Here's group invite," Zangar said, adding the mage. "New partner needs food. I have little. Not enough to share.

"No problem, I have some," I offered Marinar the pasty I had received oh so long ago from Dolgunata. At the trader's I had to stick the pasty under my breastplate to clear space in the inventory. However, the mage didn't need to know the full path this piece of bread had travelled. It was enough that it could replenish his Energy.

"So, now that we have 12 hours of life now, let's set out," I concluded as soon as Marinar greedily ate the pasty. First, we need to go visit all the teachers. Tell us, pretty boy, where did you go and what did you see?"

"Why you say 'pretty boy'?" Zangar inserted in surprise before the mage could as much as open his mouth. "Can't you see? It's woman"!

CHAPTER EIGHT

CAVES OF TESTS

"WHAT?!" I exclaimed in surprise, staring at the mage. "You're a woman?! Why didn't you tell us at once?"

"I'm a girl," the new partner babbled. "I thought you knew. I thought that was why you didn't kill me..."

The mage's loose robe concealed not only the flaws but also the fine points of her figure; combined with the mage's slenderness it confused me. As a result I had supposed that the mage was male. I actually went back and reviewed the scene of our first encounter, but even there I found nothing that provided a clue to indicate that Marinar was a girl. Even her voice as she was pleading to let her live was so full of fear and hysterics that only an extremely horny guy would have noticed the notes of a female voice in it.

But now, having finally looked at my new partner thoroughly, I could clearly see that she was a girl. Fine-featured face with aquamarine eyes, short hair that was snowy white, as if over-treated with peroxide, somewhat full lips, delicate hands with long fingers visible from the robe sleeves... There could be no mistake: indeed, it was a girl before us; but why hadn't I noticed that before?

I reviewed the video of my first meeting with Marinar once again. Indeed, all those telltale features were there. However, even Monstrichello was kicking Marinar with his boots as if he had no idea she was a girl. But why? Hadn't he noticed anything either? But he was from Earth. It's not really customary to kick and beat women – it's actually frowned upon – and Monstrichello is not the type to change his ways quickly. As if some mindwarp came over him, myself, the other Paladins who were calmly watching while we...

Mindwarp! Stop!

The scene of the first encounter with Marinar was shown to me for the third time. Dolgunata wasn't with us any more – we had managed to kill her by then, banishing her influence from our minds. But had we fully overcome the druid's influence? What if that bitch had forced me to consider that she was the cat's meow? It's not as though I hadn't seen beautiful women before... Why had it suddenly seemed to me that Dolgunata and the goddess of beauty were related? I opened the Book of Knowledge and entered "female players" in the search field. Then I stared at a very long list in astonishment... It turned out that I had previously encountered women within the Academy; moreover, I killed a few dozen during the brawl at the respawn stone. However, not once had it occurred to me even remotely that there was a woman in front of me. No – just another player, nothing else! Blasted druid! May she rot in hell rather than get granises for the Paladins! I'll come meet the group. Take them under my hand and send her to have some rest! Enough is enough!

Case initiated: "Evil Incarnate" (Slots available for: 9 more cases)

Description: You consider that the druid Dolgunata tramples the Game and/or social rules by actively suppressing players' wills and forcing them to perform actions useful to her.

Task: Investigate this case and deliver a verdict

Case investigation: Not applicable; the case was initiated by the Judge himself

Period of limitation of action: None

"Guilty!" The verdict practically jumped off the tip of my tongue, but I bit it just in time. Not now! First of all, I needed to find the Paladins, free their minds from the druid's influence, ensure their support, and only then go around delivering verdicts. I had no doubt: If I were to make my decision here and now, the Emperor would not approve it. I needed to approach this self-initiated case carefully and thoroughly. Trying to resolve it in a swoop, as I had with Nartalim, wouldn't work.

"Tell me about yourself," I asked the mage, snapping back to the moment. Enough bothering about the druid – let her have fun with the Paladins for now. Marinar blushed, lowered her eyes and then started her story, stumbling on just about every word.

Our new partner hadn't chosen a class for herself. Quite the opposite: she was that hapless kid chosen by the Game itself. She came from an agnostic highly developed technogenic world totally devoid of magic, and was used to even, friendly relations with people. Marinar couldn't even imagine that somewhere not only could a different world exist but other races as well, different from people both physically and emotionally.

It was completely unthinkable for her to realize that people were not only not friends, but rather enemies to each other by default. Marinar was confused and susceptible to the influence of those around her who were more experienced; they decided everything for her, chasing some short-term advantage for themselves and their class. She didn't know what mages were, and definitely had no idea what they could do nor of what they were capable. In her world she had been a quiet but promising biologist; despite her youth, she was very knowledgeable about physical and chemical processes occurring in living tissues and methods of manipulating them; for that reason she decided to become an alchemist. Marinar decided that the knowledge from her previous life would be a good aid in attaining mastery of alchemy and magic. That was why Marinar accepted her class with stoic fatalism: I didn't want this, I didn't expect this, I didn't train for this; but now that it has happened I'll work out how to figure it out. Once the genocide started Marinar refused to participate, so the mages wrote her off as useless. They wouldn't even allow her to go through training. But they wouldn't kill her either, having decided that death from Energy depletion was more painful than from the hand of another player. Then she met us, was scared, pleaded with me not to kill her, and, finally went through with her first training session. The players gradually left the forest; that made it possible for Marinar to train with one more teacher and practically reach level 3. But then she encountered a player mad at the whole wide world. He killed Marinar in passing, as if slapping a pesky insect. In response to my question who it was the girl simply shrugged: someone in dark steel armor. Not like mine. She didn't recall either name or class.

Unfortunately, Marinar hadn't activated video recording, so we were unable to see the player so mistreated by life. After yet another assurance that from now on the girl would follow all the instructions issued by Zangar or myself, we took her to all the teachers in order to complete her training. Amazing, but by now there was no one else in the forest besides ourselves: everyone had left for the Labyrinth. Had it not been for Marinar, who had sat for ten hours under the respawn stone bemoaning her deplorable fate, we might have not have met anyone! Next time we should plan more thoroughly. Too much had hinged on "maybe" and "off chance". There should be no place in the Game for these words altogether!

"Welcome, recruit!" We approached the attack abilities teacher and, before sending Marinar to him, I decided to complete my own training. "Have you decided to train some more?"

"Among other things," I said knowingly. "Among other things..."

Meeting Marinar showed the weak spots in my current development. Maybe it was hard to kill me now, but I was still a weakling against professional head hunters. Dolgunata could easily get into my mind and force me to either deactivate my protection or stop paying attention to other girls. It's possible that she could do something else of which I was not even aware at the moment; it was time to put a stop to that. That could be done only by one method: locate an artifact property blocking mental attacks. But in order to do that I needed to receive another level for the Book of Knowledge. Which was what I planned to do now.

As practice had shown, the artifact developed not only by receiving new knowledge, but also through processing information that had been received earlier and making correct conclusions on that basis. The main thing was, the Book was supposed to generate a record that hadn't been there earlier. That's what would augment the experience. Over the recent past so many unusual things had happened to me that it would really be a crime not to stop and review the video records. What if I missed something important? For example, would I not be interested in the percentage ratio of males and females in our sector of the Academy? What races do players belong to? What are their distinctions? How many players were there when I first spawned here and how many of them have I never seen again? How productive was the genocide of the mages? The more information I could process, the more experience the Book of Knowledge would receive. If time is not an issue at the training range, why not use just one elixir for the sake of additional protection?

Actually, it took more elixirs; now I had only 32 left. However, the result was worth it: I discovered one more "advanced" player. The panther that had killed two rogues was not Dolgunata. That cat was more powerful, more massive and on its right front paw there was some symbol that Nata didn't have. Undoubtedly, it was a druid, but it definitely was not Dolgunata. That immediately brought up questions to which the Book could not provide answers: did that druid and Dolgunata know each other? Could it be that that player, who traveled in the same manner as I, strictly along the guiding lines, had found the dorn? Why didn't I see that panther – or any other druid at all, for that matter – in any other video frames? In fact, there were only two druids in the entire sector: Dolgunata and the stranger. There were twelve different classes in our sector and only druids were so few. An accident? Possibly, but from now on I was really wary of them.

It took me a lot of time and effort to raise the level of the Book by one, but I did manage to do it. I ended up looking at the statistics of the players with long, medium and short noses, just to force the Book to generate another record. When, finally, the Game showed mercy to me and allowed the Book to jump one level up, I cried out to the skies:

"I need information on an artifact property that enables a player to block mental influence! A Judge should make decisions independently, not under the influence of other players!"

Request is granted. Access to Temple of Knowledge is provided.

"I see change in you," Zangar concluded as soon as I returned to the Academy. "You seem older. How many years trained?"

"Many, partner, many," I responded, looking at the world with different eyes. The artifact property "Spiritual integrity" at level 1 provided just +1 to the "Mental protection", but even that pittance was enough to throw Dolgunata out of my head. Amazing, but only after visiting the Temple of Knowledge was I able to break off the druid's mental control — for all that time she'd been "leading" me, controlling my every move. Moreover, I was the one who had granted her that right myself!

A new review of the video set things in their proper places: Dolgunata and the stranger (at that point it became clear that it was a male druid) helped me leave the clearing by killing the mages who rushed after me. After that the man started working on defense while Dolgunata started working me over! She appeared to me in her human form, made me lose my head and give her a link to my map; that automatically showed her my location within the Academy. Then, using the induced infatuation and secret desire of sex, she altered my consciousness: she made me forget our first encounter! In order to receive a fat reward from Archibald! Besides, she did it so well that even though I viewed the video multiple times to level up my Book of Knowledge, I had omitted that point as insignificant! I had seen it, I just never paid attention!

Now that was really scary. One unit of "Mental protection" counteracted "Suppression", but only within the Academy. I was certain that in the wide blue yonder out in the Game there were puppeteers who would be able to simply eat the druid for breakfast. To realize that right after you return you'd be always doing not what you wanted but whatever you were ordered to do... the Game stopped being all fun and games.

"Marinar, come here." I called the girl, who was still shaking with fear, and gave her an elixir. "So, here's a vial for you. You shall drink it only once you are down to 2 units of Energy. Here's what you need to do: go to the teacher and train to attack. For as long as possible. Any questions? No? Excellent! Go for it!"

"You definitely changed," Zangar said again, following Marinar with his eyes.

"Yes, sure I did. Tell me, my mysterious partner," I turned towards the necromancer, "is it not time to share some information? I still can't figure out the puzzle in my mind: there are four sectors in the Academy; yet you arrived precisely in the same one where your teacher trained. Simple luck or was there something more to it? We'll have to go together through the Labyrinth and the wastelands in order to get to the Chancellor, but the more I think about our partnership the more I see that it's not an equal one. You are using me, necromancer! In the very direct sense of the word! The Way, the traps... I am certain there's more! Maybe it's enough of one-sided play? How will we go through the wastelands if you are Light and I am Dark?"

"You are right, partner," Zangar nodded."Our partnership is unequal. You do a lot. I don't give information. I warned in advance. Not allowed to say, teacher forbade. His word is law. Either trust or we part. If we part, no reward. The Chancellor won't give it. Decide what's more important. Reward or injured pride. I choose reward."

I heard you," I said coldly. "We are together only till we get to the Chancellor, right?"

"We from different worlds. Different classes. Different teachers. Different everything. Don't see future interaction. Will help to meet teacher. He'll tell about Game. Then on your own."

"In this case, could you explain why in hell do you need me?" Marinar returned to us. "Devir kills any mage who doesn't follow his orders. His order was simple and clear: kill Yaropolk. That is you. I will not comply with it, since the agreement proscribes it. It's impossible to change class, so as a mage I don't exist any more. No one will accept me as a student. What's left is alchemy. So that's what I have to work on. But even that will not save me without an anchor point, so

I simply don't understand why you need me!"

"You are our keymaster! You help us, we help you. Everything is transparent here," I cut her off, involuntarily cringing from Zangar's words. The necromancer was right in calling a spade a spade, but damn, it was surely unpleasant to hear all that! In my head I was already making certain plans for life after the Academy, but Zangar had just destroyed them all. "Let's do this: first of all, let's get to the remaining teachers and the Chancellor; then we'll work out everything else afterwards. If no one has objections, let's set out. We are wasting precious time."

In total silence broken only by trifles like "here" and "follow this beam" we went through all the teachers, both open and hidden ones, to the point where Marinar received the status of a keymaster. Of course, we did encounter a glitch: the teacher refused to hand the first key to her, stating that the group leader was already a keymaster and there couldn't be two keymasters in the same group. We had to reassemble the group, making Marinar the leader, but even this funny situation couldn't break the ice of distrust that had appeared among us. As for the clearing criss-crossed by the guiding lines and located right at the edge of the abyss, it took me an hour to find it. It looked exactly the same as the one from which Zangar had pushed me off; the only difference was its symmetric location with respect to the bridge into the Labyrinth.

"Teacher knew this not," Zangar noted philosophically, looking beyond the edge of the abyss. "Thought there was one passage. Was wrong. When I return I can surprise him. Will get a reward."

"Throw her," I ordered and before the girl could squeak in surprise and protest, the cynocephalian grabbed her hand, lifted her in the air and threw over the edge. We heard a wild scream, a dull thump, and indignant curses, which quickly turned into a shriek. My assumption about the abyss was correct: the fear of heights was induced rather than a congenital feature for me. Zangar turned towards me, planning to repeat the throw, but I stopped him in time: "I'll manage myself. Go to her, lest she fall off."

The necromancer jumped down to join the girl, allowing me to approach the edge unhindered. The invisible road was about four meters below the edge of the abyss. Zangar, his legs stiff with fear, came up to the screaming Marinar, threw her over his shoulder and literally shuffled towards the other bank of the abyss. The cynocephalian was afraid, yet he overcame his fear, and with a determination worthy of better use kept moving forward. I took a deep sigh and stepped forward into nothingness. A jump from four meters didn't seem extraordinary any more: the years of training did help. What bothered me was another thought: would I be able to repeat the "heroics" of the cynocephalian and ignore my fear?

I was. Despite activating my "Spiritual integrity" attribute, the trembling and fear of heights appeared as soon as I landed on the invisible road. Knowing that the emotions I felt were induced rather than real, I lifted my head, saw Zangar in the distance and, holding myself up on arms that were shaking and threatening to give out at any moment, crawled after him. I didn't have the strength to stand up and walk along the road. Even closing my eyes didn't help me get rid of the induced sensations, so all I could do was clench my teeth and crawl at a snail's pace.

"You didn't train," Zangar calmly remarked, as soon as I plopped down on my back, drawing a relieved breath. "But you made it. Second attempt. Me, twentieth attempt. You are stronger."

"How do you get used to this?" I rasped, trying to overcome the shakes. Fifty meters over the abyss took its toll: I couldn't get my breath back; my heart beat madly as if trying to jump out of my chest and bounce around on the ledge spraying everyone with blood; colored circles danced before my eyes, reminding me of a kaleidoscope with colored glass I had as a kid.

"The fate of necromancers — always fight. Fight fear. Fight the dead. Fight yourself. Never give up."

"It's nice to talk about fear when you are an initiated minion," Marinar piped up in a trembling voice. For her the trip along the invisible road hadn't been easy either. "You should try it as we did, without training, without preparation without a teacher. Then try and talk about fear and fighting it."

"You're wrong, human," Zangar responded. "Have no initiation. Here we similar. I can die too."

"Oh, really? Then why..."

"Enough," I grimaced, rising to my feet. "Marinar, open the door and stand in the doorway so that it won't close. I'll try to run through the traps using the tactic we tried before. If I die, the entrance door will be opened and there will be no need to

357

activate the second key. Zangar, think: what else can you tell me about the Academy without breaking your teacher's orders? You said yourself – regardless of the prohibition from the Chancellor, your teacher found a way to get around it and convey the right ideas to you. Don't you have enough imagination to figure out how to get around that? For example, cynocephalian language is so complex ... I am telling you formally: before I entered the Academy, I had no idea about it, however remote. So if I were to suddenly see some hooks, loops and other scribbles, I wouldn't even know that it was an inscription of some sort in front of me. And note, in this case no one would be able to tell anything to anyone, nor transfer anything to anyone. Think about it. Fine. I'll be going now."

The obstacles in this corridor were practically identical to those in the previous one; that enabled me to get to the very end of the corridor without a problem. The only difference I encountered was simultaneous activation of the fire, compression and shooting traps. The shield held against the assault, but the Book took a long time figuring out a safe way to get through this; I ended up having to activate the traps multiple times to determine the pattern.

"I'm through! Wait there!" I shouted stepping over the last trip wire trap, keeping my eyes on the center of the cave. There, on a small pedestal, a thick book was sitting, somewhat similar to my artifact. Even in the dim light it shone with all the colors of the rainbow, drawing the eye and begging to be grabbed and read. Actually, that was what bothered me most: I knew firsthand what a fishing lure was. Dampening my desire to rush to explore the pedestal immediately, I lowered myself to my knees and slowly, like a minesweeper for whom making mistakes is not an option, started exploring the stone floor. Despite the last trap, the passage through the corridor looked too ordinary, without any tricks. If I had been the one entrusted with installing the traps, after the first one activated it would have at a minimum collapsed the cave and everything within it under an avalanche of stones. Because no one should hang around where they aren't welcome!

A thin wire, which continued from the trip wire trap and led somewhere to the side, caught my eye accidentally when I was already getting the impression that there was nothing scary or horrendous in the cave and that all that was keeping me from obtaining the book were my own fears. My speed dropped practically to nothing: whereas before I explored primarily the floor now I worked on the wall as well, as the wire blended into it so well as to be basically completely invisible; sometimes only my spatial imagination indicated to me where it would go next. Having circled the cave for about 90 degrees with respect to the entrance, I discovered the object of my search: a thin support between the ceiling and the floor; a taut wire was attached to its bottom end. Moreover, there were some more wires leading to the support; they went in different directions and indicated that the trap at the door was the most visible and obvious one.

The Book of Knowledge appeared in front of me practically on its own accord; it must have learned to anticipate my thoughts by now. In the previous cave I had stumbled over the wire by tumbling onto the floor, yet nothing horrible had happened. That begged the question: why? Had the trap already been deactivated by earlier players? Or would nothing horrible happen once the wire dislodges the support? The artifact started replaying the video in slow motion, and one more time I promised myself that I'd be more thorough in my explorations. My attention had been fully occupied with the book I had found; I had not inspected the cave in detail. I just looked the space once over to see if there were obvious oddities, found none and returned to the pedestal again, thinking of how to retrieve my loot. However, this review of the video showed me that even in a space explored by other players there's always something that needs to be studied.

For example, the previous cave had nothing where this one had the support. At least, so it seemed on the face of it. However, once I zoomed in, there was a fascinating sight in front of me: in the shadows cast by uneven wall surfaces there was a rough-hewn statue of a cynocephalian, acting as an Atlas. His arms raised, he held up the ceiling that threatened to collapse; the expression on the face of the dog-headed creature was more eloquent than any words. Despite the rough carving and the impossibility of zooming any closer, one could see the tension felt by the model of the statue. The sculptor was so extremely skillful in conveying the inhuman effort exerted by the cynocephalian that I was starting to feel unbidden respect for this Atlas. Unfortunately, when the fire burnt us up I was looking in the other direction and never saw what happened to the statue: had it stayed in place or was it also destroyed by the fierce fire?

Stepping carefully over the wires, I went around the support and stood in the empty spot of the statue. Something was telling me that it was standing there for a reason. Once I turned towards the center of the space, I shuddered inside: the cave was criss-crossed with yellow rays of light, randomly shining out of the walls; that was the only point from which they were visible. Logic suggested that if I were to touch even one of those rays the cave would have been buried. There was a reason a support was there. Following my instinct more than logic, I decided to copy the statue's posture. What if I had to make one like it? Then the Book of Knowledge could tell me the proportions. Having checked once more the position and emotions of the statue in the previous cave, I raised my hands and made a tense grimace. Not knowing how sensitive and fragile the ceiling was, I decided to touch it just with the tip of my fingers, simply to record the dimensions. What if it were to burst like a bubble? Following that thought, I even took off my armor gloves for improved sensitivity and a more tender touch. The surface of the ceiling was cold, hard and rough; it was obviously not going to crack or burst. After a few experiments, I placed my entire palm on the surface; however, I received no secret messages or epiphanies. The ceiling remained hard, fully pretending to be a stone. I made sure that the Book recorded the potential size of the future statue and the directions of all the beams within the cave, I extracted my glove out of the inventory and, before putting it on my hand, tapped it on the ceiling lightly, knowing that I was simply losing time with all those precautions. Something had to be punished for that; so why not the ceiling?

What saved me was that at the time of the impact the glove was not touching the rest of the armor. The tap turned out to be quite impressive: sparks flew, something crackled, there was acrid smoke, but everything disappeared in an instance, leaving me to face the ceiling and a roughly hewn stone glove. Wait. Stone? My chest contracted and my heart dropped to my boots, once understanding came: had I touched the ceiling not with my bare hand but with the hand in my glove, all my armor would have turned to stone. The Book of Knowledge appeared in front of me again and I looked at the statue more carefully. Its face was the only finely worked part of it, and the longer I looked the more certain I became that it was not stone. It was the figure of a player, desiccated to the point of looking like a mummy, trapped by his armor which had turned to stone. The Game prevented him from respawning, and just now I had barely avoided his fate of becoming one more museum piece.

Apparently, the cave ceiling, like Midas of Phrygia, turned all non-living matter to stone; the player garbed in his class armor not only could not move, but could not even commit suicide to respawn. For some reason the level of Energy for the trapped player didn't go down.

"Zangar, do you know anything about this?" I

returned to the group and attacked the necromancer with questions, waving the stone glove in the air. "Cynocephalians, as far as I understand, are not so many as to occur in such exotic places. The Book is telling me that you are actually the only representative of that people in our sector of the Academy. Or is this forbidden as well?"

My imperturbable partner just shrugged his shoulders and looked away, when suddenly Marinar stepped forward.

"Offer me a trade – I am still not very good at doing this. As far as I understand, you are an explorer, so I decided to take a video for you, as I found a very interesting rock on that wall. Take a look right now, please. You should like it. I need to know if I am a good operator or not. If not, there are plenty more stones around."

With undisguised surprise I accepted the video record from the girl, worrying all the while about the sanity of our team. One of them looks away without bothering to answer, the other videotapes rocks and then runs after me demanding that I look at her creative efforts and give her the Oscar for Best Director. Marinar was looking at me so intensely and demandingly that I had no other choice than to spend a few minutes to take a look at whatever she recorded there. In order to treat the mentally sick you need to first play along, so that they would trust you. After all, she was the keymaster, and we needed to somehow pass through the cave criss-crossed by those rays. The book processed the video and the following picture appeared in front of me:

"Oh! Yaropolk, I am sure, will like this stone!" The video started by showing a very ordinary common rock – there were plenty of those on the ledge. Apparently, our troubles had taken their toll on the girl. A pity!

"Marinar!" came Zangar's guttural voice, and it was a moment before I realized that he was not speaking in the common language. "Do you understand me?"

"No. I think Yari might not like this stone," the girl continued recording her video, ignoring the cynocephalian's question."It's too ordinary after all. Oh! Take a look at this one! It has a lot more facets!"

"That's a pity," Zangar started again. "No one to even talk to. You don't know my language. Cannot understand me. Won't tell anyone. Danger ahead. Cannot warn. Teacher prohibited! Don't know what to do. But you can't advise. You don't understand."

"The facets are not so fine; I need to film something else," Marinar went on once Zangar paused, but I didn't listen to her voice any more. That was so clever of them! The necromancer had found a way, after all, to share information without breaking his teacher's order!

The video lasted twenty minutes. While in the beginning I was all excited about the information I was about to learn, after it ended I had a persistent thought that perhaps it would have been better had the cynocephalian said nothing to me. Because sometimes knowledge is not only power, but also a major headache.

Recruits were personally assigned to the

sectors by the Viceroy based on the recommendations of one of his deputies. By the way, there were four Viceroys in the Game, each responsible for his sector: biological, energy-based, ephemeral and other-worldly life forms. Levard, Zangar's teacher, was a deputy of the Viceroy for the biological sector, and was responsible for relations with humanoid lifeforms. Based on his recommendation Zangar was sent into the 3rd sector of the Academy, where Levard had trained at some point. The essence of going through the Academy was simple: only the strongest, craftiest, cleverest or richest players stayed in the Game; there was no place in it for others, and the Game reverted them back to NPCs. According to the necromancer, souls were immortal. However, the Game would try to distinguish those who took risks: if a non-initiated player were to complete the entire sector and reach the center of the Academy, he would receive a gift from the Chancellor that would be useful in the future. Generally, the Academy was divided into four stages: forest, Labyrinth, wastelands and the Chancellor's castle. Each of the stages had both open and hidden bonuses, some of which we had found. The ones we hadn't been able to find were the auction and a couple of traders. There were certain subtleties in the course of completion. For example, it was impossible to pass through the Labyrinth without a sacrifice. Levard had entered the Academy with two initiated minions and left with only one who had been his steady companion ever since. The third cynocephalian was left in the Labyrinth. As a sacrifice. Zangar saw the lost companion of his teacher when we were in the previous cave but hadn't brought it up, as he thought that we would move along the road that was already known to him. When I decided to change the plan and found a new passage, the necromancer had planned to use Marinar as the sacrificial lamb, despite the agreement. After all, the agreement was made between Marinar and myself, not Zangar. But now the necromancer was having doubts about his initial decision, even though it was pointless to go through the case if you didn't have a victim. According to him, the best thing to do would be to go back, find another player, make him the keymaster and go through the passage we had used first. Because passing through the first test of the Labyrinth was extremely difficult.

But that wasn't the worst thing in the video describing various stones. Wasteland was not an allegoric name; that area was literally a wasteland. It was a flat land, stretching all the way beyond the horizon; groups of Light or Dark beings wandered through it. Light ones hated the Darks ones and would try to destroy them; the Dark ones would respond in kind. However, neither was in favor of "mixed marriages". A Dark one and Light one couldn't survive in the same group. That was an axiom of the wastelands. The groups traveled in accordance with certain rules, which one could follow moving with a group of some beings of the same kind and retreating in case of an unexpected battle; however, we would have to part ways in order to survive. As it was currently, our group wouldn't make it.

"Very useful video, thank you, Marinar," I said

slowly, looking steadily at Zangar. "It's a pity, though, you weren't able to cover more. I would very much like to know about the stone located in the center of this cave. There must be something valuable about it!"

"We must return," the necromancer said calmly. "Can't make it further."

"Oh yes we can – we'll just have to. Tell me rather – is this for good?" I showed him the stone glove once again. "Or will it return to normal over time?"

"No information. Teacher not mention ceiling. You could be stone. You're lucky."

"Really, I am a positively lucky bastard!" I said testily. "Marinar, do you have anything under your robe? If we were to take it off you, would you be running with us naked, or in your underwear still?"

"I don't understand ..."

"There's not much here to understand. We need to complete the cave. For this, we need a support, which would be a set of class armor. Since you aren't planning to become a mage anyway, we could undress you."

"NO!" The girl cried out, blushing deeply. "I will not walk around the Academy in my underwear!"

"That means you do have something there," I grinned, and added: "Relax, no one is going to undress anyone. I just said it to lighten our spirits. Now, we'll all go into the cave. I'll leave you at the entrance while I figure out what can be done about the rays and the remaining traps. If I turn to stone, you will send me to respawn and die in a trap. We'll meet at the respawn point."

"Why you need it? Dangerous and stupid," Zangar tried to address my sensible side.

"Because there's a book there which practically made your teacher a Viceroy. I don't know about you, but I am not prepared to pass up such a gift from fate. I am not going to rush forward without thinking, I need to check everything once again, but I need help. I suppose you can hit a target on the head from some distance? So, great then!"

Twenty minutes later I left Zangar and Marinar at the last trip wire, having expressly forbidden them from entering the cave. Then I returned to the vantage point. The yellow beams were still there, criss-crossing the cave in all directions. Having carefully circled the cave I reached its opposite side and couldn't contain my emotions: there were no supports or statues here, but from the point diametrically across from the central pedestal I gained a view of blue rays that were not in any way connected to the yellow ones. The Book immediately generated a 3D model of the cave with the rays and helplessly blinked red: it would be impossible to reach the exit from the center. Generally, the cave only had two safe areas: from the entrance along the wall to the 90 degree points to the vantage spots. Everything else was blocked with either yellow or blue rays; in addition, their concentration around the central pedestal was most dense.

"Fuuuuuuu....!!!" A horrible scream of pain indicated learning what would happen if someone crossed a blue ray. First I touched the ceiling with my stone glove, since it was completely and irrevocably ruined, but nothing happened. No explosions, no sparks, no smoke. Unwilling to lose the other glove, I touched the ceiling with my bare hand and immediately crashed to the floor filling the entire cave with my scream of pain: the hand, not covered with armor, started dissolving as if eaten up by acid. The pain was so horrendous that I fainted; when I came to, I had no hand. A disfigured and burnt stub was all the Game had left me.

"You need to respawn," Zangar noted, calmly as always, once I hobbled back to the group. The elves' ointment from a red vial helped: it killed the pain and healed the wound; however, it failed to accomplish a miracle: my hand did not regenerate. "Now you're deficient. Bad fighter and partner. Do you need help?"

"The yellow rays activate destruction of armor, and the blue ones destroy organic matter," I grumbled, unable to take my eyes away from the pedestal and the book sitting on it. A mere fifteen meters separated me from fascinating knowledge; yet right now it seemed like another abyss! "No one can provide a guarantee that there are no more, say, green rays that destroy everything altogether. But we were in that blasted cave!" By the last sentence I was already shouting, giving way to my emotions. "Blue rays were deactivated there! That means there must be a way to remove them somehow! Zangar!?"

"I have no information. Not even the kind I couldn't tell. Teacher thought – one cave. Said to go that way. We can return. Find new keymaster."

"I am not leaving this place without the book," I

almost growled, studying the 3D model of the rays. "How far can you throw me?"

Zangar thought for a while; he even lifted me, estimating my weight, then said:

"To the opposite end of the cave or even further."

"Excellent. Marinar, what attack ability do you have, and how much time will it take you to activate it?"

"Ice. About two seconds for activation." Apparently no one understood what I was getting at: both the cynocephalian and the former inhabitant of Varnax looked puzzled.

"It takes Zangar about two seconds as well." The plan in my head took shape, and now was fleshing out so actively that the Book of Knowledge that had learnt to read my thoughts formed a planned trajectory of my flight. "Then we'll do the following. Marinar, you stand in the corridor. As soon as Zangar throws me, you wait for one second, then shoot ice at me, hit me – that's most important! Don't you even think of missing! Then you go for respawn via a trap.

"Zangar, your task will be more difficult. You have to throw me like this." Using gestures, I indicated the trajectory of my supposed flight that would avoid most of the rays, "Immediately after you throw me you have to get out your staff and cast your mega-deadly curse at me, then step over the trip wire and join Marinar in the trap. I hope I die before I hit the floor... I don't see another way out that would enable us to obtain the book without one of the group dying. Oh, but we have the agreement! For the Game:

I officially allow Marinar and Zangar to inflict damage on me in accordance with the algorithm I have just outlined. The last thing we need is for you to incur punishment after all of this. If anyone has objections or suggestions, speak now because later we'll all be dead, so it'll be too late."

"This is crazy and irresponsible," Marinar stated."You are exposing the entire group to potential danger for the sake of some book. What if there's nothing there?"

"Zangar?" I looked at the imperturbable necromancer, ignoring the girl's words.

"The book made teacher stronger. Can help us. We'll cover you. Risk justified. Say when to throw you."

"To hell with you, let's try," the mage surrendered. "I'm ready. By the way, dying is very unpleasant."

"No one's arguing with that. On the count of three: Ready, set... Marinar, go to the corridor. STOP! Take a step to the side, slowly, now freeze! You nearly activated a trap! Everyone ready? One! Two!

"THREE!"

You were killed and sent to a respawn point
You lost one level
Your current level: 7
Object received: Founders' notes. Volume 2 of 3: Madonna

The space around me regained colors and I realized that I was standing next to the respawn stone. Zangar was standing next to me.

"We need a new keymaster," the necromancer said carefully, examining something behind my back. "Marinar forgot to put her hood on."

I turned around following the necromancer's gaze and was barely able to suppress nausea: the girl lying on the ground had very little left of her head. It was a horrendous sight: the acid had destroyed Marinar's head all the way to the brain at the back. Swallowing hard, I looked at my hand and my body turned cold: the hand was still a stub which did not regenerate after respawn.

"Marinar lingered before trap. Didn't want to die. I killed you. Left through trap. As agreed. Mage was scared and retreated. Acid flooded the corridor. Did not harm me. Marinar was slow. Stupid death."

She had level three!" I whispered in astonishment. "Why is she dead? This was not supposed to happen! I calculated everything! She had two more lives!"

"Acid prevents regeneration. Your hand shows that. Hard to live without head. Not everyone can. You got what you wanted. What's the book about? Was it worth Marinar's life?"

Only at that point did I realize that in my right hand I was convulsively clutching the book shining with all the colors of the rainbow. Before I burnt up – and I was burnt by the fire of the trap, not the mage's ice nor the necromancer's curse – I had grabbed the book, making it my property and an integral part of me as a game character. The book was made in the same style as the notes of Zangar's teacher: wooden boards with the text written in broad handwriting. Only this time I was able to read the text without the necromancer's help:

... Failed again! We managed to put HIM together, but something is going awry! The Game is asking for an access code. WHAT IS THAT?!

... We found the code! It's frightful to imagine the mind of the one who invented it!

... Merlin is still doubting. He considers we should wait another couple of hundred years. There is no time to wait! Humanity will die if we hesitate!

... I figured it out! We need a sacrifice! I know who that will be. All three of us!

... The Emperor felt something wrong and tried to stop us. Fool! The Game has no power over those who have HIM! We shall reach our goal!

... My beloved brought the babies. Two boys and a girl. He says we don't have to die after restart. It's possible to become part of the Game again, of our Game. We need some time to work out the ritual.

... The Emperor found us but didn't destroy us. It's funny: he is not against restart. He doesn't care, actually; the most important thing for him is to preserve history.

... We agreed on the list of players who will come with us to our new world. This is the third restart!!! It would be funny to look at the three histories combined, The Emperor says the Game will find a way to explain it.

... We will have to respawn after all. The power surge must be great, else the server won't be able to

make it. That's a pity; I had hoped to keep my current body and consciousness. The Emperor offered to help with the transfer. We agreed.

...This is the last entry, so I'll pay special attention to it. Tomorrow we are going to restart the Game and establish our order! Since we'll become different beings, I will leave a hint with the Chancellor of the Academy. Merlin and my beloved hid their books. Those who want will find them. In essence, in order to restart the Game, one needs the founder's key – it consists of three parts (the parts are described in Merlin's notes, he was working on that), coordinates of the game server (those coordinates are in my beloved's notes) and the access code (<a line of 4056 symbols>). A strong power surge is required for restart, so the one who restarts the machine must die. I hope the new world will be different from the old one and that humanity will come to its senses.

Priestess, level 796, Madonna.

"Yaropolk?"Zangar reminded me of his existence once I turned the last page and froze, staring into nothingness. Madonna wasn't a founder of the Game – Levard was wrong! "Have you become stronger?"

"He has become wiser," came the Chancellor's sarcastic voice; however, it had none of its former anger now. "Even though in his case it's the same thing. What would you say, Dark one, was the book worth what happened to you in the cave?"

"Everything is relative. What happened to Marinar?" It dawned on me only now that contrary to the mechanics of the Game the girl's body hadn't disappeared. If she had died, she would have simply faded, as had happened to many before her, returning her "soul" to the NPC pool. However, her body showed no signs of dissolving, which indicated one thing only: somehow the girl remained living. Since the Chancellor himself deigned to visit us, why shouldn't we find out from him the reasons for this very strange phenomenon?

"It seems as though she died: can't you see? In your flight you crossed both a blue ray and a yellow one. Had you spent a little more time investigating you would have also learnt about purple rays. While the yellow and purple act with a certain delay, blocking a blue ray instantly fills the cave with acid; the result of it is literally upon your heads. You nitwits, you are told when the armor is issued to you: don't take it off under any circumstances! But no, we are such smart ones. It's more comfortable for us without headgear. So one oh so smart one outsmarted herself."

"Had she died the body would have disappeared."

"Oh, she is alive! She is just being punished. Both for being slow and for figuring out the way to convey information from Zangar to you. I don't like cunning players, so now she will have to enjoy this. Her mind won't suffer; I will restore her mind from the point when you took the book. No, but what a crazy idea — jumping across the rays! Through the air! Some explorer, aren't you... I need to close that loophole to be on the safe side. And to protect against various explorers too smart for their own good."

"For the next time?" I said in surprise.

"You thought that there was only one copy of the notes? Levard was the first in the current version of the Game who obtained the notes, so I created the second cave. You are the second. So that means that the third cave will soon appear, with even more elaborate traps that will account for flying as well. At least I'll get some amusement from that."

"So the first and third volumes are not in the Academy?"

"Dark one: read the notes again! Don't aggravate me; it's already hard for me to get used to the thought that Merlin's reincarnation might be Dark. He was fun to talk to!"

"...?"

"What did I do to deserve all this?! Since you are the one who found the book, you may be one of the three mages of the past. Specifically, the one you are is: Merlin. Madonna can only return as a woman, and the third player is still alive. For that reason his name has been removed from everywhere. He survived – understand? He withheld some of his power, spared himself. That's why the current version came out so flawed. There are too many discrepancies in it; it's too far from the original plan. Thus, either you or Levard, or the subsequent player who finds the new cave and retrieves the book is the reincarnation of Merlin, a level 933 mage. The others are just lucky."

"I have question." Zangar joined the conversation. "Even two. First, how to heal Marinar? I understand she is alive. Not good to abandon partner.

Second... Not question Request. Remove constraint on information. Cannot keep silent. No hand, no head. Weak group we have. Will not pass Labyrinth."

"My constraint applies only to Levard, I have nothing to do with you. You need to resolve your issues with your teacher. Either you betray him and tell everything, or keep silent, or... Really, I am not the one to give you hints, players. By the way, it probably makes sense to warn you: if you do manage to get out of the Academy, we'll have to sign a non-disclosure agreement between us. It wouldn't be right to release information on specifics of the Academy into the public domain. Don't frown, Dark one, you'll receive your compensation. You wouldn't be able to sell it at a higher price than that.

"As for Marinar — her body needs to be restored. The damage from my acid is not removed by respawn. I took her soul into storage; right now there is no place for it to return. Bring the body to me, I'll restore it. And your hand too, Dark one, even though it would teach you if I were to leave it like this forever. So that you'd think twice before sticking things into places! She will still lose Energy, so hurry. As a goodwill gesture I'll slow down the drain rate, say, by half. Now she'll respawn every 24 hours. Did I answer your questions, necromancer? Then I have a surprise for you: by my right as the head of the Academy I am changing the terms of the quest issued to you. If you want to get a reward I'm waiting for all three of you in the castle.

"Further on you can't use any more keymasters, that's enough. You already had two attempts and you failed both times. Besides, there are no more players in the forest, everyone has left for the Labyrinth; so that's more of a formal constraint than a critical one, but I have to warn you. If you show your faces in the caves you may forget about the reward."

Quest "Visit" has been updated ...

"There was a player left in the first cave," my eyes fell on Marinar's body and I immediately remembered the statue. "Is he being punished as well?"

"It was his conscious choice. He sacrificed himself so that Levard could have the book. At that time I hadn't invented the blue rays yet, so I let him stay where he is. Oh well, and it's a little more fun for me: between the enrolments of recruits I play with his spirit. The way he screams in pain is very amusing... He's a funny guy. That's it; I'm waiting for you at my place."

"I have twenty two Energy elixirs and nine elves' ointment," I said once the pause grew long. Zangar and I simply stood and stared at each other, lost in our own thoughts. I didn't know what the necromancer was thinking about, but I was thinking about his teacher, Levard. If he were an incarnation of Merlin, it would explain his thirst for knowledge about the beginning of the Game and his advancement to unprecedented heights for a player. A potential Viceroy, one of the four players who control the Game. Perhaps the Emperor himself made him a councilor as he was worried about the possibility of another restart.

"I have ten pastries," the necromancer replied. "Enough for now. I carry Marinar. I am stronger. Give me ointment. We need to put on her head. Stop blood from dripping. You have protection. You go first. We go like everyone. Through Labyrinth. No other way."

Once the Labyrinth doors shut behind us with a resounding crash, Zangar said:

"First test. We need to think how to pass. Time is limited."

I have to admit, whatever I expected it was not what appeared in front of me. I associated the Labyrinth, first and foremost, with multilevel moving traps, a Minotaur roaming the corners, with Ariadne's thread, after all! But not, under any circumstances, with a small thriving village full of life. Literally twenty meters from the wall the houses started; smoke was rising from their chimneys. Children were running back and forth between the houses, chickens were scratching, a pack of dogs chased a yowling black cat that managed to climb a tree, and from there, from a safe height, was expressing his attitude to the dogs in general, now using normal cat language rather than cursing everyone right left and center. There was the sound of blacksmith's hammer, the smell of freshly cut grass just starting to dry... The Labyrinth looked nothing like a scary and formidable stage of passing through the Academy. Just in case I said:

"I see a village, with people,. Wooden houses, twenty in number. A crowd of villagers, simply dressed. Players, walking among them and arguing about something. Also, I sense such a pleasant smell of food that it makes my stomach rumble from hunger. Is this my hallucination or do you see the same thing as I?"

"This is not a phantom," astonished Zangar confirmed."Two cannot see wrong. I don't understand. Respawn point on the right. Players there. Can ask what's up. Find group. The more the easier."

"Then let's go. Be careful of the mages, they have a habit of first attacking and only then finding out the circumstances."

Having decided, we took just one step towards the village, when a message appeared before my eyes:

You have reached the Labyrinth, a PVP-free zone
Any aggression against another player shall be punished by instant respawn
You will need to complete four sequential tests
Test one: transfer 27 potatoes to head of village
Object received: potato

"Yari! Homeboy!" I heard the joyful cry and almost immediately was wrapped in a bear hug by Monstrichello's huge paws. "We've been waiting for yo so! Nata said you'd come soon, but we got worried. Teart thought you were plain dead. 'Cause you left the group."

"I was just concerned and warily I inquired about the others' opinions," leprechaun approached and shook my hand affably. "It's good to see you again, partner. Are those two with you? Why do you bring a mage with you? And what's wrong with him? Why can't he walk? What happened to your hand? Where's your glove? What happened to you altogether? Why did you and Nata decide to go as different groups?"

"Where is she?" I stopped the avalanche of leprechaun's, questions, tensing as he mentioned the druid.

"Sleeping, it's her turn to rest now. The first test involves providing 27 potatoes. Until you have them, the locals won't even bother to see you. They just totally ignore you. There are two teachers in the village, for profession and attributes, but in order to train with them you need to first come up with those blasted tubers. The growth cycle of one tuber is twenty four hours. One cycle yields three potatoes per bush. The potato that you planted disappears. How good are you at math?"

"It takes three cycles," I calculated at once. Or six cycles of Energy replenishment.

"We collected our first harvest today, but we have lost two levels each by now. We've organized guard shifts; now Logir and Sartal are guarding the crops, some people are sleeping and we were waiting for you. Oh, and I have to warn you right away: be prepared, here it's not like in the forest. In the Labyrinth you need to sleep; at least you don't have to eat and use the bathroom... perhaps they left that off until the wasteland. The food – Nata had food with her – replenishes Energy, but she has very little left, so we decided to save that for later. Good thing all of us leveled up above 8 in the forest. We'll go through the first test and then we'll see.

"Why do you guard the crops? If you can't fight other players here?"

"It's not allowed to fight, but there's no rule against stealing. The potatoes would disappear literally just as they were about to produce new tubers. Already now there are plenty of desperate players here ready to do anything to pass the test at all costs. They'd find your crops, try to pull out the plant and take the potato. The task of the guards is to prevent that by standing in the attackers' way and forcing them to push. Respawn here is instant – all it takes is touching another player. By the way, if you lose your potato, no one will give you a new one."

"Wait, isn't it silly to guard in twos? If one is sent for respawn even for a shove, why not encircle the crops so that no one could get through?"

"That would be a great decision, but not within the Academy," the leprechaun smirked sadly. "As soon as the number of people per crop exceeds three, a huge bird swoops in and drags everyone so unfortunate to her nest, which is in a huge tree. It's not far, about half a mile from here. She has two chicks there. Who are always hungry. Hundreds of players have already passed through their throats. Even our Monster," Monstrichello shuddered from the unpleasant memory. "And that birdie flies very fast. You never answered about those two. Are they with you?"

"Yes. Let me introduce you: Zangar, necromancer. Marinar, mage, temporarily headless."

"What do you mean – headle.. ... Bleagh!" Leprechaun was overtaken by a retching fit as soon as Marinar's hood was lifted and he saw the effects of acid exposure.

"We cannot wait," Zangar said while Teart was trying to regain his composure. "Marinar second level. Two respawns. Then death. Elixirs useless for her. We have twenty four hours. For Labyrinth and wastelands. Even less. Must make it."

"There's only one way for you to make it in time," Dolgunata appeared from behind Monstrichello, and cast an appraising look at the necromancer. "You need to kill the bird and its chicks. Then the locals will start talking to us. There are traders here, and I have money to pay. Hello, Yari. Doesn't look like you hurried much. Your slowness cost us all two levels, so pull yourself together now. You need to kill the bird."

CHAPTER NINE

TESTS OF THE LABYRINTH

"**W**ELCOME to the Temple of Knowledge, young Judge." The old man spread his arms in a friendly gesture. "It's a pleasure to see that you crave knowledge. Description for official interrogation of witnesses and suspects is on the table for you. Please review it."

I grabbed the piece of paper and started reading it. Dolgunata had finally done it. The girl's words had thrown a switch in my head and the inscription "Evil Incarnate" appeared in my mind.

So much had happened recently that this case had sort of faded from my mind; however, the girl's voice jogged my memory and thinking. While before the Labyrinth I supposed that we could coexist and complete not only the Labyrinth, but the Academy as well, after her statement, particularly given the way it was presented – as if I had broken all possible and impossible laws – had set off a frantic search for a solution in my head. Using physical force would not be an option: even if I were able to deal a fatal blow to her, that would immediately send me to respawn, and right now was really not a good time for that. My group members had too little time for me to indulge myself by being provoked like that. Besides, I would have to explain the motive behind my actions to the Paladins; again, that would take some time, and there were no guarantees that they would even believe me. I was certain that all of them were under the influence of her ability and under her full control. That was why it would have been pointless to argue with the girl. That would not have been taken well. Putting up with it and swallowing the dish served by Dolgunata of a mix of sarcasm and arrogance wouldn't do either. The others may think you a pussy all they want, but it's not right to fail in your own eyes. Self-respect is invisible, but it is too important to neglect. Ignoring the druid's speech would have been wrong as well: Teart and Monstrichello stared at me with a mute demand for me to answer the question: "Is it really true that Dolgunata is right and we're suffering because of you?" Dolgunata had not left a single way for me to extricate myself from this situation so that I would not lose face and become a "freak" in the eyes of the Paladins. That bitch was even appearing in a constructive mode: like, here – wipe the shit off your face, get up and let's go kill the bird. She did everything to discount my return to the group.

But Dolgunata had left out the most important thing: I wasn't just any player. I was a Judge! Before accusing her of committing all the deadly sins I needed to open the Paladins' eyes as to what she really was; that's why I had asked the Game to describe the principle of interrogating witnesses. As I found out, the players constantly tried to mess with each other's heads, gaining their own goals by whatever means it took. However, there should be some process or point, when the player is forced to tell the truth and only the truth. As if he were under oath. In order to make the Paladins oust Dolgunata from their heads I needed to show them what she was like for real, when she was herself. Even though the method I used was far from trivial. The Game kept silent for three entire heartbeats before it fulfilled my request and let me into the Temple of Knowledge.

"Teart, in the name of justice I demand that you tell the truth and nothing but the truth! You are summoned as a witness in the case "Evil Incarnate"," I said in a voice devoid of all emotion, as soon as I returned to the Labyrinth. It sounded like pathos, but such were the rules: that was the beginning of the official procedure for questioning witnesses. I was right: the Game actually had a protocol for questioning witnesses in judicial cases. While the suspect could ignore this procedure (no one, not even the Game, could force someone to testify against himself) the witnesses had no option to speak an untruth. You could omit things or skirt around things — that was fine, but you could not openly lie. That was punished harshly, up to final death.

"For the duration of your testimony you are released from all physical, moral and emotional binds," I finished the key phrase and Teart's eyes glazed. Apparently, a system message appeared in front of the leprechaun and he was reading it, surprised.

"Witness: state your name, class and level." I started the questioning as soon as the leprechaun's eyes cleared and incredible surprise appeared in them instead.

"Teart, Paladin, level seven," Teart said slowly, shifting his eyes from me to Dolgunata, who took several steps to the side. The druid frowned. Apparently events as they were unfolding now weren't going as she had planned. By the way, the Paladins had leveled up quite well before the Labyrinth. Where did they get so much experience, given that they'd already lost two levels?

"Teart, please explain: how did Dolgunata explain my absence from the group?" I continued my questioning.

"She said that you had agreed to move on separately, to avoid provoking the mages. That it would be easier for you to travel through the forest alone. Even though I didn't quite understand why ..."

"In what way did you achieve so many levels?"

"That's not relevant!" The druid interfered, but then fell silent, encountering my cold stare. We stared daggers at each other for a few moments, then

Dolgunata's pupils widened as she suddenly realized: she couldn't control me anymore. Headhunters really are formidable creatures if you think about it.

"Teart, I repeat the question — how did you achieve so many levels?"

"We killed players," leprechaun responded dispiritedly. "Mages, warriors... Everyone who came to hand, we never asked their level, nor if they were initiated. Yari, I don't know why we were doing that... At that time it seemed that we were doing the right thing, but... We killed all of them ..."

"Did you leave the concrete forest and enter the Labyrinth of your own will?" I kept inquiring.

"No," Teart thought for a while. "We wanted to wait for you, but Dolgunata and Sakhray convinced us that we should go on. Killing everyone we encountered along the way."

Hearing an unfamiliar name I slowed down for a moment, but immediately understood who that was: the male druid.

"Thank you, Teart, I don't have any more questions for you. In the name of justice I release you from the obligation to tell the truth and nothing but the truth," I said the official phrase to end the interrogation and turned to the next witness. It was Monstrichello – by this time Dolgunata was practically hiding behind him.

"Monstrichello, in the name of justice I demand that you..." I started the process for questioning the second Paladin, when Dolgunata suddenly screamed hysterically:

"Monstrichello! Save me! They want to kill me!

Darling, you are my only hope!"

"WHO?!" The giant roared, pulling out his shield and activating his defense. "I WON'T LET 'EM!"

"Kill them!" Nata continued to yell. "Kill them all! They aren't your brothers! They are demons!"

"BASH'EM ALL!" Monster rushed right ahead, swinging his shield for a blow. It all happened so suddenly that no one had time to react. Teart, Zangar with Marinar and I fell to the side like bowling pins. Hitting the ground took my breath away, but failed to kill me: I activated my defense even as I was flying through the air. Once the stars stopped jumping in my eyes and faded, I jumped to my feet to try and deflect Monster's next attack, but he was already gone. I barely saw the last ripples from his figure dissolving in the air: the Game had punished the tank for an attack within the Labyrinth. A couple of yards away Zangar was rising to his feet; he managed to save not only himself but Marinar as well; however, Teart wasn't there. The leprechaun was the first to take Monstrichello's blow and be sent for respawn.

"Babies," Dolgunata snorted testily, looking on disdainfully "You are so easy to control! You are just helpless kittens – the main world will eat you for breakfast and won't as much as burp!"

"Dolgunata! I pronounce you guilty of controlling the Paladins' minds, disregard of all ethical norms and incitement to murder," I said with unconcealed malice, shifting my artifact into attack mode and advancing towards the druid. "I sentence you to be stripped of initiation and final death in the Academy! This sentence is final and not subject to appeal!"

> *Verdict is confirmed*
> *Verdict is deemed harsh*
> *Verdict shall apply within the Academy only*
> *Player, level 10, Dolgunata, is non-initiated*
> *Case "Evil Incarnate" is closed. The task is assigned to the nearest Headhunters*
> *Received: reward for Headhunter: 1 granis (reward shall be transferred to the Headhunter that will deliver the final fatal blow at the first level of the convict)*
> *Received reward for verdict: character allegiance determined*

The arrow of the virtual meter that was already within the dark side now moved for the last time, and a note appeared on it: "100". A new icon appeared on the control panel and immediately started blinking and jumping demanding that I should pay attention to it; however, I was occupied. I was looking at the druid and couldn't understand her joy. It created an impression that the girl had everything completely under control.

"Oh, scary-scary," Dolgunata smiled, confirming my thoughts. "I am oh so afraid! Oh, the scary Judge, he wants to destroy me! Oh, please save me, kind beings. Ha-ha-ha!"

Agitation began in the village. Everyone suddenly started running and rushing about; a few moments later I saw Logir, Dangard and a few more players walking slowly towards us. Apparently, all the local headhunters had received the assignment and now, as if sleepwalking, led by the magic word "granis", were moving towards us.

"Silly little Paladin," the druid continued to express her mirth. She cast a quick glance at the advancing hunters and grinned as if completely unconcerned by the new threat. "In the Labyrinth you cannot inflict physical damage on other players. I have just demonstrated this to you. Logir! Dangard wants to kill me! Save me! He is the Paladins' enemy!"

Before I could stop the femorc, she dealt the mage a crushing blow and the two characters slowly faded in the air, never having figuring out what happened to them.

"I could continue this forever," the druid continued mocking. "Within the Academy there are no mental protection amulets, so I am like a goddess here! If you're unhappy with it – it's your own problem, you may open as many cases as you can stuff down your throat. There's no one here who would be able to punish me. You two! Get out, if you don't want to join the dead Paladins!" Dolgunata barked at the hunters who came up, and they ran off at once.

"Yari, I want to know how you got rid of my mental control. And until I find this out, I will keep sending Paladins to respawn time and again. The fact that you released Teart means nothing. I'll subdue him again. He is weak. Just like the rest of you."

"Worthy opponent," Zangar reminded me he was still there. "You're lucky, Paladin. If survive – will be strong. Hello, Dolgunata. I'm Zangar, necromancer.

We have met before."

"Sakhray, relax, they aren't going to attack," Dolgunata said to someone behind my back, then turned to the necromancer. I don't remember you, necromancer, how do you know me? Where did we meet?"

"Your teacher – Archibald. He visited my teacher. Two months before Academy. You were with them. I remember you. Archibald taught you much. Your brother remember too. Smelt him a while ago. Cannot sneak well. Not so strong. Was a tournament. You were in finals. Not won. Took second place."

"You're Levard's student?!" Dolgunata exclaimed, astonished. "What did you tell Yari?!"

"Everything that is not forbidden. We have no time. Partner dying. Need potatoes. You must help us. Forget Yari for now. He on my team.

"He's no one to you, necromancer! After the Academy you'll part forever. Why do you need a Paladin?"

"Yari help complete Academy. You know who I am. Who's my teacher. Need your help. Help. Reward will be good."

"Dammit!" Dolgunata thought a while, then cursed heartily, helplessly stomping her foot on the ground. "From what hellhole did you spring up here?! You broke all my plans! What do you want?"

"Need help with potatoes. Cannot wait. What you suggest. Why kill bird?"

"There's no need... simply an NPC, there's no point in it. I just wanted the Paladins to croak in pain: it's impossible to kill the bird. I can buy potatoes, but only for you and the mage. I won't buy anything for Yari. My teacher gave me very clear directions with respect to helping him."

"Agree," Zangar responded after thinking for a long time. "You buy potatoes for me. Mage. Go to second test. Yari catch up."

Turning towards me the necromancer added:

"Marinar die if we wait. Must get to Chancellor. He revive her. Then need to return. She need training. I can't wait. Sorry. You worthy partner. Can survive on your own. She can't. Little time."

"My brother and I will come with you," Dolgunata added at once. "I'm tired of coddling those Paladins, now Yari'll have to bother with them."

"Paladins' fate I don't care. Yaropolk important, he's partner. I return for him. But first other partner. Must go, druid. No lose time."

"But still, how did he escape from under my control?" Dolgunata wouldn't give up. "What did I do wrong? He has no amulet, nor congenital immunity like you do.

"Yari grew up while trained. Don't know how many years. Learnt to understand himself. Strong player. Will be hard for you, hunter."

"Training ranges. Of course!" Nata exhaled, smiling bitterly. "I couldn't maintain the control, and if he spent a lot of time there, he could have escaped from it – simple. Hm... Listen, but there's no way to counteract this! Six months of training, plus three months when the Energy level drops... Yeah, I'll have to think what to do. Fine, I'm ready. Sakhray, we are leaving."

A powerful druid passed by me, haughtily, with a feeling of his physical superiority. Some Mister Universe, if you judged him purely by physical appearance; in addition, Sakhray's movements were smooth and flowing, as if he'd been a dancer all his life. It looked like he was floating above the ground rather than walking, despite being quite huge. It was amazing that Zangar could feel him approach.

By the way, I didn't hold a grudge against the necromancer. It was unpleasant to be left on my own again, but I fully agreed; it was necessary to move on, otherwise Marinar would die. The Chancellor was really clear regarding quest and reward, so without the mage it would be pointless to visit him. I could survive six respawn cycles. I had enough elixirs.

As a dense crowd, we reached the center of the village, where an amazing thing happened. Amazing in the sense of understanding the druid's actions. She verified with the necromancer, to see if he really wouldn't join her group. Then she found the village elder and gave him two brass keys, pointing out that from this moment on her group, including the currently dead Paladins, should be counted among those who had passed the first test. I didn't know on what conditions her team had been formed, but was totally certain that Dolgunata could have stiffed everyone. But she didn't. Why – that was unclear. In my mind the druid was associated with all things negative. Nata bought potatoes for Marinar and Zangar from the same village elder, and then the four of them and the village elder went inside the house, but I was not allowed. A seven-foot-tall guard carefully moved me aside without any threats or instructions. Simply put me in my place.

"Yari?! I heard a surprised voice. "You are finally here! Where are the rest?"

Refor, Dirion and Sartal approached the house of the village elder ten minutes later.

"Logir, Teart and Monster are at respawn – Dolgunata killed them. Nata and Sakhray are with the village elder, discussing something. Did you receive information that the first test is complete?"

"Yes," Refor frowned." "What do you mean, killed? Why? How? And what happened to your hand?"

"In half an hour they'll tell you everything themselves," I said tiredly. "Did you harvest the potatoes or just left them at the field?"

"Harvested, of course. They're not needed any more, but leaving such a gift to the mages and the rest after what they'd done to us..."

"Since you don't need them, maybe you could share?" I put out a feeler. "They would come in very useful to me. Since I am not part of the group, the key didn't affect me."

"In principle, I don't mind," Refor looked at the rest, but before I had a chance to rejoice, he added: "There's just one thing. You said three of our guys were sent to respawn. What if the key doesn't work for them? We have to wait. Sorry, Yari, but we already lost two levels with those potatoes... those who are being respawned have more right to it than you. If they don't need it, then we'll give you all twenty-four of them. You said, it was half an hour? Let's wait: it's not that long. Meanwhile, please tell us what happened and why Nata activated the key. It seems we had agreed differently..."

An hour later I was in the middle of the field, carefully covering a single potato with soil. Refor hadn't lied to me: as soon as the three respawned players confirmed that the test had been passed, he gave me everything the Paladins had gathered by that time. Zangar and Dolgunata came out from the village elder with blank faces, and moved on to the teachers without paying any attention to us. Presumably, the second test took place inside the house and their group had just completed it. By then I, with the help of Teart and a constantly blushing Monstrichello, had clarified to the Paladins what the druid was really like, so their meeting with Dolgunata was rather cool. It's unpleasant when someone manipulates you like a puppet. The Paladins, accompanied by the village elder, went inside for the second test while I left for the gardening plots. In order to complete the first test successfully I needed to grow one crop. Three blasted potatoes. 24 hours in the Game.

I buried my potato and sat down on the ground. There were quite a few players around. Some were guarding their crops, some were wandering around in pairs looking for potential victims: not everyone cared to grow their own harvests. They were not interested in me: I had just one potato. But the players who had managed by now to plant their second harvest faced far more danger from the thieves: there was supposed to be a certain distance between the tubers, and if the group of players was large enough, already at the second growing cycle the area of the crops grew enormously. Since it was large, guarding it was hard as well. Within the two minutes that I had been in the field, the bird had flown over twice, dragging hapless players with it. The bird was an eagle grown up to the size of a bus. It covered the distance from the nest within seconds, then attacked a group of four players and dragged them off to its chicks. An unpleasant respawn. "Vultures" immediately rushed to the vacated spots: players, who didn't feel like growing their own potatoes. They pushed and shoved, sending each other for respawn, dug out the tubers stealing single potatoes, screamed with joy once they were able to stick their quarry in the inventory. It was all very chaotic.

A thought flashed through my mind that it would be interesting to find out what happened to the potatoes from the personal inventory of those players who met their final death, eaten by the chicks, but then the blinking icon on the control panel reminded me again that I was spending too much time paying attention to those around me and not enough for myself. Making sure there were no "vultures" around me, I clicked on the icon.

You have reached the threshold level for allegiance: Darkness
Would you like to activate it?

Threshold level for allegiance. One of the teachers had said that it was practically unrealistic to reach it within the Academy, but he had forgotten that I was a Judge, and that for delivering a correct verdict I was due some kind of bonus. Even though my sentence was so brazenly ignored. There was no sense in delaying the decision, so I calmly clicked on the "Accept" button. If I am destined to be a Dark one, so be it. Because...

Suddenly, like a tsunami out of nowhere, a wave of ecstasy came over me. The sensations were so amazing and delightful that, stifling a moan of pleasure, I fell to the ground. Sex? Drugs? Alcohol? All of that at once? Nothing could induce such feelings that overcame me. The sensation seemed to last forever, until finally the darkness saved me by drowning my overheated mind. Too much of a good thing can be dangerous, too.

"He's not dead yet for some reason. Shall we just leave him? It's been a day and a night..."

"Roll him to one side, that's all. Can't you see: his potato ripened! Three potatoes will be ours. This one can die, blasted freak. The Paladins killed so many of our guys."

Someone was attempting to manhandle me, and my body definitely disagreed with the idea. Uttering another moan of pleasure, since the memory of mega orgasm was still fresh, I opened my eyes and dug my arms in the ground, not allowing them to move me. I was lucky: when I fainted I fell right onto my planted potato. That's why I hadn't been robbed. What was unclear was something else: why was I still alive?"

"Bastard! Get away already!" The fat man that was pushing me growled angrily. Seemed like a monk, if I deciphered the class clothes correctly. One thing was obvious: he was not human. "Drgrygz, help! He came to!"

"Then whomp him!"

"You whomp him yourself! I have only one level left.

"Go to hell!" I growled, grabbing the potato tops with my good hand. They weren't trying to beat me, just to carefully move me from one place to another, that's why the Game was not destroying the thieves. "This is my loot!"

"Drgrygz!" The fat guy yelled, desperation showing in his voice by now, and another monk came up to us. "This loser won't give us his potatoes."

"Leave him!" The new arrival grumbled. "He came to, wanker crip. Let's go."

They stopped touching me and left me alone; and only then did I figure out what had seemed strange to me during my first few moments after "waking up". There was no more allegiance scale at the top of my vision field; in addition, a semi-transparent green inscription "+1" kept flashing in front of my eyes. About every ten seconds.

I clicked again at the new icon, which had stopped jumping like crazy, and stared at the amazing sight:

Location: Academy Labyrinth. Level of available emotions: 56%. Energy restore: 1 unit per 10 seconds. Current allegiance level: 1

The number "1" in the Energy restore

description was interactive. I immediately clicked on it and saw a complex formula for calculating the amount of Energy replenished, linked both to the allegiance level and the amount of available emotions within the current location as well as to the amount of available emotions within a certain distance from the player. The closer a source of emotions was located to me, the faster my Energy would restore.

"Get away!" I heard a woman shrieking indignantly. "That's mine!"

"Drgrygz, don't let her through! I'll dig everything out now!" One of the monks replied joyfully. I closed all the windows and turned in the direction of the conflict. A woman of about fifty, wearing dark steel armor, was trying to no avail to get around the monk standing in front of her in order to protect her plot with the three ripened tubers. Meanwhile, the second monk was digging the soil with his hands like a mole. Or a rat, which was more accurate under the circumstances.

"Leave her alone!" I shouted, throwing my own harvested potatoes into the inventory. The first test was as good as done.

"Drgrygz, come on, just a little more!" The monks ignored me, continuing to loot someone else's plot.

"Paladin, help!" real tears appeared on the woman's face. More than likely she wasn't initiated and now the monks were effectively killing her as she looked on. She was still walking and breathing, yet she was already dead. Losing the potatoes for non-initiated players equaled delayed death.

Initiation of the allegiance cost me 24 hours. The map indicated that the Paladins were approximately half-way between me and the center of the Academy; more than likely they were already within the wastelands. Zangar with his group had practically reached the Chancellor: according to the map they were within a very short distance from the point marked by the Chancellor as his location. No matter what I did I wouldn't be able to catch up with either of the groups; so I could as well use some time for additional exploration. Frankly speaking, I couldn't care less about the shrieking woman: she wasn't a Paladin, and I didn't like her appearance, so she was of no interest to me. However, she would be able to help me find the answer to my question: what happens in the nest? What happens to the potatoes if their owner dies? Since I need to wait for Zangar's return – and he will have to bring Marinar back for training – I needed to explore everything as best I could.

"You, jerk: stop!" the monk who was collecting potatoes yelled, astounded, as I was striding straight to the fighting trio. "Beware the bird! Oh, stop, you, idiot freak! Drgrygz, run! The Paladin's gone mad!"

Too late! With one leap I covered the distance that separated us, activated my protection and beamed a smile at the monk who was trying to crawl away in fear. The woman cried out, covered her face with her hands, and then a shadow covered us. The huge bird came down to sort it out with those who dared break her unwritten rules.

The talons of the flying monster pierced the

class armor of the monks and the Dark warrior like paper. The players' faces distorted in horrible pain, but they didn't go for respawn: the bird was experienced and wouldn't let her prey disappear too early. This trick didn't work with me: the protection would not pierce, and the talons just produced showers of sparks as they scratched helplessly on the force bubble. I grinned: my plan had worked. Now the bird will find a good grip, grab my bubble and we'll fly to the chicks. I'll also record a bird's eye view video of the village: what if there's something else useful here?

However, the bird really was tremendously experienced, as if it had previously encountered players with active defense. It squawked loudly, then seized me in its beak, flew up several dozen meters and then wagged its head and opened its beak to throw me on the ground forcefully. Like an overripe nut. All I could do was cry out when, just like a nut's shell, my protective bubble cracked when I hit the ground. The impact was so hard it took my breath away and I fainted for a few moments. Wrenching pain pierced my shoulder and thigh, bringing me back, and then I felt like I was being turned inside out: the bird soared into the air. In one foot it was holding the screaming monks, and in the other, the shrieking woman and myself. I was also screaming, as the pain was unfathomable.

I was unable to activate the protection, probably, because there was a foreign object piercing me all the way through. The blood and the sweat clouded my eyes. All I was able to see was a tall tree, a huge perch at the very top and two enormous gaping throats craving food. The chicks were so huge they seemed almost bigger than their mother, or at the very least as big. I could not see any small detail such as to find out if there were any potatoes. It was a miracle that I was still conscious at all. The entire left side of my body turned into one huge lump of pain. The woman and one of the monks were already slumping as lifeless corpses; only Drgrygz continued to scream. The bird hovered over the chicks and launched the monks into one of the gaping beaks. There was a chick's contented squawk, chomping, and two wild practically inhuman screams. Well, the monks weren't human anyway. With a nasty squelch the talons of the flying monster left my body, sending me forward to my death.

"I am the energy armor!" I managed to whisper as I was falling before the chick's beak closed over me. Fighting the bird left me with over half of my Energy level and knowledge that availability of energy armor did not make me invincible. This defense did not defend me against the laws of physics. Another shower of sparks flew as the chick attempted to chew me. A random thought flashed that birds cannot chew, but it was immediately banished by a wild shriek of pain: the woman came to and started screeching horribly once again. I was thrown from side to side, the sparks flew so brightly it hurt my eyes to look, yet the Energy bar wasn't even thinking of dropping. On the contrary, at some point it started increasing despite the crazy meat-grinder.

"Aaaaaaaaa!" The dark warrior screamed louder as soon as the grinding stopped and we came crashing down. Even though it had seemed to me that a louder and more protracted screech was impossible. I crashed into something soft and viscous, but this time at least the protection worked the way it was supposed to: a small air bubble formed around me and the viscous substance could not get in there. I automatically took an elven elixir to kill the pain, then stood up. After I took a look around I was almost overcome with nausea. In the Academy I'd already seen all kinds of death, but the nightmare unfolding before my eyes was a first. Apparently, we had ended up in the bird's stomach, and that viscous substance around us was the stomach acid. Within just two steps of me skin and flesh was being dissolved from the woman, who had been broken up almost to the state of chopped meat, yet miraculously somehow stayed alive. The acid was eating the player up and I saw a semitransparent bubble around her head: the Game kept the victim living, providing it with a unique chance to fully feel the pain of being in the chick's stomach. Terror settled in the woman' eyes, but somehow she fixed her crazed gaze on me; a single thought was in it: "kill me". Acting more on instinct than following the rational side. Even though my entire left side was numb, I rushed towards the woman, putting the artifact on my hand along the way.

"I am the Templar's blow!" I shouted, closing my eyes and driving my fist right into the middle of her chest. By then her skin and flesh were completely eaten away, showing the bubbling and half-dissolved internal organs. I feared to think what the warrior must have felt. Her head was still covered with some kind of protection, so before I hit, a thought flashed through my mind that I wouldn't be able to pierce the sphere. Expecting to be respawned, I lost my balance and crashed forward: my hand met no obstacle, so inertia toppled me forward, making me crush whatever was left of the player. There was not much left: part of an arm and a still completely whole head with its eyes rolled and tongue hanging out. A moment passed and even those remnants disappeared: the Game dissolved them as smoke, allowing the woman to rest for an hour till respawn. Or return to the pool of NPCs, if she had been a level one player.

That clarified what would happen to the potatoes: even if somehow they fell out of the inventory as a player was destroyed, in this hell nothing would be left of them. It was useless to think that some sort of loot would be left in the nest. The other thought that flashed through my mind was: it was amazingly light inside the bird. The sides of this insatiable chick let sunlight through, so I was able to glance around. A couple of steps away from me there was some strange island; there was no mucus there, so I hurried towards it right away. The moment the warrior departed for respawn, my Energy level started dropping precipitously again. The woman's emotions had become a source of power for me; moreover, it was so good that it became crystal clear as to why the Dark ones prefer to destroy worlds rather than create joy and happiness there. Inside the chick, taking into account the replenished Energy, I could count on ten to twelve minutes of life; after that I would follow the path of all the other players: dying in the stomach acid. I could not allow that.

Once I was on the island, the Energy bar stilled. The vapors ate up one unit per ten seconds, the same as the amount the Labyrinth restored for me. It turned out the island was just a normal stone – who knows how it appeared inside the chick. Once I hit the stone with my foot, the chick chirped angrily and everything around twitched. Several times a wave of acid washed over me, once it even washed me off the stone. The chick didn't like what I was doing. Well, I didn't come here for fun, after all.

"I am the Templar's blow!" I growled, shoving my fist enhanced by the artifact into the stone."

"Claa-a-a-!" The chick's cry was so loud, I fell to my knees, trying to protect my ears with my stump and the spiked artifact. The spikes screeched on the helmet, bringing up an interesting thought: was it possible at all to kill oneself? I was not eager to drown in the acid. I'd rather lose two levels. One for dying, the other for a kill, than go like the dark warrior did. Yet before testing the suicide theory I needed to figure out the puzzle of the stone. A bird would not need such ballast in its stomach; yet, for some reason it was there. And for some reason the chick was screaming his heart out every time I hit the thing.

Besides a displeased cry from the chick, hitting the stone did not cause any visible effect. I took two elixirs at once, for Energy and health, and started hitting the stone with abandon. I'd had to take the elven health elixir, as the burning pain returned in my shoulder and thigh which had been pierced through. The last thing I needed was to faint from pain shock before getting any result at all.

An acid storm stared in the stomach. The chick went so completely crazy that the acid waves were over a meter and a half tall, as if trying to throw me as far from the stone as possible. Sometimes the retreating acid revealed the stone completely; yet, there was nothing special about it. Just a normal smooth beach stone that had grown to be half a meter in size. My Energy was close to depletion and, unwilling to spend another elixir, I hit the stone one last time, then started to figure out the best angle for hitting myself on the head. The blow would have to be fast and precise, so that it would be done cleanly and surely.

Level achieved
Level...

The acid storm stopped, and immediately the angry pitiful cry of the bird filled the space around me. Information on receiving more levels was flashing in front of my eyes, and I held still with the artifact almost touching my helmet, glad that I had not been able to drive the spikes into my head. The new levels replenished Energy, and now I had another twelve minutes of life within the bird. Actually, more: the emotions of the bird which had lost its baby would not let my Energy go down even by a single unit.

You have achieved the maximum level in the

Academy (15)

You will receive all subsequent accumulated experience following completion of the Academy or at respawn

As I was rummaging through the stones I was not able to contain a grin: the Academy imposed a limit on player development. Within the Academy levels did not provide any benefit at all except for extra lives; however, in the main world practically everything was tied to them. Level of access to different worlds, participation in various contests, abilities, Dungeons, quest sequences, attitude of NPCs — everything depended on the player's current level. That's why the level was the utmost secret that the players guarded more than their lives.

"Now what's that?" I frowned, pushing aside yet another stone. In my hand I was holding a small flat silvery bar shaped like a regular hexagon. In the center it had the Emperor's seal: the black skull with three white eyeholes. There was no description for this object; the Game had not informed me that I had received anything, and that was what bothered me the most. What was it? Just a useless trinket? ...or a time bomb? Why could I not see the hexagon's properties? What did the Emperor's seal have to do with it? Altogether, what was that thing doing inside the chick? Is there another stone like this in the other chick? There were no answers. There was no other loot, either – the broken stone did not contain anything else. Moreover, the moment I picked up the hexagon the stone bits started dissolving and disappeared literally within a few moments, leaving me alone with the strange object. I turned it around in my hands and, failing to find a use for it, stuck the hexagon into my inventory until a more suitable time. I would show it to Sharda – maybe the gnome would know what it was and what it was for. Another heart-rending scream of loss sounded, reminding me where I was. Even after dying the chick would not disappear. Besides, it didn't even fall over; thus, climbing out the hole through which I had fallen in would be impossible: the distance to the throat was about three meters. Half an hour of trying to punch through the fowl's body was useless: I was not able to make even the smallest hole. All my blows, even enhanced, were to no avail. With my current level of attack ability I wouldn't be able to get out.

I was facing a dilemma. From my previous life the optimists' motto came to mind: "Even if you were eaten, you still have two ways out" and now I had to decide: was I ready to find those ways, or would the feeling of disgust overpower the desire to make another entry in the Book, and I would have to respawn? Both options involved significant delays; and I had no time for that – either an hour for respawn, or who knows how long to find a way to get out, going through with it, climbing down to the ground, returning to the village ... The only thing I would really sincerely regret was my freshly achieved 15th level.

"Claa-a-a-!" The mother bird screeched once again and suddenly the chick's side darkened: the bird alighted on the nest and... "Claa-a-a-!"

The lurch was so strong that I fell flat on my back. I was not prepared for this turn of events, so I hit my head on the chick's stomach pretty hard; sparks started dancing in front of my eyes. The earthquake finished, but was immediately succeeded by something like a roller-coaster. Up and down switched places again and again. I was thrown around mercilessly and only my protection enabled me to stay relatively whole. Beaten up, but still in one piece. The flight lasted forever: practically all of ten seconds. Subsequent impact crushed the chick flat, granting me the relief provided by darkness. Again the laws of physics overcame the energy shield. I needed to do something about that.

"Look there, there's one alive in it! Through the fog of my faint I heard an interested voice speaking with a funny village accent.

"We need to tell the village head, yeah."

"They did – sent for him already. Not every day a chick falls from the nest, and with a live person inside, right. That needs some lookin' into it, eh."

"Should we take him out, no?"

"Nah, let the eldeh decide, What if he's got a plague, or some such, that mum threw him out of the nest, she did? Talkin' to Gromana then? No, I don't want that!"

"Aggrh!" I groaned, trying to say that I was fine and there was no need to leave me inside the chick. But I didn't succeed. Moreover, I was not even able to open my eyes – I simply hadn't the strength to do even that.

"So! See, how he's spittin' blood so, eh! I tell

you, he's got the plague! Maybe we should kill him, no? Let him respawn, I say."

"Nah, the eldeh, he doesn't like walkin', and they sent for him, they did. He'd yell at us, he would.

"Where is he?" I heard an authoritative voice. Why have you still not pulled him out?"

"Well, eh... What 'bout the plague, eh ... Spits blood, eh..."

"Pull him out! Where is Gromana?"

"No need to fuss: here I am," I heard a rather pleasant female voice. "I was listening at the tree. The mother is upset: her chick has been killed. Killed, not poisoned. Today she'll lay a new egg and then will sit on it for a week. This Paladin helped the recruits of this sector, but what he did is a problem for all of us. It will be impossible to close the Academy in a week, so we'll have to serve as chick food. Many times. We'll really have to pay for the first chick starving for a week.

"That's nasty..., the elder said slowly. "What should we do with this one? Finish him off?"

"No. Since we'll have to suffer, let him suffer as well. I'll take him."

"He'll run out of Energy and respawn anyway..."

"You're blind, Vikat. The Paladin is already ours. He's Dark. There are plenty of emotions here. It'll be enough for him."

"Aggrh!" I groaned again, trying to ask what was going on."

"Sleep, Paladin." They puffed something sickly-sweet in my face. "I need to figure out what to do with you."

My awakening was definitely not pleasant: my head felt like it would actually crack. Groaning, I tried to cradle it in my hands, but did not succeed: my hands were firmly tied to something hard.

"Drink this – it'll dull the pain." I heard the now familiar female voice. Then a bowl appeared in front of me, full of a steaming beverage with a foul smell. My mouth was filled with burning liquid. Someone squeezed my nose, forcing me to take a gulp, then another. Then a third. Despite the liquid fire in my mouth and throat, a pleasant warmth flooded my body. Headache retreated. With an effort, I opened my eyes and stared at the wooden ceiling. I was unable to shake my head: like my hands, it was firmly fixed in place.

"Salmella pollen may cause not only pain, but also death. You are stupid, moving around the Academy with your visor open."

"Why can I not move?" I rasped through my burnt throat.

"Because you are tied up, is that not obvious?" My interlocutor grinned. I heard steps and then a pleasant female face framed with long raven-black hair appeared between me and the ceiling. "Swear by the Game that you are not going to kill either yourself or other players within the next seven days, and I'll untie you."

"You have no right to detain me!" I was indignant.

"Who told you such a silly thing? I cannot detain a recruit for more than one respawn.

Everything else is allowed. Torture, abuse, teaching, curses – whatever comes into my head."

"Are you a witch?" I said with surprise, hearing the word "curse". Only members of one specific class could cast those.

"She is a player, same as you." This time the Chancellor's thunderous voice was muffled, as if he was standing nearby. "Gromana, given the circumstances, I approve your request and you may hold Yari until his group returns. They should be back in five days. You can do whatever you want with him: he is in your power. Well, actually, no, I don't want to see the ritual for a generational curse in my Academy. That chick was my favorite pet; Yari should be punished for its death. A short delay won't harm him. As for you and Vikat, you know already: your punishment has been determined. You will be eaten. Many times. You must be more attentive to your responsibilities, Dark one! Don't let him go without an oath. Yari, I look forward to seeing you. Even though not so much at this stage."

"You heard it all," the woman said, surprised; apparently, she hadn't expected the appearance of the Chancellor. "Either an oath, or you will just keep lying here tied until your group returns. The choice is yours."

"What the hell?!" I exploded. "Untie me, now!"

"Your choice is clear," Gromana brought an open hand to her mouth and blew in my face. "Sleep, Paladin. We'll talk tomorrow..."

"I agree!" I growled, after waking up for the third time. Habitually swallowed the burning liquid neutralizing the effect of the pollen, and then repeated after Gromana, word for word, an oath that prohibited me from making any conscious attempts to respawn within the next two days. "You've been holding me for three days already?!"

"Three and a half." Gromana disappeared from my view and I heard the sound of locks opening." "Your group hasn't returned yet, so you can't go into the village. Besides, not all players have left it yet. You'll live with me for now."

"But you are also a player," I reminded her.

"I am," the girl agreed, helping me get up. "This is my punishment. Until this enrollment is over, I will have to stay in this – number three – sector of the Labyrinth and help the recruits. Some initiated slowpokes still haven't left the forest, so I'll have to sit here for quite some time."

"What did you do to be exiled into the Academy?"

"I don't want to answer this question, and I won't," Gromana cut me off. "Come, we need to treat your wounds. Here – you could use the crutch."

"What?" I frowned, staring in bewilderment at the stick the witch was offering me; only now did I notice the pierced steel cuisse covering my thigh. Since I had not yet respawned the armor hadn't been restored. Underneath the cuisse there was a huge irregular hole all the way through; its edges were covered with the white ointment. My back turned cold: a prohibition from respawning meant that for several days I'd have to walk around with this horrendous wound! Slanting my eyes to my shoulder,

I couldn't contain my feelings and cursed: there was a similar hole there. Even though I didn't feel the pain, I also didn't feel the entire left side of my body. As if it wasn't enough that I now had a stump instead of a normal hand, now I'd received two holes that went all the way through! Must be a reward for special services to my country!

"I cannot cure a wound like this," Gromana responded impassively in response to my angry tirade. "I can only dull the pain and prevent you from bleeding to death. You will need to respawn, but only after the group returns."

"Why?!" I came up with the strength to ask a clear question, suppressing my curses for a while. For what?!"

"Because you'll leave in two days, and Vikat and I will have to sit here until the Academy closes! While no one cares about NPCs and the Game continuously adds new ones, I will have to feel the hunger of the chicks first hand! The Chancellor has already warned us what the death of the chick will cost us. I've spoken to those who were eaten by the chicks – it's a horrible death. You saved the recruits of our sector: in the remaining three days they'll have enough time to complete the Labyrinth. Or die. But we can't get out of here until the entire Academy closes. All the sectors! This may take a month."

"I didn't know..."

"That doesn't make life any easier for me. The Chancellor changed the rules, and from now on it will be impossible to kill either the bird or the chicks. As soon as the last recruit in the sector leaves the

Labyrinth, all the NPCs will disappear; then the bird will hunt the only prey available. That's the two of us here: I, acting as the wise woman, and Vikat, the village elder. Do you still want to know why I asked the Chancellor to leave you crippled for at least a couple of days? Come, I need to dress the wounds."

Getting used to walking with a stick, I stood up with difficulty. My left leg was useless. So was the left arm. Stumbling at every step, I moved away the curtain, and from a small dimly lit chamber entered a light spacious veranda. In the center there was a massive table covered with retorts, bowls, mortars and other attributes of witches or alchemists. One of the walls was a window, wide open and offering a view of the lush green forest. The other walls were covered with tall wooden shelves filled with the same instruments and things of a wise woman. Gromana was doing something at the table, mixing ingredients in a wooden mortar and whispering a spell.

"Sit!" she pointed at the wooden stool after she finished the ritual. "I don't have the elves' ointment, so we'll have to do with what we have. It should be enough for two days.

Keeping quiet about my stock of remedies, I sat down and cringed when the witch started applying ointment to the wounds. White slop which smelt strongly of ammonia that cleared my mind better than smelling salts.

"This should be enough for you," Gromana finished the procedure and plopped the dish of evil-smelling substance next to me. "From now on do it yourself. I've already spent too much time on you."

"If I am stuck here for two days, what should I do?" I asked when Gromana turned away, returning to her vials again.

"Whatever you want!" the witch snorted contemptuously. "There's nothing of mine here. Just try not to come close to the table. I will not be pleased if you interrupt the ritual. I might get offended and curse you. You won't like it."

"So what are you doing?"

"Saving you!" Gromana cut me off angrily. "Hasn't anyone told you that curiosity is a flaw? The less you know, the longer you live!"

"Not in my case," I grinned. "I am an explorer. Without knowledge I'll just croak, so tell me, please, what are you doing? What kind of ritual is it?"

"I am making an elixir." The witch cooled off, looking at me in a different way. "Now I understand why the Chancellor defended you. An explorer. The Chancellor always liked those, even back in my training days. I was thrown into the Labyrinth immediately after sentencing. And before that there was a little skirmish with the priests, I spent a fair amount of Energy and didn't have time to get more, so now I have neither elixirs nor the elves' ointment here. There's no game trader here, so despite all my money I can't do anything. But that's not the worst; there are no components for the standard Energy replenishment potion in the Labyrinth, so I am having to experiment. If I end up inside the chick, my protection would last me about four days; the background level of emotions gives me another day or so, but that's not guaranteed: if all the recruits leave the Labyrinth, it might not be enough to restore. Then I'd have to die every four days... I figure it'll take the Academy a whole month to close, so six or seven are practically guaranteed. I don't want to be digested, so that's why I'm experimenting with the potions. Are you satisfied, explorer?"

"You are here because of the sentence?" I caught on to familiar words. "What on earth have you done?"

"Paladin, why don't you stop meddling where you aren't welcome!" Gromana was harsh, but I just could not afford losing such a source of knowledge about the main world.

"Now can I ask what I want?" I inquired, extracting an elixir from my inventory. "I need information; you need this vial. We could trade."

"One vial won't change much," Gromana snorted. "So I will die six times instead of seven. What difference does it make?"

"Really, what's the difference?" I drawled, pulling out another six elixirs from my cache. "This thing replenishes Energy fully, 100 percent, regardless of how much you have left, right?"

"That's a weighty argument," Gromana drawled contemplatively, impassively watching the elixirs disappear into my inventory. "What do you want, kid?"

"Kid?" I was surprised now. "I thought we were close in age."

"I am three thousand years old, child." In just a few moments the witch transformed from a sweet kind girl into a terrifying hag. Oh, her appearance didn't change one bit, but I felt so uncomfortable that I cringed and barely contained my impulse to crawl under the table and hide.

"Stop pushing me!" I rasped, fighting the fear. It was a good thing I was sitting on the stool before the witch attacked, or else I would have easily ended up under the table anyway.

"You took "Spiritual integrity?" Gromana said, stunned, and at that moment my fear passed. "That's really random. What kind of explorer are you, with an attribute like this?"

"I had no choice." I caught my breath, trying to still my trembling hands. "There's one girl running around the Academy who's a pretty advanced Suppressor, with an ability to control up to ten players. For some reason she developed a dislike for me; so I had to use one level of my artifact for this property."

"That's how it is..." Gromana's eyebrows crawled upwards. "A student of Areimen arrived at the Academy?"

"I have no idea who that is." I shook my head. "We have students of Devir, Archibald and Levard, if those names tell you anything. "I have not heard the word 'Areimen' in the Academy so far."

"Hunters and a Councilor," Gromana nodded understandingly, thinking of something. "All those in the same enrollment?"

"And in the same sector," I added, supposing the witch might know something else. "Our sector."

"Very interesting ... Two fierce implacable

irreconcilable hunters who've been killing each other for several thousand years send their students to the Academy at the same time... What for?"

"From what I understand, one of them has an order to kill me, and the other to protect me. However, the one that's supposed to protect me has been thoroughly messing with our heads – mine and a few other Paladins. That's the girl with advanced control abilities whom I mentioned.

"What – are you the Emperor's son?" Gromana asked in surprise. "What did you do to deserve such an honor?"

"Same question to you: what did you do to deserve such fuss? I mean the exile to the Academy. What does one do to deserve that?"

Silence fell over the veranda, broken only by the quiet scraping of a spatula in the mortar. Even as she was talking to me, the witch kept working on yet another potion.

"I am under the curse of truth," Gromana said finally, staring at me with her brown eyes. "And I was so rash as to, immediately after the battle with the priests that we won at the cost of incredible losses, to say everything I thought about the head of my class and her politics. Soluna, the head in question, is also a Judge, so I was instantly condemned for behavior inappropriate to a witch, and exiled first here, and then to the Game world called 'Earth'. To the utmost backwater of the Game worlds. Did I answer your question? You owe me seven elixirs and a clarification – why are they all hunting you?"

"Wait, we didn't agree that I would give you the

elixirs if you told me ..."

"Don't play with me, kid!" The veranda was instantly plunged into darkness, and the formidable witch loomed over me. The fear was to strong it physically pinned me to the seat to the point that I couldn't move. Something warm trickled down my thigh. The wound must have opened and it was blood, I was sure. At least you didn't need to excrete in the Academy, or else I would have just pissed myself from fear. "I need the elixirs!"

"Pr-pr-pp..." I tried to say "no", but only spit and bubbles came from my lips instead of an answer. My body stopped obeying me. I stood up, limping and leaving a bloody trail – it was blood after all – dragged myself, and then jumped from the veranda, internally screaming in pain, but did not even attempt to open the inventory and extract the elixirs. So it turned out that even if someone else wrenches control from you, personal effects are not in their power. That's a very useful thing to know!

"I am waiting for my elixirs!" Gromana repeated again, setting me back on the stool and relinquishing control over my body. The pain intensified, flooding like a river of fire, over the entire left half of my body, so I did what was the most sensible thing to do under the circumstances: I fainted. I really didn't want to argue with a three thousand year old witch at the moment.

"I know that you have come to." I heard Gromana's voice through the darkness. Get up so that we can negotiate."

"After what you've done?" I said testily, opening

my eyes. I was in the smaller chamber again. There was no pain.

"You know, when a green-ass pipsqueak starts insisting on his rights, it does make you lose your cool. I'll meet you on the veranda."

One thing could be said in Gromana's favor: after waking me up she didn't immediately attack me with questions and suggestions; rather, she allowed me to come to my senses and form a position. The witch had indicated the most important thing: she was ready to negotiate. My demonstration of seven elixirs had played its role, so now I had a rather weighty argument to receive as complete information about the Game as possible. Not what the teachers feed you, but what the players keep to themselves: where you need to go first thing and what to do right after the Academy; what you shouldn't do, what to watch out for and the like. Everything that Gromana had had to overcome on her own."

"What do you want?" the witch asked point blank, once I plopped down on the stool.

"How much time do I have till I can respawn?" was my first question. With those constant faints I was completely lost in time.

"One day till your group arrives. You are the last player in the Labyrinth, everyone else has already left. Two days till the chick hatches."

"I need information and help."

"What kind of help?" Gromana frowned.

"I need protection against mental encroachment. As far as I understood, you found the idea of the 'Spiritual integrity' attribute laughable, but that's all I was able to come up with. Surely you have an amulet or something else that would block someone from getting into my brain. I don't want to return from the Academy and turn into a puppet on a string. Your demonstration was very vivid and enlightening."

"The Game prohibits taking newly-minted players under control for two years after they complete the Academy. During this time the player either gains an opportunity to buy himself an amulet, or turns into a puppet as you rightly noted. No one cares what happens to you. The most important thing is to have an anchor in your class stronghold. As soon as a two year old player drops to the first level, members of his own class will kill him. No one will grant a free Game slot to other classes. Your teacher was supposed to have told you that even if you were found by the Game. Lesson number three, if memory serves."

"I had some troubles with training," I responded, and then told Gromana about my issues regarding developing as a player. Starting from encountering Devir, all the way through being sent to the Academy, and some things that already happened here. Without mentioning the Madonna's diary and the strange hexagon.

"Revenge?" the witch grimaced. "Devir has descended to revenging NPCs? Sorry: to a new player? That's stupid... I can't believe it! I know this mage very well, and together we... it doesn't matter, but he'd never stoop to revenge. That's way too petty for him. The druid, on the other hand, is interesting.

Archibald's student... The catorian had not taken any students ever since the re... For the past two thousand years he has had no students.

"Since the restart of the Game?" I ventured a guess and, from an eyebrow lifted in surprise and the measuring look the witch cast at me, I realized that I had hit the nail on the head. Madonna lived about two thousand years ago; the Game restarted at the same time. If Gromana was three thousand years old, she must be one of those who had been chosen to continue the Game in the new world.

"Yes, ever since the restart," the witch said slowly. "Now you have interested me as well. I can count on the fingers of one hand those who know that the Game can be restarted."

"What about the druid?" I reminded Gromana of a thought that had trailed off.

"Archibald is a very prominent figure in the game universe, even though he lives in the boondocks. Sorry, but that's the only way to describe the Earth. There are very few who haven't heard about that catorian, so I was very surprised to hear that his student was in the Academy. Normally, a minion's training lasts seven years; however, Archibald trains his recruits – well, at least he used to before – for twenty to thirty years before letting them enter the Academy. Devir was the last student of Archibald that I know about and he is sparing no effort trying to surpass his teacher in every way. That's why there's been an incessant struggle going on between them for two thousand years and counting. And yes, Devir went through the restart as well."

"So it seems I have no chance against the druid?"

"Neither here nor in the main world," the witch confirmed. "She'll eat you whole and won't even notice. Your only hope is – if Archibald had told her to take the Paladins through, she would have already left the Academy together with them. Then you can go through to the end at your leisure; all the subsequent tests and the wasteland are aimed at lowering your level by draining your Energy. That wouldn't be a treat for you. But if the druid decides to come back, no one will be able to help you. She'll crush you like a bug.

"You know how to lift a guy's spirits, don't you?" I grinned.

"I'm telling you the way it is. I don't embellish reality."

"The Paladins are still in the Academy." I opened the map and saw that the dots indicating my group were already a significant distance away from the Labyrinth. But for some reason Dirion and Refor were not among them. Had those two been killed? Or were they going through respawn? I'd have to check again in an hour.

"That means she's here as well. I even feel a little pity for you. We need to make a trade agreement. I want to receive my elixirs."

"You will get seven elixirs from me, I swear by the Game," I assured the witch. "There's no point in me keeping them. Even without the players the background level of emotions is enough to keep my

Energy full. But I need information."

"I hear you. Recruits other than you are all gone, so now we have a chance for a thorough conversation. Go ahead: ask."

"Why did you snort when you learnt that I have the 'Spiritual integrity' attribute?" I asked the question that had bothered me ever since the beginning of our conversation. The face of the witch was far too displeased when she heard about that.

"Because you are an explorer! The only useful attribute for those is 'Neuronal Network'. 'Context Search' could be useful as well, but only up to level 15, so as to download information. That's it! Everything else would be just a waste of attributes!"

"I have 'Context Search'," I frowned. "What 'Neuronal Network'? What benefit does it provide?"

"Honestly, at this point I don't remember what it has at the low levels; at level 15 video analyzer becomes available. What is your artifact?"

"Book of Knowledge!"

"Well, at least there you didn't make a mistake! At level 15 of Neuronal Network the book will start analyzing the video and determine what among the things you recorded is new knowledge, and what are repetitive and redundant frames that don't require detailed review. Oh – I do remember! From level one to fifteen you develop the neuronal network analyzer; starting from level one it will highlight things for you – phenomena or people that are not in the book. The analysis will improve at every level; then, starting from the 15th the Book will be able to analyze the video on its own. Then its analysis quality improves;

already at level 30 it will become interactive... The Book will become your *alter ego*. You could consult with it, ask it questions, et cetera, et cetera. There's something else at levels 60 and 120, but I don't recall. Ask in the Temple of Knowledge, they'd be glad to share that information."

"So, it seems like I grabbed a bunch of silly and useless attributes for myself?" I grimaced. "But if I hadn't selected them, I simply would not have made it here!"

"That's exactly why, before they leave the Academy, recruits are given an opportunity to redistribute the values of all the attributes they acquired earlier. You could take off everything you used for 'Spiritual Integrity' and add it to 'Context Search' or 'Neuronal Network' if you obtain it by that time. You cannot add new attributes during redistribution. So my advice to you, Paladin, is to bring serious claims against your mentor when you go back. They were supposed to have told you all this during the training! You are like a blind kitten now! It's amazing you even made it to the Labyrinth!"

"I crawled," I muttered, with some choice words in my mind for both Archibald and Sharda. "If you have such problems with the potions, I could go back to the forest and buy you as many as you need to survive. The only thing is, I don't have any granises now..."

"That's impossible. Did you not notice that there are no doors on our side anymore? After the last recruit in our sector left the forest, the Chancellor broke the connection between the units of the

Academy. You can't go back. But thank you for the offer. I do really appreciate that."

"Shit... Oh well, let's get back to the explorers then. As you noticed, my initial training wasn't really all it was supposed to be. Are there mentors for explorers? And if so, where does one find them?"

I am not sure I understand the question," Gromana frowned. "What do you mean by 'mentors for explorers'?"

"Well, you know... those who would teach..." I was taken aback. "Like, tell about the ways to properly level up your artifact..."

"There's the Temple of Knowledge for that. Why would one keep a special NPC or player just to clarify the obvious? Go on, explore, study... Nobody is obligated to lead you around by the hand like a child. The only exception is the initial training prior to the Academy, but that is strictly regulated as well. Nothing else! For example, the only reason I am talking to you is the elixirs. If they weren't there, this conversation wouldn't happen. It's time for you to get it already: no one owes anything to anyone in the Game. Especially for free. There's no place for altruism here. Go on, keep asking."

"Are there hidden characters or locations in the Labyrinth? Teachers, traders, auctions?"

"I have not encountered anything like that here. I know they have them in the forest. In the wastelands, among nomadic clans, you could run into a trader now and then. The Labyrinth is kind of bare in that respect."

"Speaking about the trade – how do explorers

earn granises?"

"The same way as all the other players – Dungeons, trade, quests, presents. Being an explorer is not a terrible punishment; it's just a development path. If you get bored being an explorer, you can become a hunter, a warrior, a librarian, a baker, a maker – anyone! The Game sets only one constraint: you choose your artifact before you go to the Academy and you cannot change it. Everything else depends fully on the player and his preferences at that specific moment. Well, you have to remember to continuously level up your artifact. The Game doesn't like those who do nothing."

"You mentioned Dungeons. What are those?"

"Oh, wow...," Gromana sighed sadly. "You don't even know that... That's bad... A Dungeon is a certain location specified by the assigner. Each Game world has the Sanctuary, which acts, in essence, as the point where the players gather. An unmentioned capital of the Game world. One of the Sanctuary representatives is called the assigner. It's an NPC; he provides to both newbies and old hand players their quests and the coordinates of the Dungeons. What it is, is an enclosed location with a final boss at the end. The Dungeons can be set up both for individual players and teams. The first thing you'll need to do after you come back from the Academy is to register in the Citadel and visit the Sanctuary. Up to level 30 the best way to level up is through the Dungeons. In addition, you'll get something to wear that way."

"...?" My stare must have been so eloquent that Gromana grinned and clarified:

"Registration is tying your respawn point to the Citadel of your class. The things to wear that I mentioned are amulets and Energy storage devices. You are a Dark one, so the latter will be extremely useful for you: not in every place can you find a sufficient level of emotions. Just in case I'll tell you this, maybe you don't know it: the only way to transfer Energy from one player to another is through storage devices; those, in turn, can only be charged through external world sources. You can't dump your own Energy into them. Being Dark in the Game is not easy at all."

"How did you figure out that I am Dark?"

"Three thousand years teaches you a lot. Particularly given my class. As for the amulets, they will provide sufficient protection for you, both from physical and mental damage. As for the latter: every player in the Game really must have some. You're already aware of what 'controllers' can do."

"I agree that it's no fun at all. Is there any other way to protect your mind other than amulets?"

"There are three fundamental ways of defending yourself against mental attacks: congenital or acquired immunity, well-developed willpower and amulets. Any player must definitely have one of those, or else he'll just be a body acting under someone else's will."

"But surely there's a way to figure out that a player is being controlled by someone else and help him? Put an amulet on him, for example."

"It's possible, of course. But who needs that? If a player is so weak that his mind has been overtaken, it's his own fault. There's no place in the Game for creatures like that."

"Let's get to a slightly earlier point. I am interested in the anchor point. Can it be changed? Is it possible, say, for a mage to anchor to a Paladins' respawn point?"

"It's a strange question, but I'll answer. Yes, naturally it's possible to change it, but each class has its requirements. For example, if a witch leaves the Citadel for another anchor point, she'd have to swear an oath of silence with respect to anything you studied in the library. You swear to keep silence even under control, which, as you understand, is not really possible but could get you dead anyway. Besides, those who leave lose access to the Citadel forever, so no, it's not a very popular step. Very few leave. As for the mage: definitely not. The class Citadel can anchor only one class. The mage in your case would have to go to the Sanctuary and look for a solution to his problem there."

"Well, speaking about a mage, what's the principle by which the players congregate in the main world? There are a ton of various classes and races, Light and Dark allegiance, and everyone is fighting everyone all the time. What does one generally do after the Academy?"

"Whatever they want," Gromana smiled. "A beginner player must complete several standard quests set for the class, specialty and current development path; after that you are free as a bird. If you want to fight other players, you're welcome. If you want love and adoration from the NPCs: no problem.

You want to sit flat on your ass and do nothing: sure, your choice – just remember to level up your artifact. There's just one thing, since we are bound to be in the same Game world: I'd like to meet with you after the Academy. In a Light world Dark players are better off sticking together."

"Are the Light ones stronger?"

"Objectively they are. It's very easy to disarm the Dark ones simply by throwing a source of Light at us. We, however, can't do anything of the sort to the Light ones: there's no such thing as a source of Darkness. That's our weakness, but that's our strength as well: the Dark ones have to be continuously at war with the world around them, as they are apprehensive about such dirty tricks. You can't believe anyone in the Game, but if you are really forced to, you should only believe the Dark ones. Or, in the worst case, members of your class. If you're one of us, you won't be abandoned: even the Dark ones honor that."

"One of the teachers in the Labyrinth teaches professions. Is there something within the Game that would be popular and profitable?"

"Alchemy, but only if you have the right path of development and specialty. Executioners are popular, but only among the Light ones. Other professions are pretty equal: they don't matter much, but you won't starve either if you follow your path and are determined. As an option, you could always sell whatever you create to NPCs, if not to players."

"I have a question regarding the artifact: can its level be above that of its player? If so, by how much?"

"Artifacts have no levels. I think I understand what you're asking: the amount of experience necessary to upgrade the properties is a constant. It takes a thousand units, and then you either receive a new property or upgrade an existing one. You can't delay the choice and make it later, so you need to figure out in advance what you want to do to develop. As I mentioned, you can only reset it once throughout the entire Game. Or during restart."

"By the way! Why did they get into this restart of the Game business altogether? What changed? You are three thousand years old, surely you know such people as Merlin, Madonna and some nameless player. What was his name?"

"A third one? Two players restarted the Game."

"Three," I corrected her. "I happened to see Madonna's diary. There were three players mentioned."

"A diary?!" Gromana's eyebrows crawled up, and then the witch, without as much as trying to hide her excitement, asked eagerly: "Yari, just tell me that you figured out how to use your artifact and you have photos of all the pages in the diary?!"

Yes, that's right," I confirmed, withholding the fact that the very diary itself was stored in my inventory. Gromana taught me that in the Game no one was to be trusted, so why not apply this rule right now? "My context search is at level one right now, and information downloading will only become available at the 15th, so I have a lot of leveling up to do for my artifact."

"It doesn't matter anymore." The witch offered

me a trade, and my breath caught when I saw what the offer was. Ten granises. "Yari, we definitely must meet in the main world! I know a creature who'd pump you full of knowledge up to your ears to level up his artifact and obtain a copy of the diary. This is important. Promise me that we'll meet in the Sanctuary and the granises are yours! They'll help you complete the Academy. You'll buy the potatoes, then the answer to the riddle, hire guards for tests three and four, and travel to the wastelands with them as well: they can't go any further. Just promise that we'll meet!"

"There's no threat in this for me?" I frowned as the witch's excitement seemed suspicious to me.

"No! One who wants to obtain Madonna's diary has never harmed anyone. I'll ensure protection for you if you agree to meet with me in the Sanctuary! No one will dare touch you!"

"Agreed," I responded. I did not see any sense in concealing the information contained in the diary. The diary itself would stay with me, and I was not going to follow the path Levard had taken. If someone wanted to perform the next restart, let them. The most important thing would be for me to be included in the list of players allowed into the new world. "We can meet. But you still did not answer my question: what happened during the previous restart?"

"That I'll tell you in the Sanctuary," the witch responded with a sigh of relief, as if a boulder had rolled off of her shoulders. A semitransparent message informed me that I had received ten granises, but it wasn't as though I ran out of questions. Having found out that Gromana was not going to tell me anything about the restart of the Game at that stage, I continued to level up my artifact:

"You were exiled to the Labyrinth with a note that you had done something inappropriate for a witch. Are there any strictly fixed rules of behavior for each class the breaking which will get you punished? and how do you learn them?"

"Yes, there are. The rules are divided into global – that are set by the head of the class for the entire Game, and local – that are set by the head of the class of the specific Game world. You will be told of those as soon as you complete the Academy. It's a mandatory procedure. Immediately after that and the anchoring go to the Sanctuary."

"That's if I get out of the Academy altogether. You forgot about Dolgunata and her unhealthy attraction to me." I reminded the witch of the issue that was a sore point to me. "It's possible that after the Academy I'll be able to resist mental influence for two years, but within the Academy my chances are slim to none. You said so yourself. Somehow I doubt that Nata will go out into the main world."

Gromana fell to thinking.

"I can't give you my amulet. You won't be able to return it before you leave the Academy, and I don't want to expose myself so much. I could apply a curse. As soon as someone takes you under their control you'll fall asleep for eight hours. No matter how strong Dolgunata might be, it's impossible to control someone who's asleep. Or increase your 'Spiritual Integrity' by a few more points. There's no other way out that I can see. A student of Archibald just cannot be weak – that's a given."

"Generally, what is this catorian famous for?" I couldn't take it anymore. "A common headhunter..."

"I wish!" Gromana grinned. "He..."

"So, I see. You are whispering things while I'm away, are you?" I heard a mocking voice that was the last thing I wanted to hear. Dolgunata came out from behind the nearest tree and, swaying her hips like a model on the runway, started toward the veranda.

"You are not welcome here." The temperature around us seemed to have plummeted, so cold Gromana's voice was. "Leave."

"Sure I will." Dolgunata bestowed one of her charming smiles on Gromana. "I'll just pick up my slave, that's all. Yari, get on your knees and crawl towards me. My boots need to be cleaned."

"Go to hell!" I grinned, and then the world around me disappeared. Two points were shining against the white background that appeared: resplendent Dolgunata and the sun, which was quickly diminishing in size. I fell on my knees, understanding at the level of instincts that I must not let the sun disappear: I must concentrate on it continuously. If the whole world were to turn into Dolgunata, there would be trouble. It worked: the sun stopped diminishing and even grew a little, starting to outshine Dolgunata.

"You should not have started that, baby," Gromana's voice floated from somewhere. "I need Yari and I don't care that Archibald is behind you in this."

"I know what I am doing, grandma. You should

address all your questions to the teacher. I have clear instructions as to what I may or may not do with this slave. My boots are dirty and I want him to lick them clean. I can't be cleaning them myself, after all! Yari, I am waiting! Crawl here, dearie!"

Despite all my concentration the sun blinked for the last time and winked out, leaving me one on one with the shining goddess. Drooling, I crawled forward. The beauty needed her boots licked! I needed to hurry! I hope I get lucky and she'll let me lick the sole. Because she is the embodiment of perfection!

Hell!

You were killed and sent to a respawn point
You lost one level
Your current level: 14

CHAPTER TEN

ALLIES

"LEAVE," I heard Gromana's voice as soon as the world around me regained color and depth. "I'll delay Dolgunata for twelve hours, but then she'll go after you. By then you must leave the Academy."

"Where is that bitch?" I exhaled through my teeth. My emotions were so strong that even the restoration of my armor and the healing of my wounds could not appease my anger. I only had one wish — to tear the druid into a hundred pieces with my bare hands, enjoying her blood and her screams all the while.

"Resting," the witch responded meaningfully. "The girl felt as though she was all-powerful and immortal; I wanted to show her how deeply mistaken she was. I ended up having to disregard the Chancellor's preference and send you to respawn. Dolgunata has competed training with all the teachers and can leave the Academy at any moment, that's why I could do nothing to her until she showed open enmity towards me. Now she is in my power."

"How did she overcome the 'Spiritual integrity'?" This was the question that bothered me most. Absence of worthwhile mental protection in the Academy spelled serious trouble for me.

"A gift from the Chancellor. The druid had no initiation, so she received the bonus she deserved. As for the 'Spiritual integrity' — I told you that this attribute is useless. By the way, I had been wrong thinking that Archibald trained her for twenty years."

"Was it less?"

"It was much more. Actually, Dolgunata's training continued for about a hundred and fifty years before she was sent to receive official player status. Essentially, she needs it mostly as a formality, already now she is much stronger than most players. Just her ability to hide is very impressive... I'll admit, the information on Madonna's diary impressed me so much that I didn't notice the druid sneaking up on us. It's terrifying to imagine what she'll be able to do in a couple of years once Archibald starts working with her as a player. You'll have a splendid enemy, Paladin."

"A hundred and fifty years?! But she looks like she's twenty three! Besides, she told me that she'd been training for ten years..."

"Well, I don't look so old and decrepit either,

right?" Gromana found it within her to smile, but then grew serious again. "You can safely forget whatever Dolgunata told you — there is little truth in her words. The girl is very dangerous and I don't understand her objectives. She has learnt how to close off her mind better than a witch. Try to avoid her. Now think, Paladin: why would Archibald, a player, who always calculates at least a dozen concatenations of events and always has, including his own actions and those of his students, would send his druid to the Academy specifically during this enrollment. Obviously it's not to help the Paladins. I think you are her goal. You were able to kill Devir, so then Archibald sent his student for a final test to see if she would be able to wipe out someone who was able to kill his previous student. The catorian must have seen something in you which made him willing to sacrifice a major figure such as she. You are in danger."

"You promised to protect me."

"Don't try to twist it. I swore to defend you from the time we meet in the Sanctuary until you talk to Bernard. I never agreed to become your slave forever. I repeat: you don't have much time. Reach the Chancellor and then wait for your group there. You must shake the druid off at all costs. Dolgunata has figured out a way to locate you. I was unable to find out from her how she had done it. There must be a mark of some kind, but I don't see it. Your group is close to the Labyrinth now. They'll be here in five or six hours. They are led by Sakhray, the druid's brother; he is also providing them with food, so from the Energy standpoint they are fine. We'll have a chance to talk later, Paladin, but if you don't stop dragging your feet our meeting will never happen. There are eleven hours left plus one hour for respawn. Then Dolgunata will rush after you. Run!"

The witch was so convincing that I could just clench my fists helplessly, promising myself that I'd sort it out with the druid a little later, and dash to the village elder's house. A quick look at the map showed me that Zangar and Marinar really were not far while the Paladins... the Paladins had taken off somewhere to the side of the center. What pleased me the most was that they were still alive, even Refor and Dirion. The only one who didn't show up on the map at the moment was Monstrichello. Perhaps the tank had been sent to respawn again. At this rate he'd easily comply with Devir's wish and complete the Academy at level one! Either Dolgunata or some unknown enemies – everyone tried to kill the giant. One thing was positive in all of this: he was definitely initiated, so at least he'd complete the Academy in any case.

I sold three Energy elixirs to Vikat for three granises. At a one to one rate. The player grimaced in displeasure, but paid my price without haggling. Unlike the witch, he had some vials himself, but the elder realized that it would certainly not be enough to last till the Academy closes. Another confirmation that in this Game everyone was on his own: it didn't occur either to Gromana or Vikat to ask about elixirs for the other. Everyone just thought of himself. I had neither time nor desire to find out from the man the details of his appearance in the Academy; so I gave him the potatoes and paid a granis for instant completion of the other test, which was answering a riddle presented by a strange creature in the elder's house; after that, following Gromana's advice, I spent another granis to hire two fine fellows as personal guards. The description of the third test indicated that I'd need them.

"Welcome, recruit: now I will train you to use your attributes. Harken to my wisdom!"

Learning progress: You have reached teacher 7 of 10

The next portion of knowledge about the Game was rather amusing. As it turned out, Energy was not the only numerical parameter for a player, as I had thought. Sometimes a player would manage to obtain additional records in personal properties – those were called "attributes". At that stage I had none, so the table that would show them was hidden. It was possible to gain these attributes for certain achievements, for getting into special situations or reaching special locations. Attributes would provide the player with special, intangible properties which made playing more pleasant: charisma, luck, attractiveness, immunity, etc. Attributes leveled up on their own, depending on the player's actions. However, they could level down as well. For example: if a player received charisma, it could easily be lost if he were to act at odds with the requirements set by that attribute.

The main distinction of attributes from abilities

and artifact properties was that other players could influence them. For example, if a player received "luck", its effect could be easily counteracted by putting the right type of curse on the player. Or, contrariwise, it was possible to hex someone's fate by putting some kind of curse on him: of failure, misfortune, intoxication, schizophrenia, muteness, deafness or some physical disability; besides, some of those curses could become permanent – it depended on the extent to which the character had stepped on the curser's toes. That's why in the main world protective amulets were popular. So were witches – no surprise there. Only women were able to apply curses, The male half of players did not have that ability. I would need to ask Gromana – why does the Game have such gender discrimination, and whether there are any classes that are only available to men?

"Let's go?" one of the guards said in a deep low voice as soon as I stepped away from the attributes teacher. The image of a big fellow was ideal: over six feet tall, rolled-up sleeves of a white shirt showing powerful hairy arms, wide baggy trousers, a simple rope for a belt, strange dark boots of an unknown material, and a huge club, practically as tall as I was. Some village fighter, folksy and rather dim. Given that the Game provided me two fighters who looked like clones of each other, the test in store for me would be impressive. The task was to find and kill the Boar. With a capital B.

"Not yet," I refused, and approached the second teacher in the Labyrinth. Finally the time had come to figure out the bit about professions.

Learning progress: You have reached teacher 8 of 10

"I am so glad to greet you here, young schlemazel!" a teacher who looked like a gnome said with gladness. Dressed in a funny loose robe and skull cap, the teacher greeted me with a broad open smile, completely different from the grimace of grumpiness and disdain that he had demonstrated to me literally just a few minutes before I handed the potatoes to the elder. "What is there that you came to tell me?"

"I am interested in professions." I was unable to hold back a smile. The gnome seemed all too similar to a remote descendant of David or Solomon

"Oy vey, really, what is this you're saying?! You know you came to the right place, and you are oh so lucky! Professions are my middle name! You can walk around the entire Derman and any putz will tell you there's no one better than Shlomo to put the basics of professions into your head. And get a tiny little gesheft for himself."

"Are you actually allowed to disclose your name?" I asked in surprise once the space around us had changed. Instead of the familiar training forest we were in an open workshop equipped with state of the art technology. It had all sorts of things! Starting from the standard retorts and vials to a huge futuristic computer and strange scientific instruments whose purpose I couldn't even guess.

"Oy gevalt, who said anything to anyone?! The teacher looked sincerely surprised. "Who is Derman? I know nothing! Don't try to confuse me, young man. Did you come here to learn or play with words?"

"Not just to learn." I put out a feeler. The gnome had quite openly indicated that besides the standard training he could provide something extra. "I have a couple of granises; it would be nice to put them to work. I need advice from an experienced mentor."

"Now we're talking!" The gnome even rubbed his hands in anticipation "Let's start with the unpleasant part: free training. What can I tell you: there are professions and it's possible to develop them. Well, that's basically it. Now, I would like to make you an offer..."

"Hey!" I exclaimed in amazement. "What do you mean, 'that's it'?! What kind of training is that?!"

"Feh, what bupkes did you want for free? So that uncle Shlomo would leave all his things and show you how to do creation correctly? Oy vey, that's not what they hired me for! They said right out: 'Shlomo, teach those putzes professions.' Teach you I did. Everything else is a special gesheft!"

"No, that's not going to work!" I cut him off sharply."If you want a special gesheft: no problem, I'd be happy to arrange for that. But only after I figure out the professions. No knowledge about the professions – no gesheft!"

"Oh, my mama told me: Shlomo, don't you go to the recruits!" The gnome pursed his lips in displeasure. "It's just losing time! And let me tell you: no one gives his time for free! A bissel here, a bissel there, and look, uncle Shlomo becomes an old and sick player. My grandchildren come to visit and ask: uncle Shlomo, give me a granis to buy candy, what is it I am supposed to tell them? Sorry, katze, I cannot? Recruits in the Academy are too greedy, so you have to suffer and starve? Do you not like children at all? Is there anything more important than family?"

"Leave that alone, uncle Shlomo!" I said in a really icy voice. The gnome should not have dragged family into that. Even though I had been a player for over three years, as far as I could tell, the wound of losing my relatives when they were wiping out the memory of me was still sore. "Either you perform proper training, or I'll start a case against you for professional incompetence! I will not accept being bilked out of my money in the Academy!"

"Oy vey, what is it that you are saying?" The gnome waved his hands. "What incompetence? What money? I never had in mind to offer you any recipes that are very rare in the main world. Feh! Only the standard, only the rules! In the Academy you could indeed learn one profession, or, sometimes it's called specialization. The rest you will have in the main world: well, we know – the more the professions, the less the profit?"

"What professions would be most suitable for an explorer?" I asked point blank in the same cool tone.

"Oy, that would depend on what it is that you were trying to sell." The teacher couldn't care less about my intimidation; he played his role to the end. "Information? Craftsmanship? Or maybe you are going to compete with poor old uncle Shlomo and work in the creative field? I wouldn't advise that: I got it all covered for quite some time."

"Information."

"Oy vey, I knew, I knew that!" The gnome exclaimed joyfully. "Listen to me, young mensch! First thing you need to understand is uncle Shlomo will not give bad advice. He would still like gesheft, even though you rolled your eyes so scary. Think of where you will store your knowledge! On paper? So that every goy klutz, without paying a decent price, could read what you have gathered around the world? Feh! I do want to make it so that you make money. Without decent encryption, unique materials and your own media there will be no place for you in the information market. That's one. Number two, is: for a purely symbolic fee of one granis I can make for you not only everything without which your life would be worthless, I could also make you a personal logo as a bonus! 'Dark Paladin, Judge and Explorer!' I can already see people lining up have the privilege of having you share your wisdom with them. All you need is to just pay me a granis and have your pleasure. Uncle Shlomo will do the best for you!"

"What profession are you talking about?" My aloofness was gradually replaced with curiosity. The gnome was right: if I were to become an explorer, it would be crazy to transfer information without protection. Then what would be the gesheft in all that...? Damn! It seemed to be rubbing off.

"Draftsman," the gnome replied at once. "Really, you'll be able to both copy texts for someone and encrypt them, to prevent various putzes from getting information for free. Uncle Shlomo would not advise you a bad thing!"

A table with information on levels of professional development appeared before me. The essence of drafting was simple: converting into documents everything that could be drawn, written or pronounced. Incantations, information, agreements with NPCs, which the Game totally refused to prepare on its own — draftsmen had enough work. In addition, drawing various monograms, symbols and signs was also classified as work under this specialty, so I was quite happy with it, particularly considering that there was no limit on the number of professions. That was not bad for a start.

"I accept! Let's learn drafting!"

"So that's it, folks." The gnome smiled and a message on receiving a new profession appeared in front of me. "Now, young mensch, you must decide: is there any point in talking more, or no? All the everything I was supposed to give you, I did. My conscience is clean. But my soul is in pain, because it knows you cannot use draftsmanship in the Academy. I say to myself: Shlomo, you did the right thing, all correct and in line with your job. But you can't deceive yourself..."

"Oy vey, so what is it that you have to offer me?" Not expecting it, I started talking like the gnome. For a few seconds his eyes became round in surprise, and then with obvious joy he started jabbering away:

"Oy vey! I knew it! Poor uncle Shlomo looks and cannot believe his eyes — you look like a human, but you are a true gnome at heart! Such a unique mensch should not use the standard kit that are issued to every recruit. They are just schlock! A true gnome, even though he might look like a human, must use the advanced drafting kit! Only that, everything else is for schlemazels! But you are not a schlemazel! Or is there something I don't know? Uncle Shlomo does have just one kit just like that. Got it for myself, wanted to study... But I see: here's a draftsman, way better than me. Just a bissel of three granises and the name of the best draftsman in the Academy will be yours already today!"

"How much?! Are you crazy?!"

"Oy gevalt, why so indignant?" the gnome asked, sincerely bewildered."You do want to become the best in the Academy, don't you? Uncle Shlomo is ready to arrange everything. So, what's the problem? We have no gesheft?"

"No-o-o, sir, that's not how you do gesheft. One granis for everything, plus you give me all the recipes that are available to draftsmen. Or, as far as I understand, a set of fonts for all the various occasions. Either that, or just give me the standard kit, and I will study it."

"Oy vey, you have no idea what you are asking!" The gnome kept insisting. "the kit may be worth a granis, I don't argue. But you will have taken unique monograms! No one else has them ever and any putz will see that he's looking at a true draftsman, and not yet another schmendrik player! You are serious player – or am I wrong?"

"Uncle Shlomo, no schmaltz for me, you are making me laugh." The gnome's style was making inroads in my speech again. "Either one granis for everything, or I am waiting for my standard kit. That's all I have to offer."

"Oy gevalt, you are killing me without a knife!" The gnome even twisted his hands in a futile attempt to arouse pity in me. "Fine! For just a bissel of two granises I..."

"One! Plus monograms!"

"Vas?!" It was the gnome's turn to be indignant. "Just one granis for everything?!"

"Goodbye." Arguing with the stubborn gnome was useless. "Thank you for spending this time with me. Return me to the Academy."

"Oy, who talks so abruptly without discussion?" The gnome's indignation suddenly faded. A granis – oy, fine, a granis. Why hurry? Uncle Shlomo always says: first schtup your client, then let him go. Oy, first train, then..."

"If we have agreed, I need information." I delivered the final blow. "For that same granis. I need to know how I can outdo a player whose level of training and preparedness is higher than mine, and I know it. You are so experienced! So go ahead, surprise me!"

"It's time to finish with the training," the gnome drawled sadly settling down on a stool that appeared from nowhere."There's not going to be no gesheft here..."

I was returning to the Academy with a complete certainty: the druid will be punished.

"Let's go?" the guard rumbled once again. He felt impatient to return to contented idleness, so the thug did not even take a test like the Boar seriously. Just a common overgrown feral pig: what's the big deal? He had encountered countless plenty of those!

"Wait," I told him curtly, and ran off to the local trader at full speed. First of all I needed to deplete the trader's stores to quite a significant extent. For an entire year outside of time I had worked on my professional development for "Draftsman" by carefully drawing hooks and wiggles and demonstrating the results to the gnome who pursed his lips in displeasure. He always disliked something: either the strokes were not the same as the original, then the degree of pressure was wrong, then I went overboard with the colors, then Mercury is retrograde and it has negative effects on emotional disturbances... The mentor picked on just everything! If it hadn't been for the Book of Knowledge, which helped to project an outline of the text I was supposed to write onto the paper, I would have never advanced my professional l level even to "Apprentice". The situation with professions within the Game was amusing: there were a total of 15 levels of development, from "Novice" to "Master". The transition between the levels was achieved by successfully creating a certain number of objects. Thus, to level up from "Novice" to "Apprentice Trainee Assistant" one had to successfully create 10 initial level items. To level up from "Apprentice Trainee Assistant" to "Junior Apprentice Trainee" it took already 20. Or 10 items of the level-up. And so on. The algorithm to calculate the number of minimum level items needed to pass from one level to the next was not available, but in order to receive the status of "Master" you had to create over thirteen trillion of them. My mind refused to digest that number, so I feared to imagine players who reached that level. They must be immortal monsters, no less! At each level of the profession the result of the work acquired additional properties; at the "Apprentice" level the scrolls could have up to 5 properties associated both them and their use. For example: paper became more sturdy, fire resistant, it became possible to encrypt the text, incantations written on paper were enhanced... there were many other features as well.

It was specifically the possibility to move the enhanced ability onto a scroll and activating it remotely that served as the basis of my plan to neutralize Dolgunata. I pushed awake the trader who was dozing, having abandoned any hope of selling anything in the Labyrinth, replenished my drafting kit with fresh paper and ink (they did not automatically renew); then I took out the shopping list prepared by Uncle Shlomo, and handed it to the trader.

"I need everything that's listed here."

"Everything?!" the shop owned exclaimed, stunned, as he was reading the requirements. "How am I going to get you a mental detonator in the Academy?!"

A granis and a half for everything!" I cut him off; I had finally started to figure out the pricing arrangements in the Game. A granis was really a lot. Like, really, a ton. That's why the NPCs paid each other and players using virtual money – so called granis "fractions". No one was bothered by definitions such as "two hundredths" or "three fifths" of a granis; the Game allowed the use of small amounts. The record of cash available to a player would be something like: 8.588 granis. This is precisely what I had after training for a year with the greedy gnome. In my view it was worth it.

"Right! I know I have one stashed away somewhere!" The trader looked like a different person now. "Tell me, you want the stakes with knobs? It's just we have a promotion for ordinary ones and... Never mind, I get it, I'll be quiet. Here... Oh, and we have a slight problem with self-installing stakes. I only have a hundred available, and you need two hundred... Maybe you'd consider the option without knobs? We are having a promotion right now, by the way..."

"You haven't left yet?" Vikat was surprised, as he hadn't expected to see me again. Immediately after visiting the trader I went on to the elder; it turned out the latter had not expected to see me ever again.

"I need workers. Lots of them. One granis for fifty NPCs. And I need them right now."

"NPCs can't leave the Labyrinth!" the elder reminded me just in case, but an obvious interest flashed in his eyes.

"No need. They wouldn't even have to leave the village. I just need a big hole dug in the next six hours."

"What for?" Vikat was taken aback.

"What difference does it make to you? Consider it my whim for which I am willing to pay. Fifty workers, six hours of work, and the granis is yours."

"Two!"

"One granis and one Energy elixir." I retreated to the position I had thought out in advance. "Don't forget, it's not you who is going to work but creatures who belong to you specifically within the Academy."

"Fine, where do you want to dig it?"

"Come with me, I'll show you and also clarify my idea."

Vikat laughed for a long time once he figured out the point of my plan. Calling me a pervert, he allocated, for the same price, not just fifty, but a hundred workers that were either created by the Game or instantaneously relocated from somewhere else. I was particularly glad of several manually operated digging machines; their use accelerated the digging by an order of magnitude.

"I'll give you an idea for free." After we'd been laboring away for five hours, Vikat came over to assess the results. "Make a removable cover. We'll sell you the wood at cost, I like your idea. By the way, Gromana is surprised you are still here. She says Dolgunata will be free in several hours and then you'll be in deep trouble."

"So we must make it," I grinned, giving new directions to the workers. The earthwork was nearing completion, and now we were moving to the new phase – installing the stakes. "Thanks for the idea with the cover, but I'll have to pass on that. Dolgunata received a bonus from the Chancellor, and now can make anyone do whatever she needs. Gromana was able to counteract that somehow, but I don't have any amulets, nor do I have immunity. I don't want to give her a chance to get out."

"Master," one of the workers rushed towards us, "it's time to install the scrolls."

"Here," I passed to him a huge pile of paper covered in writing, and the detonator. "Seven layers around the entire perimeter, as agreed."

"You chose to be a draftsman? From where did you get so much Energy to charge the scrolls?" Vikat frowned, but then his face brightened with understanding: "Right! You are a Dark one!"

I did not clarify it for the elder, just smiled. The profession of "Draftsman" enabled me to put my abilities on paper and use them, significantly reducing the expenditure of Energy. It took just one Energy instead of the 15 needed for "Templar's Blow". The scrolls had lots of limitations and requirements; thus, it was impossible to use the abilities of other classes; it was necessary to charge a scroll with the amount of Energy equal to default attribute activation; activation time was almost twice as long; one needed to use additional equipment in the form of a remote activation detonator, and a huge number of other unpleasantries that made using the scroll in ordinary battle very inconvenient. However, in my case it was an ideal way to revenge myself against the druid! A player who activated a scroll that was sitting on the ground did not inflict damage directly on another player. It was not his fault that some living creature happened to be in the impact zone. It just happened so. Uncle Shlomo and I had argued about it for a long time, and finally agreed that the Game would reduce him to dust if activation of the scrolls would send me for respawn. The gnome was so certain of being right that I had to agree.

"We are done!" An hour and a half before Dolgunata was to appear a pleased worker reported to me on the completion of the construction work. Vikat and I evaluated the result and agreed that there could not be a better arrangement. If Dolgunata were able to get out of the trap prepared for her, nothing would save me. Even twelve hours of lead time.

"By the way," the elder remarked. "While you were busy another group showed up. The necromancer, druid and mage. Can they interfere with your plan?"

"Only the druid," I grimaced, displeased by understanding that the construction project had preoccupied me so much that I had completely forgotten about those three.

"I can hold him for twelve hours and then send for respawn," the elder grinned." All I need is two Energy elixirs."

"Can you detain the players who completed the Academy?"

"Who said that he completed his training? Dolgunata did, that's true, and now she's learning to use the Chancellor's present. No one can prohibit her from doing it. As for Sakhray – he was a keymaster and is still listed as a recruit. If so, he is totally within my power now. If I decide that I want that."

"Two elixirs?" I asked suspiciously. What bothered me was the very low cost for open help to one of the parties.

"I am curious as to whether your creation

could withstand the push of two druids," the elder explained, smiling. "It's an interesting idea. I'll release the workers. You don't need them any more, right?"

"Go ahead," I agreed, and in the same moment a huge crowd of NPCs simply faded into the air. Together with the digging machines, axes and scaffolding. Everything that had had a grand code name: "The Big Dig of the Century: Revenge on Dolgunata" was now gone. "Where are the players who arrived?"

"Resting at my house. Waiting till you become free."

"When can you kill the druid?" I gave the elixirs to Vikat.

"Consider him gone. Technically it's not difficult, it just takes time. I'll block him for twelve hours, during which his Energy level will drop to zero. He'll respawn."

"Excellent. I hope you made the group comfortable. Let them rest. Now, regarding Dolgunata: I need to withstand her mental attack. At least initially. How do I do that?"

"As far as I understand, you don't have an amulet."

I shook my head: he was right.

"What did Gromana tell you?"

"Just one thing – that I need to run away as far as I can. That I can't win over Dolgunata."

"I see... Do you have any money left?"

"A little," I tensed.

"Buy a chain and ask our blacksmith to chain you to that thing over there. Choose a length such that you can approach the trap, but not jump into it. All I can suggest is the following: you need to better understand yourself and how to withstand mental attacks. In effect they are just common psychological manipulation. It's possible to learn to fight that. Dolgunata cannot continuously use the Chancellor's gift in the Academy: as far as I recall, at some point the Game determines that the player has already learned to use the object he received and issues a warning. The chain will help you overcome the effects of the present, and your brain will help you understand yourself. Nothing else can help you. I cannot give you my amulet – I still have to go back after all that. I gather Gromana said the same thing, and the trader has nothing of the sort."

"Where's the blacksmith located?" The elder's advice seemed quite reasonable to me. "It's time to prepare for the meeting."

I spent the time remaining till Dolgunata's appearance to review the video of my flight to the chicks. I tried to pay attention to the most minute things, even to the eye color of the bird and the chicks (they were bright red). The Book of Knowledge dutifully digested information and three minutes before the H-hour when Dolgunata was going to appear the Game brought me the long-awaited message:

Book of Knowledge has reached a new level. You need to increase the level of artifact properties: "Context search" (1), "Weapon"(1), "Protection» (2)" "Spiritual integrity"(1), <Choose value from the list >

"Neuronal Network," I whispered and the reel listing available properties started moving, rolling to the right line. Several times the Game asked to confirm my choice, and as soon as I clicked on the last button, the world around me changed. Not much, just a little bit, but oh, it was so wonderful! One of the walls of a nearby house, a picket fence and a few more things that I would normally not have even noticed, were highlighted in green, as if someone had applied a filter to a graphics editor program. The picket fence was nearby, so I spent some time looking at it in detail, and saw that it was made out of some form of plastic imitating wood rather than classic wood studs. The green highlight disappeared, and the Book of Knowledge literally purred quietly, digesting a new portion of information. I swallowed – when I see Gromana, I should do something nice for her. Information on how explorers develop had turned out to be extremely useful.

"Yari?!" I heard Dolgunata's exclamation of surprise from the respawn point. "What the... Did you do that?!"

I guess I was supposed to have answered something, but there was no time. The world around me exploded in a whirl of tiny flakes, leaving behind just one thing: the goddess. Dropping on my knees I crawled towards her, drooling as I crawled, and desiring just one thing: to touch my ideal as soon as possible ...

"BASTARD!!!" the druid's wild scream glued reality together and returned me to adequate perception of my surroundings. "What did you do, you freak?!"

The chain, stretched taut, limited my freedom of action, so I found myself just a couple of meters away from the huge pit. The plan prepared with Uncle Shlomo, adjusted using my understanding of the druid's abilities and her strength, was extremely simple. We assumed as an axiom that Dolgunata was much stronger than me, so I could not win in an open battle. That Dolgunata's level was at the maximum allowed within the Academy and – I was completely certain of that – had additional experience that she would receive once she were to respawn or return to the main world. That Dolgunata was an experienced head hunter, a player who specialized in killing other players, so ordinary and even sophisticated traps would be useless against her. In a battle of experience against desire to win, experience mostly wins.

Mostly, but not always!

We had known for certain that Gromana would send Dolgunata to respawn, and in some specific interval the druid would appear at the respawn point. If we knew the precise location of the girl's arrival, and could guarantee that in case of any respawn she would emerge at this specific place, what would we need to do? Right! We needed to dig an enormous pit around the point of her emergence. A pit fifteen meters wide and seven meters deep, and then cover the bottom of that pit with sharp stakes. Even in the form of a panther Dolgunata would not be able to jump over that distance; the Book of Knowledge calculated to a meter the distance of the jump without running up. And there was no space around the respawn stone to take a running jump. Jumping down would be sheer suicide: the stakes were placed in such a way that even the diminutive druid would not be able to fit between them. From the standpoint of a creature that had just respawned, the situation was dire. The druid immediately took me under control, but there was no benefit for her in that: the chain did not allow me to either hand her anything to cover the gap, nor kill myself by jumping in. Dolgunata could do whatever she wanted with me, but only within the length of the chain.

"I am glad to see you as well, gorgeous!" I grinned, rising to my feet. The influence of the object received from the Chancellor had now completely faded, and other abilities of the druid did not affect me. Regardless of what Gromana had said about "Spiritual integrity", now this property really saved me. The detonator was controlled through a separate game interface, so I clicked on several virtual buttons and said testily: "Oops!"

"What the hell – 'Oops'?!" Dolgunata exclaimed angrily, and at that moment ten scrolls with the Templar's blow activated directly under her. That would do for a start. Finally it became clear to me why the parameters of an ability included range: among other things this parameter specified the conditions for remote use. In order to inflict damage the scroll had to be within the distance specified in the description. In my case, fifteen meters; that was more than enough to hit the druid in any location on her small island.

"Bastard!!! A-a-a-a!!!" Dolgunata screamed in horrific pain once her protection was devastated by a combined hit, and the girl's legs turned into a bloody mess. The blow hit the lower part of her body as it was the closest to the plane where the scrolls were located. Legless, Dolgunata crashed to the ground, was unable to hold onto the respawn stone and dropped directly onto the stakes. Protection did not help her: falling from a height of seven meters turned the druid into a butterfly on a pin. Dolgunata's body glimmered and disappeared – she was sent for respawn...

An hour passed and my world exploded, leaving just the goddess. But almost immediately it came together again, allowing me to regain control over my body. I was able to see the fading silhouette of the druid in the middle of the pit. The option "take Yari under control and jump over the stakes" didn't work.

Another hour passed and the world shattered again, only to restore itself at once. And again, just the fading fog served as a reminder that a very self-confident girl had been standing next to the respawn stone just a moment ago. The Chancellor punished Dolgunata for excessive use of his present in the Academy.

Another hour passed and... the world stayed intact. Disheveled and angry, Dolgunata was staring at me glumly, not making any more attempts to take me under control. I did not want to give her time to figure out a new plan to escape my trap, so, without further emotion, I activated another ten scrolls with the blow.

"Yari, let's negotiate! Nooooo...!!! The druid's legs again turned into mincemeat and the force of gravity threw her onto the stakes.

"Hold on! We need to talk! I am not ... A-a-a!!!"

"Yari, stop!!! Nooooo!!!"

"You stupid freak! Once I get to you, you'll spit bloooo ... A-a-a!!!"

I'd been killing Dolgunata for twelve hours straight. It seemed to me that even if the girl had received additional experience in the wastelands she should have only one or two levels remaining, tops. Another two hours and the Academy would forever forget the creature named Dolgunata. Either I would kill her for good, or she would return to the main world. There was no other option.

"There is no need to kill her." I heard Gromana's voice after yet another scream from the druid died in the air. "You've punished her enough."

I looked back and saw the witch, with her arms folded on her chest, studying the pit I had dug.

"That's an interesting setup."

"I can't let her stay alive," I said abruptly. "You said yourself that she wouldn't let me finish the Academy. That she is my enemy. Is it customary in the Game to spare your enemies?"

"Even if you do kill her, you'll acquire a more powerful enemy. Archibald will not forgive his student's death."

"You suggest that I pardon her?" I smirked sarcastically. "Maybe I should also jump into the pit all on my own? Why should we make the poor girl do

463

all the work? Chase me and all that..."

"You are correct to consider her dangerous," Gromana was not going to give up. "You are right in thinking that it's easier to get rid of an enemy once rather than hide for the rest of your life. But you are forgetting one thing: we are in the Game. I don't understand why you would rather kill the druid than make her your ally. You need to level up, and who can help you better than a 150 year old player?"

"What are you suggesting?" Before telling the witch to go piss her pants I wanted to hear her proposition in full.

"The girl has no chance for getting out of your trap and she has already understood that. You can kill her – I am not going to interfere, that's between you two. But think – what are some other ways you could use this situation to your benefit? Until we meet in the Sanctuary, Paladin. I have nothing else to say to you."

Gromana turned back and stalked back to her den, leaving me with my own thoughts. I cursed: my initial plan to kill Dolgunata was crumbling fast! Despite my year of training, the witch was able to sow in my soul the seed of not even doubt, but of greed. Really, what would be the purpose of killing Dolgunata? To enjoy revenge? Ph! As a player who had completed her training the druid would be forced to leave the Academy; as soon as she entered the main Game I would have acquired a truly formidable enemy. But I could turn the situation to my advantage! If this were an ordinary world, I would not dare let the druid live, but this is the Game!

Fulfillment of oaths here is not monitored just by Judges, but by the Emperor himself!

Dolgunata appeared at the respawn point for the twelfth time and, what I liked most of all, kept silent. She did not try to threaten, ask or plead. Crouching, waiting for the next blow, the girl stared at me with hatred. Even across such a distance I felt uncomfortable. It felt like the druid was not human any more. She had turned into a monster. There still was time before Sakhray was to appear, so I decided to inform Dolgunata of my views.

"Let's talk?" I grinned, addressing the frowning monster. "Or should I continue?"

"What do you want?" It seemed like an eternity before the druid literally spat these words out.

"You wouldn't believe it – I want to stay alive! I want security! I want not to start at every noise waiting for the evil Nata to come and drag me off into some dark closet! Have you heard about such a thing as Maslow's pyramid of needs? You undermined its foundation, and now I need to build the whole thing anew. So, my golden, what we need is...

"Don't call me that!" Dolgunata flared up.

"No problem, would you rather be a freak bitch?! You like that better? Believe me, my golden, being yellow and similar to rotten dog piss is better if it's disguised. Let the others think you are valuable and important, but you and I will know what's hiding behind that fancy name."

Dolgunata said nothing.

"So, now. I am so sick of your control that I have no other choice than to enforce my own sentence personally, and receive the reward I will thus deserve for killing you. Choosing between two possibilities: to receive a granis or to leave you alone, I would choose the former. But there is such a thing as corruption in my world, and it keeps telling me that in principle I could turn a blind eye to your behavior if I were to receive appropriate compensation. I need information. I need a guarantee of security within the Academy and beyond it. I need granises. Generally, I need a lot of things, so I am waiting for your offer, my golden. And here's what I have to help you think better."

Three activated scrolls did not inflict any visible harm: her protection absorbed all the potential damage. But that's not what they were for, anyway – only to demonstrate the seriousness of my intent and show that I had enough scrolls still.

"I could leave the Academy at any moment." Dolgunata kept spitting her words out through her clenched teeth. If the hatred shining in her eyes had material force, it could have easily incinerated a few celestial bodies, resolving the problem of meteors and rogue asteroids once and for all, taking a couple of small planets with them for good measure.

"Without completing the quest Archibald gave you?" I was not trying to hide a mocking smirk. "Go right ahead – clear out!"

"You know nothing!"

"I don't need to know any of it! Come to your senses, old girl! You were trained for a hundred and fifty years for some goal that you could not fully achieve, or else you would have cleared out of the Academy a long time ago. You were too stupid to complete the task, whatever that task was. I have had the pleasure to talking to the catorian in person – he doesn't need losers. So, you have three choices: either you interest me to such an extent that I decide not to kill you, or return to the main world and explain to Archibald how come you weren't able to complete the quest, or forget about self-preservation and let me finish you off. You are welcome to jump yourself, by the way. There are no other options for you. You don't have anyone to force to get me here, and your own paws are too short for that. You have ten minutes to think; after which I will assume that you have chosen the last option. The timer has started."

"Bastard!" Having circled the respawn stone one more time, the druid froze, clenched her fists, threw her head back, roared, and suddenly let out a high-pitched scream: BAAAAAAASTAAAAARD!!!! AAAAA!!! Wretched shitfreak!!!!"

I kept silent, pointedly ignoring the frantic girl, and tapping time with my foot. Working as a stopwatch. Dolgunata's curses were not really varied, I even got bored; for some reason I recalled lieutenant Sintsov – he was a true virtuoso of obscenities. He could have turned "War and Peace" into profanities in such a way that the novel would still have remained a cultural gem; moreover, it would even have gained in popularity. Dolgunata, with her 150 years, couldn't hold a candle to Sintsov.

"Well," after ten minutes of the druid's screams I spread my hands, indicating total disappointment. "You have made your choice, so..."

If you preserve my life, I swear by the Game

that I will ensure completion of the Academy for you," the druid said in a dead and kind of hissy voice. I could barely hear her. "I swear that you will receive all the granises I have: ten and three hundred thousandths. I swear by the Game that I will tell you everything you want – whatever has not been prohibited by a direct order from my teacher. I swear not to inflict mental damage on you, direct or indirect, unless this is a quest requirement or the only way to save you. Is this enough? Or do you want to have me as a sex slave to boot?"

"Gerontophilia is not my preference." I was not going to succumb to Dolgunata's provocation. Even despite the oath she was a dangerous opponent. "But that's not all! Instead of sex, by which, as I understand, you make your living, I want you to teach me protection against mental influence."

"Fine – what else?" Dolgunata scowled, but nodded in agreement.

"Else: we have not specified what happens after the Academy. You are stronger than I, and after returning to the main world you would find me and grind me into fine dust. Or hire someone to do it for you. I don't want this and I need assurance that it won't happen, at least, on your order or instigation."

"Unless I have a direct order to kill you, I swear by the Game that I won't touch you! I swear to not accept or generate orders to kill you or wipe you out. Is that what you wanted to hear?"

"That's correct! You can be persuasive when you really try! Let me think... Fine, I accept your oath and will not kill you now!"

For some time the druid and I stared at each other, and I was certain once again that Nata had surrendered. But had not given up. People who had given up would not have such a burning stare.

"Vikat!" I shouted into the air, knowing full well that the village elder was watching all this circus. "Please send the blacksmith here! The chain is not needed any more."

"What the hell? Get lost!" the air around the respawn stone condensed, turning into Sakhray. The druid did not get his bearings all at once, so, when there was no space for him, he reflexively pushed away the obstacle. Which in this case was Dolgunata.

"Noooooo!" Another scream of pain sounded, turning into a throaty gurgle. Dolgunata departed for yet another respawn.

"Nata?! How?" Sakhray's face froze for an instant in a stunned expression , and then the druid faded into the air. The Game considered him guilty of inflicting damage on another player while in the Labyrinth, and immediately sentenced him to death.

The word that you said recently is very suitable to this situation," grinned the village elder, who came together with the blacksmith. "Very expressive and explains a lot. It's amazing that I'd never heard it earlier... Oops!"

During the hour that it took for Dolgunata and Sakhray to respawn, I was freed from my captivity of iron and a walkway was built as Vikat had recommended earlier; one end was thrown over the pit. Amazingly, the boards didn't sag under their own weight despite the fifteen yards between the banks of the pit. Once I noticed this, the Book of Knowledge immediately suggested the answer: the walkway was made of the same material as the erstwhile picket fence. It was not wood, but plastic with an enhanced strength feature. I am starting to like living in a magical world: a lot of the laws of physics don't work here, or even if they do, at least not in the way we were taught in school. Once she reappeared, Dolgunata gave a heavy stare at her brother, who dropped his head; then she walked over to the other side. Sakhray was just about to follow her, when the girl bent down and pulled the style after her. The far end jumped on the stakes, but Nata kept at it, increasing the distance between her brother and his freedom with every step.

"Nata?!" the druid exclaimed indignantly, once he figured out what threatened him. "What kind of a joke is that?!"

"You did not follow my orders!" Apparently, the druid needed to vent all her irritation at someone, and Sakhray just happened to be in the wrong place at the wrong time.

"Who said that?! He's already..."

"Not a squeak more from you!" Nata cut her brother off. "You want to die? You forgot Archibald's order? Sit here, I'll take Yari out of the Academy and come back for you. How much food do you have?"

"About two weeks' worth...," Sakhray drawled sadly. "Don't leave me here!"

"Let's go." Dolgunata ignored her brother, grabbed me by the hand and literally pulled me towards the village. "At what test are you now?"

"At the third. Zangar and Marinar are sitting at the elder's. They will come with us."

Nata said nothing, just turned sharply and strode towards Vikat's house, making me run to keep up. Judging from her pursed lips, the girl had made some decision that she didn't like but would follow through to the end.

"My oath does not apply to them." Nata stopped at the porch of the elder's house and turned to me. "I won't harm them or kill them, but I won't save them from the hordes in the wastelands. Is this enough?"

"More than enough."

"In that case. Here are the granises. That's all I have."

For a few seconds I saw the trade screen, but even without the help of the Book of Knowledge I was able to see the druid's current level: three. She died twelve times from my hand, once from Gromana and once from Sakhray... And still she has level three! How?! Where did she get so much experience that the system granted her three levels at respawn? For me, for example, after I was killed by Gromana, my experience bar has barely crawled over ten percent.

"Submission and being driven to suicide," Nata clarified, correctly interpreting my surprise. "There are NPCs wandering through the wastelands; it's allowed to hunt them if you are strong enough. You could level up quite a bit at their expense."

"So, it's not allowed to drive players to suicide?" I grinned, and the fleeting grimace told me that my guess was right. Otherwise Nata would not have left me any chances. One Templar's blow to the forehead and that would be it: I was standing next to her. "Since we are partners now, even though it's an odd partnership, I would like to warn you: tomorrow the major hunt will start. I did something a little much with the birds here... Anyway, tomorrow they will start gobbling up everything that isn't nailed down. Your brother fits the bill for that... They will eat him!"

"No matter, it will do him good to die a couple of times," Dolgunata said casually, encountered my stare, and clarified: "He is initiated, so nothing much will happen to him."

"Then another question: how did you find out where I was? Gromana said that she could not see a mark, yet you always knew precisely where I was. Another gift from the Chancellor?"

"He didn't want anyone else to use the dorn, so he offered me a deal," Nata confirmed. "I destroy the mechanism and then begin to see those whom I need. You could have guessed. You see the Paladins, after all. It's stupid to consider yourself unique."

I fell silent, as I had nothing to respond to that; however, my unexpected silence was interrupted by Zangar, who appeared in the door.

"Good to see you again. I returned. As promised. Dolgunata," Zangar nodded to the druid as an old acquaintance. Marinar appeared from behind the necromancer, and once again I was impressed by the girl's transformation. Now it would be impossible to confuse her with a teenager: literally after a few days of absence the girl had filled out and the outline of a female figure became so obvious that Dolgunata even made an offended grimace, seeing the changes.

"Hello Yari. I wanted to apologize, I was slow and..."

"Did you complete training with the teachers here?" I cut Marinar off, not allowing her to say the speech that she had prepared. There was really no need for that. The village elder appeared right after Marinar, and I immediately pointed at the two guards suffering from boredom nearby: "Vikat, as it turned out I never needed those two ruffians. You may take them."

"I took them," the village elder was beside himself with joy. He was beaming like the cat that ate a canary. "You never used their services, so I am returning your granis – here it is. By the way, why are you giving them up? They are quite reliable lads."

"With Dolgunata and Zangar here they become a pointless waste of experience. By the way, judging from your pleased face, while Sakhray is sitting at the respawn point the NPCs will not disappear. So your issue with the chicks has resolved itself?"

The elder grinned without answering. Apparently, Vikat had already blotted us from his mind, getting back to his own problems. I did not insist on a farewell speech, and once Marinar added Nata to the group we started out of the forest. The Boar was waiting for us.

"How did you make it to the Chancellor so fast?" I grumbled in displeasure an hour later. We had walked about five kilometers away from the village along a winding path through a sparse forest; however, the map mockingly demonstrated that the distance we covered was barely more than a needle's eye. By my estimates, at this rate it would take us two to three days to reach the Chancellor, and that only if we don't encounter any obstacles.

"Druids run real fast," Zangar clarified. Dolgunata had never said a word since the time we started out. Proud and solitary, she was walking silently in front. "I held Marinar. Rode Dolgunata. Rode her brother. Then Dolgunata again. Speed was great."

"I see, so this is not an option now... Zangar, I have a personal question for you. Do you know what this is?"

I pulled out the steel hexagon I had obtained inside the chick and showed it to the necromancer. It would be silly to lug along an unknown object: what if it's a time bomb and one fine day it would get me? Who if not Zangar would know the meaning of the object and ways to use it? However, his reaction was totally unexpected for me: Zangar froze in place as if he had run into an invisible wall and could not take his eyes, which became as big as saucers, from the hexagon.

"You are full of surprises. Paladin." Dolgunata quietly appeared next to us, appraising the object in my hands. "It's a pity I can't hunt you now. It would have been interesting, probably. In view of my new knowledge I have a question: who wants to leave the Academy here and now?"

"What knowledge?" Marinar asked, and I was immensely grateful to her, as I was about to ask the same question. Everyone may very well understand that the level of my knowledge leaves a lot to be desired, yet understanding and hearing the confirmation are two different things.

"Stone of attributes," the cynocephalian barked, reviving. "Activates any attribute. Or increase by one. If you have already. Great value. I understand you, druid. No, I don't hurry. Question to Yari. Whether he agrees?"

"That's what we'll find out right now," Dolgunata regained her manner of behaving arrogantly and independently with others. "Yari, what you showed us enables you to activate any attribute that is available within the Game. Specifically, what is of most interest to us now: Luck. It was previously considered that receiving an attribute within the Academy was impossible; what you are holding cannot be bought or transferred; it can only be received as a reward. It's quite hard to earn it even in the main world... So the player, who chooses or increases Luck will become an incredibly lucky creature for the span of three days. He and those next to him in the same group will be very lucky. Actually, no. They will be incredibly, outrageously lucky, all of them! The Academy is chock-full of different hidden bonuses and objects. That very Boar is just a common forest rogue that respawns every several hours. No rogue, even if it is a quest creature, could exist without its own den. But where there is a den, there are treasures. As for me, I would not turn down a chance to rummage through the Academy's storage. There is bound to be loot there – granises, objects... books," Dolgunata touched on something that was a sore spot for me. "The choice is fully yours: it is impossible to steal the stone or take it away from you. It's yours and yours alone. Besides, don't forget: there are wastelands in front of us, and in our case we will need incredible luck. You are Dark. I am Light. This pair is not yet definite, but most likely they will be Light as well. Everyone will want to kill us."

"So, the whole group will be lucky regardless of the number of members?" I narrowed my eyes suspiciously.

"Number matters." Zangar interjected. "Twenty, no more." After that luck leaves. Too many wanters. But we not many. For us enough. If you agree."

"We don't have quite a full group," I stated my thought and my allies' frowning faces indicated that I needed to clarify it: "If Luck works for an entire three days for everyone, I would like to bring the Paladins back to rejoin us. The map shows they are not far from us, presumably, at a respawn point. You want luck – no problem. But first of all we need to reinforce the group. If Dolgunata is right, and I am afraid that this is the case, our time in the wastelands will be quite unpleasant. We need additional fighters. Also, we mustn't forget that the mages will be actively hunting me."

"You suggest that I run over and fetch them?" The druid frowned.

"You can see on the map where they are," I nodded. "Bring the Paladins here and I'll activate the Luck."

"I need a day: wait here," Nata reacted quickly, turned into the panther without any pointless questions and disappeared around a turn, making huge leaps.

"You strange player," Zangar said contemplatively, looking in the direction where druid disappeared. "Paladins left you. Went themselves. Not returned for you. You care for them. Why? They are no one to you. Don't understand."

"Because I plan to return back to the main Game," I clarified. "And I will have to look my teacher in the eye, and he will definitely ask: 'Did you do everything to save your brethren and get them out of the Academy?' Given what the map shows – Paladins periodically disappear and then reappear again, in different places – they are being actively killed in the wastelands and they reemerge at respawn points. With this approach not everyone will survive, so they need help. Besides, why do you think that I was going to do something out of altruism? I sent the druid on a run so that we could calmly and in detail discuss my demands. What will I receive specifically from you and Marinar for activating the attribute?"

"Ten percent of whatever is found," the necromancer proposed instantly, as if he had decided everything for himself in advance. "For objects it would be equivalent in granises. After completion of the Academy."

"Zangar!" I exclaimed dejectedly. "What ten percent? We are partners, and this implies equal rights in everything! I don't understand your wish to take advantage of me. You said yourself that there are such things as Dungeons. After the Academy I'd just have to put the word out that I have a 3-day Luck attribute and there would immediately be a crowd of high-level players whose only desire would be to get me into their group. I am sure there are players who need to go through a Dungeon or two who have a very low chance of finding some specific object. I would be a highly desirable partner for them. Only because we really need luck in order to painlessly go through the wastelands, I agreed to activate it now. But note: I underscored the 'painless' part. We'd make it to the Chancellor in any case. Nata will not allow anyone to harm us too much, and we count for something, too. Since you showed that you were a real partner and also brought Marinar, I agree to half of the money found plus subsequent compensation for loot in the form of objects at market price that will be determined by the Game itself. And that's only part of it. The other part is that I need access to knowledge. You have a teacher of great wisdom; you promised me to arrange a meeting with him after the Academy. We'll talk, but there's no guarantee that we would be able to reach some kind of agreement, so I want you to provide me information useful in the Game. Within your area of competency and without breaking class rules."

"Thirty percent loot." Zangar responded after some thought. "Information on explorer. Information on Judges. Help in Game. Without breaking rules. Your world interesting for me. Many things unusual. Want to see. Teacher should allow. What you say?"

"Accepted!" I said gladly, and immediately the agreement generated by the Game flashed before my eyes. "Now Marinar..."

"She comes with us," Zangar stated in a tone that brooked no argument.

"What do you mean – with us? But she is a mage! As soon as we leave the Academy, they will take her and it's unlikely we'll ever see her again."

"She comes with us," the necromancer repeated. "Else no deal. Marinar under my protection. Teacher will allow take her. Will be player without class. Alchemist always useful."

I wanted to protest, but only now did I notice where and in what way the girl was standing. The Book of Knowledge instantly reviewed our entire trip and presented an amazing revelation: Marinar was always next to Zangar, and in most cases her hand was placed on the necromancer's forearm. This gesture didn't look like control; more like support. Marinar and Zangar want to be together?

"In the Game that's not a problem," Marinar finally said something. Apparently, I had said the last sentence aloud. "Zangar is a strong and powerful warrior, it's an honor for me to be with him. I have nothing to offer you after the Academy; I have no information, so I agree to the initial conditions: fifty percent of the loot is yours."

"In addition, I will require a personal discount for your work in alchemy after we complete the Academy – a 100 percent one." I found a solution. Despite my surprise I was not going to let my quarry get away. "In other words, you'll make elixirs for me at the cost of the ingredients."

"I agree," another notice of the Game came and went quickly. The agreement was made. However, as I already knew, an agreement was not a contract: it could be broken.

"In this case I suggest we allow the Game to prepare the text of the contract," I said, in my mind already rubbing my hands in anticipation of loot. Zangar humphed, but agreed to draw the contract for our agreement to take official form. Marinar had no objection.

"Wonderful. Now tell me, how did you restore Marinar's head? For I am going to develop an inferiority complex if my hand is not restored soon..."

The day that it took Dolgunata to bring back the Paladins turned out to be a busy one. Zangar, carefully searching for words, told me about life after the Academy — what would be a good thing to do and where to go immediately after getting to the main world. In some ways his recommendations were similar to Gromana's, yet there were nuances: Zangar suggested that the first thing I should do was to visit an auction and upgrade my inventory. Understanding that I wouldn't get much out of the necromancer, I asked him and Marinar to tell me about their worlds. While Zangar answered reluctantly, obviously withholding information, the mage was unstoppable. I learned practically everything about Varnax, starting from its political framework to the details of microbiology on which the girl had been working. The Book of Knowledge purred and burped quietly, digesting more information; by the time we ought to have slept the artifact had easily acquired an additional level, increasing the "Neuronal Network" to 2 units. Internally, I reproached myself: nothing had been keeping me from doing it before. Just grab any player and interrogate him, torturing him as needed to get him to talk about his world.

At the second level of "Neuronal Network", the space around me was transformed. Here and there areas were highlighted in a greenish fog. I started exploring the forest around me in detail, looking at every tree and blade of grass; that raised the artifact experience bar by another 30 percent. I owed Gromana: because of her hint it was becoming easier to level the artifact up with every new level.

"Get up, loafers!" Dolgunata's loud voice jerked me from the pleasant state I had encountered in the Academy for the first time: sleep. Over the few years of my personal time I had become unused to lying down and closing my eyes; at first for a couple of hours I just lounged on the ground, counting the stars. There were alternating days and nights in the Labyrinth. When Morpheus finally took pity on me and I sank into sleep it seemed to me that I was rudely yanked out of it at once by Nata, who was hanging over us three with a pleased smirk. "Who would ever set up camp in the middle of the road? Killing you would be a piece of cake!"

"No one here to kill us." Zangar remarked to her, rising to his feet. Stretching to loosen his limbs that had stiffened during the night, he asked: "Where are Paladins?"

"They'll be here any minute now; I decided to show up a little early. Yari, activate the stone."

"Not so fast," I cut the druid short and followed the necromancer's example by standing up and stretching. "First I want to make sure we discuss what I will be getting for that."

"WHAT?!" the druid exclaimed in astonishment, and immediately her eyes shifted to Zangar: "Is this your doing?!"

"Yari figured himself," the necromancer shook his head. "We bargained too. Your turn now. Our agreement secret. And Marinar too. No one makes you. Can leave group. Return in three days. Such is Game. Yari begins understand it."

"Somehow he began understanding it at a really bad time," Dolgunata scowled and turned to me: "What do you want?"

The bargaining with the druid took so long that the Paladins came up to us. Having understood what the issue was, they agreed without question to share half of their loot and information on their world. They mumbled something about Marinar and mages generally; the Paladins encountered a steady stare from Zangar, dropped their eyes, and finally joined the group. Seeing the current levels of the newly arrived players, I was barely able to contain a surprised cry: only Teart could boast level 2, everyone else had dropped back to 1.

"Where did that happen to you?" I asked carefully, letting Dolgunata think over my next proposal.

"Mages," Sartal grimaced. "Th-th-the was-s-stelands-s-s are full of mages-s-s. Th-th-they catch everyone. They mas-s-stered defens-s-se and it's-s-s hard to kill them now. Almos-s-st imposs-s-ssible. They s-s-search for you. S-s-so much more s-ssurpris-s-sing that you are with-th-th a mage."

"She is one of us, and we won't have problems with her," I assured him, trying to lighten the situation. It didn't work very well, but at least the Paladins stopped looking at her with open anger. The girl moved closer to Zangar, looking for protection in his shadow.

"I agree to your conditions," Dolgunata decided, and another agreement flashed before me. In addition to fifty percent of loot and information about her world of origin, I secured for myself such a great thing as help in passing through the Dungeons after the Academy. I would have to complete three of those in any case to get so-called "Dungeon clearance", so why not do it together with such an experienced and strong player as Dolgunata? I was not planning to develop as a fighter; my explorer's path was more than enough for me.

"So! Now that we have figured out our participation in future events, I have a global question: how do I activate the stone?" I asked with a grin, as soon as the last contract was approved by the Game.

"Touch seal to forehead," Zangar clarified. "Wish to receive attribute. Choose Luck. Enjoy result."

New character attribute is available: Luck
Would you like to activate it?

The steel hexagon faded in my hands like morning fog. A system message and a new record on the character qualities were the only proof that I had received a new attribute. Amazing, but there were no revelations or visions from on high.

"And?" I even managed to look accusingly at the group, who froze in place as the space around me was transformed. Previously objects and phenomena unknown to me were highlighted in green; now a red highlight appeared as well. It fully covered a small bush a hundred yards ahead.

"What the hell?" I frowned and, accompanied by the team of nine beings, approached the bush. At first glance there was nothing remarkable about it, it was exactly the same as the one growing next to it; yet the Game insistently pointed out this particular bush, and not another.

"Can anyone see what's wrong with it?" I asked, and immediately received a contemplative answer from Dolgunata:

"It's fine. Look at the roots!"

The group squatted and amazed "oh"s and "what the hell"s sounded in the air. The reddish glow disappeared, replaced by greenish fog. It covered the skull with three eyeholes that were barely visible, as it was half-buried and concealed by the grass covering it. It looked exactly like the one you could see on the icons of hidden abilities. The seal of the Emperor. Only here it was not a pattern or a flat projection, but an actual real skull.

"What, did the Emperor croak right here?" Teart stated everyone's thought out loud, and the space around me exploded with a host of system messages.

CHAPTER ELEVEN

WASTELANDS

"**D**OES ANYONE KNOW what this is?" I was holding a small tightly sealed box, carefully stifling my desire to throw it away as if it were something extremely unpleasant. As soon as I touched the skull, the latter disappeared, revealing this, for some reason distasteful, object.

"Distiller of emotions." Marinar took my find, allowing me to sigh with relief. "It converts emotions into energy that is necessary for alchemical recipes and preparation of elixirs. Zangar bought me one like that in the previous village. I wouldn't say this is a better one. It looks exactly like mine, at least at first glance."

"So it seems we don't really need it?" I asked for clarification and the mage shook her head. "How much did you pay for it?"

"Barely over one thousandth of a granis. Now to start making basic Energy elixirs I just need to collect a few herbs; I hope there will be no problem with that in the wastelands."

"So then you have the recipe for that already?" I drawled sadly, making one mental note for myself that the inscriptions we found in the forest would not yield much.

"Of course, it's one of the basic recipes in alchemy. It's provided by default."

"So, then, there isn't anything else there? Curious Teart took advantage of his short stature and poked his nose under the bush. "Just some useless piece of metal junk."

"We found a treasure, ya stupid! Shut up now! "Monstrichello boomed. "Yari'll now find a hundred of 'em for us, 'nough for all!"

The entire group stared at me questioningly, so I had to explain:

"I don't think there will be so many. After the seal was activated the Game showed the closest buried thing with a warning: that's a onetime thing. Everything else I'd have to find on my own, looking for three-eyed skulls, which could be anywhere. The more I concentrate on the detail the higher the chances that I'll find a trove, but I'd turn into a snail. We need to decide what's more important: these distillers or the speed."

The sigh of disappointment sounded over the land, and I finally dismissed the bothersome messages. I should have become used to this by now:

the Game had once again kicked me in the gut: it showed that the Academy was full of secret troves; it even revealed one of them as an example, and then clearly explained that if someone wanted to find the next treasure, he'd have to forget about moving forward and study not just every bush and blade of grass, but also look under stones, downed trees and holes in the trunks of all the trees that happened to be on the way. The three-eyed skull, which was a virtual chest, could appear anywhere, and the loot in it could vary. From a distiller for alchemists to a sack of granises. I didn't even get any achievement points for this.

"The Boar's den is a kilometer away from here." Dolgunata reminded us. "We only have three days of luck. Shall we stand here and play dumb, or shall we go on?"

There were no objections. Monstrichello habitually stepped forward, expecting to deflect potential attacks, and in a friendly crowd we moved on.

"Here." Teart transferred the video to me. "That's all I was able to find and keep accessible. I'll give you the other seven recipes after the Academy – they had already sunk into long-term storage before I learned to copy information locally. Did you find anything yourself?"

I waved my hand vaguely, studying the three recipes I received. They were written in an unknown language, which told me one thing: it was impossible to use them in draftsmanship.

No matter how much I tried, I did not see a

single area highlighted in red throughout the distance remaining till we reached the Boar. A couple of times I noticed green fog, but it covered a previously unknown mushroom and a tree. There was nothing else new or unusual in this patch of forest. Once I got free time, I should review the video in detail; it will certainly be possible to earn a few more units of experience for the artifact. It was vitally important to bring the "Neuronal Network" to the 15th level as quickly as possible.

"R-R-A!" I was looking at yet another bush, and nearly ran into the back of Logir, who had stopped, when, with a thunderous roar, a two-meter-tall Neanderthal jumped onto the path. The hairy thug barely looked human – well, he did have two legs, two arms and one head. As for everything else, apparently the Boar (the artifact definitely identified the creature) had gotten it from some kind of fire sale: long hair covering his body all over, arms with two elbows, very disproportionate face and a meter and a half club, which the Boar was swinging from side to side, making the trees nearby sway.

"I'll work on him," Dolgunata stepped forward, and softly, in a sort of purring and soporific voice, addressed the core of the third test of the Labyrinth: "Hello, my sweet! Do you remember me? I missed you. Such primeval power could not leave a girl cold, and I came back."

"R-a-a?" The Boar roared less menacingly, and stopped swinging his club.

"You are right – our first meeting didn't go too well. But I get it, and I want it to be better. You will forgive me, my dear, right?" Nata took a few more steps forward, now standing between the Boar and the frowning Monstrichello. Our tank obviously disliked what was going on; apparently, when the Paladins had tried to go through this test, the fuzzy monster had beaten them up pretty badly.

"Gra-ra!" the Neanderthal growled forcefully and swung the club over his shoulder. "Gra-gra-ra!"

Nata took a few more steps forward, stopping literally a meter away from the Boar. Next to the seven-foot monster the diminutive druid looked like a child.

"Don't roar," Dolgunata's aura of seduction was so strong that the faces of practically all the group, including Logir and Marinar, sported happy smiles, like schoolchildren who had earned their first kiss from the object of their ardent crush. Only the necromancer and I glumly watched Dolgunata clever manipulating the hairy thug.

"Something wrong," Zangar noted quietly so that I would be the only one to hear him. "Last time was faster. Animal resists mental attack. Looks like it. Dolgunata in danger."

Perhaps I should have answered something and just nod in agreement, but I decided to act. I didn't get the group together only to have it killed by some hairy freak.

"Monster, defense!" I shouted instantly. "Nata, get back! Everyone ready for battle!"

"R-R-A-A!" the Boar roared triumphantly, concurrently with my shout and, using his shoulder as a lever, swung the club and hit the druid from above. "BOOM!" There was a weighty blow and Dolgunata was driven into the ground practically up to her waist; she lost consciousness at once. Her protection saved her from the direct blow, but the laws of physics still worked. The Boar swung for a second blow, but then Monstrichello, who was about as big, crashed into him, shield forward:

"BASH'EM ALL!"

Apparently, the Paladin had completely replaced his old battle cry "All the Way!" with "BASH'EM ALL!" The Boar was thrown off a few meters and wagged his head in bewilderment: it was not common for him to encounter an enemy equal in size.

"Marinar, Zangar – kill him!" I kept giving orders. "Monster, don't let him close! Teart, Dirion – grab the druid! Logir, Sartal, Refor – hold the Monster and don't let the Boar get to us!"

I would not call myself a born leader used to commanding people; it was just that under the circumstances someone had to make decisions fast; the only other person capable of that was lying unconscious, not showing any signs of being alive at all. Logir, as practice had showed, was unable to lead the group.

"R-R-A!" the Boar grumbled, sounding almost offended; apparently, he hadn't expected such ardor from our group. Sniffling, he swung the club; with a loud clang it came down onto the shield extended by Monstrichello.

"BOOM!"

Two things happened at the same time: the

club of the chief local rogue shattered to splinters and the shield of our tank vibrated so hard that Monster sank into the ground up to his knees, as if it were quicksand. Shield vibration had turned the path flattened by many hundreds of players into a non-Newtonian fluid. My teeth hurt like I had eaten something tart: vibration was transferred to us as well, making us feel incredibly uncomfortable. The Monster stayed on his feet for a few seconds, then crashed onto the ground and disappeared a moment later; apparently, neither the material nor the energy shield were able to save him from the deadly blow of the Boar.

"Let's finish him off!" I growled, overcoming the pain, and the spells flashed from Marinar's and Zangar's hands. The hairy monster stood motionless, swaying a little; apparently, he was not feeling all that well after the joint blow. Logir and Refor unsheathed their weapons, sprung forward and pierced the Boar, shouting an enhancement incantation as they did it. The Boar, a figment of the Chancellor's sick imagination, had not expected such a powerful attack; he fell backwards. The message with great news flashed before my eyes: I had completed the third test.

"So that was the forest rogue?" I asked a rhetorical question as soon as the Boar's body glimmered and then disappeared, We had not received either loot or experience from the downed enemy, while the informational message that appeared in front of me strongly recommended that I start on the last test of the Labyrinth: climbing over Kindo Logjams, which separated the Labyrinth and the wastelands.

"Who knows where the respawn stone is; and what's going on with Dolgunata?" I finished my thought, ignoring the message. First we needed to investigate the den of the dead freak.

"Her legs are shattered; apparently, the blow ate up almost all the Energy and the druid was able to drop her defense at the last moment, so the residual blow hit her on the head," Dirion explained. "That's why she's unconscious. Her ability to survive is quite impressive – she had completed training with the armor teacher already. But her legs took the hit as the armor redistributed the blow to the extent possible, but all the impact went to the body parts that are the least useful in battle. In the druid's case those were her legs. So, it's best to put her out of her misery: as she is she's a goner anyway."

"But the one who kills her will be sent to respawn as well," Logir noted. "Don't forget, we're still in the Labyrinth. Damn! For us that jerk was calmer and not so strong!"

"Because you were here in a group of six, and you didn't have a full-fledged player with you," I clarified, guessing the reasons for the inexplicable strength of the Boar. Besides, I had another guess which I was not too eager to share with the rest: the Chancellor continued to perfect his creations. So now it was the Boar's turn. While during the first pass it was an easy job for Dolgunata to take him under control, now the monster was equipped with immunity to mental attacks. I grimaced in displeasure, realizing that there wouldn't be much special help from Dolgunata now: the groups the clever druid had killed in the wastelands would have updated as well by now.

"Why am I always the one having to pay for everything?" I quietly reproached myself for wastefulness, took out an elves' potion and poured it into the mouth of the druid, who had never come to. Her flattened and shattered lower legs looked awful – her army boots were pierced here and there by shards of bone, and bloody slush from crushed muscles and skin was seeping from their tops. It was actually better that the girl was still unconscious: no matter how I felt towards her, I would not wish full pain from this injury even on an enemy like her.

The bleeding stopped immediately, and the druid's bluish face returned to normal color.

"What?.." Nata opened her eyes, and the first thing she saw was my unshaved mug. "Where's the Boar?"

"Gave up the ghost. You sustained some damage, so we need to discuss the situation."

"What do you mean, some damage?" the druid's eyes turned into angry slits, and she tried to get up. I had to put my hand on her shoulder to hold her on the ground. "But then why do I not feel anything? Wait... What happened to my legs?"

Dolgunata twisted and sat up anyway, staring at her injured limbs wild-eyed.

"What the..."

"On the whole things don't look too good." I started describing the current situation, stepping away from the girl just in case. Who knew what kind of craziness might wander into her head? "You may slap any of the Paladins and go for respawn. In that case you'll be restored and healthy, but you will lose an hour. We did kill the Boar, so we don't really have a ton of time. In an hour he'll respawn as well, and I really don't want to have to face him again. The Chancellor will certainly upgrade him in some other way. Yes, you got it right: they do upgrade," I added, noticing the druid's narrowed eyes.

"What do you suggest?" Nata found the strength to detach from her emotions.

"As I see it, there are only two scenarios. The first one would be for you to die here and now by hitting one of us. In that case you would not be taking part in looking for the den and would not receive any of the loot if we find something. The second option would be for Sartal, as the strongest among us, to carry you on his shoulders. In that case we'd all take part in the search; then we'd get to the Kindo Logjams, pass them, and kill you in the wastelands. Or you could kill yourself after we find the den, and then catch up with us in the wastelands. In case of the second scenario we could use your extensive experience. I'd be fine with either way for you to kill yourself – it's entirely up to you."

"I don't want to be defective …," Dolgunata said slowly, looking at her damaged limbs with disdain. "But losing loot is not my way either. I don't feel any pain; did you use the elves' ointment?"

I nodded.

"So then I'll come with you," the druid said reluctantly. "The effect of the ointment should last for a couple of hours. Where's Monstrichello?"

"Resting. The Boar was an extremely curmudgeonly character and didn't wish to go quietly and painlessly. It took some effort. Sartal!" I turned to the reptilian. "You're responsible for Dolgunata. Will you manage?"

"I sh-sh-should," our long-tailed companion confirmed, and carefully lifted the girl in his arms. "Sh-sh-she is light. I'll be fine."

"Excellent! Now that the first issue is resolved, I suggest we explore the area. Let's do the following: Logir, Teart and Refor — go that way." I pointed into the forest. "Zangar and Marinar go over there. Sartal, Dirion and I will go along this road. We'll meet here in half an hour and share what we find; keep an eye on the timer. Our goal is to find the den before our hairy guy with ill intent shows up there."

"We should not separate," Dolgunata objected. "This is a very tricky area. Perhaps it does not have guards like the previous forest did, but who knows, what if the Boar had a gang? We should continue as a single unit."

"I agree," Logir seconded her, "besides, we shouldn't forget, it's not very effective shouting through the forest. We should all keep together."

"Yari?" Dolgunata looked at me for making the final decision. I squirmed from too much attention, realizing once again that I don't like managing people, and agreed:

"So we'll all go together. Zangar at the head, Logir at the back. Look where you are going and don't forget about the skulls – there should be plenty of them here. Let's go!"

We didn't have to go far: over his short career as the local Minotaur – the Labyrinth monster – the Boar managed to trample a pretty good path, which we discovered after searching for just a couple of minutes. Another short while later we entered a large clearing sporting a large pile of earth, as if a huge mole had dug it out. Once we came closer we saw a narrow passage leading underground.

"The Den!" Teart and Dirion exclaimed simultaneously. "We found it!"

"Quiet!" Dolgunata hissed. "There's someone there!"

"There are four," Zangar added; his eyesight was sharp as an eagle's, but he could see in the dark like a cat. "Three small ones. One large. All smaller than Boar. Must kill."

"I'll check it out. Get ready to catch the monsters." As the highest level player I moved forward, having activated my artifact and the energy shield. Monstrichello was not there, so someone had to act like the tank; why not me? Since we had already come so far it would be stupid to turn back.

There were stairs that led me to something like a cellar – a small cold room a meter and a half below the surface. My eyes adjusted to the gloom, and I saw the four creatures Zangar had mentioned: a meter-and-a-half-tall hairy copy of the Boar – the only difference were its large breasts full of milk and three small – about half a meter tall – balls of fur hiding behind their mother. The female Boar, as the system helpfully told me, was pushing her back against the wall, squeezing the little ones, and afraid even to move; she stared at me, and her eyes shone with terror. I saw a gleam of metal and realized there was a trap that had caught the leg of the hairy female. Caked blood and a torn chain indicated that the female had been suffering from this for some time, perhaps even before ending up in the Labyrinth. I took a closer look and grimaced: some of the exterior teeth of the trap had been covered with something nasty green in color while the female's leg was swollen and dark; it was not very obvious at first sight as she was really hairy. The female was poisoned, and, as far as I could tell, hung on by sheer willpower. It was not clear if she was allowed to respawn in the Academy or not. By the way, that explained the Boar's malice: he was trying to avenge all living things for the impending death of his woman. One of the cubs managed to crawl out from his mother's protection and rolled over on the earth floor, but then righted himself, stuck out his chest and roared menacingly: "R-R-RA!" The young Boar had such a high squeaky voice, though, that I could not contain a smile: the cub could barely stand up on its hind legs, yet tried to protect his kin.

"What's there?" The players could see that I had stopped near the entrance, and was not making any attempts to advance farther; besides, they were bewildered by the unexpected squeaks.

"Wait!" I shouted in response, and squatted down. The excited cub drummed his fists on his chest like a gorilla, trying to scare me and chase me out of the den. He even ran off away from his mother by a whole couple of meters. The mother squeaked in protest, but the cub ignored her, continuing to advance towards the enemy. Finally, there was no more space between us and the little Boar stopped uncertainly, not sure what to do next. His instincts prompted him to chase away the intruder, but the intruder not only refused to be chased away, but did not even act harshly, and even less aggressively. After emitting another menacing squeak the little one decided that he had been heroic enough, and strutted back to his mother, allowing me to calmly climb out of the den.

"So what's there?" the Paladins kept asking me, but I made a gesture suggesting they should calm down; then I came up to the druid.

"Nata, I have some questions regarding the specifics of the Game. Are players allowed to acquire pets, and what do they need for that?"

"Pets?!" There was a collective exclamation of surprise. "Are there pets inside?"

"Not as such. Inside there's a female Boar and three cubs. The female's leg is injured, and I suspect she'd been poisoned. She's not going to survive. There are three small ones: we need to do something with them, that's why I'm asking.".

"In theory – yes, that's possible, many players run with pets, but in practice I've never tried to tame a single one. You have to work with them all the time – they are worse than children, I've never had time for that. Here," Dolgunata handed me a pasty. "Try giving this to him. Maybe it'll work."

"Zangar?" I looked at the necromancer. "What

do you say?"

I have not knowledge," the cynocephalian's response was negative. "Do not need pets. They distract. Require time for them. Taming is possible, Nata right. Give pasty, try. I have surprise. Why need pet? You not hunter. You are Paladin."

"First of all, I am an explorer," I objected. "Pets and everything that's related to them would give me a similar scope of development as would visiting new places. It is a great untouched area for exploration; it would be stupid to deny myself a possibility to level up. Wait here, I'll be right back."

Returning to the den I came closer to the female and squatted again. She squeaked something in fear, but did not even attempt to get away. There was foam already appearing at her lips – apparently, she was supposed to die any minute now. Cursing at myself for being silly and wasteful, I took out the elves' potion – I had just seven vials of it left – stood up and decisively walked towards the dying Boar. The Boar's family hissed, trying to chase me away; the female even tried to swing her arm to hit me, but her eyes rolled from the effort and she fainted.

"Hang in there, furry girl! Don't you even think of dying here on me!" In a habitual movement I opened the lid of the elixir, tilted back the female's head and poured the liquid straight down her throat; I was a little startled by the two rows of sharp teeth and the black tongue. Pouring down everything to the last drop, I called Zangar, and together with the necromancer we opened the trap. I was not strong enough to do it alone.

The Paladins, as one would have expected, forgot about my request to stay outside and tumbled into the den, wanting to see the Boar's family for themselves. It immediately became very stuffy inside, so I cursed them out, telling them to get the hell out before we all died from lack of oxygen, which would prove to be a total waste of a potion. The cubs hid behind the mother and didn't come out any more, scared by so many strangers; even the brave knee-high-to-a-grasshopper hero peeked out just a couple of times, only to retreat right away and hide behind his mother, whose color returned to normal now; she started breathing properly as well.

"That's a funny little beastie." Besides myself, Zangar and Dolgunata (the necromancer temporarily had taken her from Sartal) still stayed in the den with me. "I've never even heard of them. Looks sort of humanoid, but the two rows of teeth indicate they must be related to sharks. Disproportionate arms with two elbows... The Game did pull them out of somewhere after all. This" – Nata pointed at the trap – "really does not belong in the Academy."

"I think I'll take it as a trophy." I opened my virtual shelf and grimaced — there wasn't that much space there, it was crowded with empty elixir vials. I brushed off a dozen of those, and then managed to stuff the trap onto one of the spaces, surprised that the Game at least did not burden me with the additional weight. As soon as the trap settled in the inventory it became weightless.

"R-r-ra," the hairy monster groaned, and opened its eyes. It was amusing to see the terror and fear in them replaced with bewilderment, confusion and shock. Apparently, the female had thought that she was already dead, and was very surprised to find herself not in a better world, but in the monstrous Academy, full of scary players. "Gra-ra-ra? Ry-gar-ra?"

"I may be wrong, but it seems she is trying to tell us something," Dolgunata played "Captain Obvious", stating something that was already clear: there could be no other explanation for the female Boar's gestures other than an attempt to talk.

"Yari!" I my hand on the chest and repeated once again: "Yari!" Then did the same thing with the necromancer and the druid: "Zangar! Dolgunata!"

"Rgragra!" our interlocutor figured out what we want from her, and also thumped herself on the chest: "Rgragra!"

"Fine, we have confirmed that it's sentient," the druid joked testily. "What next? Are you going to teach her the common language? Don't forget, just forty minutes remain till her sweetheart shows up, and he's really not going to like it, seeing all of us here."

"Rgragra." Ignoring the druid, I came up to the female and put my hand on her shoulder. "Rgragra."

"Iyarryi!" she responded, in turn putting her paw on my shoulder.

"I see you have already found common ground with her," Dolgunata continued to mock. "Ask where is the treasure here? Where is our loot?"

"Rragr!" The female, glad to be understood, turned around, grabbed one of the cubs and handed it to me. "Rragr!"

"R-r-a!" The little ball of fur roared, and I realized that it was that same brave offspring of the Boar who had tried to chase me out of the den.

"Here." I gave him the pasty. The cub grabbed it, sniffed, and immediately stuffed it into his mouth. I heard contented chewing, crumbs fell out of the mouth he still couldn't control very well; the little wonder was trying to catch the largest crumbs in the air and stuff them back into his mouth. It was such a funny sight that it took me a while to notice the system message:

You discovered a pet: Rragr, a delvian. Do you agree to take the pet under your control?

I had no doubts. A pet would be yet another way to develop my artifact by expanding its knowledge. It would be possible to observe his development, record special features and differences from other pets. A lot could be done and achieved with the pet, so I agreed with the offer made by the system.

Once I clicked "Accept", a new blinking icon appeared on the status bar, requiring my attention. My experience suggested that the blinking would be a constant distraction, and then, at the worst possible moment, there would be a system message suggesting that I familiarize myself with the features of my pet; it would cover my entire field of vision and leave me vulnerable to an enemy's blow. So while Zangar and Dolgunata whispered among themselves discussing something, I clicked on the jumping icon and looked at the new interface.

The first thing that drew my eye was that the pet had no levels, nor other meaningful parameter values. All the functions of working with the pet available to me at the moment were just a few buttons: "Place pet in extratemporal pocket", "Extract pet from extratemporal pocket", "Current status inquiry". That was it! Clicking on the first button made the pet disappear as if he had never existed, clicking on the other brought him back; clicking on the third produced a new pop-up window which finally contained some relevant information: name, current health status and attitude to the owner. According to the Game, currently Rragr had mixed feelings towards me. He was scared at leaving his family, but excited by the new horizons that opened up in front of him. The pet himself sat and looked at me so expressively with his jet-black eyes waiting for orders that I felt uneasy. I really needed to find out how to work with pets: at this stage it all looked extremely complicated.

"Finally!" Dolgunata sighed with relief and shouted: "Come here, everybody!"

I hid Rragr and tried to figure out what had gotten the druid so excited. Having made sure that I accepted her gift, the female hobbled to the right wall from the entrance and scratched the earth several times, uncovering a solid steel door. I finished with the pet just at the moment when the door was fully cleared of soil, and it opened with such a horrendous squeak that only one thing was similar to it: my grandfather's garden gate, whose hinges must not have been oiled ever since he built it. Behind the door there was a small storage – that was what had caused such an excited reaction from Dolgunata.

"What?" The Paladins crowded into the den, making the female fearfully retreat from the passage, trying to protect her children.

"Loot." Zangar pointed at the room inside. "Yari's luck worked. Need to change. Armor better than standard."

In the small room – literally six square feet – we found a rack with clothes. A lot of shining steel, a little lighter than what we were wearing, a greenish set of druid's clothes. Dark robe for a mage and elaborate armor for necromancer with a crystal on the buckle shining even brighter. There were no doubts: the small storage contained precisely ten sets of armor, one for each group member, including Monstrichello after respawn.

"Would you help me?" Dolgunata asked Marinar quietly. Zangar put Dolgunata over the mage's shoulder and for a few moments the girls disappeared into the room. Naked legs and backs flashed, but to everyone's disappointment no one was able to see anything more. Marinar was able not only to support Dolgunata, but also to cover the field of view.

"I'm done," we heard the druid exclaim, and Zangar pulled out the transformed girl for everyone to see. If one ignored the richer color of the clothes, the changes were minimal: a little more chainmail, additional arm guards, more feminine boots, from which the bones weren't sticking out anymore... I don't know what it did in terms of functionality, but from the standpoint of appearance Dolgunata really gained a lot with the new clothes.

"I don't really understand," Refor was taken aback, "so this is the loot we receive together with the bonus luck? A set of class armor?"

"In principle, that's true," Nata grinned, settling more comfortably in the cynocephalian's arms. I could have been wrong, but it seemed the druid liked it there. "If we were to disregard the enhanced level of protection against all types of damage compared to the standard armor, improved system of filtration, conditioning and waste disposal, availability of information panels and other frippery with a lowered visor, it's just common class armor. No, it's not a Klifand armor set, but even this set would run seven to seven and a half granises at the auction. I don't think there's going to be anything else useful for me here, so see you in an hour. Sorry, Zangar."

The druid tenderly stroked the cynocephalian's muzzle, causing Marinar to snort in displeasure, then briskly hit him on the chin with her forehead. The necromancer staggered, not expecting such a turn of events, but his cry of indignation was wasted on empty air: the Game sent Dolgunata to respawn, as a player who had broken the rules.

"Let's change." I issued a curt order once Marinar had changed one dark robe for another just as dark. Either Zangar wasn't quick enough to stand in the passage and cover her from view, or the mage didn't care that she was being ogled by men starved of female attention, or she was a habitual exhibitionist, but we got to fully enjoy looking at Marinar's beautiful body. The loose robe of the mages hid its owner from immodest glances, falling in baggy folds. But now we could see for ourselves that the people of Varnax were similar to people from Earth. Snow white lacy panties and a thin strip of similar snow white cloth across the chest was all that Marinar left on before reaching for the new robe. Turning it in her hand, as if not sure where the front was, Marinar raised her arms, causing most of the Paladins' breath to catch in their throats. Only now did I realize for how long I hadn't been with a woman! With constant training I had turned into a fierce ascetic striving to survive no matter what, and completely forgetting such a joy as sex. The robe swallowed Marinar, turning her figure into a baggy outline, but in our minds we still kept seeing the two almost invisible white pieces of cloth, which seemed to disappear on the mage's stunning figure.

"I..," Logir said, swallowing. The femorc's face, red by nature, turned deep crimson. "Get out!" I need to change..."

We reached the huge vertical wall about an hour later, after waiting for Monstrichello and Dolgunata's return. As soon as the group rejoined it became clear that three stable subgroups had formed within it. The first and most numerous comprised the Paladins and Dolgunata, who acted as the lead. They listened to her, followed her and obeyed her without question. Perhaps the druid had never removed the submission spell. The second were Zangar and

Marinar, who didn't let anyone close, and gradually wandered off away from everyone, including myself. Those two generally wandered around the area discussing the specifics of the growth of this or that tree, like two teenagers building a relationship with each other. The third included just me, which did not bother me at all. During the last several years of leveling up I had become used to solitude.

"Monster on the bottom, Sartal on second level." Dolgunata started issuing commands as soon as we approached the four-meter wall. The yellow road ended at its base, clearly indicating that one should keep moving on and simply soar over this minor obstacle. The wall was assembled of large rectangular blocks, and with a certain amount of agility and luck it would be possible to climb up using the joints as hand- and footholds. Unfortunately, I had no rock climbing skills, so had I been without the group, I would have spent a long time here working out the problem of how to climb over the obstacle. The Chancellor had thought of everything: there was a wide strip of empty land between the forest and the wall; not a single plant was growing there. Apparently, more than one player had climbed a tree and jumped over the wall, so the Chancellor closed that loophole.

"Yari: your turn!" Paladins demonstrated miraculous acrobatics. Monstrichello was pushing with his hands against the wall; Sartal climbed onto his shoulders and used his tail to help the other players climb higher still. Zangar finished the climb first, then lay on the wall, hanging down to help the rest: Logir, Dirion, Refor, Teart, and finally me. I climbed to the top, carefully making sure not to inflict any damage, and looked around. Behind the wall, as far as the eye could see, there was a grassy plane interspersed here and there with a few scraggly trees. Several clouds of dust indicated moving inhabitants of the wastelands, but they were moving away from us: the dust was receding into the distance. Clinging to the necromancer, Sartal hitched Monster with his tail and swung him up. Climbing over the "logjams" was so trivial that it made me frown.

"About fifty percent of all loners died here," Logir answered my silent question. "When we got here, there was such a crush... Nobody wanted to be on the bottom, as there were no guarantees that anyone would help you climb to the top. We actually had to walk some distance to the side in order to climb over. If before this "logjam" the player did not find a group for himself, he was not fit to go into the wastelands."

"When Dolgunata went to fetch you, she was alone," I reminded her. "But somehow she did climb over!"

"It's nice to be a panther with strong claws," Logir grinned, watching the Paladins as they were starting to jump down. Dolgunata in her panther form was about a hundred yards away from the wall, jumping and frolicking like a kitten. Suddenly Logir became serious: "Yari, what I'm going to tell you should go no further. If my father finds out what I did... it's better not to think about that. I was sent to this enrollment for a reason. I was supposed to betray you to the mages. Devir promised to take me as his student only after that.

"I know." I told the girl about the scene between her father and Sharda which I had happened to witness. "Keeping quiet about it seemed like the right thing to do at the time."

"So you know...," Logir's face dropped. And you still brought us together."

"You don't want to be a headhunter any longer? So the issue with Devir is not relevant any more."

"That's not all. My father doesn't know that I know the truth – when he discussed this with Devir, I was supposed to have been asleep. There was a sleeping potion in the wine, so by all accounts it should have knocked me out for quite some time. But the mages didn't count on the fact that I have good resistance to poisons. I watched my father and Devir. I saw their guests. I could not hear the entire conversation – the guests were careful – but now I am quite certain that Zangar was among them. He was covered with some kind of fog that only parted once, but it was enough for me to remember that scowl. Now that I have seen him go around with Marinar, I remembered that incident. That was definitely him. But he wasn't in the lead – he did not participate in the negotiations. He was with another cynocephalian, very well groomed, as if they were preparing him for the final sacrifice. Zangar goes everywhere with the mage, the mages declared war on the Paladins, we are Paladins... There are questions. What was he doing with Devir? I'd better get going – people are looking at us askance already. This is all I wanted to tell you to reciprocate your help. You can figure out yourself what to do with this information."

Logir jumped down to join the rest, leaving my faction to think in solitude. I shifted my eyes to the necromancer – he and Marinar were strolling along the wall; it seemed they were discussing something and arguing. So what do we have? Zangar's teacher first met with Archibald, then with his main enemy, Devir. Then the three of them send their own students to the Academy, and through their machinations they all end up in one sector. What do they all want? Me? Who the hell needs me?! Just one of the players, and there are thousands of those! There's something else there. Something that I don't understand, but Archibald and Devir can't live without. Should I ask the necromancer directly? Hoping for his positive attitude towards me, and a rather special sense of justice? He would tell me exactly nothing, quoting the teacher's prohibition one more time. Sad as it might be to admit it, all these creatures are strangers to me. After the Academy our roads will part. I would need to find Gromana and work out the issue with Madonna's notes. That's my number one priority, while the squabbles between Archibald and Devir may be left to their students. By the way, there should be mages somewhere in the wastelands. Dangard was threatening that he'd make us pay for what had happened in the forest.

"Does anyone wish to make a speech before we set out?" I was primarily addressing Dolgunata and Zangar, as soon as we lined up in order, ready for battle. Monstrichello was habitually going first; I even ended up having to give him three Energy elixirs from my precious reserve. It was not a good idea to venture forward without the tank, who was immune to magic. Logir, Refor and Dolgunata were following Monster. Two with weapons, one with claws. Zangar and Marinar comprised the third row in the group, ensuring elimination of enemies remotely. I, as the second tank, was at the back, to cover for some unexpected circumstances attacking from the back; all the other lightweights were between me and Zangar. Without weapons they would not be much help in open battle.

"Since no one has anything interesting to say, let's move on," I concluded. "Where's the nearest teacher?"

Five hands at once pointed in the same direction.

"Excellent! So that's where we'll go. Monster, go ahead to the right, along the wall, and then gradually move more to the left. We need to circle the sector."

There was a pause. As I supposed, the Paladins had worked out such a strict hierarchy for themselves, with Dolgunata at the top and everyone else below, that now their worldview was shattering: the druid was in no hurry to take power back into her hands, allowing someone else to be in command. I had to repeat once again before Monstrichello humphed, turned and slowly, as if unable to believe what he was doing, trundled along in the direction I had indicated. I do wish this blasted Academy will be over soon! I hate to be in command.

Some time later I became completely certain

that it was not possible to call the terrain of the wastelands "flat as a table". There was no vegetation – we had not encountered trees, brush nor even tall grass; yet the height difference sometimes reached about thirty meters! The wastelands looked more like knolls, hills or earth mounds rather than an even plane. Trying to walk between the hills we had not encountered any unwanted visitors – only once there was a fleeting shadow on the crest, which disappeared quickly and never returned. Several times I extracted my pet from his suspended existence, but other than a funny lurching run there were no new features about him; he didn't even growl as he had in the den.

"We've got a visitor!" I shouted, surrounding myself with my energy shield, and activating my artifact. Two overgrown snakes that looked like the worms in the movie "Tremors" were following us, making no sound; they were about a hundred yards behind us. Had it not been for the pet, who had slowed down and made me look back, those visitors would have caught us without any warning.

"That's something new." The druid was next to me in a few seconds. "Monster, defense! Everyone in a circle! Activate shields on my command! Marinar and Zangar – remote strike!"

"They are only moving along the foot of the hill," I noticed and looked higher up. The separation line between thick lush grass on the top of the hill and thin, barely alive at its bottom, that had been bothering me for the last half an hour, received an explanation. At the bottom it had been chewed, stomped and spoiled by the worms. Those creatures couldn't reach any higher!

"Did you hear him? Upward on the double!" Apparently I had said the last thing aloud, since Dolgunata immediately started issuing orders.

"Won't make it. Those are quick," Zangar stayed where he was, as Paladins and Marinar rushed up the slope. The necromancer extracted his spear and scowled: "Must fight. Yari, give two elixirs. I have only food. Let's trade. Want see what I learnt. You with me?" The last question, surprisingly, was addressed not to me but to Dolgunata.

"I don't think I'll have enough control for those creeps... On the other hand... Why not? Yari, I need a couple of elixirs as well: go on. Really, I need to test my abilities in battle mode."

"Do I look like a bottomless well?" I was looking from one player to the other in bewilderment.

"I'll give it back to you double!" Dolgunata waved me off, waited till I provided the desired after all, and started whispering something under her breath. The soil around us started foaming, splashing forth as a thick juicy green carpet, so favored by cows in the Alps. The druid's eyes glazed over with a green sheen; despite dead calm, her hair was drifting, as if in a strong wind; the girl even became taller, as if filling with some force. The ground twitched and started dragging me towards the druid: the green carpet was rapidly shrinking; it was sucked up into Dolgunata's feet as if she turned into a sponge. I had no idea what would happen to me if she were to touch me – what if she sucked me in as well? So I quickly ran off the grass and continued to observe her transformation from a safe distance.

Zangar was not far behind the girl as she was sucking up grass. A foggy cloud formed around the necromancer's head, just as I had heard so many times but had never seen until now. It looked disgusting, as if a dense dark thundercloud was stuck in one place. The crystal on his belt started shining like a little star, and the cynocephalian, who was already pretty large, seemed to have increased in size as well. Zangar set one foot to the side, holding the hand with the spear to the side as well, and bent down like a long-distance runner. The fog around his head prevented me from seeing the necromancer's muzzle, but I was sure that it displayed the evil grin of a fighter who is certain of his strength and prepared for a hard fight. All that, and given that unlike Dolgunata and myself he had no active protection. Only his own agility, flexibility and upgraded armor.

"WEEEE-A-A-A!"

The worms, moving as inexorably as a train engine, hit an invisible obstacle a few dozen yards away from us and stopped dead in one place, swaying madly from side to side. Ultrasound hit our ears, and the players running to reach a safe height crashed to the ground like the pins hit by a bowling ball. The only ones who stayed on their feet were Logir, Sartal and Monstrichello, who managed, just as we did, to shut the visors on their armor. There was no question about climbing up any more – those players who were able to withstand the sonic wave were preoccupied helping their partners who were not ready for the battle, and now were disoriented and screaming in horrendous pain. I took a hit too: my left arm felt numb all the way to the shoulder. The absence of one glove created a defect in my armor, and the hit of the worms affected me, although not in the way they expected.

As I was clenching my teeth trying to live through the pain and dissipate it, I figured out what had stopped the worms: thick roots sprung from the ground and wove around the bottom parts of the advancing beasts. A shadow dashed by: the necromancer attacked. Zangar was so fast that it was impossible to follow his movements. All I could see was black lightning dashing around the worms and leaving deep gashes. There was another – fruitless – ultrasound attack; after that the worms moved to the offensive: they used their four or five meter bodies towering above the ground as whips, beating the ground, trying to hit the cynocephalian who was hovering around them.

"Zatrak de valda!" Dolgunata growled in a voice so metallic and listless, that I shuddered and turned around. The druid did not even look human any more. Moving her arms to the sides, with the help of green shoots she rose above the ground, tilted her head back and was incessantly whispering something – periodically the horrid metallic voice echoed over the land. The result of her action was not long in coming: a swirling cloud of insects appeared around the worms, biting and stinging them; new vines kept shooting from the ground to replace the ones destroyed by the monsters' thrashing; a thundercloud formed over her enemies' heads, periodically spitting out lightning bolts. Dolgunata used all her arsenal of druids' abilities, that she had studied with the help of the dorn. The ultrasound attacks of the worms sounded without respite, their hitting the earth created effects similar to a 4-point earthquake. Realizing full well that I would be unable to repeat the feat of Zangar – who managed to stay alive still – and I would inevitably be hit if I were to come any closer to the worms, I took out an Energy elixir and ran up to the druid — her respawn would be a luxury we could not afford. Given that the girl's hands were restrained by the shoots she had grown, she had been unable to drink the elixirs that I had given her earlier.

Two circles of green fog stared at me as soon as I tried to approach the druid. I showed them the elixir, demonstratively opened the lid and raised my arm, indicating my intentions. What if Dolgunata thinks me an enemy and hits me with something heavy?

"Shaldan rasm de valda!" The monster that had used to be a rather attractive girl shouted something else in that metallic voice, tilted its head back and opened its mouth. Apparently, that's where I was supposed to pour the elixir. Given that her whispering temporarily stopped, I stood on tiptoe and replenished the Energy for the druid who had gone into full battle mode, in the process seeing a row of thin green teeth, sharp like a shark's. The girl had been transformed not only from the outside but from within as well. Or I had just seen Dolgunata's true appearance, while her human form was but an illusion.

There was a sigh of relief and the space around

us was again filled with whispers and periodic shouts. The worms were becoming tired and did not thrash so hard any more. The roots created by Dolgunata deeply embedded themselves in the snaking bodies, almost tearing them in half; the ubiquitous lightning – that was Zangar – did not stop for an instant, literally tearing one piece of flesh after another out of the worms. It became clear that the uninvited visitors were not going to survive. They were not even using the ultrasound as fiercely any more – that enabled our team to get on their feet and continue climbing up at a faster pace.

"Attack!" Calling up Rragr one more time, I pointed at the worms, who had practically stopped. "Devour them!"

"Rra-rgra," the pet responded voraciously, and rushed forward. I grimaced: instead of tearing at the snakes themselves the Neanderthal started devouring pieces of their flesh that had been torn out by Zangar's blade. Having filled his belly in just a few minutes, the pet strode back to me and plopped down with a satisfied face, starting to pick his teeth. The controllability of the hairy one left a lot to be desired – one could say there was none at all.

You have achieved maximum level in the Academy (15)

You will receive all subsequent accumulated experience following completion of the Academy or at respawn

The worms finally ran out of steam, one could

say, in too ordinary a manner. Their lifeless corpses crashed to the ground one after another, showering our whole group with experience. I looked at the information frames with satisfaction: while killing worms was enough to bring me to 15th level, most of our group was propelled to level five, saving them and granting them the possibility for several additional respawns.

"Rga-ra?" The pet looked at me with questioning eyes, obviously wanting something. I nodded and the Neanderthal immediately rushed towards the downed worms and dove into the nearest one headlong. Zangar, who noticed that, dispelled the fog, pointed at the place where the pet had disappeared, and eloquently moved his head, asking what the hell was going on here. So I had to shrug my shoulders and meaningfully spread my hands to indicate: oh well, my pet is still small, doesn't get it all and sometimes does stupid shit.

"Marinar, take the worms apart!" The necromancer asked the mage, having decided that the pet would not do much harm. "Should be ingredients in them. Alchemy important for us. Need elixir. Careful with heart. Should not oxidize. Normally very valuable. Here probably too. Very valuable product ... YARI!!! CALL HIM BACK!!!"

Rragr, happy and covered in blood, climbed out from the first corpse, holding in his hand a still steaming and half gnawed piece of meat. Well, actually, of the heart rather than just meat, as the system helpfully indicated with respect to the object, quickly disappearing into the Neanderthal's belly.

Rragr's little muzzle shone with contentment, joy, and – what bothered me most of all – determination; his whole appearance expressed such decisiveness not to stop with what he had, but to continue on to devour the ticker of the other downed reptile, that I hurried to follow the necromancer's suggestion, and retrieved the pet into his extratemporal pocket. It would be better for him to sit there for a while, to stay out of trouble.

As soon as Rragr disappeared, the body of the "heartless" worm glimmered and disappeared, leaving behind several vials filled with black liquid. Marinar didn't even need to demonstrate her coroner's skills – the Game had done it all for her. However, from Zangar's heavy stare, flattened ears and heavy breathing, I understood that what the Game had left us was far from optimal. Perhaps it was just a pittance that was not worth bending down to pick it up.

"I have taken my share of the loot – the rest is yours." Despite the looks of the group, I was not going to attempt to make any excuses for my pet's actions and promise that he'd do better in the future. Looking indifferent, I strolled a dozen meters to the side, in order to look at the grass, highlighted in green: my artifact should develop constantly.

It took Marinar till the end of the day to deal with the other worm, so we had to set up camp right there in the valley. It was reasonable to suppose that such worms were unique and extremely rare, while their respawn time, if they respawned at all, should be at least twenty-four hours. So we set the order for night watch and fell asleep. Unlike the Labyrinth, the wastelands did not create additional problems for us; at least there was no desire to excrete. By the way, it would be useful to somehow delicately find out more about this – don't players ever need to use the toilet? Or would we have to go through an additional rehabilitation course after returning to the main world, to help the body regain its memory of physical needs? During the time spent in training ranges a body could forget everything.

"Yari, it's your turn," it seemed to me that Dirion shook me awake just a minute after I had closed my eyes and decided to sleep a little. The lanky Paladin was yawning mightily and rubbing his eyes; the fatigue of the day took its toll. Once he made sure that I had woken up, Dirion fell on the ground where he stood and literally a moment later his loud snores joined the quiet breathing of the group.

"Zangar agreed to substitute for you." I was just about to get up when Dolgunata settled down next to me. "I promised to teach you to resist mental attacks; it's inefficient to allocate time for that while we are on the move. Why not do that now? I warn you from the start: I am going to attempt to gain control over you; I need you to state aloud that you allow me to do that; that's one of the conditions in the Contract. A couple of hours should be enough for us. Shall we start?"

Not expecting such a turn of events, for some time I tried to discover a catch in the proposition and Nata's words. As if it weren't enough that the girl had decided to teach me here and now, but she also convinced Zangar to stand my watch for me. The

Necromancer would never do anything for nothing. So something must have been promised to him for that. But what was it?

"You need learn," the cynocephalian emerged from the dusk. "Need learn control face. Distrust on your face. Too eloquent. Too easy to read. Train, is better. Game doesn't like openness."

"Nobody likes openness," I grumbled at Zangar's retreating back, while he disappeared as quickly as he had shown up; then I asked the Game not to kill the druid during the training and requested clarification: "So, what is it that I need to do?"

"Open your mind to me," the girl whispered sweetly and the world exploded in a hundred shards, leaving the goddess of beauty named Dolgunata at the center of all there was. The druid used the Chancellor's gift.

"Be still and harken!" the goddess uttered in a thunderous voice, as soon as I fell on the ground and started crawling towards her. Kept still, trying to fulfill any whim of my ideal. "You are under my control. I rule your emotions and wishes, making you do what I need, not you. You must fight that. Find a balance point within yourself. Find something within you that will always be with you, regardless of how the world around you changes. Find something that will enable you to rely on it and build your defense around you."

"I don't understand what you want." I dropped my head on the ground, exhaling raggedly, as soon as Dolgunata released control. My body was shaking from feeling how helpless I was. "What balance point? And why are you still alive? My understanding was that you were not allowed to use the Chancellor's gift any more."

"It's not allowed to use it for personal gain, but there are no restrictions on other uses. Actually, I was interested, and I was ready to sacrifice a level. Training is not considered personal gain. It doesn't matter. As for the balance point... I'll skip the full theory lecture – you can find that out from any openly available source. I'll just tell you the basics.

"Any control comprises two aspects – a psychological and a magical one. The magical is extremely simple: you obtain a special device and use it to suppress the will of your opponent, forcing him to do whatever you need. However, this type of control has constraints that counteract its simplicity: it's impossible to force your adversary to harm himself. As a result, the most popular method of blocking this type of control – well, after amulets – is to force yourself to think that you are feeling extremely poorly right now, that with every moment spent under control your body, for example, cannot breathe, cannot live, cannot exist.

"There are special hypnosis masters in the Game who can make these thoughts permanent at the level of the subconscious, so it would disrupt any such control. It's possible to counteract these embedded thoughts as well, but this is outside of the scope of our study tonight. It's important for you to understand that beside the most popular method there are some less popular but more effective ways to resist: you need to find something within yourself that would not let your mind switch off. For example: the artifact is always with you. As soon as I invade your mind your task will be to reject the image that is imposed on you and concentrate on the artifact. Visualize its dimensions, shape, color; think about the rules for its development – in your case, to leaf through the pages in your mind. In other words, do everything so that it will be at the center of your attention rather than the controller. If you can switch in this manner, you will return back to reality. If you can't... well, then this method, unfortunately, is not for you. Then the magic control will have to be blocked through hypnosis or use of an amulet. Shall we try once more?"

I nodded in agreement, and my world transformed itself once again. There were some thoughts in my head, reminding that I was supposed to think about something, but I rejected them as irrelevant. What thoughts could there be when the goddess appeared before me?

"No, that's not going to work," Dolgunata said sadly, pulling her leg away from my embrace. "Of course, I am flattered by your love for the dirt on my shoes, but that's not what we gathered here for. Did you think about the artifact?"

I stared angrily at the druid, spat the sand out of my mouth and glumly shook my head, indicating that at that moment I couldn't think about anything at all. The most unpleasant part was that I remembered very well everything I had done and thought while under her control; but I was completely unable to control myself. It was a horrific sensation.

"You must," Dolgunata stated dictatorially,

adding without skipping a beat: "Let's continue! Either you will learn or you won't. There are no other options!"

After every attempt Dolgunata took a break, allowing me to spit out the sand, catch my breath and sit in a steady position; then she activated the Chancellor's gift. Twenty useless attempts to think of the artifact and loosen her control led to the druid's shoes shining like a mirror! At least everyone was asleep, so they couldn't see my disgrace.

"Let's continue!" the druid announced once again, and the world yet again fell apart, leaving just the goddess before me. I jerked forward, wanting to lick her feet, and then froze in place. What appeared before my eyes was the smirking image of Archibald, whose entire appearance indicated that such a stupid useless giftless creature unable to overcome elementary control was not worthy of the right to... revenge! He had killed my mother. Sister. Friends. Everyone who had known me! Archibald had wiped me out from the world of NPCs, flooding the free space with the blood of the people whom I held dear! A scowl of hatred appeared on my face, and suddenly I felt as though I had been doused with a bucket of cold water: I realized my current situation. I was being controlled! The goddess was not a goddess, she was...

"Excellent!" Dolgunata rejoiced, as soon as the world regained its wholesome nature. "You have found the core that can help you hold on. Remember that feeling, and the way you arrived there. Let's do it again!"

Shards – goddess – Archibald – release of

control. Shards – goddess – Archibald – release of control. Shards – Archibald – release of control. Shards – release of control. Release of control.

"Hm..." Dolgunata frowned when after the words "Let's do it again" the world stayed whole, and only the Book of Knowledge appeared before my eyes, displaying the picture of the catorian. My artifact took an active stance in counteracting control, and did everything to help me resist it. "You are upgrading your skill way too fast. Amazing... I'd need to look into this in more detail. We are done with the magic control; the charge of the lergant doesn't allow to use it at over ten percent of capacity, but you have the main idea, that's the most important. Now let's talk about psychological control... It's what they call Neuro Linguistic Programming in your world. Amulets, hypnosis or curses will not help you if you encounter a true master of this method. Only your own willpower and adequate perception of reality. The 'Suppressor' specialty, despite its magical nature, makes it possible to enhance the effect of this method. I repeat: there is no protection as such, you just have to use your head and be aware of your actions, conscious or subconscious. So, for example, this is how one could use this method..."

Quite unexpectedly I flicked myself on the nose. Then again. And again. Having stopped this self-punishment with difficulty, I shifted my stunned gaze from my hand, which stopped obeying me for a few minutes, to the pleased Dolgunata.

"Review the video of the past two minutes," the girl suggested with a smile, and the Book of

Knowledge immediately appeared before me. My eyes nearly fell out once I understood all the subversiveness of this method! We were sitting facing each other, and then Dolgunata suddenly leaned a little forward. I repeated that movement. She leaned to the side. I copied that too. She brought her hand up to her cheek. I did the same. She scratched. So did I. Dolgunata lightly flicked herself on the nose, and I copied that as thoroughly, trying to repeat everything my "mirror" did.

"This is the whole essence of NLP. You need to capture their attention, fix it and then you can do whatever you want to your victim. From whacks on the nose right up to suicide. You were very lucky that I am not yet very good at that technique. Or else our conversation at the respawn stone would have been quite different. Anyway, this completes our training. You have learnt to release yourself from magical control, and I told you and showed everything I know about the psychological one. Naturally, all the hunters and controllers use mixed techniques, it provides a far more effective result. But we are not going to go into that now; that would be a combination of the various techniques used within the methods I have already covered. Each controller would choose the sequence he finds preferable. Please acknowledge that this clause of our contract is completed."

"Not yet," I said slowly, and the buttons that had appeared before me disappeared again. Dolgunata had managed to seriously puzzle me with the second type of control; before leaving this topic be

I needed to think it over thoroughly, sleep over the new knowledge and sort it out for myself properly. What if I had missed something important, and now the druid was influencing me using yet another technique, coercing me towards a result beneficial only to her? Wanting to shift the conversation in the direction I needed, I asked:

"Could you rather tell me about the worlds that you visited during your training? Their special features, differences, what's special about them...? Since we are not sleeping anyway it would be a useful way to pass of time."

"Useful for you," the druid snorted, yet settled into a more comfortable position and started talking: "The first world that I remember has a funny name: it's called 'Earth'. Yes, no need to be so surprised, I spent my childhood in the same third-rate world as you..."

Time passed quickly. Dolgunata's story enabled me to level up the "Neuronal Network" by another unit, making the green highlight surrounding objects, elements of terrain and generally everything that caught my eye become brighter and acquire more depth than before. Stones and sand, striving to become added to the Book of Knowledge, appeared in addition to the grass. Having collected information about the new objects, I grimaced, once again not finding even a hint of a hidden cache; then an interesting thought made me drop everything and hurry towards the waking group. It was the second day supposed to be filled with incredible luck, but so far we had not experienced not only her kisses, but not even a hint of a shy smile. Clothes and two overgrown snakes didn't really count.

"Zangar, I need you and your blade." I was panting from hurrying back so fast. "Let's go!"

To give the necromancer his due, he stood up and followed me without asking any questions. The plan that I had thought up was so painfully artificial that any adequate question would have destroyed it from the start.

"Now listen." We were at a safe distance now, and I turned towards the necromancer. "What I need is for you to ask the question aloud 'Where is the nearest teacher for the wastelands?', spin your spear around, throw it up and step to the side so that it will fall on the ground. We'll use the spear as a compass and check to what extent luck is with us. We'll launch it ten times for a proper experiment, average the direction and set out."

"That's an interesting way of checking," Zangar commented, looking at his spear intently. "That's checking not luck, but chance. They are different."

"But would you agree there's a rational thought in this suggestion?" I was not going to give up. "After all – what, is it too hard for you to do what I am asking? If I had something that could be used as a pointer, I wouldn't be asking you."

Zangar fell silent, thought for a while, then grinned, and with the words "Where is the closest teacher?" spun his artifact like a propeller and launched it up vertically. The spear hung in the air for a moment, then came down to the ground.

"Record the direction," the necromancer

ordered, unperturbed, lifting his spear and launching it into the air again.

After another couple of throws the entire group joined us, even though we had walked away from them so as to avoid accidental hits with the flying spear. While at first they were making jokes and laughing, with each throw the mirth subsided. Zangar decided to extend the experiment, and threw the spear thirty times rather than ten. At the moment when the spear landed for the last time, silence hung over the group, so thick that one could hear the sand squeaking as Monstrichello shifted his feet. All of the thirty attempts to determine where the teacher was located, as Zangar launched his spear with different strength and speed, kept indicating the same sector, within a variation of about ten degrees – the sector that was located in the direction opposite from the center of the wastelands. According the theory of probability, at least half of the throws should have pointed in any other direction, but obviously this logic did not apply in the Academy. The method I had invented clearly indicated the search area.

"This way." The Book of Knowledge averaged out the thirty vectors. "Nata, we need you to scout. Could you run straight ahead as a panther along this line and see what's there? We'll follow. The experiment showed a result too strange to be discounted. Even though the wall is in that direction, we still ought to explore this sector. Anyone have any other ideas?"

There were no objections. Dolgunata rushed forward and disappeared over the crest of a hill in a couple of leaps. We moved into travel formation and followed her, thoroughly investigating all the wrinkles in the landscape. As the forest had demonstrated, teachers could be located in the least accessible places, and they didn't have to be living creatures either. Within the Academy mechanisms could teach as well.

Learning progress: You have reached teacher 9 of 11(+1 optional teacher)

"Welcome, recruit," slowly said the creature that looked like a mushroom. Three red eyes, set right on the stem, looked from under a huge brown cap. The mysterious teacher had neither legs nor arms. Moving away an elephant's ear that grew next to the wall and was so far the largest plant we encountered in the wastelands, I settled down next to Dolgunata, who was deep in thought. The girl had gone through the training first, and now was reviewing her new knowledge. "I will teach you how to activate a combined attack. Now harken to my wisdom!"

CHAPTER TWELVE

CHANCELLOR

"**N**OW ALL we have to do is figure out how to get there," I mumbled in contemplation, moving away from the impromptu map of the wastelands drawn right on the ground. The results of looking for the teacher turned out to be so indicative in terms of checking out our luck, that we repeated the experiment several times asking more and more interesting questions. Where is the next additional teacher for the wastelands? Where is the closest hidden treasure? Where is the auction? Where are the objects in the wastelands that are most valuable for a player? Where is the Dungeon in the wastelands? Where are the monsters with the most valuable loot? Where... The group generated questions a mile a minute and Zangar barely had time to make the throws needed to make sure of the direction. Using the Book of Knowledge I drew on the ground a potential map of the wastelands in our sector and marked the directions on it. Once the group ran out of questions and the last line was marked on the map, everyone was left scratching their heads. That was not what anyone had expected.

Practically all the lines led to the center. Where the Chancellor was supposed to be located, together with his castle. There was only one deviation from the overall picture: the nearest additional teacher – in order to reach him it would be necessary to veer slightly to the right. All other indicators led strictly to the center.

The teacher of combined attack said a lot of interesting things, but the only one who could use them in the Academy was Dolgunata. As it turned out, the players could form so called "combos", which initiated several types of damage at the same time. For example, it would be possible to complement an enhanced physical attack with a mental attack which would temporarily stun your enemy, and with that an Energy destroyer; this ability does not inflict any damage on the physical body, but sucks out Energy like a good Electolux. The combined attack was activated by one keyword that you would set up when you created the whole arrangement; the use of resources would be added to each other. If it took 20 Energy to activate each of the abilities, the combined attack involving three abilities would take 60. So on the whole it seemed to be generally relevant but not really usable knowledge. It would not help us to survive in the Academy.

"In effect, we have three options," I summed up the results of the second experiment. "Either we go to the second hidden teacher and learn some other super useful thing, or we go to the mandatory teachers and calmly complete the Academy, or we move towards the Chancellor. I am sure that in his castle we'll find plenty of good loot, and probably all the teachers are concentrated in the same place. I vote for option number three."

"Agree," Zangar seconded me. "After the Academy can train. All available as here. Combine attack too. Time pockets also. One granis and a half costs half year. Now need to use luck. Go to Chancellor. Need to complete dungeon. If it's there. The throws show it is."

"This teacher was too noticeable to teach anything rare," Dolgunata was of the opposite opinion. "But suppose, necromancer: what if there is a teacher of, for example, del'onika in the wastelands? Would you be ready to miss that?"

"There can't be. Too crazy. My teacher would know. He went through all wastelands."

"Your teacher didn't know anything about luck either." The druid wouldn't give up. "Being a Viceroy doesn't mean being all-knowing."

"Stop!" I had to interfere, as the bewildered eyes of the Paladins showed that they didn't get any of that either. "What's del'onika?"

"It's a specialty that enables you to turn emotions into a source of Light," Dolgunata clarified. "It's a very rare one; in the main world it's taught by one NPC, who appears next to the person he randomly selects; it must be a brand new player. He trains the player and immediately disappears; then he reappears a month later. The Light ones guard the chosen ones like the best treasure: no one else can create sources, and catching the NPC is impossible. There were several attempts, and every time it ended quite badly. Even Archibald turned down the quest to find him; the consequences would have been too serious. What if with your luck we find a teacher like that? It won't make any difference for you – you are Dark, so a source would be deadly for you, but nine Light creatures, who would have all the development they needed for the life of the Game, pampered and doted upon – that looks too good not to check for the possibility, just in case."

"That's a thought!" The Paladins became quite excited. "The druid's talking business and…"

"You'd better tell them what happens to those from whom those sources of Light are made," I snickered quietly, but everyone fell silent as if I had shouted in a thundering voice. "How they are tortured, how their limbs are drawn and twisted in the hope of extracting a little more 'emotions', how mothers are forced to kill their children…Tell them and then we'll decide if we want to look for that del'onika teacher. What a word you made up for that: 'del'onika'. It's so that no one could figure it out, right? An 'executioner' doesn't sound so pleasant!"

"What's that nonsense you're spouting?" Monstrichello frowned. "It's just crazy! The Darks ones torture! The Light ones protect the innocent and help the poor..."

"Is that true?" Logir turned to Zangar, as the most experienced and informed player. "What Yari said about the sources – is that true? They are made of living beings?"

"No, not 'made of'. They provide the energy. Elixirs are made from living. Like those Yari has. Restoring all Energy. One life – one elixir. Also there's the distiller. It uses only emotions. Makes weak elixirs. To restore specific units of Energy. Invented by del'onika professionals. Takes much time to make a source. Takes lots of emotions. No matter what kind. Light, dark... important to have them. Torture is simplest solution. Yari said truth. Most die. No... Normally all die."

Dolgunata exhaled disdainfully when the whole group looked at her with disapproval.

"So, great then." Taking advantage of the general disarray, I took control into my own hands again. "Now, then, we have decided that we are not going to look for hidden teachers any more, but rather we'll go straight to the Chancellor. Any objections? No? Excellent. Monster: we go that way. Onward..."

Leaving behind the oversized mushroom, we started on the path we had already seen, towards the center of the wastelands. Periodically various silhouettes and groups appeared briefly here and there, but no one bothered us. From what I understood, while we were walking along the valley of the worms (who had still not respawned) we were safe. But if we were to leave it, then the troubles would begin, because...

A huge flat chunk of earth flew towards the sky, carrying the lead group with it. Monstrichello, Logir and Refor were thrown about twenty meters up, only to crash to the ground with deafening clanging, a rattle and a ghastly squelch. While they were still falling, the other group covered themselves with an energy shield, and Logir's wild yell made everything clear:

"MAGES!"

"I promised, Yari, that we'd see each other again." Part of the turf moved to the side and a dozen mages climbed out from under the ground, led by Dangard. I turned around and saw that there were three more of those "underground shelters": we were surrounded by a tight ring of thirty-two mages and a dozen hunters.

"I consider our agreement complete. I brought him," Zangar said calmly and moved to stand next to Dangard. Marinar followed him closely. "He's yours. Don't touch Marinar. She is mine. Dolgunata interesting to me. Try not to kill. Monstrichello, Logir and Sartal. Are initiated, level 5. Rest are not. Kill them. Yari level 15. Drop to three. Then to Chancellor. Need to fulfill Contract. Need to support him. Help. Till leave the Academy. We help get to Chancellor. Drop to first level. Go to two teachers. He receives return key. Kill forever before activation. Contract will be fulfilled. Devir will be pleased."

There was dead silence. Paladins looked at the necromancer, stunned, unable to say a word. No one could believe what was going on, as lately Zangar had demonstrated that he was a real partner. Someone you could rely on!

Case received: Zangar's Betrayal (Slots available for: 9 more cases)

Description: Zangar, necromancer, level 5, breached the conditions of the Contract between him and Yaropolk, Paladin, level 15. In accordance with par. 35.8 of the Contract, the Game delegates the determination of the extent of the breach and punishment for the said breach to the Judge who is located within 20 meters from the location of the potential crime.

Task: Investigate the case and deliver your verdict on it

Case investigation: 40%

Period of limitation of action: 3 months

The text of the Contract we had signed immediately appeared before my eyes. Scrolling it down to the referenced clause I could not contain a scowl: the standard contract had a reference to Judges who were within a certain distance from the location of the crime. It meant that any breach of the Contract to which I was a party would not lead to instant death and punishment of the perpetrator. Dolgunata, for example, could refuse to follow the contract and force me to dance to her music. I must modify the text and cross this clause off. Standard contract, my ass...

The first astonishment passed and I growled with hatred:

"You breached the Contract!"

"Contract says much," Zangar calmly shrugged his shoulders, stepping out of the ring of mages. "Cannot kill you. Must share information. Need help you. Need support. Does not have important things. Not forbidden to transfer. To mages, Dolgunata, anyone. I help you. Help avoid dangerous enemies. Will bring to Chancellor. I receive reward. Bring to teachers. You will train. Our Contract will be fulfilled. Then they kill you. Don't need competitor. Marinar is enough. For future, Dolgunata," Zangar turned towards the panther. "Not possible activate stone of attributes. Not possible receive luck here. I know truly. Always three stones here. Yari found one. Two remain. Yari activated his. Then three here again. I will find. I know how. Teart sees the way. He help find. If wants to live. I threw spear. My spear, my rules. Fell like I needed. I knew where teacher. Dangard said. Knew where to bring. Dangard set the ambush. I led Yari. Needed to come here. We came here. You may leave. No issues with you. Your task you failed. Kill all!"

Thirty five lightning flashes and ten shining lines shredded my protection, but I had practically reached the mage that was closest to me. Marinar, as I noticed before darkness swallowed me, was standing to the side modestly looking down, staring at her feet. As for the druid... She was galloping off, and no one was going to chase her. Nata had completely failed her assignment, whatever it was.

"There he is! Fire!" As soon as the world around me came into focus, a barrage of blows peltered the protective shield that had appeared around me. Lightnings, ice spears, arrows. I tried to take out an elixir and turned cold – I had run out! The last one I had poured down Dolgunata's throat, and I simply had not taken back the other two that I had given her before Zangar's betrayal. Protection burst and I died.

"He's appearing! Kill him!"

I simply had no time to do anything. I rolled around, jumped, put on shields, but everything was in vain. They were pressing me really hard. Every time, as soon as I appeared, a coordinated volley from several dozen players sent me to respawn yet again. Once I noticed Monstrichello, who was just plowing through; I tried to run over to him, but then our thug crashed down like a tree with over a dozen arrows sticking out of his back. The mages really did figure out a way to fight our Monster: they brought in the hunters.

"Catch him!" "The darkness dissipated once again and I found myself next to three huge warriors. They were so enormous that I felt like a midget next to them. So finally I had a chance to see real ogres! A pity that it had happened at such an inconvenient time for me. I was clasped and lifted, like a little child; huge paws firmly pressed my arms to my body. Twisting, I tried to hit with my head or feet, but stars danced in front of my eyes as I hit the shield big time.

"Careful with the hand, he uses it to activate an attack!" an unfamiliar voice stated, and then the ground under my feet started moving – I was being carried forward.

"He has level three," the stranger continued

making me frown: how would he know? My eyes dashed to the group frames, and I gnashed my teeth – Marinar had added Olzar, a mage, to our group. The frames for Dirion and Refor were grey and barely visible. Judging from the three-eyed skulls covering them I could forget those two forever. Dolgunata was not in the group. Teart had level 2; all the other Paladins were at the 1st level. The genocide had happened. By the way, while I was out both Zangar and Marinar had reached level 15. Once I saw them, I would kill those freaks!

"Ha-ha-ha! That won't help you!" Olzar started mocking as soon as I removed myself from the group. There was no need to flash my information in front of my enemies. I twisted and tried again to hit the ogre, but stars in my eyes were the only visible result. "Three deaths, Paladin, and you will be gone. What's up there?!" the mage suddenly shouted to someone ahead.

"Dark ones! Ten horsemen!" A hunter peeked out from behind the crest of the hill ahead. "Dangard's dealing with them!"

"We'll wait here," Olzar ordered and continued laughing at me: "How stupid did you have to be to fall like that into the necromancer's trap! It's just..."

The mage froze, glassy-eyed, staring into the distance. The ogres exchanged bewildered glances, unsure what was going on. Pulling out their clubs and demonstrating that in the Academy they were the most dangerous game around, the huge warriors retreated to the crest of the hill and stood in a semi-circle. Olzar and another dozen mages were left without cover. As we were already twenty yards or so away from the still group, I saw, just as a flicker, the black tails of two panthers. In just a few seconds the mages were torn to pieces and the panthers disappeared as if they had never been there.

"Why are you still here?" Dangard approached the ogres, whose hackles had risen. Taking an elixir from his virtual inventory, he flicked back the lid in a smooth movement and drank the entire vial in one swallow, replenishing his Energy. My brows furrowed: so it meant the mage had a stock of elixirs with him. So then why had he decided to strike a deal with me?!"

"Druids!" boomed the ogre who was holding me. The timbre of his voice was so resonant that it made my teeth hurt. "They killed the support."

"That bitch did decide to declare war after all?" The mage seemed surprised. "No matter, we'll quiet her too. Carry him on, it's all clear ahead. I'll check what's going on behind you."

The earth started moving and rocking again. Finally this was a time when I could think everything over thoroughly. The map showed only Teart of all the Paladins – the rest were at respawn. Also, Teart himself was close to the center of the map, presumably in the same location as the Chancellor. And where, by all appearances, Zangar and Marinar would be sitting. I opened the list of cases and was surprised to see the status of the case investigation for "Zangar's Betrayal": 40 percent. So, according to the logic of the system, I know less than half of the relevant information on the case; that makes the probability of delivering a correct verdict vanishingly small. But what is it then that I don't know? The reasons behind his action? But I really couldn't care less about them! I can see the actual fact: I am going to be wiped out notwithstanding the Contract! What kind of help and support is that? It's a crime of the first water! What else do I not know?

"Hello, fatheads!" The ogres had managed to cover only a few hundred yards when Dolgunata's brother Sakhray jumped out in front of them like he'd been hiding under ground, too. The druid looked impressive: strong and muscular, moving like a dancer, he was not at all afraid of three huge thugs with clubs. At least a mocking grin, shining on his face, indicated clearly: he had no doubts as to who was on top. "I have a feeling that you have gotten it wrong..."

A familiar picture appeared before me: Sakhray's eyes glazed, and in an instant he turned into a drooling vegetable. The druid twitched, trying to rush forward, but stopped still when grass entwined his legs. Dolgunata was somewhere close, and would not let her brother move.

"Good, the first one's here," Dangard emerged from behind the orges' backs, examining the landscape. "so where's the other one? Dolgusha! Come out! Let's talk!"

"I have nothing to talk to you about," the druid's answer seemed to come from everywhere at once, as though she had surround-sound speakers. "Let Yari go and leave us in peace! The ogres can't help you!"

"Come on, sunshine." Dangard was obviously not afraid of the druid. The mage was calm and determined. "You know very well that I cannot do it. Why do we need extra problems with our teachers?"

"I promised to Yari that I would get him out of the Academy," came the answer. "I am used to being true to my word. One punishment more, one less... Archibald will be unhappy in any case. I am not risking anything. As for you..." Dolgunata laughed trillingly, "How long can you hold Sakhray? How long can you resist me? The necromancer is not here – no one to suppress me. Shall we play?"

"Find her!" Dangard lost his calm and his demeanor changed. I didn't like the changes, however: instead of becoming nervous, jumpy and indecisive, the mage now looked like an experienced warrior preparing for deadly battle and not willing to give up even an inch. Two ogres rushed off in different directions, swinging their clubs around and plowing the earth with them. Apparently my kidnappers thought that the druid could be anywhere. I shifted my eyes to Sakhray and could barely hold back an exclamation of joy – the druid's eyes looked normal again, and he was actively getting rid of the plants around his legs. They had stopped being aggressive – Dolgunata had deactivated them.

"You have no power over me!" The mage, standing next to me, suddenly made a hoarse sound and fell to his knees. Dangard growled, mumbled something, pushing against the ground, but still held on.

"GARGGH!" An ogre's thunderous roar sounded

from the right, and immediately the thug faded in the air. Dolgunata, sleek as a cat, jumped down from where his huge back had been, squatted and looked slyly at the monster who was holding me.

"You are mine!" she purred, and at the same time the other ogre's wild low yell came from the left. Sakhray had killed the other defender. Dangard was still pretending he was a plough, trying to resist Dolgunata, who, swaying her hips, was approaching us now. "I always wondered, why are ogres immune to control? Poor imagination? Lack of brain power? Surprise me, Nurlag. Why did you decide to join the mages?"

"Stand where you are," growled the ogre. "Or I'll destroy him."

"With what? Your weak little farts?" The druid grinned not even thinking of stopping. "Yari has leveled up his defense to level two at least. Remember how long he held on every time before respawn? Ten mages could barely breach his shield. You think you have become so tough that you could kill him before I get to you? You dirty douche bag." Dolgunata came so close that she kicked the bleating Dangard and pushed him over. Bending over the mage, she grabbed his head and then yanked; it looked as though she was about to pull his thinking implement off completely; she pulled Dangard to her eye level, showing her formidable strength, and whispered:

"You are mine! You have always been mine! You always wanted me! If you relax you'll get what you want! I want you! Give yourself to me! Accept me! Be mine!"

The ogre stood motionless, and watched silently as his potential employer was turning into a puppet. However, my guard did not release his hold; he was still keeping me above the ground and blocking access to my artifact.

"If you want to be with me," Dolgunata kept breaking Dangard, "you'll have to forget about Yaropolk. This Paladin doesn't exist for you anymore. Work on your teacher's task and leave Yari alone. Then you'll have a chance. Now you will wake up and will go about your business and will leave us alone."

The druid snapped her fingers and the mage's eyes cleared. He looked in bewilderment at the ogre, Nata and myself, grumbled something like "some people don't know what they are doing", and without bothering to say goodbye rushed off somewhere to the right as if the best delicacies in the world were awaiting him there. For the mage we didn't exist any longer.

"Let him go, Nurlag," Dolgunata calmly addressed the ogre as soon as Dangard disappeared beyond the crest of the hill. "What's the point of dragging him to the Chancellor if he needs to go there anyway, and will perfectly well walk there on his own feet?"

"You killed my warriors!" The ogre didn't give up, but his grip loosened somewhat. I could breathe easier.

"Those two weaklings?" The druid's eyebrows quirked up. "As if you cared about them! Don't frighten me pretending you have become an eager supporter of your class – it's been a hard day as it is."

"Why did you let Dangard go?"

"Because otherwise he would've come back in an hour and started hunting us. While now I have at least five hours before he overcomes the hypnosis. Yes, I know he will; I taught him myself after all. Let him go – there are no more enemies around. Only friends."

"Head hunters have no friends," the ogre chuckled, almost making the hilltop shudder and unclenching his paws, letting me crash to the ground. "They have enemies and future victims. Hello, little breakneck! Long time no see!"

Stepping over me the ogre buried the druid in a hug, like an old friend! She did not resist, moreover, responded in kind, throwing her arms around the ogre's trunk-like neck and closing her eyes with pleasure.

"Nurlag," the druid chirped joyfully, as if she really had encountered an old friend. "I am so glad you are in this enrollment as well! Also because of the Paladins?"

"It seems we're all here 'cause of them!" Releasing Dolgunata, the ogre sat on the ground and set the club behind his back. "You understand that you'll have to kill me?"

"Of course, in a couple of minutes. Even you wouldn't have been able to resist me longer than that. But I am so glad to see you! Remember Zhardan?"

"Him and us against a hundred cannibals?" Nurlag brightened, and his face took on a dreamy expression. A dreaming ogre would be one of the last things I would ever want to see in this world. Slowly, trying not to draw any attention to myself, I crawled backwards until I hit an obstacle. Lifting my head I met the eyes of the grinning Sakhray. He shook his head negatively and pointed at Dolgunata, suggesting that I should join the druid. "How could I not?! I still have the head of their chief on my wall at home! Such a nice trophy – warms your heart with memories to look at it! Why do you need the Paladin?"

"I need to take him out of the Academy. Too many people want to keep him here, so I want to prove to myself that it's possible. Dangard with his pit-bulls, Zangar, you, Salvar with his hunters ... Of course, if he were the main target, at least the reason for such close attention would be clear. But no, there were people continuously milling around a simple uninitiated Paladin, so I was interested: why do you all need Yari?"

"I have no clue – I am doing what the teacher asked me. Helping the mages. I'll try to hold my guys back," Nurlag rumbled. "But I can't promise that I'll be able to do it forever. We are mercenaries, and a granis for a Paladin is too tasty a bait to neglect it. Are you taking him to the Chancellor?" He nodded towards me.

"Sure, but a little later. First we need to finish with the teachers." Dolgunata grimaced. "Damn, they have guards everywhere..."

"Here're the coordinates. He's one of the optional but interesting teachers. He teaches invisibility, but it eats up Energy like a vacuum cleaner. Dangard doesn't know about him."

"What do I need that for?" Dolgunata frowned

but then immediately beamed: "Right! Nurlag, if it all works, I owe you!"

"Oh, that's nothing," the ogre looked down. "Tell me later how it goes. Time, Nata. If we linger, there might be questions. Just do it quickly. See you later."

"See you later, Nurlag," Dolgunata purred, turned into the panther and separated the head – the ogre tilted it back – from his body with one neat motion of her paw. "Thank you; you are not an enemy …"

"Excellent performance." I rose to my feet as soon as the only ones left alive were the two druids and me. "Please explain what is going on!"

"Later." Nata cut me off. "Sakhray, put him on your back. We need to get out of here. First we'll teach him invisibility, and then we'll decide what to do next."

A hit on the head made the stars whirl like crazy and fade to darkness. The druids didn't bother wracking their heads over convincing me to go with them, following a simple rule: when someone is unconscious, you can do whatever you want with him. For example, take him to any place you need.

Learning progress: You have reached teacher 10 of 12 (+2 optional teachers)

Invisibility turned out to be an ability unrelated to class and available to anyone. The main prerequisite was the availability of an energy shield, on top of which a special field formed; it fully absorbed the light from one side and let it out on the other side. As the ogre had warned, the requirements for using this method were simply crazy: one minute of invisibility ate up 50 Energy units, plus extra for activating and maintaining the shield. After half a year in the training range I was able to lower the cost of maintaining invisibility to 40 units, but even so it was extremely high given how slowly the Energy replenished. If Dolgunata had not returned to me the two elixirs, I would have never dared use it in the Academy – the potential consequences were too unpleasant.

"You have two more teachers you need to train with – armor and general abilities, "the druid deigned to conversation, once I stepped away from the teacher, hidden in low grass. I wonder how did the ogres get to find him? "First we'll go to the armor one."

"I am not going anywhere until you explain to me what's going on." I cut her off, activating my defense. Just in case Sakhray decided to hit me over the head again. "Only this time I want to hear the truth and nothing but. We have a Contract – remember that."

"As if I cared about your Contract!" Nata snorted. "Zangar clarified to me that the standard contract had a clause referring me to a Judge, so even if I were to breach it, the Game would do nothing to me. It would ask you to choose a punishment. And what can you do? Announce again that I should be killed? Remember, no one has responded to the first verdict yet. Why do you think anyone would now? In the whole Academy the necromancer is the only one who could actually kill me; all the rest have neither the strength nor the ability to do so. So don't aggravate me more than you have to, please, by mentioning it. I am already wanting to kill you for the trap."

"But it was really well designed," Sakhray inserted, stretching luxuriously. "We could use it in the future."

"It was designed like normal," Nata waved her hand. "A standard trap, one of the simplest. If I could fly or jump it would have made no sense. Anyway, forget it. As to what's going on: I am in exile here. Archibald was displeased that I lost the tournament. Said it was pointless to train me any further as a minion; I had reached my limit. Then there came news that Paladins were selected as a sacrifice and he ordered an increase in the number of people of his class who would complete the Academy. In addition, a target was selected who was supposed to complete the Academy at the first level. That's my test. I can't tell you who it is, but it is definitely not you. The mages have a similar task – they also have a target who's supposed to complete the Academy at level one. The rest is just collateral damage from the main task. All this genocide is for fun, nothing else. As for you: Dangard was playing with you. Devir said in passing that 'it would be preferable not to kill Yari before he gets to the wastelands'. So in the forest they didn't bother you much, letting you do whatever you wanted. But here they started after you in earnest. As for me... Archibald had said that the more you're put into a difficult situation, the better you develop. My task was to get in the way, provoke, kill, but not too much, do whatever in order to continuously keep you in shape. As you can see I was doing it well. You had reached level 15, received the attributes' stone, a load of granises, found elixirs, managed to lose your hand and your glove somewhere. By the way, I'd like to hear that story. And I know that you had no information about the Academy at all. You can safely consider that whatever you have achieved here is to my credit. My provocation is your development."

"What is Zangar doing here?" I tried to dampen my emotions to the extent possible to avoid attacking Dolgunata with my fists. Blasted provocatrix!

"Controlling fulfillment of the task. The mages must do whatever his teacher needs. Who if not the cynocephalian is in a position to check the quality of task execution? Besides, the mages are players who have to do everything themselves, and Zangar would retain his spotless reputation and receive his blessing from the Chancellor. The local boss likes them Light and clean."

"Why in hell does he need Marinar? Why is he troubling himself with her?"

"I have no idea. On the face of it they look like a happy couple, but... you'd have to know this necromancer. He has no emotions at all, only calculation. For some reason he has messed with her head and keeps her close to him. It's not clear why, but definitely not just so. If you manage to find that out, I'd be glad to hear the answer to that. Because I don't know it myself. Are you happy now? Or did you want to know something else?"

"Why did you return for me?"

"Because I want to prove to myself that Zangar and Dangard, not even to mention Ahean, of whom I haven't heard lately for some reason, would not be able to interfere with me. They want to kill you – I will try to pull you through. To spite everyone. After the Academy we'll do a couple of dungeons together and will never hear about each other again."

"Why should I believe you?"

"Because you have no other choice," Dolgunata said harshly. "Whether you want it or not, I'll make it so that you complete the Academy. You want to croak – go and do it in the main world. Enough talking – let's go deal with your armor."

I didn't believe a word of Dolgunata's little speech. How should I know? Maybe it's a clever plan by Zangar and his team to have me finish training with all the teachers on my own, and arrive to the Chancellor all ready. However, Nata is right: it's not like I have a lot of choice. I need to train with these two teachers in any case; this would give me an option to leave the Academy. Then afterwards I could make the final decision about what's more important to me: to quietly leave and forget about the Chancellor's gift and his quest, thus screwing over the necromancer, or to risk it and show up at the Chancellor's, where both Zangar and Marinar were now.

"Another question." Before mounting Sakhray's back, I looked at Dolgunata. "Will you be able to beat Zangar?"

There was no answer, but for the twenty

minutes that we rushed towards the next teacher, the druid's catface looked contemplative. Before I made a decision I needed to know: is Dolgunata capable of beating Zangar, and would she be willing to do it? Because I really had no intention to forgive the necromancer for such a frame–up. Besides, he and Marinar were the only ones who knew that I had Madonna's notes. Gromana didn't count. Somehow I couldn't believe that Zangar's teacher would greet the holder of this book with a hearty welcome. Rather he'd kill me and forget my name. Therefore I needed to solve this issue here and now. I should keep in mind that this couple of traitors were not initiated.

"Yari – the three on the right are yours," Dolgunata whispered, assessing the lay of the land. Thanks to invisibility, we managed to come extremely close to the teacher, passing by the obstacles represented by several groups of guards, but as we came right next to the teacher we encountered a surprise: twenty warriors and hunters as well as a couple of mages. We happened to arrive just as the guards were changing: one dozen of guards was replacing another. Nodding silently, I activated my artifact, drank one of the last two remaining Energy elixirs, put on invisibility and rushed towards my targets. The time of the nice Paladin was past. Now was the time of the mean Paladin.

"...No one is going to show up, but keep your eyes peeled!" I heard one of the grinning mages say when, without delay, I activated the attack and drove the spikes of the Book of Knowledge straight into his eyes. Crit! The body of my enemy had barely faded into the air when I proceeded to the warrior. The enemy, covered in armor, was impressive, but I had an advantage of surprise attack and there was Dolgunata. As I hit the first time, the druid tied her enemies up with the grass, preventing them from moving; thus, the warrior could not use some of his warrior abilities. Besides, he had no weapons, only his own fists. With a nasty squelch my spikes pierced the player's armor at the third strike – that was how long his defense held. I was lit by lightning: my third victim, the mage, caught on quickly and attacked. I grinned: the emotions of fear and despair of the players who died or were dying were so intense that my Energy bar did not go down by even one notch. I was sure that even invisibility – that was lost with my first blow – would have been free to me now. I didn't have to wait long to check: I activated invisibility and stepped to the side, allowing the mage to look, wide–eyed, at the place where I had just stood. The Energy bar twitched down, but immediately jumped back: the loss was offset by inflow. I slowly circled around the mage, who was looking around frantically while trying to untangle his feet from the grass – and drove my spikes in at the base of his skull. I felt no other emotion than anger. I was so used to killing players that I perceived killing just as a given. Invisibility dissipated again from the blow, and an arrow ricocheted from my defense shield, striking sparks: one of the hunters switched to me. Knowing very well that the druid didn't need much help as she had already killed a dozen players and was dealing with the rest, I rushed towards the shooter who attacked me. I wanted to take my anger out on someone. I ran at the player, toppled him to the ground with a flying kick, and sent him for respawn with the next move, habitually driving the spikes into his face. Amazing how effective that method was! A system message flashed on reaching the next level, but I ignored it. There would be time to rejoice for level 4 later. Not wanting to delay the group, I turned away from the fight and approached the insipid old coot, indifferently staring at the carnage as if it was no concern of his.

Learning progress: You have reached teacher 11 of 12 (+2 optional teachers)

"Welcome, recruit," the old man said, and the space turned into a training range, as so many times before. "I will teach you how to use the armor. Now harken to my wisdom..."

The class armor turned out to be a rather curious thing. First, an additional button appeared in the character attributes; clicking on it enabled me to set properties for helmet and cloak: it was possible to make them invisible to others and practically weightless for me. For example, even with a closed visor the player could easily use elixirs and food without having to be exposed to ambient dangers. Once the visor was down, an additional green outline of my character appeared. My left hand was glowing red. Absence of the hand, and therefore the glove, made the armor incomplete. Leaving the visor down, I adjusted the helmet, making it invisible, and returned to the game world: the armor teacher categorically refused to talk about any topics not related to armor.

However, I managed to get him to talk a little. Even though class armor is the player's only clothes, it can be and even needs to be renewed whenever possible. There were over twenty armor sets for Paladins alone, from the initial one provided before sending one to the Academy, to Charleston armor – he was one of the greatest armor makers of the modern era. The teacher didn't even bother mentioning the cost of this armor, just hinted that all the money I had currently would not buy me even the privilege of making an appointment to talk to that master.

However, there were some variations: less famous armor smiths also could make either complete sets or individual plates, providing protection against various type of damage. Some craftsmen put antigravity devices on their armor that would enable you to fly sometimes, but one enhancement particularly popular among players was inertia neutralizers: they made it possible to survive even if you fell off a skyscraper. The operating principle was simple: if a player with energy defense was falling on the ground, for example, from a great height, the force of impact would be distributed and transformed into an impulse dissipated on the other side of the shield, protecting the player from damage and preventing him from being squished flat. Inertia neutralizers, just like the armor itself, came in different types and needed to be continuously improved, because as soon as stagnation occurs the player would not be protected anymore.

"I have a question." Even though training with the teacher lasted only a moment, by the time I returned to the Academy and looked around, the battle was over. Sakhray was stretching, as always; Dolgunata was shaking off the grass that had stuck to her dress, and the defenders of the training location were dead – to reappear in an hour. "Before we proceed to the last of the mandatory teachers, I would like to find a local trader. I am sure there is one in the wastelands somewhere. I need to buy some elixirs."

"That's a reasonable thought, only there's one thing – we'll need to fight for the trader. We have a mixed group, so everyone will attack us: Lights, Darks, Neutrals... Are you prepared for that?"

"As far as I see it, we don't have a choice – without the elixirs I can't really do much after the next teacher in the Academy."

Nata didn't ask why in hell I was planning to stay in the Academy after finishing the training with the last mandatory teacher: she was thinking again as to whether she'd be able to beat the necromancer or not. What were Zangar's advantages? First of all, his speed and physical qualities. In this respect he exceeded a normal human by several times. The presence of his artifact used as a weapon – his attack ability must surely be leveled up to the point where he could pierce my 2nd level defense with one blow. His necromancer abilities that eat through the shield like rust. The presence of Marinar, who would support her partner to the last. Extreme experience: fights that he had won while he was still just a minion. By all accounts, it would not be a good idea to tackle

Zangar, but for one thing: I have a case open on him. There was no point pronouncing him guilty and sentencing him to death: Dolgunata's example showed that if there is not a force capable of executing the sentence, it was a stupid one to begin with. We needed to think up something new, something that would enable us to best the necromancer. For example, he could be deemed guilty and the punishment within the Academy would be taking away his speed. Or the abilities he received there. Then it would be worth risking it. But still, first of all I needed to clarify one issue...

"Nata, I have another question. The fact that you are helping me now – is this something that Zangar requested, or no? I stared the girl in the eye. "If not, call the Game to be your witness that you are either acting of your own free will or following Archibald's orders to complete some task he gave you of which you never told me. It's important for me to know that nothing ties you to the necromancer."

"The more I know you, the more I understand why the teacher was interested in you," Dolgunata smiled. "You are right: I am fulfilling a task from Archibald. As for you, I had special instructions. I have nothing to do with Zangar, his plans and quests; on the contrary, I'd be happy to screw over this three hundred-year-old upstart. May the Game kill me if I am not saying the truth." For an instant a bright outline appeared around the druid, confirming that the girl was telling the truth.

It took us about twenty minutes to reach the trader, avoiding unneeded encounters. There were some groups of players we saw from time to time, but Sakhray and Dolgunata changed direction sharply and kept moving without a stop. I hung on to the druid's neck and thought of one thing only: for this crazy run to be over soon. Despite the protection, the sensation of constant jolting was hard on me. Because I was clinging to Sakhray's body, I missed the point of arrival. I just felt at some point that the jolts had stopped and I was lying on the ground, while a massive fight was underway just a couple of meters off. The druid had run at full tilt into a group of riders on the backs of green reptiles, dealing fear and chaos all around. Dolgunata made the entangling plants grow again, and that's when I joined Sakhray, hitting right and left with my artifact. The reptilians' teeth and the blows of the riders' spears helplessly slid off my protection, only increasing the great drive of the battle. I was enjoying the feeling of the killing! I liked looking at the reptiles' heads turning into bloody mess, at the riders torn limb from limb, at my enemies stomped by their own as they were falling... Fear, chaos, terror... Even though I was using my attack ability liberally, the Energy didn't drop even a little. Experience started flowing like a river, and by the time I was out of breath and put my hands on my knees, trying to get it back, not a single enemy was left around. They had all left this world, having showered me with five additional levels.

"W–what do you need?" squeaked a little leprechaun who looked exactly like Teart. Clutching the ground, the trader was afraid even to breathe.

"Goods. Amulets. Things!" I waved my hand

wildly, still unable to calm down. The adrenalin was rushing in my veins and instead of calmly continuing the dialogue it made me want to jump, run and fly.

"But you are not Light ones...," the leprechaun started, when the spikes of my Book of Knowledge flashed right under his nose.

"Are we now Light enough?" I asked menacingly of the trader, who swallowed, and then his face broke into a broad smile:

"How could I not notice right away?! Welcome to the shop of Tardal the Restless!"

The space around us habitually faded to turn into a small room stacked with different shelves. The leprechaun, wearing green velvet, took his place behind the counter and gave a surprised whistle: within the shop he had access to information on the visitors' available funds.

"In what could I interest such esteemed customers?" The trader was just about dancing with impatience, wanting to pocket my savings as fast as possible.

"Double extender of personal inventory, three hundred Energy elixirs." I got down to business right away. Casting a look at Dolgunata, I added: "For each of us. I need an amulet for protection against mental attack, scrolls with curses, slowdowns and other heart–warming functional things that would make it possible to beat a strong opponent. We need items that enhance protection, attack and level of available Energy. We need an Energy accumulator for Dark ones. We need plates for the armor to counteract a necromancer's abilities. We need scrolls or objects that would burn up the enemy's Energy – I am sure there must be something like that. Now tell me, what of the above do you have?"

With each word the leprechaun's eyes became bigger and bigger, as if the objects I had named were as rare as Hermes' flying sandals or Thor's hammer. Swallowing convulsively, the leprechaun squeaked:

"It's not allowed in the Academy..."

"But right now we are not in the Academy, are we?" Dolgunata came to my aid. "In addition to Yaropolk's list, we would like to have twenty, and better thirty, Molotov cocktails, amulets for viscous space, a source of Light, time traps and Black Death."

The trader blanched:

"Black Death is prohibited! Using it is punished by the Game!"

"I know. That's exactly why we need it!"

"Yari doesn't have enough granises for all of that." The trader wasn't about to give up, when Sakhray interjected:

"Even if we were to pool our funds?"

I looked at the druid. So that meant that not only did Dolgunata have a certain stash of granises, but her brother was also – to put it mildly – not so very poor by the terms of NPCs!

"I don't have Black Death," the leprechaun looked really pitiful. His ears drooped, his face turned grey, and even his top hat sagged, indicating extreme astonishment.

"We could take a 'Widow's Kiss' instead," Dolgunata suggested. I didn't know any of these names, so I decided to trust the druid's experience in killing strong opponents. Archibald's personal training must be worth something. May he rot in hell, blasted pussy.

"Yes!" as soon as we suggested an alternative, the trader beamed again. "'Widow's Kiss' should work just fine! As it happens, well, entirely by chance of course, I just have one! Well, let me think... Here's what I can suggest...

We bargained for a long time; Sakhray showed a most amazing affinity for that. The druid fought for each hundredth of a granis, looking over the offered items with the thoroughness of an incorruptible quality inspector. Finally we agreed on fourteen granises and a half – Sakhray paid four of those. As soon as the granises disappeared into the cash box, the space around us shimmered and we were in the midst of the reptilians we had just recently killed, the trader's protectors. The only advantage of our current situation was that they sort of stopped noticing us. After we gained access to the trader we acquired a form of immunity to them: they didn't care about us anymore.

"This is for you." Dolgunata handed me five bottles of Molotov. "Careful, there's napalm inside. Even though Zangar will have a shield, it's unlikely that he received temperature regulation at the Academy. I'll do the main hit, but if I am killed start throwing those at him yourself. Put the amulets on right away – oh, and the accumulator as well: you need to get used to working with altered parameters. We have the last teacher coming up soon; stay with him for a few years, learn to transfer Energy. Will you put the armor plates on yourself, or do you need help?"

"No, I can do it, if I figure out how they work," I nodded, attaching additional protection against both physical and magical damage. From now on even if someone were to pierce my shield they'd have a run for their money trying to get through the armor. That was a decided advantage.

In general, the visit to the trader left me in a state of euphoria. The amulets I bought enhanced defense and attack properties of the artifact by five units and the level of Energy soared to unprecedented heights: 500 units. According to the druid, the amulet the trader sold us was too simple, but there was no way he could have had a different one: it's mostly the players themselves that would be selling stuff like that. So we got one of the cheapest and most common ones. There were no scrolls with curses – things like that simply did not exist; however, we bought two Dark Will Wands each carrying five charges. Each charge would reduce the enemy's Energy level by 20%, ignoring any armor, so Zangar would get two respawns guaranteed. As for the Black Death...

"It's a banned scroll," Dolgunata clarified. "It enables you to destroy, through one respawn, either ten percent of your opponent's levels or 10 levels if your opponent's level is less than a hundred. The one who uses the scroll will also be sent to respawn and lose either five percent of his levels, or five levels. Black Death is also called the weapon of last resort... When you have nothing to lose, you hang this thing on your enemy and at the first respawn he drops quite a few levels. The Widow's Kiss works according to a similar principle, only instead of ten percent it eats up only four levels from the enemy and two from the one who activates the scroll. It's one of the favorite methods of headhunters when they are given a task to eliminate someone. Don't worry, Sakhray will work on activation. It's not a problem for him: he is initiated. While Zangar is not. That's what we can and must use. The most important thing is to drive the necromancer down to the 4th level. That's exactly why we need viscous space amulets and time traps. There's no other way to best him."

"What do you think – has Zangar already visited the trader?" I asked Nata. "If he's been here, he must have also bought lots of useful stuff."

"Hm..." Dolgunata went still for a moment. "That's a good question! You are known for those, aren't you...? I have no idea... We found this trader when we were running to save Marinar, so we didn't stop. Whether Zangar stopped here on the way back..."

"Ok, let's ask at the source. Sir," I turned to the leprechaun, who had lost all interest in us. "Could you alleviate my doubts – did one Zangar, a necromancer, come to shop with you?"

There was a pause. While a lot of stunned eyes were staring at me – from Dolgunata and Sakhray to the leprechaun and the reptiles and their riders, who suddenly noticed my presence and were staring in surprise like I was the 8th Wonder of the World. Judging from the reaction, my question had been really inappropriate.

"Yari...," Dolgunata started, but then the leprechaun interrupted her:

"How could you?! How could you think that I would tell anyone who comes to me and what they buy?! It's one of the most closely guarded..."

"Two granises," there was nothing I could do rather than insist. As soon as I stated the price, the trader choked on his own drool. "Two granises for simple information as to whether Zangar visited you or not. Another two when you tell us what he bought. All in all, four granises, basically, just so. From the kindness of my heart. So, I'll repeat the question – did Zangar, a necromancer, come shopping here and what did he buy?"

"Actually, in the main world that's a punishable offense," Dolgunata grumbled, as she was studying the list of Zangar's purchases. For the sake of four granises the leprechaun gave some ground and asked us to help him to deal with the cash register. He suspected that it was chewing up receipts. Silently swallowing the information, that, as it turned out, even the traders in the Game had cash registers, we inspected the device, and, while the leprechaun was demonstratively looking at his goods, we looked through the list of purchases over the last few days. "This is prohibited!"

"You keep teasing me about my lack of knowledge about the Game, yet you are acting like a small child," I said in surprise, having copied all the information I needed, and moving away from the register. "Are you not familiar with such concepts as 'bribery' and 'corruption'?" You lived on Earth –

there's nothing worthwhile that happens there without these two words. Until you grease the palm of the right person, you get nowhere. Besides, fighting it is futile. Those who protest against bribery the loudest are, in the majority of cases, simply those who charge more."

"The Game nips those things in the bud." Dolgunata still resisted, expecting some kind of a righteous blow to hit the leprechaun. There was none. Neither was there a case initiated on information disclosure – the Game did not find a transgression in the trader's actions, and I was not going to initiate a case. What was happening was, in my view, a common occurrence. Well, in general I was against corruption, but once the situation affected me personally, my conscience turned a blind eye. Double standards at their best. I wondered if it would be possible to bring a case against a Judge for not initiating a case? It would be useful to read up on this once I had some free time.

"So then, Zangar enhanced protection for Marinar, increased Energy for himself and for her as well bringing it to 500, and replenished his stock of elixirs quite a bit. So he's not lacking for Energy now," I concluded my review of the necromancer's purchases. "But why did he not buy anything for attack or defense?"

"Because everything that's on sale here are just child's toys compared to what he'll get from his teacher once he returns," Nata clarified. These amulets are so basic that that dog didn't even bother to look in their direction. For him they are nothing. He considers that no one could touch him in the Academy, so he decided not to waste extra granises. You are the one playing a millionaire's son; for the majority of players losing four granises is like losing half a life! But the information is very interesting. We won't be able to kill the necromancer just so now..."

"Don't forget that he'll also get some kind of trick from the Chancellor." I reminded her of that unpleasant thing. "In any case, it's worth trying, and then... You can take Marinar under control, can't you?"

"Naturally," the druid responded in surprise. "But how will that help us?"

"I have a thought..." I looked at the girl slyly. "What if the cynocephalian actually did fall in love with her?"

Learning progress: You have reached teacher 12 of 12 (+2 optional teachers)

Congratulations! You have completed the Academy and may return to the main Game world. Timeframe for return activation: 30 seconds

It took us about ten minutes to reach the last teacher. Killing the guards by attacking them in invisibility mode, I followed Dolgunata's advice and spent several years learning how to use the emotions accumulator, bringing the process of Energy replenishment to an automatic skill. One of the teachers had said that within the Academy the "Accumulator" ability was not available to a player. No point in arguing with him – I was sure he knew what he was talking about. However, for some reason he had not bothered to inform me that it's possible not only to use the artifact as an accumulator, but a random object as well. As a neutral ability I chose the option to improve my night vision. There was nothing else in the offered list of abilities that interested me.

We were going to the Chancellor's tower without too much haste, killing everyone we saw along the way: monsters, nomads, strange flying creatures, players, who decided that they were stronger than we. We had just one goal: to achieve the maximum level possible before we saw the central tower of the wastelands on the horizon. One time we even had to spend the night there, so hard and tiring was the battle with the flying monsters. They could not penetrate our protection, but there were so many of them that we spent several precious hours cleansing the world of that plague. The flying creeps would not as much as look at the grass called up by Dolgunata, and mocked us mercilessly.

As the end point of my route I was going by the location of Teart, a level one player. The leprechaun was staying in one place, so I used him as a beacon. However, when we were about a hundred yards away, it became clear that I was not the only one who did it. Zangar was standing next to the leprechaun and looking in contemplation across the mirror-still water at the enormous tower, whose spire was lost in the haze.

"I was tired of waiting," Zangar said calmly, turning towards us as if nothing unusual had happened between us. "Wondering when you'd show up. I had thought it would happen much earlier. Dolgunata, Sakhray," the necromancer nodded, greeting my companions. "It's a pleasure to see that you are alive. Let's go. We need to complete our quest. Teart, I release you. You have fulfilled your mission."

The leprechaun cast a quick apologetic glance at me, and exhaled in relief. His torture was over. But as soon as he took the first step, the necromancer's spear neatly separated the leprechaun's head from his body. Spraying everything with blood, the head rolled a couple of steps away and stopped. The leprechaun's eyes, open wide in surprise, stared at our group, and an instant later, glazed. Another instant, and blood, head and body disappeared, letting the Game color Teart's icon in grey, and putting the Emperor's symbol over it. The leprechaun did not exist any more. At least, for the next three hours; I remembered very well that he had a conditional initiation.

Emotions moved me to rush forward, but common sense overruled them. Not now. Having promised myself that Teart's death will not go unpunished for the necromancer, I shuffled my feet as if preparing to lunge when, as if called up by magic, a wall of ice appeared between us. A mocking chuckle from Marinar indicated that she wasn't too far away. Had I rushed forward without thinking, the ice would have formed around me. Oh well, we would settle our scores later.

"He was weak." Zangar clarified his actions in the same calm and confident tone. "Did not see Way. Wanted to survive. Such player not needed. Such should be destroyed. You are strong. Made it here.

Yourself. Proved you're worthy. Mages failed quest. They are weak. Will be punished. Nothing to fear here for you. No threat, partner."

"Former partner," I corrected the presumptuous cynocephalian. "You betrayed me. You are not worthy of being my partner."

"Wrong. I tested you. Only strong can survive. You interested the druids. You are strong. Our agreement fulfilled. You passed through Academy. Help meet my teacher. He is interested."

"What a touching scene of the group rejoining," the space around us rumbled with the Chancellor's voice, preventing me from telling Zangar where he could go with all of that. It took me too long to prepare an adequate answer. I should have taken lessons from Sintsov: beautiful curse passages would have been more than appropriate right now. "You made it to my castle. You have truly earned your reward. Welcome to visit me! Dolgunata, Sakhray, please join us. It's always a pleasure to talk to Archibald's students."

Quest "Visit" is complete. You are invited to the Chancellor's castle. During the visit to the castle attacking other players is prohibited

The air over the lake shimmered, to turn into a spectacular crystal bridge leading to the central tower on the island. On the bridge, just a few yards away from the shore, a tall blonde man wearing a dark robe was standing, tilting his head to the side with interest. Appearance in the Game had nothing to do with real age, so I did not even bother to guess how old the Chancellor could be. For us he chose the image of a handsome thirty year old man whose red eyes seemed to pierce one through, and turn one's soul inside out.

"How interesting." Even though he was there in person, the Chancellor's voice made each member of my body vibrate. "You seriously believe that Marinar is an incarnation of Madonna? You believed your teacher's words to such an extent? That's funny... very funny... I am changing the rules! Dolgunata and Sakhray: come with me into my castle and enjoy a pleasant conversation. As for the three of you – only two will step on the bridge. I don't care who it will be – the necromancer, the mage or the Paladin. One of you will die here and now. Each of you is at level fifteen. I take off all the extra experience; you will receive it when you make it to me. If you make it. All three do not have official initiation. Fight. Battle. The task is simple: to kill one of you with finality. Or two, it doesn't matter. The winner will receive a reward. I will tell you from the start: you cannot make an arrangement so that one of you leaves the Academy. In that case everyone will lose and no one will receive a reward. So watch carefully, so that your enemy does not have time to activate his return. I think that's it. Come, druids. This show does not concern you."

"Here!" Dolgunata whispered, quickly passing to me everything we had bought from the trader. "I hope you figure out from the first attempt how to use all of this. Don't you dare die! I'll kill you personally if you do!"

CHAPTER THIRTEEN

FINALE

NEVER believe anyone. The Game does not forgive trust. It's created to test the loners; everyone else is weak by default and must be destroyed. That's the main principle of the Game and I fully absorbed it with each death the mages and Dolgunata dealt me. There is no place in the Game for friendship, relations or attachment. Only cold calculation and profit.

I did not know the true reasons why Dolgunata and her brother were helping me. Perhaps because of Archibald's orders, perhaps because of Dangard's demands, perhaps for some other reason... So, after returning from the training range of the last teacher, I limited myself to simply saying that now I understood the operating principle of the Energy accumulator. That was enough. What actually happened during the five years was known only to me and the teacher, sitting there in a meditative trance and completely not caring what was going on.

I was preparing for battle.

My history of using exploding scrolls showed that they were horrifyingly effective, even though their range was limited. I knew that near the Chancellor's place I would have to battle Zangar, and possibly even Dolgunata and her brother, so I had prepared to both potential scenarios. In any case, I did not believe that the druid would fight the necromancer. They all knew each other too well to interfere with each other's plans for the sake of some strange Paladin. Therefore, I would have to take care of Zangar myself. The time slowers and viscous space amulets I had received from Nata during the last few seconds before the battle were too untested a thing for me: I would never rely on them. As for trust – what did I know, they could block me as well. I couldn't count on Molotov cocktails either – I simply had nothing with which to ignite them, and hoping that the throw would generate a spark and that the mixture would ignite by itself would be stupid and inadvisable when your own life is on the line. There was only one thing which would enable me to survive in the battle with the necromancer: scrolls. I decided right away that it would be useless just to put them on the ground: Zangar was so fast that as they activated he would not only be able to run out from the impact area, but also to drag me in there as well. So the scrolls had always to be next to the target. I even grinned, stuffing the thick pack of scrolls I'd prepared into the empty arm guard on my left arm. The Chancellor had not bothered to restore my hand before the battle, leaving me defective against two formidable opponents. Apparently, he'd already made the choice for himself and now just wished for it to come true as soon as possible. So I'd have to disappoint him.

I activated invisibility, but literally in an instant the energy shield exploded in a shower of sparks; I was thrown a couple of meters back: Zangar did not wait for the formal signal to start the duel and attacked first. The cynocephalian couldn't care less whether he could see me or not. Years of training paid off: the necromancer was running on autopilot. I fell on my back, rolled to the side and immediately a wall of ice crashed into the place where I had been a moment ago. Marinar followed her partner in everything. I scowled angrily: the hit of the spear ate up 120 Energy units. Had I not had the amulet for enhancement, there would have been my corpse fading in the Academy, my body cut in half with one quick blow. Rolling over once more, messing up the mage's aim, I felt one more horrendous blow, then another and another: Zangar figured out quickly that my resistance level was pretty high, so once again he turned into black lightning, dashing around and periodically striking sparks from my shield. One blow would take 60-90 Energy units depending on the speed and trajectory of the necromancer's movement. He was working on me expertly.

It would be suicide to stay in one spot; Marinar

was creating boulders of ice every ten to fifteen seconds. The Book of Knowledge came to my aid: boulders appeared above me, casting a shadow on the ground, and the artifact granted me literally just one second to leave the impact area. Missing one blow that nearly flattened me and gobbled over 300 Energy units taught me to react to the mage's attacks way faster. The elixirs disappeared at a scary rate: only a minute had passed since we started fighting, and I had already had to take five vials. According to all the rules the outcome of the battle was determined before it started. I was not given a single chance to survive; they were methodically and systematically robbing me of Energy.

There was just one "but" – this couple did not take into account that I came from a third-rate world called "Earth". The world that knew the concept of self-sacrifice. The world that created the kamikaze.

The necromancer's speed was awe-inspiring: even after a minute the Book of Knowledge could not predict where he would appear in the next moment. It could only determine an area with a precision of several meters. In any case, even this was enough for me. Thrown to the side once again, I did not take an elixir – the remnant of Energy would be quite enough to live for a few seconds. Clenching my fists, I waited the signal of the Book and clicked the detonator button. Five seconds. Four. Three. Two.

One. Swing.

Blow!

You were killed and sent to a respawn point

You lost one level
Your current level: 14

With my good hand I grabbed from the inventory another roll of scrolls and stepped forward, hugging the necromancer who appeared next to me. He was stronger. He was faster. He was more powerful. But I needed just five seconds to hold him within an area of fifteen meters. The cynocephalian's arms started moving like pistons. Beating the breath out of me even through the shield; yet I felt better than ever. Because just one second was left and...

You were killed and sent to a respawn point

Step forward. Embrace. Activate. Five seconds of pain. Respawn. Step forward. Embrace. Activate. Five seconds of pain. Respawn. Step forward...

I had plenty of scrolls. Rightly believing that the necromancer's defense was much stronger than that of the druid, I put the entirety of forty Templar's blows into one bomb. Due to the amulet for attack enhancement, the scrolls were a lot more powerful than before. All that I needed was Zangar's presence within the impact area of my home-rigged charge. Given that I died first, and therefore respawned first as well, the necromancer had no chance to extricate himself from my clinging embrace. He appeared in the Academy already in my arms. Another explosion and another respawn cycle. I was not going to spare either him or myself.

The respawn stone "printed" me yet again and

with my habitual move I hugged the necromancer as he was appearing. He had nowhere to go: he could not push me away, nor run away, nor jump over me. Well, he could have, but it would have taken him much more than five seconds. Zangar could face and beat a hundred, if not a thousand enemies, but apparently he had never run into an enemy who would be willing to die just to kill his opponent. The cynocephalian didn't know what to do, and it worked in my favor. Because sooner or later he would want to talk and it would give me an additional break. Which I needed like a breath of air.

"Yari, we need to talk!" the necromancer rasped, trying to unclench my hand. "This is pointless! There will be no winner! We'll both die!"

"So we will," I growled in response, extracting another scroll from the inventory literally with my teeth. Since Zangar had started talking it gave me a faint chance of victory. "We'll all die, some sooner, some later. I have decided that we – you and I, my partner – will do it together! A worthy completion of the Academy!"

The Game started asking me questions verifying if I really wanted to activate the Widow's Kiss, so that didn't improve things. It was hard to struggle with the necromancer and at the same time carefully read everything that flashed in front of my eyes, but I had no other choice. Clicking on the buttons without thinking could lead to unexpected consequences.

"Let's make peace!" Zangar suggested as he suddenly stopped struggling. Apparently, he also counted the required five seconds and, seeing that there was no explosion, decided that I was interested in negotiations. Naive cynocephalian: I would need a minute to activate a scroll! Suppressing an urge to jump with joy, I pretended that I was interested in listening to Zangar's proposal, asking him directly:

"How can there be peace between us, if the main goal is to kill one of us? You've heard it – leaving the Academy is not an option. No one will let me go, because then there will be no reward."

"We'll kill Marinar," Zangar said calmly as if it were an obvious solution. "I was wrong. "Chancellor helped me see. She's not incarnation of Madonna. OK to kill her. Pass the bridge together. Receive reward. Help meet my teacher. Help develop. I like your approach."

"WHAT?!" The girl's stunned voice sounded from somewhere to the side. "Zangar?! What are you saying?!"

"Need to admit mistakes," the necromancer replied, not at all embarrassed by the girl's reaction. "You are weak. Thought you were strong. Don't like mistakes. You will die."

"But I believed you!" There was so much indignation in the girl's voice that I was spellbound, and nearly missed yet another message from the Game. It would not settle down and kept asking me to confirm that I really did want to use the scroll.

"Your weakness. Game not forgive that." It seemed like the necromancer didn't care for anyone at all, except for his own precious self. He had been working with the girl so closely prior to our battle that hearing this admission from him was quite unexpected. Marinar confirmed this impression by dumping a pile of ice on us. Minus half of the Energy, but plus a few additional seconds needed for the "Widow's Kiss".

"Useless, Marinar. Resign. You die soon. Don't have to resist. Come, Yari. We kill her. Become equal partners. I tell you all. Explain why mages want Paladin. For what ... WHAT IS THIS?! NO!!!"

The cynocephalian's wild roar was probably heard throughout the entire Academy. The Game, finally, took mercy on me and activated the "Widow's Kiss". Given that Zangar, like myself, had level 4 now, the news of the scroll activation was quite unexpected and unpleasant for him. The new bomb scroll appeared in my hand, the detonator discharged and the countdown began. The countdown on Zangar's life.

"YARI, NO!" He screamed, with the last of his strength, trying to unclench my hands, hitting me every which way. "STOP! NO! DON'T..."

"I don't like traitors!" was all I had time to say, before the world was filled with red, and replaced with absolute darkness.

You were killed and sent to a respawn point
You lost one level
Your current level: 2
Case "Zangar's Betrayal" has been closed, due to the final death of the suspect

Roll over, jump forward, activate the artifact

and... Nothing happened. No one tried to kill me, crush me with boulders of ice, immobilize and send for respawn. Looking around I saw a slumping Marinar a few steps away from the respawn stone; she was sitting on the ground and staring aimlessly at one spot. The girl didn't even move when I came right up to her.

"Do it quickly...," I heard her whisper. "So that it doesn't hurt."

I lingered, not expecting such a proposition, and finally Marinar lifted her head. Her eyes were red and full of tears.

"Take everything that's left after him." The trade panel appeared, the girl offering me to take twenty three granises. "Elixirs. Inventory extender. Amulet for protection and for Energy. We found one more teacher – he trains in additional attack ability. Here are the coordinates. I have nothing more. Please, Yari, do it quickly... I don't want to stay in this rotten Game any more!"

The spikes entered the base of her skull without resistance: the mage had no protection on. The girl bent backwards, drew air convulsively, and immediately faded into the air. Marinar had made her choice; she had decided not even to leave the Academy, so I did not deny her last request. The Game turned out not to be her thing. Fourteen hours later, angry, tired and barely dragging his feet, a second level Paladin was moving along the crystal bridge with determination worthy of a better use. I had questions which the Chancellor simply must answer. Otherwise I would break to pieces everything breakable in his tower and I wouldn't care about the ripe old age or strength of the host of the castle.

"Come in!" The huge double-leafed wooden door to which the bridge led, opened, and the Chancellor himself came out to meet me. The vampire's red eyes measured me from top to bottom, causing me to tremble with a feeling that I was being examined piece by piece. Snorting with satisfaction, the Chancellor added: "We need to talk."

I silently followed the head of the Academy, looking around furtively at the tower. The Chancellor's castle was just a very tall building that seemed to scrape the clouds and took the all the land available on the island. The vampire gestured, inviting me into a futuristic elevator, and we, at breathtaking acceleration, rushed towards the skies. In passing I noticed that there was a spiral staircase snaking along the wall. That made me think a little better of the owner: given his mean character he could easily have made me climb up on my own.

"Have a seat." The elevator brought us to a spacious room, and the vampire pointed at one of the red leather armchairs facing each other. The floor was covered with a thick green carpet that looked more like grass, and for a while I could not force myself to step onto this wonder of nature or example of someone's brilliant work. "While you were busy killing, Dolgunata and Sakhray received the answers to their questions and left the Academy. They wanted to wait for you, but I was very persuasive. Are you coming in, or are you just going to stand here at the door?"

Reproaching myself for momentary weakness, I decisively moved towards the armchair.

"Who would think," the Chancellor grinned once I settled down in front of him, "that the incarnation of Merlin would be a Dark one! In the past you were one of the most devout fighters against the Darks, you killed them whenever possible, so how did you manage to become one of them?"

"Did you tell the same to Levard?" I responded. "Don't you think that it's impossible to have two incarnations of Merlin at once?"

"There's a lot you don't know, young Judge. Levard is a cynocephalian; Merlin was a human. A human can return only as a human. I admit, there was a point when I thought that the Game had changed its own rules, but now everything fits the picture. You are human, you have Madonna's notes, just like Merlin, you don't care about your own life ... The battle with Zangar was quite telling. In an honest and open battle you would not have any chance at all, but neither the necromancer nor myself could have even imagined what you did. That was clever and interesting. Quite in the spirit of Merlin. So yes – I am more than certain who you were in your previous life."

"If I am Merlin, then where's my book?" I grinned.

"With the keeper," the Chancellor answered with a serious face. "You have to remember who it was, find him and take what belongs to you. Then you will be able to gain part of your former power and strength. But until you find the true Madonna, nothing will matter."

"What will not matter?"

"The Game will stay defective. Lies, betrayal, hatred, desire to kill those close to you and advance through their deaths – those were the point of the last restart. Find yourself, find Madonna, teach and train her. When the third one shows up – and he will, as he is attracted to Madonna – break him and restart the Game. Make the world better. Then your life will have meaning."

There was a pause. The Chancellor made a face as if he just said a speech full of pathos and it was supposed to immediately make me want to run off and throw myself on the enemy's grenades. Apparently, he was confusing me with someone else.

"Let me recap in plain terms everything that you've just told me," – I hadn't even noticed that I had become quite informal with the Chancellor, ignoring his impressive age and status. "Train, find this couple of lovers, break them and then die so that everyone's lives would be great and full of joy. Did I miss anything?"

"In general that's correct."

"Great motivation for work! Most important, the goal is precise and clear."

"You were an NPC," the Chancellor said calmly, completely ignoring my sarcasm. — "Did you like the world in which you were living? Corruption, lies and treachery? You became a player – did you like the foundation of the Game? All the same, only taken to an extreme. Your verdicts are indicative: you can't tolerate any of that. Now think, how long will you survive in a world which is based on treachery?

Nothing to say? So I'll repeat myself – your thought that you will croak so that life may be great and full of joy for all is correct. There's no other way for you to survive. Now let me work on your hand. I don't like it when someone is defective."

A greenish glow encompassed my left wrist, and literally out of nowhere a whole and healthy hand appeared there, devoid even of the scars I had earned as a child. I clenched and unclenched the fist several times, as I was reviving the habit of using the limb I had lost; then I took the glove out from my personal inventory, set it in place, and the world was transformed once again. There was a barely audible click when the glove connected, and suddenly I realized that until that moment I had been in a rather stuffy and uncomfortable room. The outline of the human on the armor icon turned fully green, indicating it was now complete, and, to my immense surprise, it activated an air conditioner, ensuring an optimally comfortable environment.

"I can see you really like one of my gifts," the Chancellor, noted, observing the changes. "An intelligent being that destroyed one of my birdies is quite rare; not every enrollment can boast one of those. So the upgraded armor is yours by right."

"Gifts?" I frowned, regaining my critical thinking. "So, this is not the result of activating the Luck?"

"No, of course not. Zangar was not lying: it just doesn't work in the Academy. When you activated the stone, it gave you a glimpse of what you would have received, had you activated it in the main world; also, your attention sensitivity improved somewhat, but not more than that. You veered from the main course, found the cave and completed that practically ideally, Actually, I was planning to give pets also to Zangar and Dolgunata, but for some reason they refused. Decided that they were not prepared to take on such a responsibility. So you were the only one who received a pet; the armor is just a nice bonus, no more. Not only you get to bring me joy; sometimes I could cut you some slack, too."

"That means there are three stones still somewhere in..."

"Don't even think of it!" The Chancellor cut me off. "From the tower you have one way only – to the greater world. No dungeons, attribute stones, or anything else. You've got enough already."

"I need to help Teart," I said emphatically. The leprechaun had survived, after all, though he had lost his conditional initiation, and now was actively moving away, further from the center of the Academy.

"He betrayed all of you by agreeing to help Zangar. Why do you need such a weakling?"

"You are not in a position to criticize him, and I don't want to. Let him be punished or exonerated by those who speak for the law of our class. As for me, I need to do everything I can to ensure that as many Paladins as possible finish the Academy."

"Teart has to train with one more teacher." The Chancellor thought for a long time before decisively dotting all the i's. "As a gesture of good will I will make sure that he finishes the training and leaves the Academy."

"Why do the mages need Paladins? Why do you allow such bedlam to go on in the Academy altogether?"

"I don't care why they are killing you," the Chancellor snorted. "Dust eating up other dust. Why should I care about it? As for the bedlam – I am preparing them to face life. If not myself, who else? That's my duty. Are you happy with the answer?"

"More than happy. Who else, other than Zangar and Marinar, knew that I had Madonna's notes?"

"Looking out for your well-being?" The Chancellor nodded approvingly. "Good thinking. Don't worry: no one else knows about you. As you already noticed, Zangar was not a talkative player. He kept this information to himself. Only Gromana knows that you've seen the notes, but actually she will be the one who can help you find the keeper. Now about you: in accordance with the rules, I am supposed to present a non-initiated player with a gift. However, there is a problem: you are initiated. Therefore, no gifts for you, as you understand."

"It's a conditional initiation. In effect, it's just an extra life..."

"What difference does it make? The operative word is initiation – everything else is immaterial. Besides, remember: the number of players and NPCs never changes. Nartalim was an officially initiated player – he was sent to the Academy specifically in order to overcome the three-level ceiling. By your verdict you took his initiation and, as you can guess, became quite an officially initiated player. There were no precedents of that before, but I am sure: had

Zangar been able to find a way to counteract the way you were killing him, you would have stayed stuck at level one. A pity there was no chance to check."

"You said all three of us were not initiated!"

"So I was wrong, can happen to anyone," the Chancellor was obviously having fun. "I could not say definitively whether you would die or not. So I proceeded based on the information available. According to it, you should have died."

"So then now why are you proceeding on a different basis?"

"Because those who work in the Temple of Knowledge are unanimously saying that you are initiated. I am inclined to believe them: in recent tens of thousands of years they have never been mistaken."

"Tens of thousands of years?" I frowned and suddenly was hit with a stunning idea. "How many restarts of the Game have there been altogether?"

"Oh! What an interesting question! One could even say "unexpected". To which I have been leading for the past several minutes of our conversation. I was already thinking of becoming desperate! I will answer that. Even Levard does not know; during the time of its existence, of about seventy five thousand years and a bit, the Game has restarted four times. And every time it was done by the same essential beings. Two men and one woman. All human. Two of whom loved each other. Does it remind you of anything?"

"Then another question: who was it that created the Game altogether? And what for?" The news regarding restarts was shocking, but to some extent it was expected. But I was interested in something different.

"That's two questions, but I will answer. The Game was created by the creators, and they did it because they could. They were just amusing themselves."

"Are you one of them?"

"Me?!" The Chancellor even laughed, obviously not expecting that question. "No, Paladin, I am just a tool. Half machine, half living being, half Light, half Dark, crazy but knowing how to control himself. I am not a creator of the Game. I am its mechanism. Like the Emperor, but the Chancellor. Hm... That's a funny play on words... I should write that down..."

"Are the creators still alive?"

"Hmm... That's questionable. Two are definitely not, the state in which they are can hardly be called a life. Nirvana, nothingness, uncertainty – go ahead and pick a word; it will not describe even a fraction of what their current existence is like, anyway. As for the third... Yes, he is definitely still alive. When you restart the Game, you will meet him. It's unlikely to happen before that, so the name will not tell you anything. It will lead you away from the main path."

"He takes active part in the Game?" I asked in surprise.

"Oh, sure he does! Seventy five thousand years is not a reason for idleness, you know. I, for example, became aware of myself during the creation of the Game and still have not lost my interest in setting up training."

"If you've been involved in training for so long...

then why is it so easy to pass through the tests? You make everything more and more complicated all the time, right?"

"Because if I were to make the tests even an iota harder, you would have all just died here! I grant the non-initiated players a chance, even though it's an ephemeral one, to complete the Academy. You may consider me a benefactor. The last restart didn't work out right; before that a lot more players completed the Academy. There wasn't such chaos. And of course there was no sacrifice class. Only a truly depraved mind could have come up with such a thing... So I jump through the hoops of all these constraints, trying to help as many players as possible complete it."

"Who knows the name of the third one?"

"Madonna does: she is the only one. It's possible that Gromana does as well, but I would not bet on it – the witch was too carefree at the time; she could have simply not paid attention. The others definitely didn't care about him and his desires. Find the keeper, receive your book, and you will understand how to find Madonna. I think it's time for you to go back. I will not tell you anything else anyway; you can learn everything else in the Citadel. By the way! Your experience. What, did you think I'd forget that?"

Information flashed in front of me, notifying that my second level was just history now. I was going to leave the Academy as a level 11 player.

"So, I can't train in something special with you?" I asked just in case.

"No. I don't do training, that's what teachers are for. But really, I can't just let you go with nothing! Here, take this and don't you dare say that the Chancellor of the Academy is an evil creature who hates Darks. First of all you are Merlin, and only after that a Dark one..."

The Chancellor disappeared for a moment, then returned with a thick book bound in dark leather.

"That's the book of the explorers. Read it in your spare time, figure out where you should go first and what to study. I hope it helps you develop. Now activate the exit key. Your time in the Academy is complete. I will accept no objections. No matter what, from here you will go out into the main world. This is my will."

I didn't feel like arguing. Hiding the gift in inventory, I silently clicked on the button, confirmed several times that I really wanted to leave the Academy and, finally, stared at the long load bar with its countdown:

29... 28... 27...

Thirty seconds, during which I had to stay still.

... 3... 2... 1...

I finally finished this blasted Academy!

"We hail our new brethren in arms!" Once the darkness around me lifted I heard the pompous booming voice of the Viceroy. "This month one thousand and seventy eight players completed the Academy! Thirty six non-initiated beings were able to prove that they are worthy and from now on have a full right to be proudly called "players"! Glory to the Game!"

The general roar of everyone's exaltation and approval exploded in the arena, in the center of which there were a thousand tired, swaying, slumping and embittered players. I was even surprised: the faces of many Academy graduates broadcast anything but joy. I met Logir's eyes. The red-eyed femorc was swallowing tears; not for a second did I think that those were tears of joy. Grief, pain, disappointment – anything but joy.

"Mages, over here!" The moment I started towards the femorc to find out what had happened, the loud order from the master of ceremonies interfered. "Under the blue banner!"

"Hunters, over here! Under the green banner!"

"Paladins, over here! Under the red banner!"

The crowd swirled. The players ran into each other, hurrying to the banners of their class, trying to forget, as quickly as possible, the nightmare they had just escaped. No, one wouldn't say that all the players were depressed: some really beamed, knowing they made it back, but there were only about twenty percent of those. Mostly they were having the blues.

"Paladins: over here, come to me!" A long-eared elf vigorously waved his red banner, looking for someone in the crowd. Sharda, grinning, was standing next to him, counting the arriving Paladins on his fingers. Logir's father was also there, barely able to stand still, eager to embrace his daughter and ask her questions. Other Paladins started to join that motley group – one, two, five, ten... Twenty three Paladins returned from the Academy, and as far as I figured from general conversation, only Teart, standing with his head bent down, was not initiated. I no longer counted myself among the non-initiated.

"Logir, where's the group?" Sharda asked pointblank as soon as all of us had collected in one spot. "Tell me, please: where are the rest? At least two brothers, after whom you were instructed to watch, are not among those who completed the Academy. I would like to understand..."

"Where is Nartalim?!" The elf who had been holding the banner lost it, looming over the hunching femorc. "He was in your group! Why did he not come back from the Academy? He was initiated! Where is my son?!"

"He was stripped of his initiation and killed. It was done on my command," I said coldly, defending the femorc. In any case, very soon the truth about Nartalim would become widely known, so at least let it be known from the source. I had no intention of hiding behind the backs of other players, who had already shown their weakness. Nor was I intending to interfere with Sharda's instruction process. Logir was nobody to me. Even worse, she was one of those who had tried to make sure that I never left the Academy.

"WHAT?!" Grygz and the group of Paladins echoed the elf's astounded exclamation. Only Sharda refrained from expressing surprise – just tilted his head to the side in contemplation.

"Are we here for a while?" I asked the gnome calmly, ignoring the elf's angry shouts. If the father was the same arrogant twit his son had been – after all, Nartalim must have inherited it from someone – there was no point in talking to him.

"What did you do with my son?!" The elf flared, but then help came from quarters I had never expected.

"You just heard it, in plain Game language – he was stripped of his initiation and killed," Archibald appeared out of nowhere next to us, accompanied by Dolgunata and Sakhray. The druid nodded to me, just barely, in greeting, and then immediately restored her "Snow Queen" face. "What is not clear?"

"It's impossible! It's prohibited!" The elf kept protesting, but Archibald was not listening to him any more. Turning towards the group of new players, he pointed at Logir, Sartal, Monstrichello and myself with a curt command: "You are coming with me, the rest go to the Citadel with Sharda."

"They all must go to the Citadel, brother," the gnome frowned. We need to set up the anchor and level them up at least to level ten."

"Tell that to the Viceroy's Counselor," Archibald was not even looking in the direction of the gnome. "There he is, by the way, looking for us. I'm afraid if I don't take them with me, this moment, we'll never see these good Paladins again. Sharda, cover us! Yari managed to repeat what I did."

"You're not for real?!" For the first time in our short acquaintance the gnome lost his Olympian calm and his eyes bulged at me. A surprised gnome was a truly scary sight.

"Damn! We can't make it – they've noticed us. Sakhray: take Monstrichello and Sartal. Nata: Yari and Logir are yours. Portals at the arena only work in portal rooms – get everyone there. Bring them to the Citadel!" Archibald started issuing commands, forgetting about everyone else present. "I'll deal with the necromancer!" "Levard, what brings you here?" The catorian smiled broadly, whipped his tail angrily through the air several times, spread his arms and made several quick steps forward, as if wishing to hug the cynocephalian who was advancing towards us.

"Run!" Dolgunata hissed, pulling myself and Logir away from the Paladins. Sakhray was busy with the Monster, who was stubbornly resisting like a donkey, and refused to leave the group. Sharda cast a glance at us, Archibald and Levard; then he rushed towards Monster and whispered something to him, and Monster relaxed, allowing himself to be dragged to the side.

"Levard, I heard your student also joined this enrollment!" The gnome turned his wide back to us, and somehow appeared to stand between us and the necromancer, who had just extricated himself from Archibald's clutching paws. "So how is everything going?"

"He never returned," the future Viceroy barked, his gaze fixed on our group. "I want to know why he failed. I trained him myself. Zangar could not die."

"Come on, slowpokes." Dolgunata did not waste a single second, and kept dragging us further away from Levard. Sakhray with his bunch kept up with us, and within just a couple of seconds we had left the arena, disappearing into one of the numerous passages in the stadium.

"They won't be able to delay him long – his level is too high!" Nata said quickly to her brother, peeking out into the arena from around the corner. "Quick – the teleport to the Paladins is on the third floor below ground! We need to hurry!"

We ran after the druid as fast as we could. Apparently, she was very familiar with the layout of this stadium; she never stopped even to look around to get her bearings. No, Dolgunata was running forward with determination, making Logir and me follow her. We were running so fast that I was barely able to move my legs fast enough.

"Hi everybody!" I heard a long-forgotten voice as soon as we turned another corner and ran into the stopped druid at full speed, dropping her on the floor and creating a huge pileup of Paladins and druids. Jumping to my feet, I immediately activated my defense, attack and invisibility, trying to get away as soon as possible, but it didn't help: a thick ring of ice formed around us. Devir, pleased, was enjoying the sight of downed and frozen Paladins and only now did I realize that Dolgunata and Sakhray were not moving: they were literally frozen into the ice. "It's so nice that you are all here. I won't have to chase you all over the world. Yari, my congratulations – you were able to complete the Academy, I hadn't expected this. Logir, you disappointed me. I had thought you were interested in becoming a Headhunter. Sartal... you know it yourself. You were sent to Earth hoping I'd never find out, but I have good informers. You are caught, Paladins. See you soon! Take them! Keep the druids alive, I don't want to aggravate Archibald more than I have to."

A wall of ice formed around me, and the world exploded in a myriad shards when the cold penetrated my shield and reached my unprotected body. The darkness mercifully engulfed me almost at once, but before I fainted, some sarcastic part of my mind noted that we had not been killed. Somebody wants us alive, even if not quite undamaged. It's unlikely that after you turn into a piece of ice you can stay even relatively intact.

Darkness gradually faded, turning into something shapeless and dark red. My head felt like it was breaking to pieces. Making me moan; I needed to take an elves' potion right away, or else this kind of pain was liable to make one go mad.

"Yari, are you alive?" Logir's voice was terribly hoarse and raspy. I tried to answer and realized it was really hard – I could barely inhale, let alone say anything. I tried to open my eyes and failed: I was lying face down and had no strength at all to turn over. But I needed to let the femorc know, at the very least, that I could hear her. I found a way out and mumbled:

"M-m-m!" The headache intensified, making complex circles float in front of my eyes.

"Sartal, are you here? Monster?" There was silence. Either they weren't here, or they hadn't come to. Or maybe they had never been with us.

"I can't move, Logir said pitifully. "We are

sitting in some kind of cage. There's a large empty room. There's an altar a couple of yards away from us. And some strange writings on it. Something weird is going on. Yari, say something already!"

"M-m-m! Gr-m-m!" I was able to extract another sound and tried to at least roll over onto my back. It didn't work and I nearly threw up even from this minor effort. What was going on with me?

"My father will find us!" The femorc kept weeping. "And Archibald! He always finds what he needs. They will find us, you'll see! The mages let us out of the Academy at just the first level! I don't want to die..."

The femorc started crying silently. Gathering all my willpower, I made a superhuman effort: rolled over onto my back and opened my eyes. Something crunched, but I did not pay any attention to that. I was much more concerned about the glum picture I saw before me: Logir was sitting with her back to me, half embedded in a boulder of slowly melting ice. Bending my head down I saw what had crunched: my legs were turned to the wrong side in a very unnatural way.. There was no pain – it was simply dulled by the ice in which they were. Apparently, they were frozen all the way to the bones; that's why my body was so unnaturally fragile.

The location where we found ourselves looked more like a gloomy cave than a room: it had rough stone walls, long stalactites were hanging down from the ceiling... but part of it had some signs of civilization: there were tiles on the floor, the walls were painted gray, there were even a few torches on the walls dispelling the dark. The snow-white altar was the center of that civilization, and that's what the femorc was looking at. What upset me most of all was that I couldn't kill her. In principle, I could have reached her with the artifact if I tried. But it would be the girl's final death, and I really didn't want that. On the other hand, giving the mages an additional fighter would not do either. I should think of what to do while no one is here.

"Yari – don't just sit there!" After another minute of silence Logir lost it and started weeping again.

"Grm-gr," my throat still refused to form sounds into words, despite all my efforts. Pain started seeping through the cold that numbed my lower body, fighting with the pain reigning in my head. At first it was just an echo of pain, but I realized very well: the more time passes, the worse I will feel. Twisting one more time, I pulled an elves' potion out of my inventory and poured it down my frozen throat. Welcome warmth spread through my body, and finally the pain left it. I had given myself at least twelve hours of healthy and adequate interaction with reality.

"Logir?" Another attempt to say something was finally successful. It was a little hard and my throat itched a little, but I could talk. "Are you OK? Did you have any damage?"

"I can't move," the femorc replied through her tears. "I can't feel my arms and legs. I can only look forward."

"The most important thing is you're alive; we'll

deal with the rest." I started wriggling from side to side, trying to free myself from the ice. I heard another horrible crunch, as if a dry branch was breaking in the forest, and my legs completely lost connection with the rest of my body. Had it not been for the armor, part of me would have stayed in the ice. I could not sit up to break the ice with my fists or my artifact, so I dared to try the last thing I could do at the moment: brought out my pet. Even though he was pretty uncontrollable, I was going to try and convince him to break the ice. That was the most important thing. After that we could deal with Logir and the cage.

Rragr appeared in all his glory: a half-meter tall prowler, looking for something to grab and stuff into his face. I had been naïve enough to think that having eaten the worm's heart would improve his qualities – for example, make him bigger, stronger, smarter and more agreeable – but none of those dreams came true. My pet had just gobbled up the heart without any visible effect, and now was on the lookout to gobble up whatever else. Seeing that there was nothing edible in the vicinity, Rragr settled next to me, upset, and stayed still, waiting for instructions.

"Break the ice," I pointed at my legs. Noticing that it did not elicit any reaction whatsoever, added: "I'll give you a treat."

"Gra?" The furry wonder showed some interest, rising to his feet. A few moments later he repeated demandingly: "Gra?"

"Ice first," apparently, the only word Rragr understood from my sentence was "treat" and now he insistently demanded one. Having received no answer from me, the dismayed Neanderthal sat down on the floor of the cage and whined quietly, telling the world of the unjust and dire fate of the Paladins' pets. He was not showing any intent to break the ice.

"What an interesting thing you have there, I see," I heard a surprised voice and immediately hid the pet. The last thing I needed was for him to be killed before I even figured out how to control him. Devir came up to the cage and made a face, seeing my legs. "Aren't you a masochist, Yari! Does it hurt?"

"It's bearable. You'd better think about what happens when Archibald finds us. Then everyone will hurt!"

"You are hoping for the connection that Dolgunata created? I hasten to disappoint you – it only worked in the Academy; don't hope that my teacher will appear here in a minute. First he has to deal with my present." The mage shrugged his shoulders, walking around the cage. "But in general, I am now interested in you. Not everyone can bring a pet from the Academy. Actually, it's the first time I've ever heard about such a thing. Besides that you were able to get away from my mages, even though the druid helped you with that... I always liked extraordinary individuals. In effect, I am not going to hold you back: you can go wherever you want, but only after the ritual. I don't want the catorian to interfere with it."

"What ritual?" I was taken aback totally, not expecting such unprecedented generosity from my main opponent. I was surprised that Devir even deigned to talk to a common Paladin, but now he was saying he was going to let me go. Somehow that did not fit in with my impression of the crazy player.

"You will see," Devir responded with a smile. "You have front row tickets to the show. After it's all over I am inviting you to the Sanctuary – let's have a talk. I am not such a demon as you wish to see me, and I know how to take a loss. By getting out of the Academy you beat me, showing that my students were inadequate. I understand that very well, and don't hold a grudge against you."

"What will happen to my group?" I looked at the back of Logir, who was sitting very still and hanging on to our every word.

"Since when did it become your group?" Devir asked in surprise. "They betrayed you, tried to trade you for their own lives, framed you... They will die and it doesn't matter who will clean the Game of this trash: Archibald or myself. I'll do it quickly and painlessly – something I cannot promise from the Paladin. He would have to punish members of his own class as cruelly as I am going to do now with my transgressors."

Devir turned around and shouted:

"Let's begin!"

A motley procession appeared from behind a large stalactite which apparently covered the entrance to the cave. Two groups of mages were bringing in the unconscious Paladins, whose hands and feet were tied: Sartal and Monstrichello. Next to be brought in were Olzar and Dangard, tied up even more elaborately than the members of my class. Throwing the tied-up victims down next to the altar, the mages dispersed around the cave, trying to avoid the upgraded part of it. New participants in the proceedings appeared next. A grey-haired elf mage stepped out from behind the stalactite, strutting regally and looking arrogantly at everyone including Devir. A long cloak train behind him was not touching the floor: it was held up by two servants. The elf approached the altar, and magically a soft armchair appeared, with elaborately carved armrests. Sitting down and casting a contemptuous look at the tied-up bodies, the grey mage seemed to turn into a statue, ignoring the outside world. At that moment another mage appeared from behind the stalactite, looking at everyone just as arrogantly. Then another. And another... Seven high-born mages – that was all I could think to call them – settled around the altar, and all became stone-still waiting for the show to begin. I had thought that all the actors were already on stage, but I had been wrong: the mages started coming out, running, not wanting to delay the noble guests; the mages spread around the entire cave. As far as I could tell with my lack of experience there were about two hundred of various beings that appeared before the inflow of visitors trickled down, and then HE appeared. Someone whom I had not at all expected to see here. Levard, Zangar's teacher – the cynocephalian necromancer who was almost the Viceroy of the Emperor – honored the mages with his presence. The necromancer was immediately provided a dais a couple of yards away from my cage, to give him the best view of both the altar and all the participants of the proceedings.

"Brethren!" As soon as Levard had taken his place, the first of the high-born mages took the floor. "This session of the Minor Circle of the Mages Of the Harti Sector is now open! Today's Minor Circle will be held in the presence of guests: His Highness the noble necromancer Levard, and one who is a reason for this session: Paladin Yaropolk.

"Why is the Paladin still alive?" suddenly asked one of the high-born mages, whose race I did not know. Green skin, three eyes, a very disproportionate mouth, no nose at all and webbed hands. Sort of an oversized frog that had grown to the size of a human and learnt to walk on two feet. "Do we need witnesses?"

"We would all like to know that," a gnome, another high-born mage, seconded him. There was not a single human among the seven mages sitting around the altar, so one could say with certainty that nothing good could be expected from that bunch.

"The paladin is a guest rather than a sacrifice for one simple reason: my students failed." Devir responded, bending in a deep bow in front of the high-born ones. "It will not be possible to kill Yari. Despite my orders, my students were unable to prevent Yaropolk from gaining level 11 in the Academy. At this point even the "Black Death" won't help us, so I am calling on everyone here to accept the fact that we have two guests, and not just one as we had initially planned."

"You shall deal with him immediately after the ceremony is over," the elf ordered, and Devir bowed his head."

"Whatever you order, Your Highness. Your will is the law for me. Paladin Yaropolk will be declared my personal enemy immediately after the ceremony. Only the Sanctuary can protect him from my wrath."

"We have no doubts of your qualifications, master," another high-born rumbled. He looked like a huge monster made of earth. Was he an elemental spirit, maybe? "I accept the right of the necromancer Levard and the Paladin Yaropolk to be present at this session of the Minor Circle."

"I accept the right...," six more confirmations sounded in the cave, when Levard interrupted:

"I want to talk to Yari. After the ceremony. I will decide his fate myself. I release Devir from the quest. From now on Yaropolk will be my concern. I hope there are no objections?"

High-born mages exchanged glances in bewilderment, losing their aura of arrogance just for an instant. But then they nodded silently. No one dared to object to one of the most important beings of the Game.

"Let's start the ceremony!" The elf proclaimed after administrative issues were settled. "The floor goes to master Devir!"

The unperturbed mage strutted to the altar and pointed at Olzar. He was immediately yanked into the air and placed on the altar.

"Olzar was not one of my students," Devir began, "but he was supposed to replace Ahean, who happened to be assigned to a different sector. Olzar failed to follow my instructions several times. Started an open struggle with the druid Dolgunata, a student of Paladin Archibald, which brought the entire plan to the brink of failure. It doesn't make any sense to list his transgressions; it's simpler to state what he did well. The answer to that is simple: nothing! I consider him unworthy of representing our class, and ask the Minor Circle to make the decision on his fate. He has been brought down to level one."

"Soak the altar with his blood!" The elemental was the first to react. "Olzar is not worthy of being one of us!"

"I second that!" The gnome was in agreement. "Only death!"

Each of the high-born said his word, convicting Olzar to death. The new mage thrashed on the altar, his eyes bulging, and only a tight gag protecting us from him screaming wildly. One of the assistants presented the ceremonial blade to the headhunter, and silence fell in the cave. Even Olzar was still, staring crazily as his death loomed close.

"May this sacrifice benefit the mages!" Devir said with pathos, and the silence succumbed to monotonous humming: the high-born mages started singing. Swaying like pendulums they hummed a melody they alone knew. The altar started vibrating to its rhythm, like a hungry living being waiting to be fed soon. All this looked so enthralling that I missed the moment when the ceremonial blade cut Olzar's throat, and the blood, pulsing, started leaving the immobilized mage – the victim didn't even twitch, as if he were in a trance. Contrary to what I expected, the blood was not absorbed by the stone; that would have made the ceremony even more horrifying. It simply drained to the bottom of the altar, to disappear into the drain holes. However, there was something strange: not a single drop of the blood of the mage, who became desiccated like a mummy, stayed on the altar. It was pristinely clean. Devir brushed the remains to the floor with a grimace of disgust, and indicated for the assistants that Dangard was next. The new victim was placed on the altar.

"Dangard was my personal student. For thirty two years I trained him in everything that I knew myself, but that was not enough. He was unable to complete a minor assignment. As a result, Yaropolk achieved level 11 in the Academy. It is important to point out that due to Dangard's selfless actions the main target returned from the Academy at the first level, making it possible to hold the ceremony today. As a headhunter Dangard does not deserve to be my student, however, I believe he is a worthy member of the class and I plead with the Minor Circle to decide his fate. He has been brought down to level one."

"Let him prove himself worthy as a mage!" The earth monster was again first to reply.. "I consider that we can grant Dangard a second chance!"

Another six votes granted Dangard life, and Devir cut the ropes tying the victim with a fast flick of the ceremonial knife. Actually not a victim any more, but a level one player: mage Dangard. Putting the dumbfounded mage on his feet, Devir said:

"You have been granted life; prove that the Minor Circle was right in this decision. Find yourself and become great. As a teacher of headhunters, I reject you. Leave: you don't belong in this session!"

The ceremony attendants appeared like jacks-in-the-box, surrounded Dangard and literally pushed him out of the cave. Devir pointed at the sacrifices silently, and in just a few instants both Logir and Sartal were placed on the altar. The femorc was ripped out of the ice so carelessly that part of her leg and back was left there – her spine was showing How the red-skinned girl was able to stay alive and somewhat conscious with such wounds was beyond me. One could not continue with this level of damage, even as a player.

"Two first level Paladins," Devir continued. "My gift to the class. By killing them we will receive two new player slots. Besides, the father of the reptilian is an old enemy of the mages, so we will deal him a crushing blow. I want to pour the blood of my enemies on the altar and ask the Minor Circle to agree to this sacrifice."

Monotonous humming came again instead of the answer: the high-borns resumed their singing. The Paladins' fate was determined as soon as the altar started vibrating: two quick sliding blows of the ceremonial knife committed Logir and Sartal to history. The Paladins, like Olzar before them, turned into desiccated mummies immediately brushed to the floor and, finally, Monstrichello was heaved up onto the altar. Unlike Logir and Sartal, Monster was fully conscious. At least he blinked in bewilderment, and kept trying to rip the ropes. But they held fast.

"A first level Paladin – a human – whose very existence was predicted by our guest." Devir turned to the necromancer and bowed to him. "A fully immune creature is born once in a millennium, and we have a unique chance to exalt the class of the mages above everyone else. We will become first, and the Viceroy will help us in that."

"Future Viceroy," the necromancer corrected Devir. "Enough speeches. We have waited too long. Begin!"

My eyes nearly bulged out once I saw what appeared in Levard's hands: it was the all too familiar book, the Madonna's Diary. Putting it on the support in front of him, the necromancer started pressing on its cover, making me rejoice once again that I had the Book of Knowledge working for me: after the cynocephalian's manipulation, the cover of Madonna's Diary changed its color to bright red. Nothing else happened to the book, so I dared to attempt an incredibly silly thing: I took out my own set of notes and repeated Levard's actions, precisely repeating his movements. I was so grateful to my Book of Knowledge! Not only did it help me to light the cover with that red glow, it also helped me conceal my actions: I put Madonna's diary right into the book of Knowledge, so it seemed that I was just studying my artifact, nothing more.

The high mages made the altar vibrate for the third time, and with the quick swipe of the knife Monstrichello's game was over. But unlike in the previous killings, the big boy's blood did not pour to the floor: the stone absorbed all of it to the last drop.

Levard's palm fell on the cover of the diary, and I repeated his motion precisely, hoping that no one would think my actions strange. A second passed, then another, then a third... I was starting to think that nothing was supposed to happen anyway, when the reddish glow of my book's cover changed to green.

"Why are you not activating?!" the necromancer's angry shout broke the heavy silence in the cave. His book never changed color, still lighting the space around it with a bloody glow. The mages were silent; they obviously hadn't expect the blood to be absorbed by the altar, and now stared in awe at the stone, whose color had changed from stark white to blood red.

"Blasted hell! Too late!" The space around me suddenly exploded loudly, throwing ice in all directions, and Archibald appeared in the center of the cage. Looked around, cursed, and literally spat out: "Magic freaks! You'll answer for the Paladins! Levard: the Viceroy will definitely find out who was mixed up with the death of the immune one! You won't be able to hide behind the mages!"

"Stop him!" the necromancer screamed, but the catorian had started acting already. He threw something like a flash bang grenade through the bars. With a sharp move he pulled me out of the ice prison, activated the portal, and the world around me instantly turned into a hundred rainbows.

We had escaped from the mages, but that did not cause me much fear or concern. After all I was not afraid of death: I would respawn... somewhere. A different thing scared me: by repeating Levard's actions I had earned a headache that would make all the squabbles between mages and Paladins look like a child's play. Because even through the iridescence of the portal there was a funny notification hanging in front of me and not going anywhere:

Sacrifice is accepted; Madonna's Diary is activated.
Preparation of Game restart has been initiated.

— END OF BOOK ONE —

Want to be the first to know about our latest LitRPG, sci fi and fantasy titles from your favorite authors?

Subscribe to our **NEW RELEASES** newsletter:
http://eepurl.com/b7niIL

Thank you for reading *Dark Paladin!*
If you like what you've read, check out other sci-fi, fantasy
and LitRPG novels published by Magic Dome Books:

Reality Benders LitRPG series by Michael Atamanov:
Countdown
External Threat
Game Changer
Web of Worlds
A Jump into the Unknown
Aces High

The Dark Herbalist LitRPG series
by Michael Atamanov:
Video Game Plotline Tester
Stay on the Wing
A Trap for the Potentate
Finding a Body

Perimeter Defense LitRPG series by Michael Atamanov:
Sector Eight
Beyond Death
New Contract
A Game with No Rules

League of Losers LitRPG Series
by Michael Atamanov:
A Cat and his Human

The Way of the Shaman LitRPG series
by Vasily Mahanenko:
Survival Quest
The Kartoss Gambit
The Secret of the Dark Forest
The Phantom Castle
The Karmadont Chess Set
Shaman's Revenge
Clans War

The Alchemist LiTRPG series by Vasily Mahanenko:
City of the Dead
Forest of Desire
Tears of Alron

Moskau by G. Zotov
(a dystopian thriller)

El Diablo by G. Zotov
(a supernatural thriller)

Mirror World LitRPG series by Alexey Osadchuk:
Project Daily Grind
The Citadel
The Way of the Outcast
The Twilight Obelisk

Underdog LitRPG series by Alexey Osadchuk:
Dungeons of the Crooked Mountains
The Wastes
The Dark Continent
The Otherworld

An NPC's Path LitRPG series by Pavel Kornev:
The Dead Rogue
Kingdom of the Dead
Deadman's Retinue

The Sublime Electricity series by Pavel Kornev:
The Illustrious
The Heartless
The Fallen
The Dormant

Citadel World series by Kir Lukovkin:
The URANUS Code
The Secret of Atlantis

You're in Game!
(LitRPG Stories from Bestselling Authors)

You're in Game-2!
(More LitRPG stories set in your favorite worlds)

The Fairy Code by Kaitlyn Weiss:
Captive of the Shadows
Chosen of the Shadows
More books and series are coming out soon!

In order to have new books of the series translated faster, we need your help and support! Please consider leaving a review or spread the word by recommending *Dark Paladin* to your friends and posting the link on social media. The more people buy the book, the sooner we'll be able to make new translations available.

Thank you!

Till next time!

www.ingramcontent.com/pod-product-compliance
Lightning Source LLC
Chambersburg PA
CBHW052340020726
47503CB00001B/46